CW00920277

A Deadly Vow

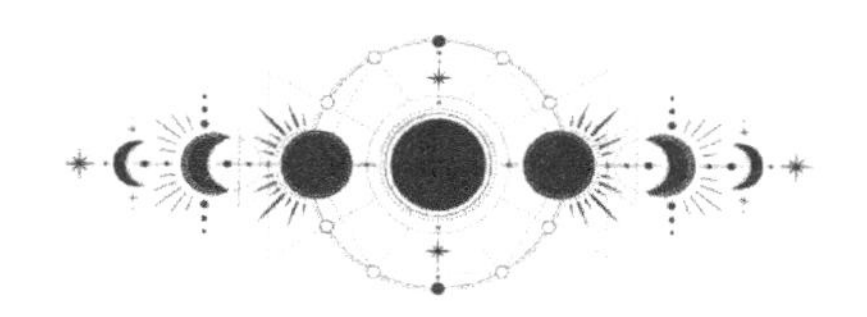

THE FATE OF VENGEANCE

J.D. RONAN

THE FATE OF VENGEANCE

J.D. RONAN

First published in the United States of America in February 2023 by
Dark Throne Press LLC
www.jdronanauthor.com
ISBN 979-8-986989-40-2 (ebook)
ISBN 979-8-986989-41-9 (hardback)
ISBN 979-8-986989-42-6 (paperback)

Book cover design by Storywrappers
Character Art by Alice Marie Power
Map by Cartographybird Maps

To be kept up with all things in the Fate of Vengeance Series please visit www.jdronanauthor.com and sign up for our newsletter.

To my sister, for all the times I wanted to show you I loved you too, but couldn't.

I pinky swear it.

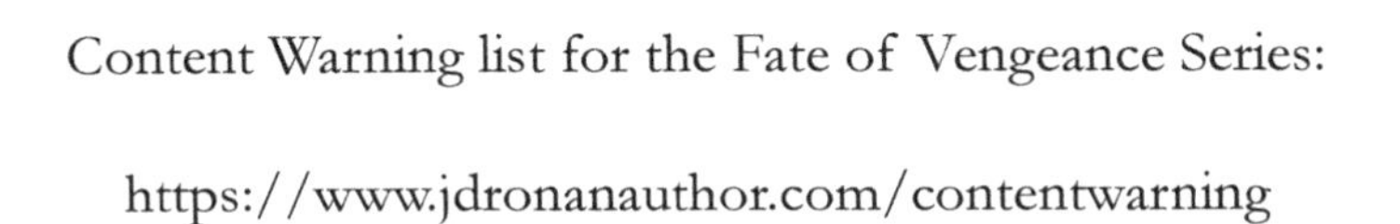

Content Warning list for the Fate of Vengeance Series:

https://www.jdronanauthor.com/contentwarning

TO THE
FAR NORTH
SOLSTICE
THE KINGDOM OF SUN AND FIRE
THE VEIL
OF SEVEN
THE VALLEY
OF ARCANE

NOVEAR
THE KINGDOM OF LIGHT AND STARFALL
CELENIA
THE KINGDOM OF MOON AND WATERS
TELLURIAN
THE KINGDOM OF NATURE AND LIFE
TO SOUTHERN WILDS

In The Beginning

The Gods created our kind knowing we would die.

It was only for the Gods to be reborn.

For life was an illustration of an illusion we were never meant to fully be a part of.

It was a cataclysmic event that turned dust into stars, an explosion of chaos creating life as we know it.

Just as the universe could be destroyed, it could be reborn again.
Stitched together by something that was never meant to exist.

It bloomed from destruction in a harmonious lie, where stars that learned to paint the night began to fade.

The sun and moon who danced with their rise and fall found that all life was at its will, and the earth that had produced life found death at its door.

Slowly knocking, not once, but twice.

The Realm

The Solstice Kingdom: The Sun

Rhiannon

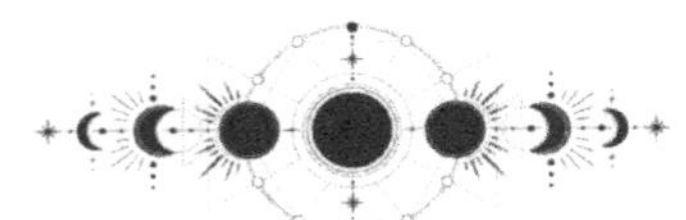

The Celenia Kingdom: The Moon

Selene and Twyla

The Tellurian Kingdom: The Earth

Lycus and Neith

The Novear Kingdom: The Stars

Astrea and Eos

Pronunciation Guide

POV Characters:

Keahi Aldeer, Prince of the Solstice Kingdom

KIE (RHYMES WITH PIE DAMMIT . . . Sorry) ALL-Dear

Sabine Azterrin, Princess of the Novear Kingdom

Sah-Bean Az-Tehr-In

Character Name List:

Kane (Cane), Drakkon (Drake-ON), Elias Griselda (E-Lie-Us Greh-ZEL-duh), Iahni (E-AH-Nih), Zehra (Zeh-RUH), Ossian (Oh-Sigh-Anne), Emric (Em-Rick), Rhiannon (Rye-uh-non), Astrea (Uh-Stray-uh), Eos (Ee-ohs)

Kingdoms:

Solstice

Cellenia (Sel-LIN-E-Uh)

Tellurian (Tell-LUR-E-In)

Novear (No-VARE)

Locations:

Kallhani (Cuh-LAH-Knee)

Chapter One

Keahi

There was no scar designed to be unfelt, and no burden heavier than the sacred truth I deemed myself unworthy of. I would always be on the opposite end of a knife. An instrument of war which was not my own.

The pieces left of me were unable to be stitched together, unarmed against the icy chill piercing through the seams of my tent. Winter was not within the valleys, but the violent trek across our mountains burrowed a premature cold within our bones. Exhaustion prevailed as we raced to the border of our territory.

After we set our camp, Elias had been working to repair my wounds for hours, to no avail. The strain between his eyes deepened, along with my guilt, because we both knew it was not war creating these wounds.

"Weapons do not heal," Elias repeated as he did with each line my father appointed the Healer to mend. My skin curated into a book of scars.

No, weapons do not heal.

They become what they have been made for.

A weary sigh left his lips as he patted the edge of the bandage with his fingertips. "I cannot guarantee it will last the length of your travel to the border. Take supplies with you once we part our separate ways."

"It will," I said firmly, despite knowing my uncle's work was futile. "We are almost there."

His eyes flicked back to me as I hesitated, holding the bunched edge of my black tunic in my palms. I sucked in a breath and slowly lifted it over my wounded torso, attempting to avoid his watchful concern with every sliver of pain I revealed. I wished he would allow me to do the same. My uncle's words were scarce to me after we departed from the capital.

"Hmm," he grumbled under his breath.

My wince was not hidden well enough.

There was always a lesson from him, even when he chose to stay silent. So far, he had been uninterested in any conversation dancing around the inevitable.

"How long?" I bit out as I worked on my leathered chest plate. A shallow attempt to hide another huff of pain, letting the weight settle over me.

Elias tugged the end of his white beard, a shadow cast over his face, and a snide remark at the tip of his tongue. "If it is my response you want, I will need to know what you are referring to. If it is your mind in which you would like me to read, then I am grateful to not have the ability."

"How long are you going to be angry with me?" I shook my head. "My title as Prince does not eliminate my responsibility as General. The Novear Kingdom has closed in on our borders unexpectedly, and I will not allow them to test us for future attacks. Bandages have never stopped me in battle before."

The movement of the Novear Kingdom's troops had become erratic, more spontaneous than ever before as we scouted their defenses, hovering over our lines. They were desperate to invade us without proper revisions, even as their numbers doubled in size from the raids. I needed to find out why they had finally chosen to close in on our borders after all these years before it was too late.

"This is different, Prince Keahi. Your father continues to bleed you dry of your magic. The wounds you carry are no longer healing as they once did—something has changed. The power harboring in your veins does not make you invincible."

I loosened my jaw. "Elias, you have known my father for a long time. If I refuse him now, it will only cause more chaos within our own Kingdom. I cannot object to him in the middle of a war. Especially when there would be no survivors if I start one within our own."

The tremor in his hands worked into his voice. "I cannot watch you yield yourself to him any longer just because he fears the magic in your veins. Inflating his power with your blood. There is nothing to be gained by the throne of lies he sits on. Your mother would not have wanted this."

A vested assumption my uncle reminded me of each time we circled back to this conversation. Even if it was his sister's intentions he claimed to know for her son, Elias could not argue for the dead. My mother was not here to tell me what she would have wanted. I know only what she thought of me before her passing, and it was not much.

"Elias, please." I bit the inside of my cheek, preparing the lie I hopelessly gave him year after year. "One day, I promise. Maybe. . . it is time to appoint a different Healer in the meantime. . ."

"No." His eyes wrinkled against the distant thunder. "No more. If your father requests the magic in your veins, Keahi, you must refuse him. Just look at you! Your brother and sister have already told you they will fight by your side if a rebellion unfolds."

"It is not that simple." I sighed.

"Do you want to become our enemies? Is that what you want? To destroy everything in our paths for the sake of magic? We both know that is not why you are here, and it is not why you have let your father slice you open like an animal bred for slaughter. Do not let it become what you fight for."

The wind howled, battering against the silence that ensued. Elias never knew when to give up. I might have heard him say the same of me once, but I had learned it from him. His stone blue eyes searched the rare sight of my bare face. The gold rim around his irises dimmed as he mulled the dark fabric of my mask between his thumbs.

"This was never something that you were meant to endure, even if it has turned into a choice." He spoke softly. "You cannot hide from yourself forever, Keahi. There are some scars I cannot heal."

The fold of my tent settled as Elias slipped off into the night.

Releasing a breath, I shamefully slipped my hands underneath my tunic before he could change his mind, quietly sifting between my armor as I tightened the final band—spotted with fresh blood.

The Volkan warrior creed I was sworn into symbolized the resilience of the sun's flames. Resilience, though, was just another defamation of honor to me, and I was reminded of it each time my father's knife dipped into my veins. I stared down at the black mask Elias left me to choose, to hide behind, as my father cut me open at his will. Marred before I had the chance to fight for the Kingdom of Solstice, or what was left of the realm before the war began.

There was too much blood on my hands to be hidden by a thin shield of black fabric, and I could not blame it on the war in our realm alone. It served as a second skin as it molded to my face. The hollow slit in the fabric permitted only my eyes to be revealed to others, glowing with my element of fire. I was not hiding behind a mask; I was its willful prisoner.

The portal for our Gods to re-enter our realm and breed new magic be damned—*what was lost, was lost.* I did not become the General of my father's army because of the closure of the Veil of Seven. I fought for what was left after the King of Novear destroyed the veil, to conquer a realm that was not entirely his. It was rare for me to believe something was worth saving. My Kingdom, the people of Solstice, could still be saved.

If the Novear Kingdom was brave enough to cross our lines in the coming days, I promised myself to be the one to remind them.

The white elm's bark crackled and lifted warm smoke through the brittle air. I stepped out of my tent, careful to secure the wind-tattered frame in its place. I did not wish to patch it in the middle of the night when rest was already a scarcity.

My boots toed against the edge of the fire's glow within the center of our camp. Kane, my second in command, did not startle as I drifted beside him. He poured the heat of his magic into the core of the orange flame, solely focused on the warmth.

The Volkan warrior creed, an honor bestowed upon Solstice's most valiant of sorcerers, did not allow us to see each other's faces often. Our appearances were hidden beneath black cloaks draped to the earth, strapped in leather harnesses to carry our silver weapons, and a mask we rarely departed from. We learned to sense the smallest shift in each other's movements because of this, even to our own detriment.

My chin dipped low. "Something on your mind?"

I readied myself as a meager sigh parted his lips. There were few others besides Kane who refused to withhold their honesty toward me. The title I carried did not deter him. I would not wish it any other way. Those who said what they felt were far less dangerous than those who did not.

"Yes, there is something on my mind. Not that you would be inept to hear it," Kane said as he shuffled his feet into the moss-covered ground.

I stifled the irritation in the back of my throat. "Get on with it. Elias had his turn already."

"As if you listened to him. Why would I waste my breath?" Kane peered at me over his shoulder and back.

"I was not aware of how much of a busybody you are, clinging to overheard conversations," I shot back. A bitter hum in Kane's chest served as a warning to my remark. The campfire glared with revived heat in front of us as his annoyance toward me flared with his magic.

"Though it is your job, isn't it?" I continued, a smirk forming beneath my mask at his rile. "It is unfortunate that chastising your gifts would be contraindicated, given the circumstance."

There was very little Kane did not observe compared to most, a useful talent when politics were interwoven with war. The council meetings with my father never proceeded smoothly without him. His talent for persuasion was even more formidable, considering he had coerced me into one of the few friendships I maintained outside of my brother.

"I do not overhear your conversations at my enjoyment, believe me. It is a torture to hear you be so painfully stubborn," he said sharply. "Stupidly arrogant on top of it, but the two go hand in hand."

"Is it my pride you think I bow to?" The calm left my insides, blistering with a fever. "Do you think I allow my father to belittle me for the sake of my enjoyment? Push my men beyond their breaking points at every turn because I fear the Novear Kingdom will have us running with our tails between our legs finally? It would seem blatantly obvious that pride is the least of things I feel."

"Do not make me say it." Kane fell into a hush. "The only fealty I have sworn to is the Solstice Kingdom. Do not give me the opportunity to slander your father when you know I hold no loyalty to our king. Elias is not the only one who has had to watch you suffer."

Kane's words bit beneath my armor, striking exactly where he intended to. His honesty toward me held too few limitations, except for one. Kane was the only sorcerer outside of the royal family who knew of the Solstice King's secret regarding the source of his power.

"I won't then." I swallowed thickly, barely able to produce a sound.

Sweat beaded underneath my hood, and a bizarre ache singed the skin above my heart. My nerves were not as easy to control in front of those I trusted. They lifted the weight I bottled my emotions with, and I felt more than I allowed myself to in private. . . but this feeling was far beyond my control. The wound my father curated from the last draining had not appeared to be infected, but it radiated with stark heat. I stumbled back from the fire. My hand neared the building discomfort in my chest. It had just skimmed the surface as it drove deeper—*piercing.*

My brows pinched as a slash of torment slammed into my breath, threatening to send me to my knees. I had sustained enough torture over the years to know—*something was very wrong.*

Kane stilled, sensing my movements. "I should have forced you to rest. You've pushed yourself too far this time. Go back to your tent. I will send Elias back in to look at your wounds again. . . Keahi?"

A blinding pain struck the back of my head.

My surroundings fell victim to the magic, pulsing like a drum-beat in my ears, submerging my senses. It roared through my blood, coating my veins, until it synced with my heartbeat. I felt a presence capsize me, forcing me under. My eyes opened in a body that was not my own. At my feet, I stared at a blade slick with blood dripping down the edge of a knife.

"Is that the best you got?" The window of the soul I looked through growled as vulgar cheers and chants erupted.

I felt her strength splinter underneath, within my chest. An army of soldiers that were not mine surrounded me, snarling between torches lit within a perfect circle.

"Have you grown weak after all these years?" She rasped against the cool boulder she was bound upon. Her vision slowly trailed from the tip of the red knife, and up to the two hands strangling the hilt—and then I finally saw his face. "Finish it!"

"Kane!" I screamed against the magical connection, attempting to dislodge from its grasp. "Elias!" The knife rose above him with a smile made of venom and promise. Wrath set fire to my blood and chilled my spine. A crown of dark and hollow stars bloomed along his veiny forehead, plastered with long white strands of hair, staring down at the woman who was to be his sacrifice. I did not have to find the King of Novear after all—he summoned me instead through her.

The knife came down.

Their cheers rang louder as the echo of the woman he sank his knife into grew distant and frail. The King of Novear carved her back ruthlessly against the connection, solidifying the link between us that would anchor my soul to hers forever.

Terror coursed through me as I searched for solid ground between my fingertips. I blindly tore at the damp mud, desperate for an anchor to appear within my physical surroundings. I threatened to rip the realm in half when it did not let me go, but it answered me instead. My vision returned to my body.

The forest around our camp lit with wildfire as flames poured from my hands. "The King of Novear—I know where he is," I rasped. "We are close. I saw him. . ."

I saw her too.

My soldiers fled from their tents as Kane shouted orders above the wrath of my fire, their weapons sheathed to prepare for a war they could not come with me to fight.

"Send word to the nearest base at our border. I need a small search party to scout the perimeter before we get there. We are coming for him, even if it takes us all night." Kane and Elias flanked to my side at my commands.

Their panic did not rival my fear when I could still feel hers, barely beating through her heart, against the thread of magic suspended between us.

Chapter Two

Sabine

The realm refused to cradle me to my death. For it was known, peace required a mercy I had not earned.

"Tell me where your king is!" The Solstice infantry soldier who had found me upon their border shouted. My father and the rest of his army were long gone, fleeing toward the safety of the Novear Kingdom's territory.

The white of my hair touched the ground as I raged for a single breath, and the ends turned a shade of crimson. "I have no king."

He hummed low in his throat as he leaned over me. "Renounce your blood all you want. It makes no difference to me—they already know you are here. Tell me where the King of Novear is, and I will make death easy for you. Refuse to answer me, and I will hand your broken body over to them alive."

I slowly peered up at him through blood-soaked lashes. I had been traveling the border of the Solstice Kingdom for days now, awaiting my imminent fate.

"Who said I wanted to live?"

The soldier's fist slammed directly into my jaw with a solid *crack*.

Do you hear us now? The Gods who did not answer mocked far out of reach as a metallic taste pooled inside of my mouth. The rope fibers tied around my wrists from the ritual burned, overpowered by my body's instinct to lurch forward.

An echo of my father's voice waded past the ringing in my ears as pocketed blood dribbled between my lips. The Novear King had whispered my sentence to me as he dragged the blade down my back—the King of Solstice would find me and kill me.

I would not have to endure this life for much longer. Crackling like a flame caught in a storm, the magical connection from the ritual was engulfing the distance.

Death was as impatient as I was, though. I did not plan to wait for it this time, even if it was prowling straight toward me. The loss of blood forced my sight from the realm. It sputtered around me with an implicit memory I wanted to forget, emerging from the quiet it had been hiding within in one violent streak of shame down my cheek.

"The Gods allowed our people to suffer at my hands, but it was you, Sabine, who allowed them to suffer their fate by disobeying me. Let this be a lesson for you daughter—there will be no God to save you. We can only save ourselves, and in the end, we will still burn for it."

They did burn—my people.

After years of being tortured under my father's rule, I was going to finally burn with them. It was what I told myself as I looked up into the night sky and counted every prayer which had gone unanswered. Then, I selfishly added one more. For it was not the stars shining against total darkness above me, but the embers of my people that glowed in the shadow of their own memorial.

The soldier's fierce hand gripped my burning throat and forced my vision to return to its destiny. I sensed the hatred he beheld against his palms. His callouses scraped against my neck, handmade with suffering. The soldier was purely barren of magic. Sorcery he had not been given after my father destroyed the Veil of Seven. It was the only thing my father had ever done right when he prevented the Gods' return to our realm.

He wanted to become one, and I wanted them to never exist. Anything touched by the Gods, even magic, did not outweigh their selfish act of creation.

"You are quite a long way from home, are you not?" The soldier flashed his teeth. "I know you did not make it this far to the border of Solstice all by yourself."

"Is it my bleeding charm that confuses you, so?" I drawled lightly. "It seems your ability to conclude is as strong as your ability to land a solid hit. Maybe you should try harder—"

A streak of fire ignited my opposite cheek, and stars erupted in my vision with the promise of home. My chest heaved, and his grasp tightened on my throat.

The soldier's brown eyes darkened as he leaned in close. "If I hand you to them alive, I promise you will beg for the death I offer you now. Do not waste it."

I was not wasting anything. It was he who wasted my time by feeding me lies, but I was going to make him an honest one. I wanted to die before I was found.

I forced myself to raise a brow. "Do I sense pity, Soldier? Or is it fear?" My head tilted to the side. "What will your king do to you when he finds out that you ignored the trail of the King of Novear's magic still in the air from the ritual?" Drops of my blood fell from his knife as he walked away. "And instead, you stayed with the victim he left bound for you?" I smiled, deliriously bright and bloody. "I will take my chances. Just so I can watch you die first."

A new fear danced in his eyes at the mention of his own death, a fierce motivator for feeble men who did not live with honor. He gripped me closer, and my knees dangled in momentary relief.

"Where is your king?!" He spat through his teeth.

I smiled brighter, just before I spat back.

The soldier stumbled to the side with a wince. My laugh was low and dark in my throat as he smeared a matching crimson streak across his forehead. "You fucking little bitch!" His hand raised, and I closed my eyes in wait, unwilling to yield. I prepared for him to land the hit I knew would solidify the crack formed in my jaw, but the final blow never came.

I was too late.

The air changed around us. An irrefutable sensation emerged—darkness was coming. The way it clung to your skin and dissolved your senses, only allowing you to see what nightmare it created, as your mind made monsters out of shadows. They rose like my own personal hell from the ashes. Smoke loomed around their figures, pooling from the burning torches it circled me within.

My father's spell ignited my back, sending shivers down my spine as I forced myself to watch. There were three of them, their black cloaks cascading over their figures. I knew the one who had come for me in an instant, deep within the ache of my bones. Even in the night—*the King of Solstice had found me.*

The King in the center slightly tilted the top of his hood he hid behind, and his auburn eyes glowed like embers in the night. Fires raged in my vision, reminding me that my people's deaths would haunt me until my final breath. The fallen Novear Sorcerers my father had killed, wrapped in an eternal volatile flame.

The soldier's grip tightened in their presence, and a small, strangled sound came out of my throat. The King's gaze flashed to mine in response, watching me struggle as his gloved hands flexed at his sides. All it took was a single nod from him, and my knees crashed to the earth with a solid thud.

A shriek escaped me as jagged rocks cut into my skin, shooting a bolt of pain to my hips. I paid them no attention as I quivered against the ground, almost completely bare before them. The front of my shredded night gown was crusted in blood, the back of it ripped wide open from the ritual. Only the bonded ropes my father had spelled around my ankles and wrists truly covered me as I drank in their stunned silence, letting them look their fill against the torched glow.

There was no answer that I could give them, not one they would want. I did not know where my father was now after he had left me here, the King of Novear. He had irrevocably damned me beyond return, and this very moment was the least of them, despite the finality.

I would not be afraid to burn, just as my people had done when they faced my father's corruption. I would not let my head fall as the King of Solstice prowled around me like I was some captured animal—*the hunter and his prey.* He was no hunter.

My father had made sure of that.

I knew he had found what he was searching for when his footsteps halted behind me. I wanted to see his face then. To see the realization that every inch of my scarred back damned him just as much as it did me. There was only the shake in his breath as he slowly exhaled. It tasted of fear, causing a crazed laugh to crawl its way through my throat in response.

All of them were to blame for the measure of this war. There was no kingdom left pure when they had watched my people suffer. They deserved to see the extent of the corruption they were too late to defend.

The soldier snatched the top of my head, yanking it back to uproot the strands of my white hair. "How dare y—"

His mouth moved frantically, but there was no sound, like the soldier had lost the ability to speak entirely. The Solstice Kingdom's silver armor clattered against the boulder of rock my father had sacrificed me on. His eyes bulged with wide-eyed horror as his arms crossed the expanse of his chest. It was not the chill of late autumn causing his breath to fog, but dense black smoke charring his lips.

I sensed the moment the King's eyes lifted from my back through our connection, prowling into my peripheral vision with slow, devastating purpose. His long black cloak dragged over the rocks as his attention averted to the man kneeling before me. The soldier was so close I could feel every shudder burst through him, gasping and gnarling for a single breath. My throat felt tight at the sight.

"I have a question for you, Soldier," the King said. My skin went crawling, ready to depart from my body entirely as he lowered himself to the ground. The King's red glowing eyes pierced through me as he peered over him. "How many of those marks were made by you?"

The night's wind picked up as the soldier and I stared at each other in disbelief when the King's eyes slid across my blackened jaw line.

"I—only was trying—to get the truth out of her. I would never betray my Kingdom. I had found her like—this, believe me! Her back—" The sound in his throat died.

The King's voice plummeted. "I believe you. What I cannot believe is that you felt the need to take punishment into your own hands."

A single gloved finger reached out, lightly tracing the side of the soldier's jaw line. It was the exact location of where he had smashed his fist into me. My jaw flinched as if the King of Solstice had been the one to touch me instead.

The soldier squirmed in place, unable to move away despite not having a single hand laid atop him. "If I remember correctly, that is not within your status. . . *It is within mine,*" he hissed. "But since you took matters into your own hands, what would you have me do to her?"

If death was reaching for me, I could not will it to come any faster as the soldier lowered his eyes and angled them back up, gleaming with revived hatred. "Kill her. Kill that Novear scum where she kneels. Make her—beg for it."

The King's dark laugh skittered across my skin, and I could not fight the full-bodied tremble as the flush drained from my face. I nearly lost myself entirely to fear until I repeated my mantra of strength.

Whether I served it to myself or those who truly deserved it, I craved what could only be provided in the sanctity of it all—*Death.* I would no longer be what I have done, what I could not come back from under my father's volition.

There was no running away as I held the fury in his eyes and met his wrath. "Just. Do it." My voice shook. "Just kill me."

The King's head tilted in a predatory glance, searching for something I could not give him even in death. His weight shifted into the dirt. I could have sworn I caught a small glimpse of a smile as he stood, drawn underneath the shades of his cloak—*but I was wrong.*

This man's entire face was covered except for his burning eyes, hidden behind a mask as he drew closer to me in the night. Every king I had ever encountered wore their crowns and reveled in the power they held over you. The only mask they hid behind was in the glamor of their rule. *Why then, had the King of Solstice come to find me, hidden within his own territory?*

"You heard her," he whispered, willing smoke into his palm until a silver blade flashed its metal against the moonlight. "She wants me to end this."

The promise in his voice forced my eyes shut in a flash of remembrance, like the coward I had always been—*like my father believed me to be.* The song of my undying belief softly whispered to me, pleading for me to remain with the realm.

It was a suffocating reminder of a hope fate had not destined me to have. Not as my father, the King of Novear, had stood in his castle bleached clean of corruption in pearlescent columns of stone while his people turned to ash. His reign was hand-crafted to reflect an innocence he could no longer retain after destroying the Veil of Seven.

No amount of ivory plated armor could remove the portrait

of betrayal I saw my father as, what I saw myself as—*an abhorrent shade of blood-stained red.* It washed away clean in my final moments, challenging the freedom of death I had always begged for. Because it would always be the same to Gods who did not listen: *desire, need, wanting.*

Each of which was writhing to the surface to be wielded by forces of no benevolence. Desire was a sin, need was a weakness, and want was an idea which would never come to fruition. It was a canvas of the Gods' design as my last prayer went unanswered: I *needed* to die, but it never meant I had not *desired* to live.

I lifted my chin to the stars glittering above me in their sea of darkness. A trail of cosmic light shot through the night, leaving a path for me to follow my people home as I closed my eyes and listened to the sound of my skin slice open in one fluid motion.

Chapter Three

Keahi

Even the stars mourned above us, their light piercing through the forest from realms away.

I stood motionless, surrounded by a ring of torches staked into burnt layers of moss, emitting a residual curtain of dense smoke from the ritual. Scarlet and amber hues bounced off the boulder they cursed the woman upon. The flame's glow cascaded over her unconscious frame as my soldier's blood pooled beneath my boots.

The damning proof of the vision was written with a spelled knife upon her back in inflamed lines. It exposed a secret even the realm was not supposed to know of. The King of Novear had needed our troops within reach for an attack which did not need soldiers. It had all been a game to draw us out—*to draw me out.*

Warranted fear had incited from their newfound strength as they pressed up against our borders. Their troops had grown too powerful after invading the Tellurian Kingdom, forcing their sorcerers to resign to their submission and join their ranks. Those who did not were executed according to our spies, and I had refused to allow the same fate for the Solstice Kingdom.

I promised myself to be on the frontline, if or when he finally seized the opportunity to invade us. I had not been the only one aware of my promises, though.

The woman's flesh I was connected to was maimed black and blue. A symbol of magic drawn by the tip of a spelled knife. Identical to the symbol I had been born with on my skin, and it represented the hidden truth of the magic pulsing within my veins.

The King of Novear had used my seal of power to generate a rare type of magic during the ritual, initiating the link between us as he carved my symbol until it formed a sorcerer's bond.

I have many scars because of the symbol I was born with above my heart, sustained enough pain to last several lifetimes as my father drained the magic in my blood, but there was no scar more painful than this. The sorcery on her back etched into a mark she would be forced to forever wear like a scar—*because of me.*

My heart thudded against my sternum. A vile stain of dark magic misted through the air, and the trees lashed to rebel against what we knew could not be undone.

Madness reverberated against every bone in my body until my palms twitched. It trickled into my fingers as Kane cautiously lifted the woman from my vision. Her head lolled back weightlessly, and a crimson stream trickled out of the corner of her mouth. Her blood dripped like an offering she had not chosen to give.

"Keahi. . ." Kane's whisper trailed off when he shifted to support her head.

My eyes turned up from her blood, tracking the subtle movement of his grip tightening around the base of her neck. His hesitant fingers pulled back to graze over the top of her spine, far above my symbol engraved on her back.

The sudden arrest of his chest forced me to freeze in place. His eyes clouded over as he brushed his fingertips over her neck once more, repeating the movement for a third time, each pass gentler than the first. Kane's eyes slammed shut.

I braced myself as I watched a man who I had not only known for almost my entire life, but who had also seen the terrors of war beside me, curse a rattled breath.

"There is a siphoning crystal embedded in her neck. When the

King of Novear initiated the link between you . . . even if she wanted to fight against the ritual, she—"

She didn't have the chance to.

The King of Novear owned this woman's magic. Trapped her free will in a barbaric form of treason all other kingdoms upheld despite our differences. A siphoning crystal was an enslavement of power. The sorcerer forced to wear the crystal beneath their skin was at the mercy of the owner's control—the complete and utter loss of mine. This torture she endured was different. I felt the knife glide through her skin through the connection.

My symbol on her back. The power I did not want. Power I *willingly* gave away.

'Finish it,' she had screamed through the connection the King of Novear tied us to—I now knew what her words had meant. She had known there would be no other choice but to suffer as the blade came down when the link between us formed.

I slowly looked down at my soldier, who had put his hands on her after she had already been beaten. My own hands rattled with a shrill demand as the leather of my gloves met the untamed snarl erupting from my lips.

'Finish it.'

The front of his neck sliced clean open by my blade—*too clean*—as it mixed with the blood he spilled when the King of Novear had already defiled her.

'Finish it.'

Her echoed cries snapped through my body with a shudder. The blatant need to feel it coursed through me, the crunch of bone hitting bone without a barrier.

'Finish it!'

The memory of her screams grew louder between my ears—*desperate.* I ripped my gloves off with my teeth, uncaring that it had been years since anyone had seen my scarred hands. All ration departed as my bare fists rained down upon the soldier's pulseless body.

The copper in the air prickled my knuckles with the need for more. I beat the face of his corpse until I felt the crown of his head cave against solid rock, but it was not enough—*I was not finished.*

My scarred hands grasped the mold of his skull I had designed for my own sick demolition. "I'm going to kill him for this!" A dull vibration wracked against my palms as I bashed the soldier's face against the stone, envisioning the King of Novear under my merciless will. "I do not care what it takes. What I have to give!" I hissed through my teeth. Blood splattered against my cloak, my mask.

"General! Control yourself!" Kane commanded too late. The soldier's skull shattered, and his beaten flesh sloshed against the rock with a final blow.

Kane lowered his voice as I attempted to control my wild and staggered breath. "Keahi, I need you to listen to me. Zehra left us the moment you confirmed the carving on this woman's back to track them. I know you do not want to leave Zehra, but we need to get to the nearest base Elias fled to after the vision."

The hollow ache in my chest heaved as I studied the bloodied path the King of Novear had left, and Zehra had followed it on her own.

Kane traced his thumb along the ridges of the siphoning crystal beneath the base of her neck. "She's so pale. The loss of blood. . . I do not know if there is anything we can do, but if she has a chance of surviving the initiation of the link between you, Elias will know what to do."

I fitted my blood-soaked fingers into my gloves, my decision locked in place long before his debate.

"We have to leave her," I rasped painfully at what had to be done.

Kane tensed as I ripped off my cloak and covered the Novear woman's body. Relief flooded the fire in his eyes as our forms dissipated into smoke, scarcely loosening his grip as he realized who I was choosing to leave behind in this moment.

It was not the woman he held in his arms.

Chapter Four

Keahi

Miles of mountainous ridges snaked along the border between the Solstice and Novear territory. It had protected us from invasion so far, but not all wars could be won with brute force.

I had ruthlessly torn us through shadowfire until ash coated my lungs, traveling to the military base embedded within our first pass. The Colonel we found at the fissure in the mountain led us deep into the tunnels. I fought to inhale against my mask. Sulfur swelled in potency the further we descended into its core.

The muscles in my back sparked with tension. Yellow eyes flicked their suspicious gaze toward my cloak in Kane's arms, shielding the unknown identity of the woman he carried. It was the fifth time the Colonel had looked over his shoulder since we had entered the base. If he made it a sixth, it was going to be his last.

I bit back the growl in my throat as Kane stepped on the back of my heel. It was already his second warning to me since our arrival. I was so on edge I had nearly sliced the man in front of me open when he asked if the soldier he so proudly sent at my request was coming back.

The Colonel had flinched. The bright yellow in his eyes lost their curiosity from what I was sure to be a deranged look in my own. *'As long as you do not mind picking up the pieces to carry him back here, I'm sure he can,'* I had explained. He had not braved to ask another question out loud since.

"How close are we?" Kane strained to ask as he called over my shoulder from behind us.

"Not too much farther," the Colonel claimed. "The Grand Healer was last seen in the abandoned holding bay we had once used for prisoners. The red-headed infantry Healer with him did an inventory check of our medical supplies. He was rather. . . insistent that we were not to disturb them after that."

Rusted iron bars cut through the side walls, some corroded into a jade green from the moisture trapped this far below.

"You have brought us close enough. We will take it from here," I said sharply, halting both mine and Kane's footsteps.

The Colonel's gaze dipped to the single drop of maroon blood that fell between Kane's boots, giving us a hesitant salute before he took his time in walking away. I peered out of the corner of my eye to find Kane shaking his head back and forth at my unspoken thoughts—*I would have to replace the Colonel later.*

Before I turned on my heels, I tilted my head. "I will not kill everything that walks. . . at ease."

"They do not have to still be walking, apparently," Kane shot back as he followed me. "I have never seen you like this before. Do not hold it against me for not wanting to take the chance."

"How thoughtful," I mused between gritted teeth.

He blew out a breath as we picked up our pace, searching for Elias on limited time. "Keahi, you've never even. . . you've not even—"

My head whipped around. "Do not bring that up at a time like this. Not when you never braved to do so before—especially not in front of Elias."

Kane's shoulders lifted as he breathed a second harshly extended sigh. I pretended the popping in my ears from the growing pressure was muffling the string of curses he let out. "*It's-not-like-he-doesn't-know. . . Elias-always-knows.*" After I continued to ignore him, he possibly added, "*Fucking-idiot.*"

I drowned him out completely at the sight of an orange glow gleaming near the end of the black tunnel. We rushed inside the enclosure the light came from, and Kane set the woman on a wooden bunk in the center of the prison cell. A white sheet Iahni must have borrowed from their infirmary was thrown over the top of it. Once the woman's back settled against it, her injuries bled into the fabric like ink on a page.

We straightened above her body. A high-pitched creak swung behind us. I realized as the groaning metal clicked; Elias had set up his supplies in the only prison cell with a functioning lock. Kane and I slowly looked at each other, pausing for a moment, daring the other to ask first.

"What. . . are you doing?" Kane's chest heaved up and down as he turned.

The acid crawled up my throat and pressed against my windpipe. I did not have the ability to speak. My hand flexed as I stumbled to brace myself against the nearest cave wall, closing in on me.

"We have to keep it locked for when she wakes. The King of Novear knows too much already. We cannot apprehend what he might have learned beyond the mark you were born with, Keahi, or who he used as an anchor to create the link between the two of you." Elias ripped off my cloak covering her, but Kane's hand snatched his wrist before he could assess the damage.

"Stop," Kane growled. "There's something you need to know. . . we found a siphoning crystal in the back of her neck."

I was not the only one unfamiliar with my friend's ways. He had never exerted the faintest amount of force unless it required punishment to our enemies. Elias gently grasped his hand, giving him a slow nod as he released the firm hold. Kane's fist shook and remained in the air, still molded to the shape of his wrist.

Elias's white beard whipped toward me before his face did, unkempt brows ridden with shock. "You still brought her?" he whispered.

I shook my head, my gloves scraping against the soft gravel sinking beneath my fingertips against the wall.

His golden staff thudded as he crept toward me as he said, "Then you know what I must do to heal her. . ."

My eyes pinched closed. "Elias, I don't know what I want. All I know is that I could not leave her there."

I looked over to her swollen face, uncovered in this cell, streaked with morbid discoloration. It did not matter that I did not know her, not when I felt responsible in part of it. It was *my* symbol she wore.

Kane reached his hands to the side of his mask, clumping the dark fabric into his fists. "Elias, you could die if you remove the siphoning crystal. Is there any other way to heal her without attempting to remove it?"

Elias grimly shook his head. "There is a reason she looks the way she does. You both know this. I can try to heal her, but it is unlikely the owner wanted her to live long enough to see you truly linked to her. Not with the risk of it being successful."

"And if it is successful?" I swallowed thickly.

"There are many stages to complete the sorcerer's bond, even if I remove the crystal." Elias lowered his voice. "I do not need to remind you what they are."

Kane flicked his widened gaze toward me, abruptly wrenching it away as I stilled.

The blunt end of Elias's gold staff churned into the dirt before he continued. "If you kill her now, it will have a minor effect on your magic compared to if we follow through with this."

"No—I cannot. . ." I lifted the front of my mask. The compression suffocated me as I gasped for air.

Elias stared at me for a long time as I clutched the tops of my knees. What did he want me to say? Even in my current state, we both knew I could survive the severing of the bond at this stage. My survival was not what led me to bring her here—it was hers.

It had not killed me to feel someone else under the knife. Instead, it awoke a part of me so jagged it collapsed the moment I laid eyes on her.

"Then it is my choice," Elias said into the quiet when I did not elaborate; he did not need me to.

"No," I rasped past the burning in my throat. The reality settled over me like a gavel. "Heal her the best you can. If she does not survive. . . then I will live with it." I always lived with it. The guilt. . . I would keep living with it.

The ring around his stone blue eyes sparked with a golden fury. "I said. . . *it is my choice*. I am tired of watching your definition of living."

"No—" I croaked.

He stopped me, pointing a long pale finger. "You brought her here knowing what I would have to do to heal her for the sorcerer's bond. I have watched you make your choices, Keahi Aldeer. You will watch if I choose to make mine to save your future wife." I flinched back against the cave as his words struck me.

A sorcerer's bond created a magical bridge to ignite the merge of each other's powers and intertwine the two souls together upon marriage—consummated by blood, body, and soul. In an unformed bond, the risk of power depletion became deadlier in consequence as the threads of fate fully weaved the sorcerers together.

I had known the consequences I would face in order to save her life the moment I saw my symbol on her, but I did not know the gravity of it until Kane found the siphoning crystal in her neck.

The sorcerer's bond could not begin to truly form if she was enslaved to another, and her injuries the King of Novear had meticulously placed along her body could not heal unless removed. The King of Novear, however, underestimated the power that stood before me, just as I once did.

I looked toward the hands which had mended me, frail with age from his incessant efforts to piece me back together. It was my fault because I had never done it myself. I did not feel the same anger I wished to when I had asked him to stop healing me over the years; instead, I was terrified. I would not forgive myself if Elias died for this.

It would be a loss; one I could not sustain.

The choice I had made to bring my bonded to him was fragile, but it was still a choice I had ultimately made when I did not have the time to question it.

Elias did not soften his gaze as it left mine and turned toward Kane. "Flip her over. Show me where the siphoning crystal is. Keahi," he said over his shoulder, "I need you to help him." Kane was already at her side, one hand braced gently behind her knee.

Sweat pooled beneath the leather of my gloves at the mention of touching her mangled form. "We should find Iahni. I cannot do this," I said.

"Iahni is busy elsewhere!" Elias shouted. I winced as the end of his gold staff whacked against my side rib. "Zehra is nowhere in sight, which I do not have time to figure out on top of everything else. I am the one left to heal her with the two imbeciles who once thought it was okay to use poisonous moss to pack their wounds!"

"We did not know it was poisonous!" Kane groaned. Elias would never let us live it down, even at a time like this.

"Believe me, I know. Since I am still asking the two of you for your help, maybe take that into consideration. . . *hmm*?" He tugged the thin white hairs at his temples. "Kane, you are going to have to grip her a little tighter than that if you are to be any help."

Kane thrashed forward as he braced on the woman's legs, but not before he threw a frustrated expression at Elias, or at least what he could, through a mask.

Elias's right brow shot up in defiance. "Don't give me that look. She's not getting any deader, is she?" He cursed under his breath. "Keahi. . . move your damn legs since your mouth does not seem to work well enough to fight me. . . *now*."

I reacted on pure instinct and shoved Kane out of the way at the base of her legs, but he refused to budge. Our boots scraped against the dirt as he set his feet wider to defend his stance. Elias reached over her torso to claw the back of my mask, along with a fist full of hair underneath.

They yanked me toward her upper body. I hovered over the top of her, trembling. The barrier between my hands was far too thin as I searched for an area of her skin that was not mottled. Kane cursed low as he watched me struggle beside him.

Elias stabilized his palms on both sides of her neck. "On the count of three. . . one . . . two. . . Keahi, I will not ask again. . . three!"

The room released a collective hiss as we flipped her over. My hands numbed against her as I glimpsed the siphoning crystal in her neck.

Her white hair had matted against her nape when I found her, clung together in a mixture of sweat and dirt. It was still somewhat difficult to observe. The ruby crystal beneath her pale skin blended in with the angry welts leeching the blood vessels underneath.

Elias's mouth thinned as his hands hovered over her back to assess the damage.

Icy dread shot down my spine. I watched him wipe his face clean of feeling until it was devoid of emotion. It was the same look I had seen him give me many times before as he healed my wounds into scars. This was different. I was not the one on the table.

"Hold her down," he commanded.

There was no hesitation this time as we pressed her extremities into the wooden frame. A sphere of gold glittered as Elias summoned his gift between his palms, almost as if he held the sun itself. He lowered it until it tapped against the siphoning crystal beneath her skin.

Electric ebony waves of power jolted inside the glowing sphere from the crystal. The dark magic crackled against the encapsulation, trying to escape the hold Elias had on it, but he had just begun.

His fingers tensed as he stretched at the shape of his magic to compensate, fighting against the pressure to expand it. Even past the singe of repulsion hissing through the air, I heard Elias's breathy sob. The golden orb in his palm fizzled in patches, but he revived it before he lost control.

A tear dropped from the sea of his eyes. "Do you want to know her name?"

"Elias," I stammered.

Removing a siphoning crystal would force him to see her memories until it dissolved. Her skin blistered against the touch of his magic as he gained further access to them.

"Please, you do not have to do this for me."

Tears assaulted his face as he said, "Her name is Sabine Azterrin."

"That's impossible," Kane muttered.

"She lives," Elias claimed softly. The opposite of the power he poured into his palms.

The Princess of the Novear Kingdom had died. An entire city burned to the ground by their king, along with the sorcerers who had rallied to fight against her father after he destroyed the Veil of Seven. *She was supposed to be dead.* My breath labored as I made the connection. I was walking straight into another trap.

"We have to stop this. If she survived the fires, she would have had to surrender to him, or worse. We do not know how long the crystal has been inside of her body. For all we know, she could have helped him do this!"

Elias absently shook his head, lost within her memories. "Not after what I just saw. . . I have forgiven you for many things, Keahi. Know I will not forgive you if you try to stop me." I did not have the chance to ask him what he saw.

The ring in his eyes capsized with a golden flare.

"This is my choice," he repeated. My grip tightened on her arms as Elias slammed his magic against the siphoning crystal. Her body seized violently against the wood.

Kane jumped up on the end of the cot, pressing his entire body weight against her flailing legs. A chilling scream tore from her lips as the spindles from the orb of his magic wrapped around the crystal beneath her frying skin.

A metallic dome boomed around us, draping like a veil of the sun's warm light as Elias struck the very bottom of his vessel. He swarmed the siphoning crystal in gilded waves, pulsing through his fingertips. Flecks of ruby and gold exploded inside the cave cell.

The siphoning crystal refused to let her go as dark magic sinisterly coiled around his streams of magic.

He screamed a fatal cry as it burrowed into his palms, but Elias would stop for no one. Not even death as I begged him to, knowing he would not have the chance to forgive me.

Chapter Five

Sabine

Even in my death, the only thing I ever had left to hold on to was grief. My screams rippled against the plane of inky darkness fate banished me to. It pooled in endless directions, blanketing around me. The cold had never felt so empty as it furrowed deep into my core, claiming me for an eternity. It did not stop until it found the one thing I begged it not to—*I had been too late to save them.*

My sins emerged out of the lightless sea. Pulsing, blinking in an illumined haze, until the stars punctured the night I was trapped within.

The charred faces of the fallen Novear sorcerers, from the Kingdom of Light and Starfall, surrounded me. They stared back at me through hollow eyes. Soot fell from their cheekbones as fire crackled underneath, their bodies continuing to burn in the afterlife, even outside my father's reach.

"Please, believe me! I didn't mean for this to happen!" I desperately pleaded with them. "I did not know my father would do this!"

My people did not want to hear my cries, nor did they want me to burn with them after what I had done. The stars faded into the darkness of night, disintegrating in rows, one by one, in piles of fallen ash.

A pressure built within, right beneath the base of my neck. The layers of the body I had left behind shredded itself from the inside out. Left alone in this dark hell. Time was deemed irrelevant against the pain I was to sustain here forever. I fought through each idle wave of icy pain that followed, but then—it *stopped.*

A golden sheen swept through the void I was to be punished alone in. I watched as the sun rose beyond the night's eternal horizon. Its blinding rays streamed out toward me, spreading warmth through this frigid hell.

Its amber glow pulsed like a beacon in the night, like it was begging to find me. There was no doubt in my mind. Somehow, I just knew as I watched it gleam in the distance. The sun had risen to save me when I did not deserve to be saved.

The power disturbing the dark was still too far out of reach when I started to crawl on my hands and knees. "Wait for me!" I cried as the darkness threatened to pull me under. I was weighted down by the truth of what I rightfully deserved, but I used all the strength I had left to fight against it.

The golden orb flared as if it heard me, slowly turning until it shined down to where I was hidden. Turbulent night cowered as the golden light, irrefutably mining a path straight toward me, pierced through the vacant tundra.

"You're almost there!" I panted as I dragged my useless legs behind me.

Darkness rattled against its gilded fury, but it was not enough to stop it. Night coiled around the beam of shimmering light. Panic wrenched through me as I stretched my hand out toward it, watching it continue to fight even as it wavered.

If it was going to fight for me, I was going to fight for it.

"I'm right here!" I screamed.

Spindles of gold weaved their path around the dense night as it began to break, sparking away from the beam of light, stretching themselves far too thin as they made a feeble attempt to wrap around my fingers. I cried in agony as the spindles slipped straight through them, and then there was nothing.

The darkness swallowed the light whole.

My lips quivered as I whispered into the emptiness, "Please, don't leave me here."

There was no end and no beginning as time stretched thin. My breath fogged in front of me as I lost myself. So lost, I did not stir, even when the darkness whipped and howled violently around me. An eternity could have passed, and I would have never known.

A hopeless void had already taken hold of my soul when a voice spoke softly in the distance, "I won't."

The dark did not fear what had come for me in the sun's place—it bowed to it.

Smoke funneled around me as a phantom hand wrapped securely around mine, interlacing itself between my fingers. It was cautious, but firm in its touch, as it brought awareness back into my body.

I let it take me, as it gently carried me out of the darkness.

Chapter Six

Sabine

I was in my grave.

My eyes opened within the body I had left to decay. Stale air hit the back of my throat, my ribs expanding against a solid surface beneath me. The soft glow of an oil lamp barely lit the cold, damp room with a ceiling entirely made of stone.

There was an opening ahead of me, barred with rusted iron rods. Piles of damp cloths dripped with blood in the room's corner, muddying the dirt floor as they hung off the side of a wooden bucket.

All of which became faded concerns. The presence behind me was so ominous and powerful, I felt the room spin. It crowded me from mere inches away.

"You are not dead," his voice drifted over me. Blanch-able heat seared all the way from head to toe, as familiarity struck me when it shouldn't have.

My knuckles turned as white as the sheets I held on to. "If I'm not dead. . . Then I'm sure I will be soon enough. That is why you brought me here, is it not?"

I kept myself still at the sound of his boots grinding into the dirt. The power that dripped from him with each step he took. There was no accusation in his voice when he asked, "Is there a reason you should be dead?"

I did not need to lie to him. The King of Solstice must have already known what my father achieved.

"Yes," I whispered.

The power I felt behind me fractured. His breath shuddered upon inhalation, as if it had struck him down to his knees.

The King of Solstice held an undertone of raw hatred he had not borne before. "I could not kill you even if I wanted to at this point. Your father has made sure of that. Though he has made sure of a lot of things over the years, hasn't he?"

I resisted the urge to curse under my breath.

He somehow knew *exactly* who I was.

"My father left me."

Carved my body like a leftover carcass. He was the only person left in my existence who was supposed to love me, and he never did.

"What would he have gained from the ritual? I know for certain he did not exactly leave you to die on your own now—do not lie to me." The thunder in his voice cracked. I could feel him drawing closer, waiting for me to respond, *but I could hear them.*

The insatiable cheers. Their shouting as he tore open my skin, as he bound the magic to my back. How they praised their king for the sacrifice he was making.

I never mattered.

I never mattered to anyone.

"Answer me."

My head snapped in his direction, but he was still hidden within the dark corner of this cell. "Answer what?" I seethed.

I was nothing to him.

I would always be nothing.

The words came out forced because I felt so much weight on my chest. "I remember every mark he made, every jagged line he spelled into my back. The raw heat of the magic seared my flesh as they all stood by and watched him. Is that the answer you want from me?!"

The King of Solstice flinched against the dark, causing his shadow to bend against the oil lamp. "Why would he do it?" he pressed.

My mind was spinning in violent circles, sickened by his incessant need to pull the information he already knew.

"Your kingdom continued to flourish with magic compared to the rest of the realm," I rasped. "I do not know what vile means Solstice had to succumb to just to sustain it when the Gods are not here to do it themselves, but it was not worth this."

I thought I heard him bite back a grunt of disapproval at my ridicule, but he remained silent. My neck was unbearably stiff as I shook my head and said, "My father grew desperate enough to steal it from you."

"Steal it?" Ember eyes glared back at me from his dark corner. "In what way is he trying to *steal* my power now?" The King's patience wore thin as he crept closer, but not enough to come out into the light. "I would argue he has risked the opposite."

Nausea roiled in the back of my throat.

"The same way the Gods allowed him to kill my mother through a siphoning spell." It was easier to fail her than it was my people. I never had the chance to know her.

He lowered his voice to a simmer. "Enlighten me, will you? How would *your* father's actions have anything to do with the Gods? They are not even here anymore because of him!"

I breathed, meeting him word for word. "The Gods made us with the same power to destroy us. His search for a greater power destroyed my mother. My people! If you had any sense to listen to me, you would know he is doing something very similar to you at this very moment."

"Your father is *weak*! That speaks nothing of the Gods—" The sound in his throat died as I fisted the front of his cloak. The King of Solstice had blindly put himself within my reach. I did not have the strength to pull him the way I did, but the surprise of my touch alone had rendered him. The wall of his chest shuttered against my shaking hand.

I half expected him to be hiding behind the mask I had seen before, but instead, I was met with every stark detail of his face against the oil lamp.

A scarred white streak broke up the light brown shade of his skin, running from his jawline all the way through the center of his left eye. It was jagged, like lightning had cracked all the way through his skull. I had seen enough in this war to know only one type of blade could cause such a scar–a sorcerer's blade. It had taken away a stripe of color from his midnight hair. A soft white curl fell in the front of his face.

This man was not the only one rendered. I could barely pull myself away as I took him in for the first time. One side of his mouth twitched as if the direction of my gaze physically touched him.

It took everything I had to keep steady. "Yes—my father is weak in the sense that he is beneath even the vilest of creatures, but the Gods are no better."

I watched the notch in his throat bob as he pressed his full lips together. "And who might I be for your father to siphon power from?"

How young he looked for a king. It was all too quiet, as my words echoed through the cave. "The King of Solstice."

A chill ran up my spine when he smiled, stretching his white scar. The power rippling off him said more to me than the mask he was wearing.

Dark laughter climbed up his throat. "The King of Solstice will want you dead for this," he said through his teeth. "But it is not the reigning king you are bound to."

His hands drifted up to the collar of his cloak, pulling it down just enough for me to see the emblem planted over the left side of his chest. I knew every line, despite it being the smaller version. I had felt every single marred scar ingrained.

"It is the crowned Prince."

The Heir of Solstice, one of the most feared generals among sorcerers, was standing right in front of me.

"Then you are the one to end my life."

His brow furrowed as he looked at me like I was a soul out of touch. Like I could not comprehend the slightest bit of severity that had unfolded.

The General dipped his gaze to the hand I had placed at my throat. Where I had been so sure he had dragged a blade clean through. Nausea roiled within me further as I pulled the memories out like knives.

"There will be no ending your life, at least not anytime soon, I can assure you." He shook his head, his scowl flashing in the amber light.

"You are an ignorant fool. It will kill you if you do not break the siphoning!" The Prince's ignorance would surely kill me faster than his knife.

My father may have enslaved me through a siphoning crystal to contain and will my magic to his greed, but it was my mother's power he stole from until it killed her. She did not have the chance to break the siphoning spell he cast upon her, but he did.

This was just the beginning. I was only a display piece my father shelved as a reminder to the Solstice Kingdom of what was to come. The King of Novear would eventually obtain the power he truly sought in their lands.

He leaned toward me, enunciating his speech. "Do I look like I am drained of power. . . *Sabine*?"

My breath shuttered—audibly, at my true name in his mouth. I knew he heard it from the slight quirk of his lips. Unadulterated rage coated the power I had sensed within the room earlier as he straightened.

"The spell he carved into your back was not one to drain my power from, at least not in the way he intended. He did not perform a siphoning spell. . . of any kind," he claimed.

"Then what kind of spell did he perform as he mutilated my body in front of his soldiers for the sake of this so-called power *you* possess?" I unraveled, my control splintering. "What part of his soul has my father traded me in for this time?"

The General walked toward the rusted metal bars meant to house his prisoner of war. My father, at the very least, had traded me from one familiar cage to another.

He tilted his angular chin over his shoulder. "You will know soon."

I shuddered.

There were far worse things than death. I realized this long ago. "I thought. . . I was finally dead."

He turned away from me. "I am sorry to be the one to tell you that you are not."

I had been so sure. The knife moved across my neck, slicing through the air. The thud of a body that I thought was my own.

"Where is the soldier who found me?"

He threw his hood up over his head and walked through the bars as if made entirely of smoke. "He's dead."

Chapter Seven

Sabine

Time merged, fading into thousands of torn memories. I wanted the impossible. To grasp the golden threads of fate—and tear it apart.

My shallow breaths were not enough for me to hold on to as I pulled at each of their voices. I shoved it as far down into my mental space as I could, but they were too loud in my memory. Not a single one of them had tried to stop my father.

There had been no point in my life where I could brave the idea of friendship. The closest to me I held at a calculated distance. My father's thumb pressed upon those who joined his cause, but not once did I believe they held so much hatred in their hearts to cheer him on. War changed people. It changed what I could have been. Their silence would have been a blessing.

The General of Solstice would not have to break me to get what he wanted from me. I was finely broken. Death was not the relief I thought it would be, but life was still far too excruciating to bear. Not everyone had the strength to live with what haunted them. All I needed was one final push, and I could make it all go away—the voices, the pain.

The newly found scabs prickled and stretched as I feebly sat myself upright. I just had to make it across the room, and it would all be over. Determination set in. I bit the inside of my lip so hard the metallic taste of blood rushed underneath my tongue from the strain as I stood. My destination mocked me from fields away, and I took my first step.

Dark, blood-stained waters reflected what my father had done. My arms shook as I grabbed the ridges of the wooden bucket and slowly lowered myself to the ground, one knee at a time. I glanced over to the pile of crimson-soaked towels, methodically wringing them dry over the bucket. Silently sending useless prayers underneath my breath, hoping that no one could hear me as I worked.

I tied each one of them together, testing the sheared cotton fabric until I was satisfied. Forging a makeshift strand of rope. Finally weaving the threads of my own fate. I investigated the waters once more as I held it up to my neck and paused.

'He's dead,' the Prince uttered before he left me in this cell.

I pulled the loop taut.

It should have been me.

I froze, watching a small ripple slosh through the bucket of water. It sent out small indicative waves. I fumbled with the end of the rope, panicking as I gathered it in my hands. I cursed myself as the door to my cell swung wide open.

Their staff connected to the earth, thudding in time with my raging heartbeat.

My grip quivered against the cold noose when their stone blue eyes, crinkled with age, found mine against the water's reflections.

He whispered, holding no accusation. "Is this what you want?"

I swallowed against the rope, unable to respond.

A low hum sounded over my shoulder. "I would like to ask you a question before I let you do it." Confusion rattled inside me as I gripped the rope tighter, not wanting it to be taken away. "You want something, and you have stayed alive long enough to keep wanting it. Why choose now?"

My eyes tightened. "You are asking a prisoner."

The old man shifted beside me, dipping the end of his golden staff underneath the other end of the rope. Analyzing it. He released a sharp breath. "Despite what you believe to be true right now, you are not our prisoner. Though you have been one for some time. . . *so why do this now*?"

The answer rallied inside of me to be set free. I ached to feel what settled beneath my heart; a quietness against the rush of my mind. It searched for every opportunity to take the pain away, even if it was my life. It was so loud, even when I was entirely still. A melody that followed even when I did not know how to dance to the music. Emotions I had, but felt foreign to, because I did not feel like I deserved them. It was hanging on the edge of my lips when a bright flash descended through his staff. It swirled with a shimmering glow until it captured the end of the rope and obliterated it.

I stared at the left-over debris of the pathetic rope in my hands. A small sound of defeat died in my throat as my source of alleviation disintegrated to ash. I smashed the side of the bucket with just enough force to tip it over. I collapsed from the effort instantly, cool water splashed into the muddy pool I had created.

"*Damn you.*"

He shrugged his shoulders, unfazed. "You took too long to answer me."

"I would be doing your kingdom a favor," I seethed through my teeth, my ribs contracting.

His eyes flickered. "It would be no favor to us. I can assure you." He stepped in front of me, kneeling against his golden staff. The tip of his long, white beard barely hovered above the water. "It must have been there for some time," he muttered softly. All other feeling left my body, as I fixed my focus on the base of my neck. "You must be too weak still to feel its absence."

I shakily reached up to that spot, drawing my fingers over the crystalized ridges that were no longer there.

I felt. . . nothing.

"What have you done?" I gasped.

His hands twisted around his staff. "I did what was necessary to keep you *alive*, and I am just as surprised to find you are not the slightest bit relieved."

"*Relieved*?! I—I could lose control. I—"

"Is that really what he told you after placing that crystal in your neck? *Hmm*? He shouldn't have been able to do that to anyone, let alone a *child*. I saw everything. The moment he had forced it within you as I ripped it apart." He spoke with a fury I could not comprehend, only to silence it with one sentence. "What has he been hiding underneath that you are so afraid of?" A part of me feared he already knew the answer.

"You do not know what you've done," I rasped.

He straightened, bearing his weight against his staff. "I know exactly what I have done. It is you that needs to accept it now."

No– I could not live like this again.

"Why would anyone in Solstice risk their magic by destroying a siphoning crystal—strip your magic bare in the process? Why do you people need me alive so badly you will go to such lengths? What more can you take from me that my father has not already?!" I screamed.

I would not make it this time.

He slammed his staff into the ground, cutting off my thoughts. "I am not here to hurt you. Despite what you may think right now."

A dark, hollow laugh racked its way through me. "Are you so sure? Because I had been told the same thing before a dagger was dragged down my back." His mouth thinned into a straight line as I turned to look him dead in the eye. "But what is one more?"

His eyes cut to the wall behind me. The unease in his stance was obvious, but he spoke with clarity. "I would do it again, Sabine of Novear, even if my kingdom did not depend on it. I would have done it ten times over, because *no one* deserves to be enslaved by such magic." It felt like someone slapped me. My face prickled despite the absence of physical touch. His words hit the same. "Do not look for a regret you will not find."

"You will one day find it when you come to regret the decision of keeping me alive. When you could have just let me die." I meant every single word.

He stretched one hand out to me. "I do not live life looking for regret, even if others tell me I should."

The tops of his hands were spotted and frail with age, and yet I still feared whatever magic he possessed within them. The power it would have taken to release me from my father's enslavement. To still have *any* magic left inside of him, let alone be alive, was something worth fearing.

My nails dug into the mud. "Where am I?"

"You are not far from Solstice's border. . . where you had been left. We are deep within the tunnels of our first mountain pass," he said.

"And *who* are you?"

He leaned his hand out further. "My name is Elias Griselda, the Grand Healer of the Solstice Kingdom." I hid my shock.

They had sent for their Grand Healer to save me?

"What is it you want from me, Elias Griselda?"

The Grand Healer's face tightened. "I want nothing from you. The Prince, however, has a deal to offer you. I will take you to him once you are prepared."

A deal? "If he wants information on my father's plans, he will find himself disappointed. I have nothing to offer in exchange for my life. He will have wasted his efforts in saving me."

"But you are wrong, Sabine. You have something," he said. "We all do."

Again, he held his hand out and patiently waited for me to take it.

There was something unalloyed about Elias's presence that made me reach for him this time, like a moth drawn to a flame. Though his magic did not exactly resonate like fire, the element of the Solstice Kingdom. It did not look like destruction as his golden staff glowed with a soft aura of the morning sun—it was exalted rebirth.

The golden ring around his stone blue eyes drew me to safety. It told me I could come home without grief. It did not matter what sins caused me to drown as the storm coupled with the sea. Elias calmed even the wind to a whisper, assured the waves to bring me to shore, and told the sun I was still worth saving.

The resistance in my chest unfurled as I hesitantly wrapped Elias's rough palm with mine. My brows pinched together. The memory I sought out of reach.

A soft, knowing smile lit his face. "Close your eyes."

Elias's staff clashed against the ground two times before I lost sight of the room.

Smoke poured over me like rushing water, guiding me beneath the surface as it overtook my senses. Heat trickled over my skin as the smell of burnt coal singed my nostrils and reddened my eyes.

We appeared in a small, bleak, changing room. Just in time for me to find a place off to the side to expel the empty contents of my stomach. The fumes swirling in the air from our travels floated around me.

Elias stood, waiting as he held me up with one arm, bracing heavily into his staff as I heaved. He let out a rough sigh. "You did not close your eyes."

Small footsteps pattered out of the corner of the room, a cool damp cloth on my forehead. "She can barely stand, and you thought it was a good idea to travel through shadowfire?"

Her gentle hands guided me into a musty velvet chair as Elias grumbled off to the side. "Her current state is exactly why I had to—not *choose* to do so, Iahni." The room spun around the two figures before me, and I snapped my eyes shut. "We need to get her ready—*do not* look at me like that," he grumbled.

Ready for what?

"She needs more time," the young woman snapped.

A silence followed, as they carried an exchange while I attempted to ground myself to my surroundings. Heat flared into my face as the woman stepped over the bile I had emptied on the floor and kneeled beside me.

A bright red strand of her hair fell in front of her face as she patted my forehead with the cloth. "We have to be quick," she said in a hushed tone.

Elias pulled on the ends of his black oversized robes. "Iahni will help prepare you. Do not avert her. I promise you will find her far more pleasant than what lives in these caves."

Like I had such capability right now.

He nodded once toward us. "I must go. I will see you both soon." His staff clashed twice before he vanished, leaving a trail of smoke as he went.

Iahni rolled her eyes as she swatted at the swirls in the air. Hers were strikingly blue as she leaned back down to me, almost the exact same shade as Elias's.

"The man is a profound Healer and yet he cannot even stand the sight of bodily fluids. It is rather hypocritical if you ask me." Her pink lips lifted into a soft smile. "Let's get you cleaned up. He will be waiting for you."

I was too sick to object, or even think. Everything felt like it was going in slow motion around me. My body was still trying to adjust to its new location as Iahni worked fervently around me, gathering supplies. As she returned, she shoved a small silver vial into my palm. "Drink this. It's not food, but it will help."

I eyed her, taking a split second to consider whether it was poison. Until I concluded, it would not have mattered either way. I pressed the cool rim against my cracked lips and tossed it back. It soothed the aching parts of my throat with a cherry warmth.

Iahni stared at me, fresh bucket in hand. "Better?"

My voice was rough. "A little."

"Good." She wasted no time. "I need to get the blood out of your hair. I did the best I could while you were unconscious, but the wounds on your back took precedence."

My eyes widened. "How long have I been out?"

"For quite some time. . ." Her freckles bunched across her forehead. "Forgive me, we have been traveling a lot here recently. The days are blending."

I forced my head to nod.

When I looked back up, she had been standing there waiting for my permission, a privilege I was not accustomed to. "Go ahead," I mumbled.

Warm water ran down from the crown of my head in streams. As much as I wanted to resist, I eased into the heat with little reluctance. She scrubbed my hair from root to tip, pausing at the ends, working through the clumps in my hair that had knotted from a mixture of dirt and dried blood.

I felt dazed as it eased my nerves, feeling her take time to not cause me any further pain. I tensed as she gingerly patted the damp cloth over my back. To my surprise, I did not wince at the touch. There was no feeling of pain when there should have been. My father had carved my skin until it was completely raw. The rag stilled on my back, lifting in cool contrast away from me.

She pulled the sides of the thin makeshift gown someone had placed me in while I was out. Our eyes met for a moment as I gave her silent confirmation once more. The fabric tugged over my shoulders. It dropped to the floor with an abnormally heavy thud.

I felt the momentary urge to force her away, to retain whatever could be left of what was entirely mine. I did not want to tell myself another lie. My body had not been mine. The sunken realization my enemies knew it too, that not even the core of my magic had ever been mine to possess. It was taken from me before I had the chance to fully mold it for my own.

The feeling of cool silk slipped over my lower extremities as she guided it up over my navel to my chest. The feeling did not travel to my back; it was completely bare. Scars I knew I had, but had never laid eyes on, on full display. My focus grew heavy on the thought, how even out of my father's reach, he had left his mark.

Iahni quickly braided my hair as I became lost trying to regain myself, the woven strands hanging down the center of my back. She came around to face me, squinting as she picked out white pieces to frame my face.

"This will do," she said. It felt like she was reassuring herself as she continued. "You are beautiful," I heard her say, but it was doing nothing to reassure me why my appearance would matter so much to them.

Chapter Eight

Keahi

The ground faded beneath me the moment I left Sabine alone in the prison cell. Nausea roiled inside my gut. It forced its way forward until acid burned through my shaking core, and I convulsed into the first bucket within arm's reach.

My cloak snagged against the rocks as I offloaded the pressure against my forearm. The other hand cradled the edge for support as blood welled with each agonizing lurch forward in the empty tunnel. The unhealed laceration seeped through the binding around my chest, trailing to my hips.

This was at the very least a familiar pain, one I knew how to endure. My father, at first, needed one drop of my blood to maintain the ruse of his inflated power to our kingdom. I should have known from the very beginning. Long before the greed to maintain his image went past the point of insatiable. Without the Gods' presence after the Veil of Seven was destroyed, he needed more, but it would never be enough.

All magic required balance, even to those who thought they were above it, and to the Gods who were no longer here.

My blood was not supposed to be his, and over time the balance demanded defrayment. The King of Solstice's punishment for the taking was his addiction to the power in my veins. There was no balance when I did not stop him, as he required more.

My scars did not disappear. The cuts were now too deep to fully mend. The pain I felt was so raw, I drank myself to a blatant stupor most nights to avoid Elias's attempts to heal what was already broken.

Power was not synonymous with invincibility. I kept giving myself away like my body was dismantled, because it was the only thing I knew how to do. To give away my magic so I did not hurt anyone else but me and yet somehow, I had failed at that, too.

This physical pain was fleeting compared to each lash of Sabine's unbridled misery. My soul now connected to hers for what would be an eternity. . . if she could live that long. Sabine had barely survived the removal. The siphoning crystal had been so far embedded, like it had lived there for *years*, ingrained to be a part of her.

My neck pricked with spiked heat at the memory of Elias's hands working over her. I begged him to stop as his palms turned black from the dark magic she harbored, but he refused to let go of her.

'Get away from me!' Elias yelled, shoving off my grip as I tried to pull him away. Tears streamed down his face as he rallied with the magic that refused to let go like it had been its final command.

'I cannot leave her,' Elias whimpered as he struggled to wrap the golden streams of his magic around the broken pieces until he finally collapsed. I shook him, as his face paled and his eyes lost their blue. The fear of losing him fevered a sense of panic I did not know existed until his hand faintly cupped my jaw.

'She was just a child,' he breathed as a tear welled in the corner of his pale eyes.

Those were the last words he had spoken to me, even as I lifted him. *'It's over. It's over,'* I murmured into his shoulder repeatedly. His eyes had glazed over with no direction; lost within the seal of her memories the crystal had contained.

I decided I could not know what Elias had seen—because as I returned to check on Sabine I looked down upon her swollen face and realized that if I did. . . I would lose every ounce of frail control I had left, knowing this happened to her because of my seal of power.

The door to her soul was now held partially open after the initial link, but her very presence was stronger than before. The removal of the crystal had unlocked a part of her to me through the sorcerer's bond. I could feel how her body shook with icy pain even after Iahni had tried to keep her comfortable, whispering over her unconscious body that she was going to be safe.

I could not withstand it. So, I did something I did not know how to do. Touch was like a memory which could only be forgotten if I removed my skin. For as long as I could withstand it until she woke, I held her hand.

It was an effort to just breathe as a sliver of guilt edged its way into my rib cage and labored my breath. I wanted to believe she was innocent as she made her claims, but what other reason would the King of Novear have to intentionally bind his daughter with his enemy?

The risk he took did not match unless he had a contingency plan if the sorcerer's bond went through, and she survived. Yet Sabine had mistaken me for my father, and I could not refute the rumble of shock I felt from her through the bond. If the King of Novear knew of my seal, he also knew my father did not have the amount of power he claimed to have on his own.

There was a betrayal in our midst. The seal on my chest was known to few, or at least I had thought, as I watched the King of Novear ignite the sorcerer's bond between us through Sabine's eyes.

When, there would be no if. I let the word clamor inside of me because I planned to do far worse to those responsible. When I found out who revealed the truth of my seal to the King of Novear, they would wish seeing it happen was the worst of it.

Volatile—that was the only way I could describe the residual ache of her emotions coursing through me now from afar. Despite my desperate attempt to create distance when I left, her feelings magnified, as if they were my own. It infected any rational thought I had as the pain she carried from surviving drove deeper.

Misery lashed out at me, every feeling heightened, and I was the one that felt like I was invading her. Sabine's confusion was evident, because she had not felt when her soul fused with mine and the link snapped in place. If she had felt it as I did, she would have known I was as translucent as glass on the brink of shattering.

A part of me believed she never would feel it, the sorcerer's bond, depending on how she healed from the siphoning crystal she had been enslaved by. Selfishly, it was a relief. It would be easier this way, I was sure of it.

I struggled to swallow the lump in my throat. The look of utter defeat on her face had nearly brought me to my knees to beg for forgiveness, even if I was not initially the cause of it.

She *wanted* to die.

Her face was made of stone as her internal screams sliced through our connection when I told her the truth she hadn't—and I just left her there.

Tremors racked their way through my core as I clung onto the bucket, listening to the echo of her cries as punishment from a distance, because I was too much of a coward to tell her I was the reason she was still alive. The pain she had to endure was because of me, and I would never forgive myself for it.

The air shifted beside me, as warmth stole the damp cold in curls of ash and smoke.

"Elias, please just leave me here," I said weakly.

He crunched his staff into the dirt. A telltale sign he would rather twist the end into my skull. "How could you leave her there like that? What is wrong with you?"

I cleared the grittiness from my voice. "I—It was too much. I never—"

"*Boy*. You're going to have to *speak up*," he rumbled through his teeth.

I pressed my eyelids tightly.

Elias was never one to be *truly* angry, but when he was, he had every right to be. The man I have become is far from the boy he raised to do and be better. I failed him at every turn. The only good pieces left of me were entirely because of him; it would be a disservice to say otherwise. My father with certainty had no part in it, and my mother was not here to see the monster she knew I would become.

"I could feel it. . . everything," I half-whispered, riddled with shame as my head hung low. "I could not take it anymore after she woke."

Elias huffed a drawn-out sigh, wringing the handle of his staff. "It's funny. I found her in a similar position as this." I nodded my head slowly as he continued. "Except she had wrung every cloth dry in that bucket we left. Each one connected knot after knot, a loop formed at the end, holding it up to her throat." My skin iced over as every hair raised in my body. "You know better. You, of all people, know better."

A hoarse sob released from my throat as I fought to hold my chin up, but I crumpled under the weight of the image of finding her dead in the hold. An apology on my lips I would not have the chance to give for a second time, when the first one had been too late, as I cried out over my mother's grave.

"She isn't." Pinpricks hazed my vision. "She is not dead. I would have felt it."

"No," Elias bit out. "But you are lucky I found her in time." Time that was not given after my mother had killed herself.

A hot tear marked its hidden trail beneath my mask. I stood up to face him, wiping the grime at the corner of my lips before I lowered it to my neckline. "It will not happen again. I promise."

The gold rim along Elias's eyes flared. "I most certainly hope not. I will not lose you too. You may think you are invincible, Keahi Aldeer, but you are not."

He lowered his eyes to my chest. The hitch in my ribcage with each breath was a dead giveaway. The pressure from my ailment had ripped the wound Elias did not have enough time or strength to heal; *good.* I wanted to feel it, anyway.

"On a different note, we have a wedding to prepare for, it seems. I rather enjoy them." I gaped at him as he shrugged. "Kane enjoys them too, apparently. Iahni told me he was rather upset when you sent him back to Kallahni with the rest of the Volkans."

My eyes anchored themselves to the floor. "Elias, we need to wait. She is in no position to make this kind of decision to finish the sorcerer's bond."

His gray eyebrow rose. "And you are? *Look at you.* If you are feeling the effects, just imagine what it will do to her if we delay further. She is barely hanging on as we speak. The lack of connection from the bond might tear her apart if we do not follow through with the bindings. You have never been sick like this a day in your life, even with walking around being sliced open from your father."

I straightened. "It does not matter what I want in this. I will not force her to marry me, Elias. *She must choose.* I did my part to keep her alive just as you did to give her the chance to say yes or no. I will sustain enough power to keep alive. . ."

But she will not.

A thought I had to violently suppress. I could not see another person choose death because of me. There was very little else I wanted outside of that fact.

Marriage had never been on the table for me, regardless. My father had never been against the right match for our kingdom, but he never opposed my refusal. A powerful match would become our advantage, but was it worth risking the truth?

He knew as well as I did.

What was I to say to a woman when she saw the forbidden seal of my magic for the first time? How was I supposed to explain the ruins on my skin from my father's blade? The secrets I wore were hidden, not confessed. Nothing good had ever happened to those who learned the truth.

Elias's blue eyes darkened. "You must let it go, the guilt that lives inside you."

"That's not what this is about."

"She was not in her right mind, Keahi. The things your mother said before she took her life were not true. She was sick when the veil closed. You cannot carry the weight of something that does not pertain to the truth of who you are now. *Stop punishing yourself.*"

The realm was punishing me right now; I did not have to do anything. Not when her blood spilled because of me. Sabine's nature did not reveal an ounce of what she felt, but I could sense it through the connection. To hear from Elias that she had almost. . . taken her own life. I did not know if I could relive another death like my mothers, not again. I slowly looked back up, our gaze a collision course of opposition Elias had not once backed down from. A loyalty I did not deserve.

"How much time do we have?"

Elias's features hardened. "By the end of the night. I have taken her to Iahni to prepare her the best we can for the ceremony, but she can barely stand. The healing potions we have given her will not last forever."

Ice-cold dread pooled in the pit of my stomach. "She is going to hate me, and I am going to let her."

"Be honest with her Keahi, she has been through too much to deserve anything else but the truth from you. It is not her fault, *or yours*, the position that you are in now. Her father's plans will be revealed in time. The tide of the war is about to *change* because of this; you must look forward."

My thumb circled the inner portion of my left palm, rubbing a hole through the third set of gloves I had this year. "You do not know her enough to trust her," I painfully argued in retreat. "Sabine could be aligned with him still, preparing to tear our forces down from the inside out."

Elias's hand landed on my shoulder, the wrinkles around his eyes crinkling with a somber laugh. "I believe that just as much as you do right now. I do not feel it as you do Keahi, nor can I imagine, but I saw enough to know what it could feel like as I watched her father place that *thing* in her neck. Believing in what you feel from her does not make you weak. Trust what she is telling you when she does not have the strength to speak it."

"It could make me weak." I tugged at the collar of my mask that felt too tight. If the sorcerer's bond was clouding my judgment, it was strongly taking effect. Because right now, I was listening to him. "I would deserve nothing she gives me once we fully seal the sorcerer's bond. That much I know."

Elias shook his head. "The fates do not control the realm's cruelty we are subjected to. I believe they can only forge their powers in search of the moments in our lives when we least expect it. When the realm breaks us, the fates find the moments that make us want to live. This is your chance to live, Keahi. Do not break now, not when the stars have finally spoken."

I brushed his hand off my shoulder.

"The fates are no friend of mine."

Chapter Nine

Sabine

The Prince of Solstice cheated my deal with death in exchange for his own vigil. If I would not be his prisoner, then his offer to me would be another burden I was forced to accept.

My legs resented the ability to stand. The warmth of the potion Iahni had given me blunted the pressing ache of my exhaustion, just enough to hold my weight. The crystal had been removed, but my soul, the vessel of a sorcerer's magic, felt fragmented within me.

"We are not going far," she said easily. "Go slow if you need to. The tunnel system beneath the military base is not trafficked frequently."

I furrowed my brow, acutely aware of how hard I was panting. The room had stopped spinning at the very least.

"I may not look like I can put much together right now." I relented as I braced my arm around her shoulder. "But I find your claim hard to imagine."

An array of silks and tapestries colored the stone walls of the small changing room. Antiquated chests with keyed fastenings piled on top of each other in the corner. A fine layer of dust staled the dresses Iahni had splayed across the velvet chair next to me. Otherwise, the space did not appear to be occupied.

Her laugh was light and melodic. "Traveling through shadowfire has overtaken your ability to smell the musk strangling this room," she said as we brushed through a fine red tapestry hovering over the door frame.

"This area was once a sacred ritual ground before the war had claimed it. The soldiers believe this area is now haunted. They refuse to take anymore prisoners, alive at least, to prevent coming down here." Iahni's grip loosened on my arm as I straightened when we approached the end of the dark corridor.

My eyes went toward the only source of natural light I had seen in what felt like days. We entered through an archway leading us into a massive cave dwelling. "What exactly took place down here?" I asked.

"Ceremonies. . . of sorts."

A small opalescent beam pierced the center of the room we emerged into from thousands of feet above.

The moonlight revealed a mosaic of a slumbered dragon curled upon the cave floor. It demanded the entire room's attention; crafted of ruby, obsidian, and clear quartz crystals glittering against the lunar rays. It was an entrancing presence, as if the very offspring of the earth's finery was alive with magic.

So much so, I had not noticed the man at the edge of the room—*the Heir of Solstice,* staring at me with an intensity that burned the rest of the world gray.

My entire body sent streaks of fire through my nerve endings in protest as his magic suffocated my soul. This power he beheld was so overgrown it was physically painful to be near, tapping against the broken edge of my magic. I could sense it through the link my father had carved on my back, sparks of his magic igniting the outline in an unpleasant heat.

I stared at my infernal executioner, unsure as to how he made it this far without being drained of his sorcery entirely. No, he was not the King of Solstice, but the power he beheld was everything my father had been looking for. A trade that would work in my father's favor if he did not end me before it was too late.

The Prince had changed from earlier into what I would think of when looking upon a Solstice royal. Power dripped like arrogance. A red cape bellowed across his broad shoulders. There was no mistaking the metallic armor belted around his muscular thighs, the house crest of solstice on his center breast plate.

"I want you to know. . ." his voice echoed against the walls despite how quietly he spoke. "I did not want it to come down to this. We must continue the ritual before it is too late."

The cave walls crumbled with the force of an avalanche. My blood beat against my ears, rallying their distant screams of glory as I was bound to the rock against my will.

"*Finish it then*, but only if you kill me, General."

His eyes flickered like a flame in the night, weighing my words like a decision he did not know how to make.

"There is another way," he hesitated. "I have no intention of hurting you."

"*I would rather die.*"

What was life if I was forced to live for anyone other than the person who had to wake up every day in this wretched body? Death was a painless alternative. There were very few that could escape it outside of the Gods.

The side of his jaw ticked as he took a step into the sparkling light. He slowly lowered his gaze to my neck. A slow devastating agony broke over me, the memory of the noose circling my throat grew tighter.

The Prince's voice was barely a whisper, "As I am fully aware."

I searched his face, expecting to see a rueful smile, to find him baiting me before he tortured me further. Those who did not understand what it was like to have the thought their life was not worth living had the privilege of a life they wanted. I would not be shamed.

Every muscle in my body locked itself in place when I found nothing of the sort. He wore all vulnerability and emotion in the crease of his brow.

It was the opposite of indifference.

Compassion was not something I had been dutifully trained to accept. It scared me how I discovered it just by looking at him unmasked, without ever learning the definition of sympathy prior.

The Prince prowled directly in front of me; the light descending fiercely on his scarred face. His throat bobbed. "He ignited a sorcerer's bond."

A choked breath released from me.

"*Liar*," I hissed.

He could not refute the power I felt pulse through me during the ritual. The rush of magic claiming me for its own was standing right in front of me.

I fisted the satin of my dress. "Do not be blinded when you bear the truth of the siphoning magic on your chest!"

"The mark we share now is not what it seems." He shifted his weight carefully. "Has the King of Novear ever used another person to complete the siphoning ritual?"

A tension gripped my chest, making it hard to breathe. My father had told me he was going to siphon as much power as he could until the King of Solstice came to kill me. He wanted to taunt them with my discarded existence, symbolize what he had done, but it was not the King of Solstice who had come for me in the night. I searched my memories for an answer I already knew—my father had not once used another person to siphon power from.

When the King of Novear had siphoned magic from my mother, it was through a relic to contain the power she beheld. Just as he had done with the siphoning crystal, but hers had broken apart, ending her life along with the spell.

He searched my face, waiting for the realization to fall into place, but it did not.

The magic he was speaking of was ancient, unfathomable even before the widespread drought of our magic, when the veil was closed for the Gods to return. Any evidence of bonded sorcery burned in the Kingdom of Novear with my people.

"There may be consequences to your survival if we do not close the channel. . . to *our* survival," he said, correcting himself. I heard the weight settle into him at the same time it did me, at the severity of his accusation. "You must know, in order to complete the sorcerer's bond ritual, we have to—"

"I know the laws of magic." The sting in my chest grew. I was only worth something when it was tied to a motive. It was time I learned his weakness through the one thing all powerful men feared, the opposite of what I craved.

"What makes you think I care if you die?" I pressed. "I have been waiting for death to find me for far too long. I will take you down with me if I must."

The Prince approached me with desperation in his step. Heat

rippled off him, corrupting me to the flames, forged by his own element of magic.

"Because if I die, then you have also died for nothing. Your mother died for nothing." His words were sharp as he spoke. Tearing me to shreds as he used the only thing he could against me. What I had foolishly given him.

"My people may have been painted as your enemy, Sabine. I may still be, depending on what side we end up on during this war, but do not base your life on your assumption of me." He stopped at the edge of the crystal dragon unfurled beneath us. "I cannot promise you much, but I can promise you I have never seen the sight of someone as wicked as the man you call your *father*. I am not a good man," he rasped, "but I have never surpassed such cruelty."

I closed the distance between us, uncaring of the line I crossed to reach him. "Then what cruelty do you offer me, Prince of Fire?"

I threw one of the few titles I knew, for his name had been kept hidden among borders. *Heir of Solstice, Prince of Fire, The Serpent in the Shadows.* All names every sorcerer outside his kingdom knew well, except for his actual name. A name that I hoped I would get to know and curse all the same.

His nostrils flared, gritting into his teeth as he raised a single hand. There was no crystal to hold me in place, but I remained its captive. I flinched out of instinct, waiting for his palm at the side of my face. A light leather-worn touch gripped my chin instead.

My face turned with little resistance.

The Prince of Solstice did not take one step closer. His ember eyes were on the gloved hand that was holding me, pain written on his features as if the contact tore him apart.

"My face might say otherwise." He let go of my chin. "But I am not a violent man to those who do not deserve it." Heat rose as his slow gaze dragged over every inch of my face, almost as if he gained to memorize it. "Still, you have every right to fear me."

I noted every fine detail. The way his features shifted as quickly as his own shadow. It lingered upon the walls behind him while it danced in the gleam, refracting off the crystals. How his eyes burned with a vengeance that made me want to believe him—desperately.

"What if I am the one you need to fear?" I whispered. It was a simple question. One I did not expect to say, as I had not had that type of freedom in a long time.

The corners of his mouth rose slightly, his eyes smiling with every bit of hatred I had seen before. "I am afraid I already do."

I did not flinch this time as he raised his hand, motioning to the figure that had been waiting for us.

Elias stepped between us, holding a red sash. He was dressed in ceremonial robes embroidered with a gold dragon braided on one side, curling its belly across his shoulders, and its tail draped down the length of the seam until it flowed to the floor.

"We cannot delay further—you are already feeling the effects of our unformed connection because of your weakened state." The Prince urged me while the Healer remained silent. "If you agree to this, a sorcerer's bond must be brought before the Gods to—"

"The *Gods* are not *here*," I spoke slowly, cutting him off. The very mention of them caused my blood to curdle. I did not seek approval from Gods when they had never sought mine. "They have not been for decades, even before my father destroyed the veil."

Elias interrupted calmly. "Some magic does not fade, Sabine. There is sorcery so deeply embedded within our lands, even without their presence to sustain it. We cannot undo this once their magic gives blessing to this union of power."

I lashed out. "It can be undone if I refuse the ritual."

The Son of Fire passed a worried glance to the Healer and back, but Elias had kept his stone eyes trained on me.

"You have run before." I stilled as Elias pitched his voice lower, shaking his head. "Do not run this time. Not when you finally have the power to change it. Our kingdom has never supported your father in this war, and it is very apparent you do not either. Our goals are the same."

Elias's words struck like a viper to my chest. I stared at him, not wanting to know what else he could have seen when he removed the crystal from my neck.

"The magic you speak of is ancient, and you truly expect me to believe you? You speak of heresy," I cursed.

There was very little history of sorcery I had privilege of outside my father's control. According to the few legends passed down to me, magical bonds between kingdoms were forbidden by the Gods, and rarely accepted within their own kingdoms when they were here to grant it.

"I speak of nothing but the *truth*," the Prince growled. "Allow me the chance to prove everything that I have been saying to you holds nothing but verity. Their residual magic will not give blessing to the sorcerer's bond if I speak falsely."

The seriousness of his proposal, and the underlying hint of hopelessness as his voice strained, turned my blood cold. He proved something vital in his admissions. I did not know the laws of magic well, but I did not have to.

A sorcerer's bond was as foreign to me as rumors were to the whole truth. I did not need to expose my ignorance to get what I wanted from him if what he was saying was true. There was nothing to gain from vulnerability. It was perhaps the most valuable thing my father had ever taught me.

On the days my father was eager to punish me, I memorized my failures to learn to avoid them. For every time he raised his hand at me when I could not prevent his anger, I studied the reaction he wanted to lessen the strike. When my father screamed at me, I learned to be quiet. In my silence, I learned how to listen.

The Prince of Solstice wanted to save himself, but he needed me in order to do it. There was no king, or future king, who would beg for my consent unless it was required to complete the ritual. I felt my strength gather, my anger fueling me as I closed the gap until I grazed his chest.

"If you are lying to me. . ." I smiled. His breath hitched against the feel of my own brushing against him. "I will make you wish you had left me for dead. Just like he did." There was no crystal shoved in my neck now to prevent me from killing him otherwise. I vowed to remind him as often as I vowed to remind myself from this day forward.

My brow arched. "What are you waiting for?"

Our gazes collided as I pointed a single finger to the ground. He parted his mouth slightly, his face puzzled. I knew the second he understood what I wanted from him as he placed one knee on the ground. Any man who wanted power from me would have to beg on his hands and knees for it.

The Prince of Solstice dropped to one knee. "Sabine Azterrin, Princess of the Novear Kingdom." He firmly grasped my left hand. "Will you continue the sorcerer's bond ritual with me?"

There was no part of my being that wanted to accept what he could offer through the bond, except that which was his underlying message—*revenge*. I craved it so deeply, more than the air I breathed, more than the idea of death.

If his claims to me of the sorcerer's bond were true, then I was going to kill my father with my bare hands. Relish in the light, leaving his eyes with the power he coveted, claiming it for my own, just like he did to my mother, my people. So, I said the only thing that made sense, to fulfill what had been torn apart and pieced back together.

"Yes."

It was at that moment I felt the small mask he beheld slip. Power that tasted like the aftermath of fire, smoked out by destruction, rippled with the tangy aftertaste of fear.

I devoured it.

The Prince stood, resisting the urge to leave my eyes as he towered above me.

"Let us begin," Elias resounded. His voice was laced with sorcery, whispering prayers in a language that I could not understand as magic eddied into a pulsatile sensation around us.

"Keahi Aldeer, Prince of the Solstice Kingdom, prepare to take your oath upon the center stone of Rhiannon, the Goddess and creator of Solstice."

Keahi slowly stepped over the heart of the dragon laying before our feet at Elias's command.

"Sabine Azterrin, Princess of the Novear Kingdom, please come into the light. For the fates have chosen you to unite our kingdoms. A unity that the Gods had forbidden."

Heart hammering, I met him an arm's distance apart.

"Intertwine your hands together to symbolize a force that cannot be broken," Elias proclaimed.

I followed Keahi, mirroring his cautious movements, interlacing opposite hands. The warmth of his fingertips pressed into my slick palms through his gloves.

It was a small win, because he could not feel the difference between my fear of the unknown and my mind's refusal to back down. This was finally my choice, and nothing could take it away from me this time.

Elias stepped forward to wrap the fine red cloth around our arms, tying the leftover silken strands at our wrists. A strike of a match sounded. Crackling fire set ablaze, rebounding off my soul.

Firelight reflected within Keahi's eyes as a ring of flame met around us in a perfect circle, levitating above the crystal dragon. Sparks dived and flicked at our feet. Heat roared in a blazing frenzy, causing my eyes to glass over in retreat from its sting.

I did not so much as falter, and neither did the man locked in front of me as the heady sensation of magic flowed between us. The sash intertwining our fates caught fire. There was no sting as it wrapped around in line with the silk. Only the warmth of the magic flowed until it flaked to ash between our feet, swiftly dissipating into a curling smoke.

All the light in the room died as a glittering moonlight took its place. The crystal dragon dispersed its shimmering gaze upon us once again.

"You may release your hands," Elias said, stepping through the fade.

We lingered for a moment, carefully releasing them in hesitant unison. The feeling of the ritual still charged through my fingertips, electrified with the promise of fatal retribution.

Elias lifted two blackened objects out of the fallen ash. He turned to Keahi with a deep affirming expression and slipped a blackened ring with a molten stripe over Keahi's left finger. The remaining object was placed in his right palm. A mutual bow shared between them before the Grand Healer stepped away.

"Hold out your hand," he said in a gruff whisper. My mind numbed as I stared at the tiny object cupped in his palms.

Keahi's black and white curls cascaded over his forehead as he rounded toward me. The intensity in his gaze maimed the rage I had been blinded by, pushing me forward until this point. An obsidian, diamond-shaped crystal was shakily placed on my third finger. A thin, matching molten strand lining the middle.

Did all bonding ceremonies require a ring?

He straightened, thumbing over the top edges just before letting go. A faint spark ran through me as he did. Keahi's eyes escaped to the floor and never returned—*no, please no.*

I begged him silently to look back up at me as Elias lifted his hands. "The ash of your union has been carved into the stones you now wear. Rhiannon's residual magic, the Goddess of Solstice, has blessed the bonding. The foundation is as strong as the will of the objects forged. May the Gods bless the Prince and Princess of the Solstice Kingdom, for you are now a pair of sorcerers bonded."

What have I done?

Elias nailed his hands into the rock, my vision spinning while the air shifted. Magic smothered my senses as spindles of smoke grayed between us. The sorcerer who was now my bonded was the only thing that remained constant.

Chapter Ten

Sabine

Fire emerged from the blaze of smoke, lighting the four torches at the corners of the room we appeared alone in. The space itself did nothing to prevent the pit in my stomach.

Unfathomable power was revenge in its purest form, taunting me as I solidified my answer with a single phrase as I accepted his offer.

'Yes.'

There was a separate portion I had completely ignored for the sorcerer's bond. I had not weighed the consequences when I bargained without knowing the conditions. My one shot at freedom gained another chain in the form of a small molten lined ring on my left finger.

My heart knocked against my sternum, begging to be released as I made sense of my surroundings. Elias's voice rang through my ears, dousing my newfound strength. *'The Prince and Princess of Solstice.'*

The room was completely barren. . . except for the single, small bed pushed up against the side of the room.

I twisted the obsidian ring.

Keahi headed straight toward the bed. The last of my fears flickered to me in the dark as it whispered, *'and now you will pay the price for power.'*

My eyes pinched closed. *It was nothing,* I assured myself. This would be nothing compared to what I had already sustained against my will.

My virtue was long buried under the tangled bedsheets of men and women I spent my nights with. Allured by the small window of indulgence as their eyes became lost in the pleasure. It meant nothing, but it had been mine.

I jerked my head, forcing myself to face what would one day be a minute inconvenience in the grand scheme of my undoing. I told myself at least this time it was my choice, and it was no one else's debt to pay but mine.

I could just close my eyes.

Turn it all off.

Keahi went deathly still as he stopped at the edge of the bed. It was several moments before he finally turned, as if I had spoken my thoughts out loud into the silence.

The hitch in my breath was audible as our eyes met. His jaw hinged shut. It did nothing to calm the terror roaring in my bloodstream. His lips moved, but I could not hear the sound they produced.

"Sabine. . . I need you to breathe," Keahi said for a second time. It was firm, a command filled with his own set of fears. My lips trembled with broken admission when my chest did not move at his instruction.

"I am not here to claim you," he said. My fear spiked with his urgency, calling me back into my body. He pointed underneath the bed, kneeling slowly on one knee as he stretched a hand underneath the frame. "I just need to retrieve my satchel. We cannot stay here tonight."

My voice cracked in my throat as I reclaimed air. I attempted to clear it silently, but I knew he had heard it by the way his shoulders tensed at the sound. I was spiraling completely out of control, barely having the ability to force myself to hold on.

The moment you appear weak is the moment another dagger is at your back, Sabine.

Change. Be anything else but this. They do not know who you truly are. You can be anyone, anything but this.

I snapped back into myself.

He rummaged through his pack on the ground, hurriedly setting out a set of clothes and a separate fleece cloak on the bed. That was no doubt for me. The size of it was entirely too small for his stature. He had continued his conversation with me, but I had not been listening. "We cannot risk being seen together right now, not this close to our borders. I will—"

"—You will do nothing until you tell me what the meaning of all of this is." I fueled myself with anger until it surpassed my uninvited fears. "Nothing more until then."

You will not be weak.

Keahi's dark brow raised at my own commands, either in challenge or curiosity. His response made me feel transparent, and I knew then that I was going to have to lie better than that.

"What? Did you think I was going to agree to finish the sorcerer's bond with you, and then go along with your every command?" I asked. Keahi's features dropped, and his entire body went rigid.

I held out both of my wrists to him. "If that is the case, then lock me in chains because you will have to drag me there." Triumph built itself a new home inside me at the break in his composure. The shock of our union I let slip past my hold was now hidden behind his own discomfort.

His footsteps toward me fell unnaturally silent. Keahi's eyes darkened as he looked between my outstretched arms. "Are you testing me, Novear? Because lying will do you no good here; your false claims bear upon you as if written into your skin."

The blood in my face drained. I wanted to believe his words were a threat. Wanted to find my own threatening words to respond with, but there was something else which terrified me more. The wall

I had built crumbled on the glassy edge of his concern, which said otherwise.

My momentary lapse of triumph dwindled at a rapid pace. I would not cower at a man, no matter how deadly he might be. Never again. The General behind the mask may have built his reputation on the battlefield, but he was going to have to earn his when it came to me.

"What lies do I lay so humbly at your feet, your highness?" I sneered.

He pressed my arms down to my sides. "You have no idea, do you? How easily your lies sing to me." He went still within the erratic movement of his shadow behind him, as if it were alive. "You have no idea what you have agreed to. That much I know for certain now."

I took him in fully, continuing to track the movement of his shadow circling him, grinning wide as it died at my following words. "You underestimate me then. It offered me a power I could not refuse. The rest is simply collateral."

"Collateral?" He cursed under his breath.

If he was attempting to gain my full confession from his valiant charade, he would fail. "Tell me, how far do you think I was willing to fall for power as I accepted the sorcerer's bond? Since I can see you are quite eager to do so."

My father's words flooded my mind intrusively. '*I want them to know just how far I will go to win this war. Do not take it personally. . . I killed your mother far slower.*'

It was my father who underestimated how far I was willing to unravel for revenge. There were a lot of things I did not understand, questions I should ask, but right now I only cared about one thing. I had nothing else to lose when I never had anything to give. I just needed to survive long enough to take it, and I was going to keep taking until I got what I wanted.

"What do your people know of the sorcerer's bond then?" he asked, interrupting my thoughts, unwilling to give into my games. So, I played his, with the retellings I could remember from when my kingdom had been fully intact.

"That it is a sacred bond of powers, rare, even when the Gods were here to sustain our magic," I said.

Keahi's hands tensed at his side and nodded, but I could tell it was not the answer he was looking for. A gloved hand reached into the root of his hair, tugging the strands away from his face.

"It is not my people, or even the King of Solstice, who will not accept we are bonded. They would not dare question a magic so rare. What they will question is *how*."

I knew what he was referring to. The Solstice and Novear Kingdoms were rivals among each other, more so than any of the other kingdoms, even prior to the death of the veil. My father made sure of it when he burned every village outside their mountains to the ground.

"You place blame on them for questioning? There has never been a pair of bonded sorcerers from separate kingdoms, in any of our histories, let alone any type of civility between our own," I said.

He placed his restless hands behind his back. "I do not, but we cannot afford to leave room to question how the bond came to be. If my father found that the King of Novear ignited the link of our bond, he would not let you survive."

I bristled. The very thought of my revenge escaping me wrenched its way down my spine. "So, you plan to lie to your own father? To your entire kingdom that our powers are bonded?"

The temperature within the room plummeted as if he stole all the warmth to feed the power in his veins. "I will lie every day of my life if I must. Spin whatever set of lies I can afford because no one else can know the truth."

I waited for a sign. Any sign that what he was saying was not true. The length of my funeral gown trailed behind me as I circled him.

"And while we are drowning in our web of lies, how do I know you will not be wrapping your threaded silk around my neck? Tightening every inch with every lie you tell? I dislike liars, Prince."

I never have because I was the biggest one of them all.

He followed my pursuit. "You may not see through my lies now, but one thing I know for certain is that I see through yours. You have only told one, and you are wearing the threaded noose around your neck like it was made for you," he hissed.

There is no way he could know. Running my mind over the conversation I had with Elias in what was supposed to be my final moments—what the Grand Healer saw beneath the crystal. "And what lies have I told?"

He cocked his head to the side. "You promised to know the laws of magic. That you were fully aware of what the sorcerer's bond entailed. . . but I realize you do not. If you knew the laws, you would also know whatever lie I tell, whatever lie you tell, we are wrapped together all the same." The glow in his eyes flared. "You are not the only one willing to sacrifice to get what you want."

Unease brushed over me, coated with my failure. "Why did Elias call me the Princess of Solstice?"

Keahi looked away briefly, his shoulders full of tension. "As my bonded, you now have the right to the throne as much as I do."

I hung on his words, unable to speak.

Keahi's gaze frantically dipped to the ring on my finger and back up. "We are not married," he blurted suddenly.

My lips parted. It was a small gift to be spared, but I would not take it for granted. Life had not molded me to love. Marriage was not meant for someone like me. He tracked my movements, missing nothing as he said, "But we are going to have to pretend to be."

Our eyes clashed instantly.

"It is a truth within a lie," he continued. "Believable, as to why I brought the daughter of the Novear Kingdom into our territory. We will hide the truth of our bond for as long as we can. After the destruction of the veil, it is a powerful source of magic to behold in this drought. We cannot trust others with this knowledge. It is too dangerous until we can wield it for ourselves."

The Prince did not have to worry about my trust. It was a power I did not give myself, especially now, because I nodded in agreement as I held the weight of his stare. He clutched the moment away and turned on his heels, his red cape lashing behind him.

"It will take us several nights to travel to the inner portion of Solstice. We are at risk being on the edge of our border, and I cannot protect you out here. . . not alone," he admitted, spoken as if we were already on the run, but I did not ask *who* he needed to protect me from.

"I am not as weak as I appear to be, Prince," I said.

Two rival heirs from enemy kingdoms were now bonded by sorcery. Our enemies would find us regardless of the distance, but we needed time to strategize for the fight.

Keahi's hand went to the side of his hip, drawing a blade. It glinted in the light, revealing a silver dagger with scales winding around the hilt.

I hated the way I held my breath as he turned the fabric covering his hand red. Keahi sliced straight through the center of his palm as if he had done it a thousand times before, grasping the pool of blood forming through the ripped seam of his glove.

The Prince of Solstice walked over to the bed, throwing the sheets off in disarray with intention before he let it drip slowly onto the mattress.

"You are far from weak," he said distantly.

He tore a piece of white cloth from the bed to wrap around the wound he had created, fumbling with it against his chest as he tied it off with his teeth.

"Do not let anyone see your face. Do not speak to anyone you may see, no matter who or what you hear. I will let you know when it is safe."

Keahi stepped around me, farther than necessary, as he gripped the door handle with his bleeding hand. "I hope you will be well enough to withstand the coming travel."

"I will be," I said, as he gave me a parting glance.

I have to be.

Chapter Eleven

Keahi

There was outright torture, and then there was suffering in silence. Torture was undoubtedly my preference. It had been two whole days since we had begun our travels into Solstice, and Sabine and I had not spoken to each other—not even *once*.

I continued to tiptoe around her the best I could while setting up our camp for the night. The anticipation slowly ate me alive, but I was set on giving her as much space as she needed, despite how painful it was.

Sabine crossed her legs and eased herself onto the grass as I created a small fire with my magic. She quietly watched the flames flicker against the wind, her hands folded tightly in her lap. For a split second, I thought she looked up at me. I tore my gaze away and shuffled through my pack, attempting to avoid making her uncomfortable. The crickets seemed to lull each time the contents clinked together, causing my shoulders to flinch.

After preparing the rations Iahni had made for us, I hesitantly gathered the courage to walk over and place it in front of her. I neatly unfolded the edges of the cream-colored cloth, separating out the dried nuts and fruit. My body tensed as she shifted her eyes from the fire, a white brow arched as she stared down at my gloves.

I fumbled and watched a portion of her food roll onto the ground. Snatching it back up to blow off the dirt, I stopped at the slight tilt of her head. *What the actual fuck was I doing?* I quickly tossed it into the fire over my shoulder as I backed away to sit on the opposite side, my face a bright furnace.

She did not look up.

She did not eat.

She just sat there.

Sabine made me feel like I was some wolf prowling in the night. She, in fact, was the gray wolf, and I was the doe-eyed bunny in a fluorescent snow-white coat waiting to be eaten. I could have sworn my thoughts were so loud I inadvertently kept her up the previous night. Neither of us had slept.

I gave up on trying to eat, grimacing with each bite as the echo cracked into the slumbering forest under my teeth. It was too soon to look back over to check on her, but I did it anyway and regretted it.

Sabine *still* had not moved. I held my gaze longer than I should have, just to make sure she was still breathing. My eyes shot away when the corner of her mouth twitched. I cursed under my breath.

I needed to get it together.

Not wanting her to feed off my raging discomfort, I forced my restlessness into submission. I have killed men with my bare hands with more confidence yet waiting for this woman to speak to me made my vision dust with stars. There was nothing I could do but take a deep breath and busy my sweating palms.

My horse, Aires, had been brushed so meticulously by the time I finished grooming him, his hoof jabbed into my shin to stop. Aires, at least, spared me some embarrassment as I grunted from the sharp sting. The beast waited for Sabine to disappear off into the night without her saying a single word before he kicked me.

After I realized she had lied to me, I was so sick to my stomach with nerves. I dipped back into the tree line myself and wretched up the empty contents of my stomach for the sixth time since we left the base.

So much guilt pressed upon my shoulders, and I did not know

how much longer I could withstand it. I settled back in front of the campfire to wait for her.

Emotions transformed into muffled sentences as the sorcerer's bond between us strengthened after the ceremony, but it was not enough to hear her every thought.

The ones that passed through wrecked me.

Sabine's very nearness as we rode horseback through the last of autumn was a whisper of what she had repeated to herself when we were alone in that room. Rustling in the wind, I heard it repeatedly in her silence.

'I could just close my eyes.'

'Turn it all off.'

Her truth was now on full display.

When Sabine demanded me to kneel before her with my proposal, it had given me falsified hope. I was ready to burn with her until it was extinguished with realization. She did not know the *'laws of magic'* as she claimed regarding the sorcerer's bond, or what had just unfolded when she accepted it.

Even then, I would have been a guilty man before I let her go without a fight after she initially refused to continue. It was the mistake I allowed myself to make when I truly looked at her for the first time. I scoured the edges of her blackened jawline. The pale contrast of her face, still swollen and angry after days of being subdued. I raised my hand out to the side to call Elias over toward us, because I could not bear to see her in pain like this any longer.

The subtle gesture of my palm was enough to cause her to flinch the other way. Sabine's cheek turned as if I had already struck her, and her reaction toward me burned when I had never felt what it was like to be caught on fire. I was the last person who would ever want her to be marked by my hand, or the knife her father drove into her back with my symbol.

My mother's voice rang through my ears as I stared at her. *'You are nothing but a monster'*—it was the first time in my life I refused to listen, ignoring her perception of me past the grave she put herself in. When I had reached for Sabine, I hoped to assure her I was not one.

Instead, it all but confirmed to me she was everything I did not deserve as I held her at a distance, tilting her chin gently toward me. Her eyes held the sun before it set, swirling with pools of honey-colored skies that ached with a sense of home I had chosen to forget.

When I dropped to my knees at her command to ask her to continue, it was because I would have begged her to take me, regardless of who I was otherwise. I would have stolen her from death's arms. I acknowledged it too late. The mirror image of my soul stared back at me through her and vanished.

Sabine had not chosen to marry me through the sorcerer's bond. Not knowingly at first. This woman had been a sacrifice for others for so long she did not question it when she made herself 'collateral.'

The worst of it transpired when she realized it, too. Sabine looked at the bed over my shoulder and prepared to subject herself to my touch. Panic had struck me senseless as I heard her thoughts. I felt her slip away from her mind, turning to see her breath labored and eyes empty compared to the fire I had seen before.

Mourning had no place in matrimony. I did what I told her not to do. Accepted the consequences. Ignored every warning I had been given to tell the truth and hoped she would find a way to kill me before she found out we were married.

I lied to her, and I vowed to keep it like it was the truth. The sorcerer's bond would remain unfinished, but it was enough to sustain her life. I would force the fates to make it enough, no matter how deadly.

Elias sent communication to my father, announcing I would not be returning home from the border as previously planned. The King of Solstice would eventually not take my refusal because of his dependency on my blood, but there was no part of me that wanted to risk returning.

Sabine and I were not intertwined fully. The sorcerer's bond required three bindings after being ignited. We had only completed one through the ceremony. A minor injury to me could prove fatal to her during this stage, when I still had not healed from the last time he took blood from me.

There would be another war, but this time it was my own. If my father came to drain me of my magic, I would be the one holding the knife.

Elias insisted upon adding I had married in the letter to my father. He was sure if there was a chance of settling him over my refusal, it would be this, but I still did not trust him. Several days of travel were ahead of us, pushing us toward the safety of the Volkan warrior's stronghold to keep out of my father's reach.

Kane had been preparing for our arrival since the moment I sent him there ahead of us. It had already been decided. No one else could know the truth of our bond until we found out who had betrayed us by exposing my mark.

The Volkan warriors would naturally suspect our marriage given my history, but sharing our union was the better option out of the two, rather than risking others learning of the sorcerer's bond. If there was anyone who could convince them I had taken a wife, it was Kane. Our marriage was not a lie, but it would be to her.

I stilled, pulling abruptly away from my thoughts.

Sabine's footsteps crept softly upon the brush at the edge of the camp as she made her way back. My shadow whipped around me in alert. It did so every time Sabine was near, and it annoyed me to no end.

Stop circling around my head every time she breathes. It's not helping, and you are giving me a headache, I mumbled under my breath. She was watching me through the pines, assessing my every move.

Sabine had done the same thing the night before, never turning her back as she disappeared into the tree line. It unnerved me how quiet she was as she inspected me in secret. Taking the time to study me.

I was regretting my choice to not wear my mask while we were alone. It was not for her to find trust in me. I could not be the one to earn it after I lied to her. The emotion I hid beneath my mask was different, and I needed her to know I was terrified, too. There was no part of me that trusted her, either. Except for what Sabine told me through the sorcerer's bond without her knowledge.

I scarcely even allowed myself a breath as she continued to watch me. My shadow had a mind of his own, though, morphing behind me to place a faint hand on my shoulder. I exhaled through my nose.

Yes. I'm fine, stop asking. I growled with a low warning as I felt him tip his head behind me. *I did not ask for your opinion though, now, did I?*

My shadow swindled through the campfire smoke, winding in the wind. *Why should I be the one to talk to her first? She doesn't want to talk to me. She can barely look at me.*

He floated with the sparks, drifting in the night, and morphed back into my shape behind me. *If that's the case, why don't you talk to her?*

Oh yeah, that's right, you can't—

A branch snapped in the direction Sabine was lurking from.

My shadow vanished.

Coward.

Chapter Twelve

Sabine

I stood motionless, hidden between the crested pines as the firelight illuminated the scarred half of his face.

There had been just enough light to catch the soft murmur between his lips, lulling its restless form to his command. I thought it had been my imagination at first. My body pushed to the brink of exhaustion through days of travel and injury.

It was the whispers though, sounds that could have been mistaken for the howling wind which had kept me up the night prior—until I finally saw Keahi whisper back. It was the shadow morphed into the shape of a man who heard me first, when a mortifying *snap* alerted them from directly underneath my boots.

Keahi's piercing eyes shot through the dark. "Are you alright?" he called out, appearing not to be startled.

I picked up the fallen branches that had given me away, collecting myself before I headed over to him. "I was just getting wood for the fire."

He regarded me for a moment, scrutinizing what I knew to be a pathetic pile of twigs between my arms.

A scarred brow arched in amusement. "I can see that, though you might have noticed last night, I did not use the kindling you collected since I have the ability to wield fire." A blush crept up my cheeks as the corner of his lips twitched. "I appreciate the. . . sentiment."

"Sorry." I bit the inside of my lip. "It just looked rather small from far away. I do not feel like freezing to death tonight."

I should have bitten my tongue instead.

Heat slammed into me, whipping my head away from the fire that erupted between us. My face threatened to melt off as it lashed out at me.

Keahi shifted from one hip to the other. He cleared his throat. "Better?"

I squinted at him through the blistering waves, making my eyes water. I would have thought his gesture mere sarcasm if I had not already begun to further explore his obvious discomfort toward me.

His incessant need to coddle me started the moment we left the base. The more I ignored him, the more he fidgeted under my gaze. *How did I have that effect on him?* I did not care. I did, however, continue to exploit it to my advantage.

"Just fine," I grumbled.

A chill swept through our camp despite the unbearable warmth he had created. I had half a mind to take off the oversized cloak he had loaned me, not wanting the sweat to dampen the clothes underneath.

The ride had already been excruciating enough, and I did not need to add frostbite to the list of aches I had already gained. Regret sunk its way through me as pain dug deeper between my shoulder blades, knowing I should have asked Iahni for a second tonic before our departure.

"You need to rest—I can take watch if it makes you more comfortable." A grimace broke through the lines in my face. He sighed. "I did not waste my efforts on keeping you alive just to drag you out into the middle of the woods *to kill you*. You did not sleep at all last night; you will need your strength if you want to make it another day's ride. I, for one, would prefer it if you did."

I rolled my eyes. "Take your own advice. If I didn't know any better, I could have sworn you were talking to yourself a minute ago."

Unease trailed its way down my spine when he did not form a response. *Maybe I needed to rest, but that would require admitting he was right.*

I shifted uncomfortably, feeling the weight of his stare when I turned to see he had appeared beside me, smoke trailing over the expanse of his broad shoulders.

"It is not a 'watch' if you're going to be staring at me all throughout the night again," I shot back, unwilling to let him see my discomfort as his gaze intensified.

It was odd having him watch me sleep last night, especially when I realized he was staring intently at my chest. He mumbled softly with each inhalation, and after what felt like hours, I made the conclusion he was counting them. It was true he wanted me alive for the sorcerer's bond.

I, *for one*, preferred if he could be less subtle about how he proved it. If we were to be convincing, it would be something we would have to work on collectively. Watching him struggle was rather entertaining, though. I needed something to keep me occupied, considering he was an even worse conversationalist.

His mouth parted slightly. "You can *see* it?"

"You will have to be more specific." My gaze cut behind him involuntarily. As if summoning it, the night moved around him.

"My shadow," he said stiffly. "You can see it."

I swallowed, brushing off the residual debris the twigs had left on my cloak. "I have not slept well, remember?" *And neither have you.*

He mulled the soft leather of his gloves together. "No one has ever seen my shadow before."

It was my turn to go still.

I turned myself away from him, cringing internally as the far end of the log I had found groaned from his weight on the other side. The nearness of a long day's ride with him alone was unbearable. I argued with myself about whether to continue my silence because of it.

He was constantly fidgeting behind me in the saddle, stopping during the middle of our rides—multiple times—to do Gods knows what. It sounded almost like he was getting mauled by a bear every time he hid between the trees. How his divisions made it anywhere in a timely manner was beside me.

"This is not something that you can mention to anyone," he said sharply.

I chuckled, breaking up some of the tension in my shoulders. "As if I will have anyone to confide in once we reach the capital outside of your allegiance."

He scanned my face, showing no amusement on his own. "We will not be going to the capital. . . not yet, at least."

I turned to him. "But—"

"I do not trust we can convince an entire court of our relationship, and I think you could agree with that," he confessed.

Reluctantly, I admitted to myself Keahi had a point. Self-awareness was a good quality, but it was useless if he did not know how to fix it. Whatever confidence he had previously worn when I first met him was crumbling in the palm of my hands. The edge I had on him to make him squirm from my presence alone was something I aimed to maintain thoroughly behind closed doors.

"I will take you to Kallahni. My most trusted forces have made camp inside the city," he finished.

"Ahh," I said. "So, we are taking into consideration the fact they might kill me on sight at the capital, I assume?"

Keahi locked his jaw. "Maybe not on sight, considering our forces thought for some time that your father had. . ."

"Murdered me?" I had been waiting for him to ask since he had discovered me. "Unfortunately, he kept me alive." I threw one of my twigs into the fire, watching it crackle and pop as the flames devoured it.

I shifted closer toward him before I could shy away, smiling to myself when the proximity made him just as uncomfortable.

"And what of you, General?" I questioned. "Our scouts have failed to report to my father that you have been back on the front lines for some time, though your scars say differently."

"*Hmm*," he murmured.

Keahi kept his glowing eyes on me as he reached between my feet, barely having to stretch despite our distance, and picked up a branch from my pile.

He tossed the bark in his hands, testing the weight before he launched it into the fire and said, "We are not going to be subtle, are we?"

I attempted to determine if that was a warning not to question him further or just the truth of the situation. I decided it was both.

"Why should we be?" I asked thoughtfully. "As you said several nights before, secrets between us will do us no good."

"I did say that, didn't I?" he grumbled. Keahi tilted his chin, flashing his scar so I could see it fully. "I received this mark several years ago during a raid on one of your camps. It was not one of my best nights, as you can imagine, though it will not be the last scar I receive."

My gaze shifted back toward the fire, unable to look at him. I chose my next words carefully. "I thought the King of Solstice had been the one to raid that camp, and if I remember correctly, my father told me one of our own had marked him before they barely made it out."

A bead of sweat trailed down my spine underneath my cloak as he leaned forward to grab another branch. He snapped it, causing me to clench my fists at my side before he sent the last into the fire again.

"The King of Solstice had been nowhere near the camps that night. I was the one who led the raid. Your scouts do not seem to provide that valuable of information." The corner of his lips lifted. "Maybe I have been giving them more credit than they deserve?"

My shoulders relaxed slightly. "I would not sound so confident. Neither do yours, apparently."

His mouth thinned.

I tucked away the mental note to bruise his military standing further at a later time and seized the opportunity to change the subject.

"What was your response then, when Elias told you that the heir to the Novear Kingdom was still alive after removing the crystal?" My hand instinctively reached for the nape of my neck. It was still sore, a constant ache heating my spine.

It was no selfless act what Elias had done. Many healers in the same position as him would have refused their king outright.

Although I was still cautious of Elias's motives, I would not forget what he had done for me, even if he claimed it was for the man sitting next to me.

"I did not want to believe him." Keahi sighed tensely. "Especially after the magic created during the ritual. I saw your father with you. . . through a vision of some sort."

"How much did you see?" I asked. My voice was barely a whisper. The thought of him seeing me at one of my weakest moments shredded me from the inside out.

"Enough," he said, softer than I would have liked. "I had sent word to find you the moment I realized what was happening—that he was igniting a link between us for the sorcerer's bond. I apologize for not being the one to find you first. There had been no order to bring you harm."

"I see," I said absently. I wished he had not given me that piece of information. The look he was giving me now confirmed that he was thinking the same.

"There is no need to look at me like that, General," I recovered. "I was not always a damsel in distress. They did not keep me within the castle walls, but I will reluctantly admit that I was my father's prisoner."

Keahi's back straightened, and his knuckles cracked as he flexed his hands. "You will not be Solstice's prisoner. When we go after your father, even if you wanted to lock him up for an eternity, I would support it. Though I would rather kill him myself."

My brow arched. "You almost make it sound personal, General. I want him to pay for everything that he has done, just as you do. I crave the day I get to feel his death, but it will be my hands that kill him. . . not yours."

The Serpent in the Shadows curled his lips into a bright and malicious smile. "If it pleases you so—as long as I get to watch."

My brows pinched as I fought the urge to smile back. The conversation took its toll when I did not know what to make of it. I braced myself to stand on sore legs from the day's ride.

He stopped me before I walked away. "Can I ask you something without offending you?"

I spoke over my shoulder. "You do not appear to be the kind of man to ask such a question when you rarely use your words at all. Do not stop on my account."

The tops of his cheeks flushed, and I stopped my frown from creeping out of its place. Keahi hesitated before inching over to me. We stood side by side as he said, "I do not feel . . . your magic. . . through the bond. I thought, after Elias removed the crystal, I could feel your power more."

"I was born a sorcerer, though it was not mine to wield because of my father. I'm not sure what effects from the crystal linger on my magic after the removal. If I even still have any of my own power left." My mouth suddenly went dry. I pulled on my cloak to hide my face. "Why did you remove it?"

"You were dying," he said distantly, slowly turning his attention to the wood behind us. "Elias could not heal you because the crystal blocked his magic."

"And you decided it was worth the risk?"

To risk his life.

It was a sacrifice I could not repay. The feeling of owing him felt worse than if Elias had been forced against his will to remove it.

"Sabine—"

"He could have died—" My objection was cut off.

Keahi's hand clamped around my mouth, crushing me with his massive body as we hit the solid ground with force. He was close—*too close*, and panic flared inside me with his breath hot on my ear. I squirmed underneath him.

Every bit of his nearness repulsed my body, nausea burning the back of my throat. Keahi forced his entire weight onto me, struggling to keep me down. My resistance toward him slowed when he did not attack me further. I was too swept up to notice that he had snuffed out the campfire maybe a little too late in an attempt to shield me, as a hissing sound snaked through the forest.

"What. . . is that?" I muttered into his glove. Keahi sent me a side glance that told me I should not be asking right now.

"They found us already. . ." he whispered into my ear with a bit of disbelief. Meaning more than one, and I was completely dead weight right now.

"Listen—you can hate me later for this, but we are both not in the position to survive an ambush. I am begging you not to fight me on this one," he said.

I quickly bit back my insult at his remark for later use. Keahi slid his hand against the dirt under me, wrapping his arm securely around my waist until his palm flattened above my navel.

A second hiss rattled off in the distance, this time closer. The horse that had carried us thus far scraped his hooves into the ground and bolted off, leaving us behind. My eyes went wide. "I think I can manage not to fight you until later."

That was all the confirmation he needed, as he ripped the surrounding air apart. Shadowfire wrapped around us like we were in the eye of a storm as we landed on the horse that had been sprinting ahead of us.

His grip around my waist grew tighter as we put distance between whatever creature we had been running from, prepared to launch us forward at any moment.

Chapter Thirteen

Keahi

A shrill scream startled my senses awake. I had only been asleep for an hour. One Gods' forsaken hour after we had fled our first camp for the night and did not settle until I was sure we were safe.

"Help!"

Not just any scream—*Sabine's.*

I was on my feet in seconds, fire at my palms as I burned a pathway toward her direction. I cursed through my teeth—surely, they had not found us again.

"Help!"

I struck the ground hard as every muscle in my body ticked with dread—but what if they had? I had detoured us back, changing multiple directions to put distance between us before we finally settled for the night—but what if it wasn't enough?

The brush withered as I blasted out into the open, sinking into a gritty mixture of sand and mud. My eyes scanned the edge of the stream—snagging on what I found recklessly splayed upon the ground.

The vein in my forehead pulsed, blurring my vision as I stared at the only clothes I knew she had with her on the ground. Every spark of magic I had trembled, as I bent it to my murder fueled will.

"Sabine!"

Water splashed upstream, and I tore through shadowfire as I tracked the small sound.

"Go away! Go away!" she screeched.

I was going to rip every bone out of her attacker's body one by one and force them to remain alive to feel the blood leave their arteries. The fire in my veins charred as I materialized into the air, fueling my attack—

On a *frog?*

I gasped between harsh breaths as my soul flighted back into my body. Sabine's eyes flashed over the top of a boulder; her wet hair flattened against the top of her scalp. "Don't just stand there!" She pointed at her *attacker*. "Do something!"

My jaw dropped like a weight was attached to it as the tiny, yellow-spotted frog leaped in between my boots from a rock it had been perched on. Its purple eyes sparkled with a bit of mischief before it hopped onto a twig and headed downstream to float away.

Did that frog just. . . mock me?

"What took you so damn long?" I turned back as she waded toward me, neck deep, her white hair weaving through the cool waters behind her. "Someone could have risen me from the dead and stabbed me *twice* by the time you found me—some general you are."

Did she just. . . insult me?

"This was some test?" I growled. "You sounded like you were dying for the Gods' sake!"

She paused in the middle of the stream, bobbing down underneath and back.

"Maybe."

A smirk almost formed on her lips as she tracked the twitch of my eye.

"So, you were screaming at the top of your lungs. . . for a test?" I asked tightly.

The honey in her stare caramelized. If she was preparing for another insult, I hoped it was quick. Her screeching had been a hammer to my throbbing head, and I did not know how much more

I could tolerate.

She rolled her eyes. "Jeremy was cute, but he refused to leave me alone."

"Jeremy?" I peered at the woods behind her and dipped back to the dull chuckle bouncing off the water.

"The frog. His name is Jeremy," she stated, as if it was supposed to be obvious.

"You named the frog?" I lowered my voice, no hint of amusement in my tone. I thought she was fighting for her life by the way she had screamed.

"He seemed nice at the time." She shrugged underneath the crystal-clear surface, and a small set of ripples followed in suit. The corner of her mouth turned down. "Jeremy seemed rather okay until he got. . . testy for such a small thing."

I dragged my hand down my face and stopped at the bridge of my nose. This woman was going to give me a full-on aneurysm before we could even make it to Kallahni.

Water trickled down the bank in tiny streams, as I looked down between the spaces of my fingers. A small pool of water had formed underneath my boots, and I followed the trail until I found the ends of Sabine's white hair glistening in the sunlight. I had not seen her get out of the water, but as she bent over to wring the ends of her hair, a mortified heat electrified me from the ground up.

She was *not* naked—but I almost wished she was, at the way her white tunic accentuated every dip and curve of her body. The soaked, translucent material adhered against her pale-pink skin.

My breath shuttered against my palm as my eyes betrayed me when they drew over the peaks of her breasts. Her nipples hardened beneath from the cold. I quickly spun around on my heels and my grip tightened along my jawline. Hopefully, it hid any of the shock that was burning from the tops of my cheeks to the tips of my ears. I had never seen a goddess up close, but I found one in front of me.

Sabine was so beautiful that I would have to be hit over the head *repeatedly* to not notice. I wish I hadn't, because I could not blame it on the effects of the sorcerer's bond, though I am certain it did not help.

"Is there something wrong?" she asked suddenly.

Sweet fuck.

My back straightened—no, it flinched. I flinched at how close she stood behind me, her breath tickling the back of my shoulder even through the layers of my clothes. Her approach was far too quiet against the noise of my thoughts. I fought every urge to dissipate in the shadows as I cleared my throat.

Speaking—was not an option. I felt her round at the corner of my shoulders, and I jumped a step forward, out of view.

"I thought I saw Jeremy again," I stumbled out in a manic rush.

"Where?" Her fears flitted against the bond at her formidable attacker's name.

"Behind that rock." I pointed to the farthest one I could find as I disappeared through a puff of smoke. Sand slung beneath my feet. Sweat dripped down my body faster than the water rushing behind me. I frantically bunched the clothes she had left in the dirt, tripping over her pant legs trapped beneath my boots.

What the hell is that noise? Jeremy? I heard her say down the bond and cursed when I found enough balance to stand. I released a breath and shot back to her location.

My voice wound tight. "Here. Get dressed before you make yourself sicker. You've been groaning—" *Poor, such poor choice of words.* I closed my eyes. "Nonstop the entire ride and I do not want to add a cold to that."

She stood half naked in front of me, but I was the only one who seemed off kilter. Sabine grumbled as she took the clothes from my arms. She whipped them against the wind as I shielded my bare face against the grain, and then she paused.

"I do not remember setting them in the dirt." She hummed, deceptively conducive to my pride.

Of course, you don't. I swiftly turned to start my walk back as I ignored her, eager to create as much distance as possible.

This was not a daily encounter for me, and if I stood here any longer, she was bound to notice how the bond affected me. Sabine was always watching far too closely. She did not need the bond to tell her how much of an idiot I became in her presence.

"Meet me as soon as you are done," I said as evenly as I could.

"Wait."

A flood of humiliation extinguished the escape dangling in front of me.

"What now?" I snapped with irritation, but it came out breathless. Maybe I could not blame it entirely on the bond as I stilled at her command, her own ways of affecting me at work.

"Did you seriously rub these in the dirt before giving them back to me?" she asked. Her tone was lethal with the accusation of a different crime.

Thank fuck.

"I dropped them, so what? You shouldn't have been out here by yourself. You could have been hurt," I insisted, and I could sense her eyes narrow on my back again.

I had not done it on purpose, more out of desperation. Her aggravation was somewhat of a happy accident. The alarming wake-up call of her voice, the least of her vices. She thought I had not noticed when she placed twigs behind my back in the middle of the night, but I had.

Clearly, it was the only reason she was still insistent on "collecting firewood," only to torment me as I rolled over for it to stab me awake. Her punitive attempts to strike at me had induced pity. She was stuck with me, with no way to defend herself from the stranger she was forced to travel with and had unknowingly gotten married to.

The way her tongue clicked behind me sent a shiver down my spine, but my shoulders eased as I heard her shuffle into her clothes. "You are going to make it very difficult for people to believe that we are married if you keep looking at me like that."

"And *how* do I look at you?" My patience was on the verge of collapse.

"Like it is painful to gaze in my direction," she said simply. "I undoubtedly prefer it, but the others will not if I am to be believed as your wife."

It was painful, but not for the reason she thought. It was a surprise on my part for me to notice how beautiful she was. Wanting was not a simple luxury for me. I often forgot I could, but the sorcerer's bond surely thought otherwise.

"Let me worry about that," I grumbled.

I already was.

"If you say so," she said as she stepped past me, but a roil of nausea slammed into my gut. The assaulting sting in my nose made it hard to breathe.

I pinned my eyes to her back, her shoulders raised as she walked toward the path I had created. *Something was wrong.* She tilted her head as she scrutinized the burnt edges of the grass and strolled between the trees, out of sight.

I caught up to her. "Are . . . you well?" There was a slight hitch in her step at my question, but she pressed forward.

"I'm fine."

"You don't—"

Her feet dug into the ground. "I dare you to finish that sentence."

What? I ran my hands through my hair. "It is *freezing* out. I do not understand how you were swimming at this time of year."

"Hell does that to you. Though I would not recommend visiting," Sabine added. She swung the branch at me, and I ducked.

"I will keep that in mind," I said, materializing in front of her. Sabine's half-truths were worse than her blatant lies, but now was not the time to push her as she crossed her arms, undeterred, as I blocked her path.

Her golden eyes drove stakes through my armor from head to toe. I was a feared general among kingdoms, a commander of an entire army, but how I measured up to that *damn* frog right now belittled my ego as I stepped out of her way.

I needed to get us to Kallahni *immediately*.

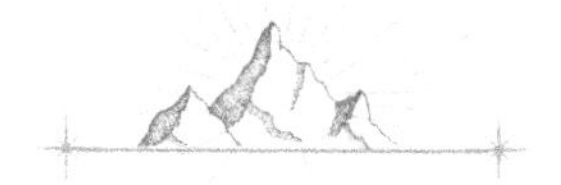

We had barely been riding for an hour before I braced my hands on my knees and forced us to make the second stop this morning. I dipped into the woods, double checking my bandages underneath for an infection.

The wound my father had curated to harness my magic had not healed yet. It was frozen in its current state, not any better or worse than it had been before, but that was no comfort, given the way it ached with the smallest amount of movement.

I steadied my breath as I walked back to find Sabine splayed atop the onyx stallion. She twirled the ends of her white hair in the warm amber light dawning through the last of the fall leaves. Her body gave no tell of my approach, except for a labored sigh of annoyance as she transitioned herself to straddle the horse's back and I stilled.

Never, in my entire life, have I known that horse to be so content as she separated a piece of its mane and tucked it behind his ear. It was an effort to keep my jaw locked as it nuzzled into her palm with peculiar exploration.

This was the same horse that berated the ground and chased

someone as gentle as Kane. He had been in the wrong place at the wrong time, choosing the apple the horse had clearly wanted for himself. Aires had pursued him relentlessly, even after Kane flung the apple through the air and screamed at the tops of his lungs when the horse did not back down.

I had let it go on for longer than necessary, but it was such a spectacular display I had never seen from Kane that I had a hard time catching my breath in between laughs to call Aires off. He kept his distance even today. She must share the same affinity, I suppose.

"You know, if you stop pulling us off to the side, we might get there faster," she chided, continuing to brush through the winded knots of my horse's mane.

"Is that so? I would have never known," I countered. I attempted so far not to feed into her too much, considering she was always watching to use it for later, as I recently found. It was almost sad, though there was something about the way she rolled her eyes that made me stroll a step forward past the patience I was giving her—*perhaps* it was the lack of sleep.

"If I would have gotten a decent amount of rest last night, I might not be so indisposed. You wouldn't know anything about that, would you?" I asked.

Sabine ran her tongue over her front teeth. "Is that an accusation, General? It is you that ran us through the night, was it not?"

I did not back down from the merciless creature showing her true colors before me. The same woman I had vowed to keep alive for what felt like the beginning of a *very, very long* eternity. The bond had pushed me in that direction in hindsight, despite my own grievances.

"You should be thanking me. I know my limits, and I would not have been able to fight them off alone," I said against my pride, but it was true. It was too much of a risk with my injury. Her bored, jaded sigh had me grinding my teeth. "It is only a mere assessment. What fragile sleep I found to maintain my strength was ruined by those twigs you strategically placed for me to roll over on."

She yawned, but I caught the coy smile she tried to cover up. "Maybe you are more observant than I originally had given you credit for. Though it is *my* assessment that you should have caught on earlier."

"Is that so?" I stiffened as she jumped down from her vantage point.

She knocked the dirt off her palms. "You barely take the time to breathe in my presence, let alone make a sound. Since I cannot feel the bond the way you do, I was beginning to worry there was nothing up here." Her finger tapped against her head twice before she crossed her arms. "Besides, *you* should be thanking *me*."

"Thanking you?"

"Precisely. The twigs I so *strategically* placed underneath you were to relieve certain pressure points. It helps with a multitude of ailments."

Is she being serious? "What ailment do you think I have then? Which must involve prodding me in the middle of sleep?"

She shrugged. "It seems you are cursed with a stiff and intolerable demeanor. Clearly it is working, as you retch with each stop to get rid of whatever poison that strangles any ounce of emotion you have."

I huffed. "I'm sorry. Are you confusing my lack of emotion with your ability to only know one? Your disdain will only get you so far, and it is you who lectured me earlier about maintaining convincing looks when you've been secretly *torturing me*. Besides, the stream water you bathed in this morning, wafting into my face, certainly does not help."

She flipped her hair behind her back. "Maybe you should have gargled some of that stream water in your mouth, considering the acid crawling between your teeth is far worse." I snapped my mouth shut.

My shadow swirled around me, wrapping itself along the bottom of my leg and up my torso before it appeared behind Sabine. She missed nothing, even how my own shadow was on her side.

"You've got it wrong." She continued with confidence, my shadow trailing behind her—*traitor*. "Wrath is what fuels me, but you will find it has a range that you are only beginning to discover. I will be able to pretend, but it is you that will not."

I looked around the forest, throwing my hands up. "Yes, because we are graced by an audience at this present time."

She spoke low. "I will warn you, again and again, until you finally get it right—I only care about one thing. I will not let you ruin it by your. . . brooding tendencies. We have what? Less than a day's ride until we reach your camp. I need them to be sure of our agreement if we are to play this right. Acting like a distressed mother hen around me will not cut it, amusing as it may be."

That was one way of putting it.

I clasped my gloves, bending at the hips. "What would you suggest then, Princess? Since you are so concerned about my ability to show affection toward you. You make it *so easy* for me to do so."

Her golden glare flicked up and down my frame twice, spinning on her heels to go through my satchel. I released a breath, and she chuckled at the exact time I caved.

"Close your eyes," she called out.

"Not a chance," I growled back.

"Suit yourself then." She walked back over with her hands clasped around the object she retrieved and handed me an apple. My eyes immediately went to Aires, but he appeared wholly undeterred by her taking his next meal.

"And what am I to do with this apple?"

"Ask me to share it with you. *Woo me*, if you will."

My scar twisted, looking down at the apple in my hands. "You want me to *woo you* with a piece of fruit?" It was highly objectifying, but I decided best not to comment on that.

"Let's just say we are starting small. If you can do this, then it will prove to me I have been overzealous in my attack to rid you of such tension."

I glared at my reflection in the shiny red peel. I cleared my throat. "Would you like to share. . . this apple with me. . . Sabine?"

Her jaw ticked. "Gods. That was just as painful as I expected it to be."

My shadow winced behind her. She snatched it back from my hands, tossing it in the air a couple times, weighing her next plan of attack.

Sabine's arm extended, the apple upon her fingertips. "It does not matter if this is an apple. This is the only tool you have been given, just like our circumstance." She drew it back, staring into its core. "We will start off with walks, longing stares of affection. Anything that has to do with you opening your mouth will be far too challenging."

"As if you could do any better," I grumbled.

I had felt no magic from her, but the challenge that sparked in her eyes felt undoubtedly similar as she lifted it to her mouth. Her soft lips formed around its side, sliding across its shape as she indulged in the taste of it while directly staring into my soul. Her thumb caressed the glisten from her bottom lip and placed it into her mouth as she approached me.

My mouth went dry.

"It feels almost forbidden, doesn't it? How something so divine is hidden underneath, and that is what others will see when they look at us."

She held out the bitten apple. "Do you want a taste of what the others will want to discover?" My head heavily turned side to side. "You may not see the appeal, but the moment we step through those doors, be prepared for the others who covet to know the truth of how we came to be. . . when we were not meant to." Her fingers detached the stem of the apple and offered it to the horse. "Protect that, General, just as you have asked me to, and we might survive this."

"Understood," was all I managed to say.

She made her way onto his back. "One more thing."

I followed up behind her, giving as much space as I possibly could. "I am sure it is not just one more thing but go ahead."

My hands tightened on the reins when her chest paused. "*That*—is how you are supposed to look at me, when the others are around."

Chapter Fourteen

Sabine

We had charged through the forest by storm. Keahi had pushed us on relentlessly, making up for as much distance as he could from the detours and inconvenient stops. The sky turned a light shade of pink as we peeked through the forest's dark umbrella.

Keahi leaned forward. His black curls tangled from the wind; the lonely white strand of his hair caught in the storm. "We are almost there."

The term 'camp' appeared to have been used loosely. There were no tents, no soldiers gathered around their morning fire, taking their first bite of bread. We did not come upon a bustling army loaded with their weaponry.

"That—is the camp?"

He chuckled lightly against my back. "Do not sound so disappointed. I can turn around if you would like."

I drove my elbow behind me, stopped by a wall of solid muscle.

Keahi inhaled a sharp breath. I had hoped to chide myself for his misery at the contact, but the playful gesture seemed to have oddly caused him pain.

The Volkan 'camp' embedded itself within the side of a mountain. Abandoned castle archways claimed its jagged rocks, cracked with stone ruins as towers surged above the fresh snow-covered peaks. The size of it made a mockery to the sky as it claimed its rightful home, aged into a layer of earth. I had never seen something so hauntingly beautiful before.

There was no doubt this could belong to anyone else but the Solstice Kingdom. The way the sun woke the forgotten castle with its rays, gradually reducing its shadow as the sun rose higher within the sky.

"I did not know Solstice had such extravagant tastes for their war camps," I said with a smirk. "It is really beginning to intrude on your hardened image." I attempted to turn around as I spoke, but the motion brought on a rapid dizzy spell.

"The outside is deceiving, I'll admit. It is one of very few entrances into Kallahni," he went on, looking at me once over. Up ahead, I could see the base of the mountain emerging, but only solid earth stared back.

Keahi jumped off the horse, lowering me down next to him with pinched brows. Upon landing, my knees buckled, and gravity melted me into the soil. A sharp pain traveled through my bones, sending heat into my limbs. It took several breaths for my head to clear from the vertigo. I jumped back, noticing the forceful grasp I had placed on Keahi's arm, but as I retreated, what little strength I maintained depleted along with my ability to stand.

He swiftly placed a firm grip underneath my arms, keeping my body from collapsing in total. It took everything I had to breathe through the proximity. My tolerance for it rapidly declined. Keahi's gaze raked over me. "Are you okay?"

"*I'm fine*," I forced out with such exaggerated confidence it only made him step closer. "You are not the only one who needs to rest, remember?"

His ember eyes were the only feature on display now. The hoods the Solstice Kingdom's army wore covered nearly their entire face. It kept their expressions hidden beneath them, but the eyes continued to tell more stories than any other part of us.

He did not believe me.

Not even a little.

Every time he touched me, the sickness I pushed through worsened. I stood taller, eager to push him off.

I gaped up at the city above. "How are we supposed to get all the way up there? I don't even see a cave entrance." His eyes turned wicked, and I knew there was a matching smile to go with it underneath.

He placed one of my hands on the horse's saddle to grasp onto and walked over to the side of the mountain. I sucked in a curse as he slid off the glove covering his right hand, praying he did not hear me. Even from a distance, I could see the scars he wore, equally brutal as the one that streaked his face.

They were completely marred.

The jagged scars stretched far underneath his sleeves, aged with the same resilience of the mountain above us. A chill battled its way over my skin as my own hands stung; circling, memorizing the lines of his haunted hands.

He placed his palm on the rock, settling himself into the feel of the mountain as he took a deep breath. As he exhaled, fire scattered across the mountain's crevices. Lines ignited, crossing into sizzling patterns I had seen only in the pages of books that were turned to ash in my father's reign.

Solstice's symbol.

A dragon wrapped around the edges of the sun, breathing fire into rays of sunlight. The horse startled beside me as the rock moved from its resting place. It pushed back like an open door on rusted hinges, screeching as it came to a complete stop.

Something in me had changed. I could feel it screaming in the wind as I approached the base of the mountain. It warned me as it blew the white strands of my hair across my face, catching the truth on the corner of my lips.

I did not want to be underground again. Whatever power still left within me was actively trying to tell me I couldn't. It begged me to stay where I could feel my power, not because it wanted me to, but because *it needed me to.* Like I would not live without it being near.

It was strange to feel its presence again yet feel so paralyzingly weak at the same time. It only grew weaker as I walked past Keahi. Damning myself as the world was once again shut off from the light, I became encapsulated within this beast of a mountain. A thudding echo drove through my heart like a death sentence as the cave wall shut us in.

I barely saw the glow of a flame ignite before the world flickered with it. I grasped my neck as a sharp pain blinded my vision, trying to hold my airway up as I felt it all leave my lungs.

Everything around me felt like it was moving, invading every part of me as the darkness suffocated me. "Sabine, what has—"

I felt a palm lift to my forehead, flipping to the back of their hand several times. Large, gloved hands gripped my jawline, pulling my chin upward. My lashes fluttered, the weight of them overpowering. A light leather touch lifted my eyelids, looking underneath.

Keahi?

An unwelcome heat rushed to my face as I found myself completely wrapped in his arms, tangled beneath him.

"*You're sick*—you are even worse than before," he muttered frantically. The sudden fear in his voice sent a small pang to my chest, as his concern lifted the curtain of pain slightly. "You've been sick this whole time. . . I should have known. . . I never get sick. . . not like that," he said breathlessly to himself.

I just needed to catch my breath. That's all.

"I'm fine," I drawled. My head lagged with my speech, rolling until I felt his grip catch at the base of my neck.

"No, you are not," he hissed through his teeth. "Why didn't you say anything?" Irritation coursed through him. I wanted to respond, to tell him to just leave me here, but I could not feel my face anymore to speak of my own accord. I did not have time to brace myself as he threw me over his shoulder and began running. *Sprinting.*

To where? I didn't know. Right now, I only had one task. I used every bit of leftover adrenaline I had to slam my fists into his back, knowing if I yelled at him. . . I would probably make the situation worse.

So, I opted for the quieter alternative.

I'm sure he appreciated the latter, but it didn't even phase him. I could feel him whisking me through the dark, my body lolling side to side each time we turned directions inside the tunnels.

"Let me go!" I tried to scream, but it came out as a broken whisper.

We stopped in a torch lit circle. The mountain domed around us with no other exit as we appeared at a dead end. He pulled me over his shoulders, cradling me into him as I went limp.

A numbness approached me, dragging me deep within my mind as I tried to keep my eyes open. My chest was heavy, trying to expand my rib cage to get a frugal drop of air. I had been too weak to stop the simple phrase dangling on my lips, breaking through the cage it resided in. "I'm sorry," I muffled into his chest.

I didn't know why I had felt the need to say it—because I needed to feel like someone would care if I died right now? As if it would make me feel like I had mattered to anyone, at least anyone left—

"—Look at me!"

My body acted before my mind did, eyes flying open. He searched my face with fierce desperation. "Sabine, do you think you could withstand one more? I'm not leaving you—*I won't*." I could feel his chest heaving against mine, much faster than the faint pulse within me.

"*Pleaseee*." I was slipping, tears dripping off the side of my jaw-line. "Just let me go this time. I promise I'll be okay."

The ground shook underneath us. Unleashed power flowed through our connection. Something raw and unbreakable cracked inside of him. The force alone tore me from the inside out. "*No*," he said tightly. "I'm afraid that's not good enough."

I was thankful for the pounding sensation expanding inside my head because it distracted me as his magic singed my lungs. It took away anything that I had left as I went into a coughing fit, trying to breathe through the shadowfire. Tears streamed out of the corner of my eyes at the potency.

I didn't know where we were now, but I knew just by the way Keahi's entire body jolted still that it was not good. I opened my eyes to see where we had materialized and quickly closed them. The room spun in vicious circles.

"Brother, I've been telling you to bring a girl home, but I didn't think you were *that* desperate."

"Drakkon!" Keahi snapped, the rumble deep within his chest pressed against me.

"Is—*is she drugged*?? If I knew my teasing would lead to this, I would have said nothing. Keahi, this is not the way to go, I promise you; I could have an escort here in minutes—hopefully. . . she isn't one?"

"*Drakkon*!" The temperature of the room threatened to scorch me from the inside out. There was not a rebuttal this time. "I don't know why you are in my room when I gave you your own, but if you don't shut the fuck up and make yourself useful right now, I will very well remember this."

A tired chuckle escaped me as I dangled over his shoulder, the blood rushing to my face. "You're *realllyyy* kind of an ass, aren't you?" My throat was sore, but I fought to finish my sentence. "I married a sorcerer with a very large torch up his ass—at least I won't be alive to see it."

Keahi took a steaming, exasperated breath underneath me.

"*Your what. . .*" Drakkon forced out.

Keahi was moving now, pushing through a set of doors. "I don't have time for this! Elias won't be here till tomorrow evening. If you will not help me—*Get. Out.*"

Drakkon halted his questions. His footsteps followed closely behind Keahi's. I was flung out onto an enormous bed. Keahi averted from looking at me directly. His hands removed my coat furiously. I felt paralyzed watching him.

My pride rivaled with the thought of two men I did not know undressing me. They stripped me down to the thinnest layer possible without my skin showing underneath. Keahi grabbed a water pitcher within reach, sniffing it before he flung it over me. I shot up, shrieking from the cold water he doused me in. That woke me up—*briefly*.

He pushed me back. "Help me flip her over."

Someone tossed me sideways until I laid flat on my stomach. A cool metal tip struck the back of my neck, the sound of fabric sheared all the way down the back of my shirt. Drakkon let out a rigid breath, and with it I lost any fight I had left.

"It's not her—It's not her mark. . . I thought it might be infected, because of her fever. . . It's not." Keahi was in a full-blooded panic.

"What is that?" Drakkon's voice mirrored Keahi's.

"She still has a piece in her neck," he whispered to himself. "We have to get it out."

No, no, no. It can't be.

There can't be.

A small whimper escaped me. I didn't want to see the looks they were exchanging behind my back as they communicated in complete silence.

"Sabine."

I was shaking, trembling as the memories flooded. They flashed intrusively in broken pieces, *over and over*. His hand went to my sweat slicked hair. Steady as he brushed it behind my ear. My mind rushed back through the mere contact, in memory, like he had already done so to ease me once before.

"I'm sorry."

I felt Drakkon's hands firmly press my limbs deep into the mattress. The weight he was exuding told me more than enough about the act about to unfold. I braced myself for what I knew came next. A tear silently made a path down the side of my face.

"I never wanted this," I rasped. A sharp sensation tapped against the base of my neck, preparing me for the inevitable. The blade sang with heat against my skin. *"I never wanted this!"*

"I'm so sorry," Keahi whispered again. A blood-curdling scream thrashed its way through me as scorching metal sank into my flesh.

"I can't get it out!" I heard in the distance as a string of curses erupted in the background. The edges of my vision swooped in.

"I can't get it out!"

Chapter Fifteen

Sabine

There was no hesitation, no spark of fear when I sensed my power unfurl awake inside of me. At first it had been a gentle warmth, blooming in my core with its own hint of disbelief, tentatively exploring the boundaries of its broken cage, drawn out of exile. It reached for the base of its home it had been trapped within, but it was not enough.

It had starved.

It probed deeper with an insatiable need, ripping through the integral home my magic had been abandoned in, melting away the layers of my soul I had deemed forever out of reach.

My sorcery tunneled with a vengeance as the crystallized edges of the siphoning crystal lost its sting. It pushed beyond the threshold of its existence and transformed into a chasm of power which was all mine.

Not my father's magic to wield through the siphoning crystal, not the Gods' who gave it to me—*mine*. I wanted to bottle it up, savor it for an eternity, but it begged me to take what it had created out of banishment from its beholder.

'Take it,' it whispered sinisterly as I approached the magic within me. *'Take what is yours.'*

The light inside me cleaved into a frenzied rage, and then I set it free without a second thought, immobilizing myself as the light barreled toward me with crackling energy.

"I will," I promised. "Only death will stop us."

Chapter Sixteen

Sabine

I woke to an iron barred skylight angled above; the sun warming the side of my face as it cascaded through filtered pieces of glass. It touched every surface with an amber glow only the first of dawn could produce, drifting across large oaken beams which arched into a rocky ceiling. Each beam boasted a set of burgundy tapestries that flowed from floor to ceiling, hovering above the marbled floor that glittered under streams of light.

A roasted, nutty aroma flavored the air, coaxing me from a warmth the bed cradled me in. I cautiously turned myself into the mattress, prepared to feel the residual ache, but it felt as gentle as the turn of a page. That weighted sensation, the one which had buried its way into my bones, was gone.

He was gone—my father's control over me from the siphoning crystal vanished. This power answered to me, and I would not let it falter. Freedom was a force to those who had not been gifted it.

Inherently, what my father had done would always remain. I knew I could not change that. The thrill down my spine from my power insisted otherwise as I pushed the soft fur cover over my shoulder.

"I wouldn't do that if I were you," a deep voice behind me insisted. I snatched the blanket straight up to my chin, reaching out to the nightstand where a glass pitcher had been sitting. I shattered it. Broken pieces skated across the marble floor as I jumped on top of the bed with broken glass in my hand.

The intruder stared back. His composure leaked a sense of calm that made me more uncomfortable than I wanted to admit. He sifted through a stack of yellowed papers in one hand, and slowly used the other to stir the rim of his mug with a simple wave of his fingers. His boots crunched on the shards of glass as he let them drop from the desk with a sigh. The desk was angled precisely towards my bed.

Gold-rimmed eyes flicked up at me before his face did. "I'm not cleaning that up."

"You will be cleaning your blood off the floor if you do not start telling me who you are and why I am *naked* underneath." My fist tightened around the glass handle as I shifted the furred blanket up higher.

"*Of course,* you would not have any recollections of the event," he mumbled under his breath. He tore off a piece of his toast and threw it at my head. "Here, eat something, you need to—"

Glass shattered against the stone fire pit behind him, inches away from where his head had been. I jumped off the bed and scrambled for a new weapon.

"I'm not a dog, *answer me.*"

His stare never wavered from me, sizing me up for the first time as his head tipped to the side. A grin formed only in the lower half of his face. "No, but you are a bitch, apparently." He popped the last piece of his breakfast in his mouth, ending his meal with a sweep of his tongue across his bottom lip. "The Novear traitor who ensnared my brute of a brother. I never realized his tastes were so. . ." He looked around at the scene behind me. ". . . Untamed."

Mischief lit in the golden tones of his mahogany eyes as the events came back to me. "Where is he?" I snapped.

"Away," he responded leisurely. "Can you put that down? I'm not really into the whole knife to the throat thing." I jolted forward, and he placed both his hands up in surrender as I prepared to jump over the desk. "He is currently in a meeting, and could not watch you sleep your way into the third day of being comatose—so do excuse him, will you? I've heard forgiveness is an important part of marriage, including not killing the brother-in-law."

"Take me to him."

"Like that?" His eyes flicked down. "Where others could see you? Never, if I want to live."

"Then *get me* some clothes," I snarled. "I need to see him."

His growing smirk tested my patience. "That I cannot do. A traitor to one kingdom is a traitor to another. You will not be allowed anywhere near our tactical meetings if I have anything to do with it."

He leveled with me, making his stance known as the space between us grew heavy. I did not fear him. I had grown accustomed to his type of interrogation. This kind in particular was met between words, which would later be used as weapons. So, I became the lie I needed to tell, and my power eagerly flared inside me.

I had not realized how far gone I felt with the remnants of my father's crystal embedded within me. *'No one can know the truth,'* Keahi had said. That truth was to be easily spilled if I did not find an outlet—*soon.*

"Traitor?" I said, rolling it over my tongue. I smiled, slowly and deliberately, drunk on my newfound freedom I possessed. As I rolled my shoulders back, I ended my brewing pause. "I like the sound of that, actually. Do tell me what you have heard so that I can live up to it."

So that I knew exactly how much to say.

This man had no shortage of prowess as he leaned closer. Strands of his dark hair fell against his chin. "Sabine Azterrin, the last Princess of the Novear Kingdom." My name rolled off like an unpleasant taste in his mouth. "It was rumored that you were dead, and now we find that not only are you alive, but. . ." His grin widened, reaching the corner of his mouth as he said, "If I'm not mistaken, it is Sabine Aldeer now? If that is even your real name."

I looked down at him. "It is my name, and I hope you like getting used to it."

"Is that so?" He leaned forward, putting both elbows on the table, resting his chin on clasped hands. "And what would my brother say? Because I find it odd—he has done nothing but avoid my questions about you."

"Then you should simply figure out why you are not asking the right questions."

He chuckled darkly. "I am asking the right questions, and you are giving me quite a few answers right now. Please, tell me more." If I had not heeded his threat before, it was going to be this one that I paid attention to.

"And what exactly might I be telling you?"

He leaned back, calculating a response in the deep furrow of his brow. "That you have just as much to hide."

"I do not hide, nor do I cower to any form of man. I do not give information to those who could easily obtain it themselves. Do not misplace your anger upon me, when you could very well have found out by asking your brother *yourself*."

Dark laughter left his lips. "You are good, but I would do no such thing. For I already know my brother too well. He's as good with women as he is with words, and that is not very well as you'll come to find. . . or maybe you already have?" He shrugged. "But my question is to you alone—why would the Princess of the Novear Kingdom turn against her own?"

Keahi was going to pay for this interaction.

I snatched his mug across the table. He let out a small puff of annoyance as he tried to retrieve it. I took a step back, raising my eyebrow at him over the dark liquid. "It seems you do not know your brother at all, then. A man who has little to say generally knows what to do with his hands the most." I lit a fire within the mischief his eyes carried. "If you are looking for the traitor, find out what he has done before you seek them from me."

I took a sip, relishing the warmth as I watched the moment his pupils widened, just before he burst out into a fit of laughter. My face flushed in an instant, but I held the steam to my face in hopes of a natural cover up. I knew that I had chosen well, at the way he slid his hand down his face.

He shook his head, something playful taking over within him. "You are not the first woman to tell me I need to keep my mouth shut, and hopefully you won't be the last." He flattened the papers he had been holding on the table and reached out his hand. "Pleasure to meet you, Princess. My name is Drakkon Aldeer, the bastard of the kingdom and brother to yours truly."

I did not reach out to take his hand, knowing that it was in no way a peace offering. "Anything else?"

His gaze darkened as he retracted his hand. "Yes, actually. Your husband was supposed to be here, *hmm*, several hours ago, and I am already late. . . but of course, he is nowhere to be found." He stood up, making his way over to the door. "I do find it curious though, for someone so newlywed at least, he finds himself elsewhere when you were clearly injured upon arrival."

Bastard, yes, the title fitted him well.

"He is to be crowned king? Is he not? I am not a woman easily hurt by frivolity." Although something pricked at the back of my head, wondering why Keahi had revealed this truth to the others so easily. Drakkon irritatingly had a point. I could only deflect the truth as good as the lie it was hiding behind.

Drakkon let out a *humph* before I stopped him in his tracks.

"You cannot seriously believe Keahi would be okay with you leaving me here by myself after I was *gravely* injured, do you? Therefore, he left you here as a babysitter, I presume?"

"First name basis? *Intriguing*." Drakkon padded his toes at the doorstep. "You seem to be feeling better. I am not too concerned," he said. I prowled behind him, sweeping tiny shards of glass with the blanket I carried around me.

The time I had spent with Keahi had been minimal. Keahi had barely spoken to me outside of what needed to be said in our alliance, but when he did speak. . . he fought with his words. This man threatened to win. He needed me to do that now. At least we could share that.

I just hoped I knew this part of him enough to be right. "And what would he say if he found out I had been injured in your absence? All this broken glass. . . whoever had broken in and tried to attack me. . ."

Drakkon swung around. "You look *perfectly* healed, Princess, believe me. He made sure of that."

I slipped the tiny broken piece of glass I had been saving underneath the fold of the blanket and held it up to my neck. Light reflected off the glass and glared onto Drakkon's face, causing him to take a step back.

"*Try me*."

He studied the glass at the soft part of my throat. "Where I am going might frighten a Novear woman such as yourself."

I glossed over the insult, pushing the jagged edge further. "Do I look frightened?"

"You should be, Novear," he shot back. "This castle is not the same one I'm sure your father locked you up in." *I almost wished he had,*

I wanted to say.

"Then let's test that theory, shall we?" I glanced at the wardrobe and headed straight over to it, hoping I could find something to wear at least. As soon as I cracked open the hinges, a hand slammed the door shut.

"Did you not hear me the first time?"

My hands were unmoving against the iron rings. "I did. You said a woman such as myself would be frightened." My knuckles turned white as a pulse beneath me flared. "I'm not."

"Are those injuries getting to your head or are you threatening me?"

"If I was making a threat. . . you would know it." I met the hatred in his stare halfway. "Besides, thank you for your subtle inquiry over my well-being, but I feel fine." *Better than I have for almost my entire life.*

"Do not say that I did not warn you. Just be happy I enjoy pissing my brother off enough to let you try to work whatever little scheme you are planning in my favor. Don't be stupid enough to think I won't be able to see right through you, even if he does not." His features hardened, easing his hand off the wardrobe.

I swung the door back open, hoping to knock him off balance this close. "And I will be waiting when you realize we are on the same side."

Chapter Seventeen

Sabine

The clashing of metal echoed through the castle hallways so loud it threatened to numb my teeth. Keahi's brother had impatiently waited for me to get dressed, shouting on the other side of the door about how he was already late for his daily trainings with my *husband's* soldiers. At his ever so thoughtful manner, I went slower each time he opened his mouth and twice as slow when he pounded on the door.

"By the way you woke yourself from the dead, I know you can walk faster than that, darling," Drakkon said as we headed toward massive, iron-plated doors.

"That's the problem. Death's embrace did not wake me. It was my husband's. . ." I eyed him up and down and continued, "brother staring at me like I was some agile prisoner."

"If I had it my way, Novear, you would be," he said. "Whatever my brother excavated from your neck, which he refuses to discuss with me, clearly was not attached to your attitude. Or maybe it was caging what was underneath? What a nice little surprise he is in for."

Flames ricocheted like that of a wild brushfire trapped within, pulsing underneath the door in tidal waves of heat that could outmatch hell itself.

"It's not a surprise, believe it or not—he actually prefers it," I said with a smirk.

Drakkon shoved the doors open, and the heat heightened as twelve pairs of red glowing eyes stared straight through me behind their masks. Each of the warriors dressed in the same black cloaks and face coverings as Keahi when we entered the mountain. Realization threaded through me in bursts of fear. These were not just any sorcerers of Solstice, *they were the Volkan fighters.*

They racked their various weapons lined along the wall, walking across the massive training floor to form a unified line as their gazes remained on me. Several battle rings spread upon the floor for hand-to-hand combat, and a sizably larger ring captured the center in the form of an infinite dragon wrapping around itself.

The man that I had seen in my rooms was only a fraction of how deviant he appeared as he crossed his arms behind his back.

"We have a lot to prepare for in the next coming weeks. We must ready ourselves for the worst in order to carry out our plans." Drakkon nodded over to the farthest soldier on the left. "Kane will dispute the matches. Today we will invoke Volkan's ring."

They found their positions knowingly. The Volkan who Drakkon had instructed eyed the two of us carefully, sighing deeply before heading toward the center ring.

"You could not even afford an introduction?" I said to Drakkon as we watched them, my arms crossed.

"Giving them your name would be like handing out your obituary, Novear. They do not care who you are, they just care to see you dead."

I brushed off his remark. "Solstice still has many powerful sorcerers from what I can see, more so than any other kingdom, including my own. I was not the one to close the veil to the Gods magic—it is my father you are speaking of."

Drakkon turned slowly to face me, scowling as he looked down at me through gritted teeth. "Tell that to them, when there are only thirteen of the Volkans left after your father closed the veil—your *husband* one of them. It does not matter how far removed you think you are from what he has done. They see you all the same."

He walked off shouting commands, leaving me to seethe alone. What he did not know was I already knew that I was nothing. I had been greatly reminded of that my entire life, but I was going to leave a mark on this realm by the end. I would take my father and his entire kingdom down with me, no matter the cost.

"Hand to hand combat, no weapons!" Drakkon shouted, pacing against the edge of the center ring with two warriors in the middle. "If the round does not end within five minutes, magic is fair game."

Kane remained at the outer edge of the ring. He knelt low to the ground, fire igniting in the palm of his hand as he touched the chalked outline. It sparked, dispersing to opposite ends as the line of his flames searched to greet one another. The two opponents, trapped within, unleashed themselves as the fire connected into a complete circle—vicious and unrelenting.

It was obvious they were highly skilled, throwing a series of maneuvers at each other that could easily take out any other opponent—but not them. One fighter had finally gotten the upper hand after several minutes, his fist connecting with the other Volkan's jaw. It threw him off balance just enough to seize a killing blow. The winner's fist halted right above the other's chest. Kane released his hold from the ring of fire he maintained during their challenge, and ash fell around them.

We proceeded to watch a series of guards, all of whom showed as much strength and skill as the initial soldiers. None of them had fought to the five-minute marker yet. Drakkon came back up beside me after some time, running his hand through his sweaty hair. The room was sweltering, and their flames did nothing to help the rising temperature.

"Have you seen what you needed to see, Novear?" Several of the Volkans cut a glance toward me as Drakkon spoke. "I would love to know what you are storing in that head of yours right now, to report at a later date when you have finished off my brother, no doubt."

Yes. I had seen everything, and I was more than terrified. *Maybe not for the reasons he was thinking*, but I did have something to report to him.

"Impressive," I said, as his incompetent smirk grew. "Although I noted some weaknesses. They are quite minor, of course."

"Weaknesses?" Drakkon scoffed. "These are some of the best warriors in all the kingdoms."

"Every soldier has a weakness, Drakkon." I stepped away and looked toward the center ring, smiling to myself. "Easily being riled is yours. Though, I'm sure there are more."

"You have no idea," he said, glowering. "Just as ignorance must be yours. There is no doubt with a ruler such as your father that you nor any other female in Novear has stepped on a battlefield because of his prejudices. Know your place here before I find it for you."

I held my tongue, buzzing energy tingled my skin, begging to be released. *My power answered to me, only me, and no one else now.* I reared back at him. "I will ask this of you again, Drakkon—do I look terrified to you?"

"No, but I feel it is time for a demonstration." His grin turned wicked as he motioned toward Kane, who was already on his way over to us. "It would seem our new *Princess* has found some weak spots in your training, Commander." Kane's eyes seemed to flicker for a moment as he looked me over. "If that is the case, I am sure she will find it in your technique," Drakkon said flatly, grasping my shoulders as he pushed me toward the center ring.

Kane positioned himself across from me. His calm demeanor unnerved me slightly, but my blood roiled underneath for the challenge I hoped to match. Drakkon ignited his palm, and my heart jolted in place. Orange flames rushed behind me, entrapping me in the circle with Kane.

He moved around our enclosure, testing my initial response to his movement as I mirrored him. I stilled every part of me that wanted to react as Kane rushed at me, analyzing the power radiating from his steps. Whatever weakness that ailed me prior was consumed by my magic. I crouched down, holding one arm out for balance. Our eyes locked right before he made contact.

I lifted myself into the air as I swung my legs over my center, landing behind him. He was quicker than I wanted to admit as he rounded the moment my feet hit the ground, rebounding fiercely with enough power to knock a man over three times my size.

This was the type of fighter that never underestimated his opponent. I cursed myself for that minor setback, but it was not the worst I have had to endure. I blocked a series of blows that he rained down on me, sweat dripping off me as I threw my first punch. He snatched up my wrist like he saw it before I had even thought to make the movement.

I acted on pure instinct, twisting myself behind him, attempting to grab hold of his neck, but he had already calculated my intent. He jerked my wrist over his shoulder, and I felt the bone *snap*. Fury broke through me as I saw the color red. My shoulder drove into the ground as I rolled over with a groan. I used every bit of momentum I had to smash into his legs. I threw him off balance, giving me just enough time to create distance.

As I reclaimed my stance, I saw Drakkon in my peripheral vision. The intensity in his gaze produced a deep monovalent sound in my chest as I circled the outer rim, banking that our time was almost up.

Kane looked as if he was ready to tear me limb from limb as Drakkon stood, holding up a hand that hushed the entirety of the room into a palpable silence. I watched the rise and fall of Kane's chest, refusing to take my eyes off him. Fire simmered in his eyes, and my power reveled with its own response.

Taking a moment, I ripped the belt I had used to cinch in the oversized shirt I had found, and I sent it clattering to the floor. My sweat-slicked tunic slopped down beside it, and I was covered only by my wrap. I shook out the wrist Kane had grabbed, *broken. . . definitely broken,* but I barely felt it compared to what was rushing through me. It charged me with a burning intensity, and soon I would have to make my own fire.

"Ready!" Drakkon yelled over the cracks of the raging flame. Kane took his stance, revving his magic in his palms as they bloomed with a sinister heat. His magic prickled up his forearms, ready to be ignited, but I stood still. I watched Kane in what felt like slow motion, demonstrating the movements to breed fire.

Pity, I was not even going to give him the chance to use it. Closing my eyes for half a second, I connected with the piece of myself I could finally claim for my own, and it came running to me with open arms. My eyes glowed a bright white, my vision turning into a kaleidoscope pattern that allowed me to see every beam of light in my path.

Kane was finishing his motion now, preparing to blast me off the ring, but as he went to finish his movement, the flame died in his hands as they came forward. A solid thud erupted as his knees hit the floor; his breath that once appeared controlled, now rapid. I walked over to him with slow purpose, drawing out my attack. Drakkon and the Volkans completely stilled off to the side.

I had brought their most valuable soldier to his knees. It would be a warning I might come to regret, but I felt infinite in my power. I felt in control as every eye in the room watched it unfold.

It was my father's favorite technique to use before he stripped away another sorcerer's power by siphoning. The strain it placed on my magic was heavy, but I pushed through it with force. I refused to ever be seen as weak again.

It. Was. Mine.

I surveyed him as I kneeled behind him. I spoke into his ear with a soft hush that only he was supposed to hear, but I knew the sorcerers surrounding us picked up on every muttered detail as the room reached its boiling point.

"There is no weakness in your training, Commander, for I would know. What I do know is that you have clearly never battled one on one with a *lightbringer*. For if you did. . . you would have never stepped inside this ring. I can control the very light that allows you to see." I leaned down closer, pinning my eyes on Drakkon as I trailed a single finger across Kane's throat. "That gives me the ability to kill you, and you would have never known the moment I brought death upon you."

His whole body shook, cowering in the emptiness I created for him. Their eyes burned into me, as I held their commander on his knees.

Their stares grew numb as a new presence emerged from the shadows. I felt as if there was a phantom string attached to me, so faint, I did not understand how even my own power could not resist the urge to look. Kane gasped with air beside me as I let go of him. Directly in my line of vision, a thirteenth cloaked figure appeared.

He sent flames down our connection, with every ounce of bleeding wrath that I could not see from his exterior alone. Our eyes clashed together as if the rest of the world was on fire. The magic suspended between us was irrefutable—even more so than my own power, what I had finally laid claim to. It infuriated me, knowing I had felt nothing of the sort when I first met him.

I sent my own blaze of wrath down that invisible line because it did not matter if he was my bonded sorcerer or not. *This power is mine.* I would never cower to anyone ever again, let alone a future king.

Do you want to be next? I inclined, wading through our connection I irrefutably sensed fully for the first time.

Keahi was as still as night, but a whisper traveled through the room that rattled my power to its core.

I would like to see you try.

Chapter Eighteen

Sabine

Envy ground my teeth to the bone, fighting my power's betrayal as it flared from his response. My power was not invigorated by a threat, but a challenge as I watched Keahi's cutting gaze slice down my form like a knife.

He harbored enough rage in one look that I almost argued if it was as insatiable as my own. I crushed the sensation with a fist as I ripped myself away from him, severing what I could of the bond.

I did not hate him for the sake of knowing he was a fragile alliance at best in the path to my own desires, but I despised his very essence. Keahi would always be my enemy on the fault line, a betrayal in hand when the realm tore us apart. I have never held the expectation of loyalty to anyone, let alone those whose fates were sealed by the Gods.

For the Gods and all they embodied would be the rival I hoped to destroy in the end, with or without him, until I was nothing, but dust shed upon this realm.

Kane's palms lifted heavily from the floor as I turned to him. Each breath staggered to regain control. I would not fault him for any transgressed plots against me for what I had just done to him. Darkness made one feel isolated until it beckoned what had been hiding within the depths all along. I should have seen anger when he looked up at me, but it shadowed his eyes with an emotion I did not fully understand.

There was no sign of defeat in the brief appearance I could gather from, as the Commander placed one solid foot on the ground. He forced himself upright and crossed his forearms against his chest. His two forefingers lit on fire as he bowed to me.

Kane did not rise from that position, not until I turned to see that it was not just him who bowed, but the rest of the Volkan fighters as well around me. Their respect I had earned, but it was their fear I wanted. I kept my head lifted, knowing I had failed.

The Volkans righted themselves in unison, following their commander's lead as he nodded toward me and walked outside of the ring. A hint of what I could have sworn was a smile lingered in Kane's eyes.

The others followed his movements, continuing their training in the outer rims. I willed my fists to remain calm as the warriors went on, as if nothing had even occurred.

The opposite was to be said about the half-brothers hovering behind me, exchanging tense unspoken glances between each other. I refused to look at them just yet, giving myself enough time to recover.

I casually strode to where I flayed my shirt to the ground. The outer edges of my scars from the ritual were on display, peeking above the top of my wrap as I leaned down to retrieve my shirt. It chilled my skin as I drew the soaked material over my shoulders. I quietly hissed through my teeth as I made quick work to latch the belt I had found in place.

A broken wrist was nothing compared to what I had handled before, and it tingled with a familiar numbness I found comfort in.

Drakkon and Keahi stood side by side behind me, muttering quick and harsh words to each other I could not make out with my back turned.

Drakkon had an unfriendly twitch at the corner of his lip as I made my way over to them. "That was quite the party trick, wasn't it, brother? I think we now know why she had been held in her father's captivity."

I straightened the bottom of my shirt, brushing off a bit of ash that had fallen on my shoulder. "Why does it not surprise me you would talk about women in such a way? Does it make you feel more. . . powerful?" I raised my brow. "Besides, I have been told that it is everyone's favorite."

Drakkon reeled forward, his breath hot on my cheek. "What is it exactly my brother has picked up on our doorstep? A traitorous woman who thinks she has something to prove?" He mocked, lowering his voice. "Do you think your petty act made them fear you, Novear? It just made them hungry for your blood, and I cannot wait to see them drain it from your neck."

My voice remained calm in comparison, despite the light that flared in my palms. "Are you scared I will have you on your knees too, Drakkon? Because I can make that happen if you wish."

"Threaten me all you want but know I will not bow to a whore who no doubt got on her own knees to get here." The light in my palms I had summoned flickered as he shot back. His laughter braised my cheeks as he witnessed it.

"*Enough, Drakkon.*" Keahi stepped between us, disrupting his watchful silence.

"*What*? Am I not allowed to say what we are all thinking, Keahi? You may be blind to it, but I am not. If you will not get to know your wife, *I will*."

Keahi's shadow seeped out of him, crawling up his form, wrapping around his lower half. If Drakkon noticed it, he did not let it show, but his face changed as Keahi looked down at him.

"If you so much as insinuate my wife upon her knees like that again, I will finally demonstrate to you the ways I have killed men who can withstand fire." Drakkon flinched, as if Keahi had struck him directly across the face. "You will see a side to me you wished you knew to be dead, but I promise you. . . it is very much *alive*."

Drakkon's face dropped to mine, his mouth slightly parted. He looked between us with a hint of confusion as he took a small step back. He attempted to clear his throat; conviction written across his face.

"I understand," was all he said as he turned to rush out of the room without another word. I fumbled at the swift change in composure, but I did not have a chance to linger on it long.

Keahi single handedly dragged me out of the room by the hook in my arm, putting on a display even though he could have used his shadowfire to remove us from their view. I did not dare look back to see if anyone was watching, knowing that I could not hide my utter shock and annoyance.

As soon as the doors closed behind us, I pushed against him. "Let go of me!"

His cloak flew the opposite direction.

"*Who. Trained. You?*"

I mockingly leaned in closer, but it was to my great displeasure to find I was no longer repulsed by his proximity. The last of the crystal's removal was an unexpected counterattack to my senses.

The sorcery he possessed overwhelmed me in a whole new way as his amber scent swarmed around me in an intoxicating smolder. It flushed every inch of my skin in an inviting warmth to discover the wicked and untamed nature rising within him to a fever pitch.

Keahi's head tilted to the side, his chest shuttering as he inhaled deeply against me in a trance. His thick eyelashes fluttered, plagued by the same carnal affliction. Our powers diverted their loyalty under the same maddening duress in search of each other.

I was about to fix that.

My lips lifted with an aggravated smirk. "Is it not obvious who trained me, General? *My father.*"

The flames in his gaze turned to coal, so brief I almost missed it as we set course down the hallway. He tightened his grip and yanked me closer. "It is not safe to discuss this here in the open. Either I drag you or you pick up your pace."

I attempted to shove him with my shoulder, but it felt like I had rammed it into stone. A dark chuckle in his throat appeared at my wince and abruptly cut off. I did not have time to brace myself as he slammed my body against the castle wall.

Keahi yielded my groan, cutting me off with a gloved hand. Our bodies pressed together as he began dragging me across the wall until we were completely out of sight, tucked behind a corridor. I riled against him, attempting to fight him off until the sound of boots sprinting through the hallway thundered beside us.

"*Shhhh.*" He put a single finger up to his mouth. "Are you *ever* quiet?"

I proceeded to resist the urge to bite that finger off and feed it to him, as we listened to the sound of our own breathing before the final set of footsteps faded. Keahi cautiously released his hand from my mouth, but he did not move, his lower half pressing against my body.

"Well, hello to you too, '*husband*'," I lowered my voice to a hush. "Should I be thanking you for my rescue? I'm sure that is what your brother thinks I'm doing right now. If this is how you want it, you're at least going to say please." One hand slammed beside me as he kept the other on my shoulder with a tight grip. I slowly turned to his gloved hand on my skin. "Now that's not very nice. Though I do tend to like the possessive and aggressive type."

The only recognition he heard me as he began melting into his shadow was a small huff of air that he did a poor job of hiding.

"Drakkon may have all the bite harbored in the world, but he rarely acts on it despite what he has so thoughtfully demonstrated," he said gruffly.

My lips parted as Keahi lowered himself down to me. I whispered, "Isn't that the excuse they all give?"

"You never let me finish what I need to say, do you?" He shook his head. "It is how we are in this exact predicament in the first place."

"You tend to not say anything at all. How should I know what you are thinking?" I looked down and back up. "Or maybe I do?"

Keahi's growl was terrifying, but only because my magic found it alluring.

"*Especially* when it is something Drakkon thinks is important. He tends to act out. I had no choice but to leave you with him, and he was the only person I could trust on such short notice. The last removal knocked you out cold, and I did not think you would wake anytime soon."

I tilted my head and pouted my lower lip. "Well, you were wrong. Please tell me you are not that dense. I did not even have a fighting chance when I woke up. He was loaded, ready with questions that *you* left him with. He could have killed me while I was asleep!"

Keahi shoved himself off the wall and looked me over slowly from the ground up. "I think you managed to stay alive well enough. Let's not continue with the dramatics."

I felt the urge to roll my eyes, but I didn't have time. I would have lost sight of him as he ushered us down several hallways and brought me into the same room I had woken up in. As soon as he clicked the lock on the door, he threw his hood behind him, gripping it so tightly I thought he was going to shred the fabric in two.

"*Now*," he said, releasing a breath between his teeth. "Do you want to explain to me how the last time I saw you, you had been on your deathbed for the second time that I've known you in the past week. . . and now you are putting on a parade in front of my troops?"

The accusation did little to cool my newfound temper. "Should you not be asking your soldiers why it was so painfully easy to take them down instead of lecturing me? It is not my fault they made it look easy."

"*Oh*. I plan on it, but we are talking about you, Sabine. Do not avoid the question. I am not in the mood for whatever game you are playing at."

You will play the game if I want you to, I said to myself.

"I had some time to refresh, as you can imagine." I walked over to the bed, dragging my fingers across the seam of the ruffled comforter. "You would have known. . . if you would not have dropped me the *second* I became useless to you. I do not think I imagined this going any other way, though."

Keahi ripped off his face covering, exposing the bladed fury underneath. "Let me explain it to you then, '*wife*.' Since we did not have the appointed luxury of getting to know one another, I am going to ask you something that I expect an answer to."

He prowled toward me, and the back of my legs hit the frame.

"*Are you working for your father?*"

I snarled at him and pushed him out of my line of sight. "You really have the nerve to ask me that? After you have claimed to see him torture me through your own eyes?"

"Does it look like I'm joking to you, or do I need to continue to spell everything out for you? I would be more than happy to, but you fight me before I can finish a sentence," he growled.

I sent up a very dedicated finger as I threw back a glass of water that was sitting on the nightstand and spat it right back out. My eyes burned; hot fluid flooded my nose. I picked up the glass and threw it into the stone fireplace with a begrudging sound in my throat. I wiped my nostrils on my sleeve. "Your brother is apparently trying to poison me now!"

Keahi's shoulders shook with a silent laughter. "It is poison, but not the kind that can kill you unless you have too much of it. Not a fan of the drink now, are we?"

When I popped it open to inspect the clear corked bottle, I nearly gagged at the smell. "I would say not." I slammed the disgusting liquid back on the table. "Why, in your right state of mind, would you accuse me of working for someone who had imprisoned me and left me for dead?" Pure, undiluted rage wreaked havoc in my system.

"Do not act like anything you just did was out of innocence," Keahi bit out. "I have every right to question your motives."

I threw my arms out. "Why would you need to question me? If my lies are so easily spoken to you, what motivation would I have to hide it?"

"They are not '*spoken*' to me. *I can feel it.* Not every thought is broadcasted. So, I am giving you the chance to tell the truth, even if it is something I do not wish to hear," he rasped.

Keahi searched my face for an answer he might have already feared. That I was working with my father. That I was just as much the villain in this story as he had been to me my entire life. I cursed myself the moment the first tear fell, not from sadness, but from a hatred I would never recover from. The pain I did not want to feel came alive within the place I had buried it.

My palms shoved against his chest repeatedly, and he stood there and took it all. "Let me remind *you*, you know nothing about me, '*husband*.' I did not sit there and take it! He paralyzed me with the crystal." I shuddered against him with his cloak in my fists. "All I could do was watch as he held me down with my power! Fought against every part of me that had given up so many years ago as he laid me down bare in front of my people, marking me as I heard their cheers with each line he carved."

My mind and body detached from itself, and my voice broke with it. "I begged him! I begged him to stop! I even begged the Gods to look down upon me just once. Not even to save me, but to see just what kind of monster they created in their absence. If you think for one moment that I would willingly trade my soul from that of one monster to another. . . it is you who are mistaken. I have heard of your sins, *Son of Fire*, and if you think your threats evoke fear in me, know men like you are all the same to me. It is *you* who kept *me* alive. I will not apologize for exploring a power that is *mine* when I was challenged by your brother in your absence! If you regret ripping away the muzzle my father had placed for your kind to control me, just say so."

Those last words left me without thought and ripped a hole in my chest. Images sliced across my vision that I tore away silently against my mind. I grappled with the room I was in as it threatened to fade away in place of unwanted memories.

Keahi stared straight through me as I felt myself shattering within. His shoulders dropped as he turned away from me, the tip of his ears red hot. I braced myself for an angered response when his ember eyes looked back up to mine, but he took two steps back.

"He has been spotted, your father. I had to ask. . . I had feared the worst. Thought maybe you were working with him." He grimaced as he reached up to rub his chest, as if the pain caught up to him. "When I saw you with Kane, it just was not the best of timing," he said weakly.

My mind changed routes entirely, and I swallowed the lump in my throat. I released him from me. "Do you think he believes me to be dead?"

"No, I do not," Keahi said flatly and walked over to the fireplace. Those ember eyes clouded over with thick black smoke. "He has probably realized by now he has not weakened the King of Solstice and is looking for an answer as to why."

Acid burned its way down. "He's. . . looking for me."

And he would find me. He always did.

Keahi nodded, placing a gloved hand on the blackened stone. "The Novear King had to realize you survived since his target is still on the throne. He just may not realize the gravity of it yet."

Pain settled into my chest and numbed my body with subdued panic. The residual feeling of using my power had taken its toll; emotionally and physically. I had forgotten what it felt like to be in control. It was brief, and it made me feel alive. I would not let go of that this time.

"Tell me what I need to do." I leveled with Keahi, ignoring the tears rolling down my cheeks.

His features nearly softened, but it seemed impossible for him with the scars that possessed his face. "Right now. . . I need you to sit down and let me look at your injuries." I went rigid, backing away as he said, "There is a gigantic bruise forming on your wrist where Kane reached for you, and I just want to look at it."

I paused my retreat. "How long had you been watching me?"

"Long enough." His mouth thinned.

"I do not trust you." I grasped my broken wrist.

The throbbing ache re-surged. When I thrashed against his chest, I had not noticed a single drop of pain. Keahi reached his hand up and wrung the side of his neck in circles.

"I will have someone bring you to Elias first thing in the morning. He will heal it. They finally made it here yesterday while you were asleep. The creatures who tracked us in the woods delayed them. . . Elias was quite worried about your recovery upon arrival."

I needed to get out of here, out of this room.

Get away from *him*—soon. I strode to the door and opened it for him. "I will see Elias in the morning if you promise to just leave."

Keahi replaced his mask. Halting under the door frame, he said, "I will never regret removing that crystal from you—never."

I spoke with an honesty I had not had the privilege of admitting. "I wanted none of this. Not before you, and definitely not after you."

"I understand," he said softly.

My grip tightened on the knob. "*No. You don't.* I have nothing to go back to, Keahi. I don't even remember who I was before my father placed the siphoning crystal inside of me. If there is anything I want in this lifetime, it is to make him pay for what he has done. That is what you can depend on from me, if nothing else. Do not question me on it again."

I shut out the roil of his regret toward me down the bond. The tinge of his sadness burned a hole in my chest; I was already feeling too much of my own when I slammed the door in his face.

Chapter Nineteen

"So, can you at least tell me her favorite color?"

Drakkon leaned up against the wooden frame of my study. I ignored him, writing the same line over and over again in the notebook on my desk.

I had to get my thoughts down on the page before they ran away from me. Before I was alone with them elsewhere, or worse, used my unfiltered thoughts to hurt those who did not deserve it.

He sighed. "Considering that you've fallen in love with the enemy of our kingdom, General, I would at least expect you to know her favorite color."

The tip of my quill snapped, exploding droplets of ink on the page. "I do not—" I stiffened. *No—that was not a sentence I could finish.*

"Yes. . . I care for her. . . and it would be important to remember the next time you chastise my wife," I painfully recovered.

"*My wife*," he taunted as he walked over to sit on the edge of my desk with a low chuckle. "Is that what you are writing in that cute little notebook of yours? *My wife. My wife.*"

My gaze gravitated to the corner of my desk he was sitting on. He had purposely chosen the side with the largest stack of papers, knowing it would annoy me to no end as a deliberate smirk rose in the corner of his mouth.

Drakkon huffed. "I wonder what Zehra would have to say about it if she were here, but no matter. It seems you are taken by Sabine since you nearly threatened to cut my head off."

I firmly pressed on the edge of my papers, hastily scooting them out from underneath him. I straightened them, knocking the edges against the desk three times before I sat them on the farthest corner away from him, and picked up a new quill.

Drakkon's lips parted with a drawn-out sigh. His eyes roamed over the contents of my desk, fingers fumbling through the air in search to find an object to move a quarter of an inch.

I clenched my teeth, the quill scraping harshly against the page. "Drakkon. I have work to do."

He tipped his head, flaying out his fingers before he withdrew his attack on my papers, and scratched the outline of his neat beard. "Yellow might be a suitable color for her, don't you think? It might match her eyes. . . they are beautiful."

My fingertips heated with magic, browning five holes into the page I was working on, and I cursed between my teeth. The sweet singe of the burnt page lifted through the air before I ripped it hastily from the notebook and set it on fire. "Do I need to provide to you a list of your thoughts that I do not wish to hear? I do not want to hear you talk about how pretty you think she is."

Drakkon's dark brow rose as I tensed.

His curiosity was insatiably inconvenient and excruciating when you were on the other end of it. His smile softened the longer I held my glare. "Now come, brother. You know she doesn't exactly suit my. . . tastes. Let us not lie to one another, we tend to do it too often. I do not want to do that now."

I shifted back, my hands cautiously drumming against the edge of the desk. "Is that what you wish to speak on?"

He shook his head thoughtfully. "I would rather watch your eyes *smolder* every time I speak of her. It is quite endearing."

A bitter laugh tensely made its way out of me. "It is a shame that I grew a soft spot for you when all you do is exploit it till my ears bleed."

Drakkon's voice lost all its playfulness as he looked me directly in the eyes. "Happiness looks good on you, brother. I feel guilty that I have never noticed what it truly looked like on you. The woman is obviously a threat, but if you like that." He grinned. "Who am I to stop you?"

Drakkon shifted off the table and paused. "Give me time to warm up to her. You know more than anyone I always do." He held up his hand in a fist and slowly lifted his last finger. "I offer my congratulations on your marriage—you deserve this."

Happiness must look like agony on me then, I thought, as I mirrored his truce.

My last conversation with Sabine eroded my guilt into a vivid shame. It was like the bond had allowed me to see myself through her.

The news I received of her father had caused dread to sink inside me, swirling with the possibility she had been involved in igniting the sorcerer's bond through the crest on my chest.

It was my rash and unwise response that fell like a hammer on the unhealed edge inside of herself, and I had been the one to drop it.

The power she displayed did not scare me. It was how she used it that did. I assumed before I could understand, and our fears drove us both to react in ways that made us feel in control. I did not want to be a monster, but in Sabine's eyes, I had already become one.

Or maybe it was always what I had been.

Fear was a condition I had not known was a sickness. It had never forced me to feel what it truly felt like from someone else. How it mangled with my own and created the worst combination when all we were trying to do was protect ourselves in the end.

I shook my head, unable to not give in to my brother's ways, as I released the hold on myself. Drakkon reached out with a heavy look in his eye. The sides of our palms met as we crossed our small outer fingers together in the unspoken promise of our youth.

I had attempted to avoid his embraces at all costs as we grew up together, but there were times when I could not refuse him. I could not tell him *no* with his arms wide open and eyes pure with joy. His only intention was to share it with others, and I could not bring myself to tell him how painful it was for me. That every time our chests connected, and he held me tight, I felt the scars beneath me.

I could not tell him no.

Not even during the last time he had ever tried to hug me. Drakkon had frozen himself in place. The joy in his eyes melted into a hurt I wanted to take away, when he noticed for the first time how I braced myself as he opened his arms.

He slowly pressed them into his side. His lips parted as he stared at the blood that had soaked through my shirt and up to the door to my father's quarters behind me.

I closed my eyes, listening to his footsteps grow near, as my heavy arms trembled in an attempt to lift them toward him—*anything* to take away how he looked at me with a silence I had never heard from him before.

'*Please.*' I had begged him.

I could feel the shake of his breath as he stood in front of me. He placed his hands on my forearms instead, defeat threatening to pull me under, because it was so gentle it hurt when he lowered my arms for me.

'*Hold out one hand to me,*' he quivered.

I gave it to him without question, roiling with regret at the connection he made. *Would he always see me this way? Would he always hesitate to love me? Would he no longer love me now?* I had thought as the tears dripped from my chin. No one, until then, had ever seen me cry, and to this day, he was the only person who ever had.

He shook as he folded four of my fingers into my palms, hooking the remaining one within his own, and that gentle touch transformed into the strongest I had ever known.

> *'This is how we will tell each other, brother. I do not need more from you. Stop. Giving. Too. Much.'* He stifled a broken sob, but his voice did not waver. *'This is my promise to you.'*

His hand pulled away from me now.

I watched him quietly walk toward the door.

"Drakkon?" I hesitated. "She would look beautiful in anything, but I think red would suit her the most."

Even if I couldn't see his smile, I felt it.

"I think. . . you are right."

Chapter Twenty

Sabine

There was no soldier more loyal to my father than the one he created within my mind. Trained to assault me at my weakest, tightening its invisible hold around the base of my throat. Every inhale, at mercy to memory. The fear before the fight because I have only known survival through the means of failure.

The Prince of Solstice's gruff voice, a constant in my head, long after I had shut him out. Where my bonded's anger lost its sting in the quiet beat of his breath, laced with his fear and my inevitable. '*He's been spotted, your father.*'

Those deluded by corruption were still feigned with clarity. My thoughts were no longer corrupted with my equivalent of hope. The King of Novear was looking for me. It was not a question. My father always knew the outcome of his price. Even his risks were calculated.

So, was I the risk he never planned to take when he sacrificed me, or was I just another price?

Was this freedom from the siphoning crystal the same freedom my people had? My mother before that?

Most confounding, was the freedom my father searched for, risked, worth the price of destroying the Veil of Seven? The Gods seemed to think so.

The Veil of Seven was the Gods' entrance into our realm, the connection to our magic, but it had also been their escape. It was destroyed by my father's hand, a pardon for their crimes, as the Gods disappeared without a fight.

Our sorcery was designed by the seven Gods of the Beginning. The four kingdoms of the realm were reborn of the sun, moon, earth, and stars, where there was only one sun, one moon, and one earth to share the sky. But it was my people, the Kingdom of Novear, who were once the sorcerers of the stars.

There were many stars, but I was alone, my soul buried with those who had dared to step foot in his way in a field of ash.

No death since then had ever sounded the same. Not when I had survived, and my people did not. When I had heard the absence of their screams within my own numbing silence.

Death was a hollow sound in the abyss, and I had felt it the moment it created its home. Deep and irreparable, until the darkness swallowed me whole.

The thought of my father finding me eclipsed my ability to reason. Moonlight took over the day, shadows curated in the pits of the very room that seemed like a breath of fresh air. Where I had found my delusion. The disdained belief I had a fighting chance, and fate was on my side. Where I had woken up without the edges of my father's crystal cage clawing at my skin. Where I had felt my power for the first time in years—*mine.*

That's where I saw him.

Every corner I turned to, darted toward. . . *looked like him. . .*

The silhouette of his lanky figure. A flash of his fanged scowl, hollow glimpses of his grating cheekbones, and gray piercing eyes. The change of his breath when he was angry, something I had learned to pick up on in a crowded room not by sound, but by the way his shoulders pinched higher. My father's white hair was iridescent against the night, but his presence loomed as dark as a shadow.

The King of Novear crept out of the darkness, holding the shattered pieces of the siphoning crystal. The one he had placed many years ago to control me on the night of my people's deaths. Its shattered ruby pieces swirled in his palm as he approached me, staining the white marbled floor with my blood.

I could feel the crystal burrowing into my skin. The blood trickled down my spine, just below the nape of my hair. The scabs on my ruined back from the ritual scraped against the wooden surface as I frantically searched for the knob behind me.

'Let me fix you.'

My breath shuddered at the sound of my father's voice. It snaked down my body with chills, pounding in my ears. Too close, he was too close, and he could not command me this time to stay still.

"No—*not again*, not again," I cried out as I rammed my shoulder through the door, wasting precious seconds when it had not been locked. I sprinted past the burning furnace and into the dark tunnels of the forgotten city inside the mountain.

He's coming for you, I told myself as panic rushed through me. My too-heavy footsteps synced with my heartbeat, heels striking against the uneven rock floor. *Don't look back.*

The only viable way out of this mountain was through the base. My lungs burned as I turned toward every corner deemed south, descending multiple flights of stairs. My nails scraped into stone as I tumbled over the last five steps, making it one.

If you stop, he'll find you.

My injured wrist shot warning signals as it recovered from the contact of the wall. I used my other hand to press myself off in a clumsy attempt to right myself. I lunged forward as I grabbed a torch off the wall and pushed myself beyond the shrieking pain, copper rushing under my tongue as I bit back a sob.

If you rest, you're done for.

I could hear him. The footsteps that were in tandem with my own. I increased my pace, but there was no fuel to sustain me. No magic for me to summon, as I had ignorantly made use of it for a power play instead of an actual threat. I just wanted to feel it for myself, but he knew. He knew if I ever used magic on my own, I would be starved enough to burn through it.

So, he could find me.

My father was gaining on me, and it was only a matter of time before he caught up to me as I heard his pace slash through time.

The impact of magic hit me before I could fight it, wrapping around me like the distance I had created was futile. I flung my torch in the direction I felt him attack me from, waving blindly through the smoky haze, hoping to give myself enough of a diversion to run.

It was a final attempt that came to a smashing halt as the torch stopped mere inches from my attacker. Gripped by a hand that flame could not scorn, and eyes that swallowed the wrath of fire whole.

"Sabine?" Keahi said my name like he was out of breath, but we needed to hurry. I looked over his shoulders, spinning, tuning into the silence of the hallway—*nothing*, but I knew within my bones my father had been here.

I saw him.

Keahi followed to where my eyes flew wildly, but he was wasting time. We needed to run before it was too late. The anger I had felt toward him vanquished by the thought of my father taking us.

"He's here. He's here," I muttered frantically, trying not to be too loud. My father had been close. I clutched hold of Keahi's arms, tearing at his cloak and thrashing against his broad chest as I dug my heels into the ground, but like the mountain we were within, he stood still.

Keahi wrapped his arms firmly around me, unmoving, and refused to let go. The itchy fabric of his undershirt pressed against my hot cheek, and my fists dug into his side, desperately trying to push away; just enough to speak, to warn him.

"Don't let my father take you too," I pleaded when the room circled, and the air grew thin. The thought of the crystal suffocated me, but I refused to leave him.

For years, I had wished that someone, anyone, would have stayed for me. Even though I knew there had been no one left. "Please, you don't know what he's like. *Don't let him.* Don't let him take you too," I rasped.

My forehead fell back against the cool fabric of Keahi's shirt soaked with my tears, and I lost my breath. "He was—he was here," I whispered, my voice quieter by the word.

Wasn't he?

Every inch of my skin iced over despite the warmth he wrapped me within. The memory of my father faded into an echo of the past, overtaken by the sound of our ragged breathing and a dying torch.

Emptiness dipped its brush into the black stain I concealed

myself within. An antidote that breathed life into my shame. Layer by layer. Numbness painted over me like watercolor, spreading through the base of my fear until I was just one shade, transformed into a spectator of my misery within this empty hallway.

Exhaustion burrowed its strain into the shell of who I was, and I knew even if my father had been looking for me, I would not have made it far.

"I'm here," Keahi whispered into my hair. He carefully lowered himself for me to see—familiar ember eyes with enough warmth to melt away every shadow that was not his own until all I saw was him. I shivered, tucking my arms around myself as he carefully let go.

"He was here." I swallowed, refusing to believe it had been anything but real.

Keahi's shadow floated through the space between us. A phantom touch I could not feel, but somehow felt protection from as it folded its form around me. "I won't let him hurt you," Keahi said softly, with no argument. "I promise. . . I'm going to help you, okay?" I did not care where he took me as long as it was not into the nightfall of that room.

Keahi gently pressed his hand into the small of my back as he led me in the opposite direction I had been running from. I fought to return within myself, but my own body did not feel safe enough for my mind.

We traveled through several corridors by torchlight in unhurried silence. We passed through an arching set of intricate wooden doors that creaked open, and a woody aroma blanketed any sense of worry still coursing through me. It drew me to wake from this spell as the lingering scent of marked pages met me like an old friend.

The bookshelves lined the jagged cave walls from floor to ceiling. The space seemed endless in this cylinder-shaped labyrinth of a library as it tunneled above and below me, leading through an archway formed on the opposite side.

Its ceiling domed around us when we passed underneath it. Exposed rock formed into the shape of another tunnel the farther we descended into the center of the mountain, traveling until we came to a set of sheer crimson curtains. The cool silk glided over me as Keahi pulled me through to the other side.

The small space was dimly lit with the clutter of well-loved pages piled neatly in whatever corner seemed available. Freshly spilled ink coated the topside of a writing desk, dripping onto the pages that had fallen to the floor in disarray.

Maps and tapestries of all the four kingdoms covered the walls. It was beautiful to look at, to see their colors and landscapes merge in the way the Gods intended. To be built side by side, in unison with the elements that sustained our world.

Keahi guided me over to a tiny cot that leaned against the farthest wall. My legs collapsed under me, and I fell on the mattress flush to the floor, but several layers of white furs softened my landing. He opened a small chest with brass latches at the head of the cot and took out a small silver vial to press into my hand.

"Drink." He left no room for a rebuttal.

"Where are we?" I asked weakly, pressing the cool, tarnished vial to my lips. I hoped it had a similar enhancement to the one Iahni had given me.

"That does not sound like drinking," he said almost militantly. His voice had an undertone of a command, a coherent sound in the chaos, as if I was one of his soldiers in battle. Keahi's shoulders stiffened as if catching himself.

He reached down into the trunk beside us, clattering a set of fine potted mugs and a tea kettle. His only visible discomfort was within the tremor of his hands, and then he quietly added, "Please, drink it."

I gave him a cross look as I scented the bitter liquid before I shot the potion straight back. The rancid taste hastily coated my tongue, and I had to hold myself back as my stomach adjusted to the flavor. It was not like the potion Iahni had given me.

Keahi held the tea kettle from the base, and steam rolled out of the spout just before he tipped it over and began filling the two mugs with a jasmine steam. He forced the mug into my empty hand and motioned for me to take a sip. "Wash it down with this."

I had never been a fan of hot tea, but I did not have the energy or taste buds to fight him on it. I took a sip and savored the warmth that flowed through me instead, letting it bring me fully back to life. Between sips, I took time to catch my breath and inhale the sweet floral notes. I consumed every drop before I finally lowered my mug into my lap, thumbing the ceramic rim in circles.

"It's not what it looked like," I said before he had the chance to ask. Heat crept up on my cheeks with embarrassment. It was not what I had wanted to say—to start off with denials after I had wept into his shoulder—but I could barely look at him now.

Keahi did not answer me immediately, tipping the kettle to refill my drink. "What do you think it looked like?"

There was no accusation in his tone, but he stated the question too calmly, like he was prepared for me to give him a lie. I decided I was going to give him some of the truth, even if it made me weak, because I was too tired. There was not enough left of me to pretend.

The siphoning crystal's power held no control over me now, but it was the memories I ran from. To escape the phantom pressure against the base of my neck, burrowing into my skin as my father repeated his promise to me. *'I will fix you.'*

"Today was the first time in my life I felt like I could breathe, but then *I saw him*." I cleared the rasp in my throat. I had been rampant with paranoia, but I had been so sure my father was there. "Everywhere I turned, even within my mind."

Keahi blew softly on his tea with his legs crossed in front of me, focusing on the task of cooling it down. He had his mask rolled up just enough to where I could see his mouth thin.

"Every sorcerer is aware of the damages a siphoning crystal could have on their life," I continued as he quietly listened with his shadow on his shoulder.

Most sorcerers could not survive a siphoning spell, the detachment of their magic from their soul too powerful. My mother did not survive my father's attempt on her magic, but I did. He imprisoned me within its ruby glass walls that the core had built—the earth had never intended for something so pure to be misused. Together, we were tarnished by my father's control.

"This survival does not feel like a blessing when I still feel trapped, despite knowing he is gone," I admitted. My nerves settled in my stomach, waiting for him to tell me how much of a coward I was when he had found me running away from the man I had sworn fiercely to rid the realm of. I tried to wipe the tear escaping before he could catch me, but he was already pressing a small silk tea cloth into my hand.

"It is my fault, and I take full responsibility," Keahi finally said. "I should have waited to tell you my scouts had seen your father. . . I should not have accused you the way I did."

Tea splashed off the side of my rim as I stopped mid-sip. "You do not owe me pity," I rushed out, stumbling on my words. I would have preferred him to call me a coward. "This reaction. . . was not caused by you."

The cord in my chest tensed through the bond, and his dark eyelashes fluttered as if he sensed my panicked uncertainty. This need to seek my forgiveness took me aback when I was far from someone who held innocence.

"It does not matter when I played some part in it," he softly argued. "We are in this together. . . I have made my vows to you, and I will uphold them." The leather of his gloves squeaked against the side of the mug, and his jaw tightened.

Keahi's words sounded sincere, but no apology I had ever received came without conditions. It stirred the anger I found my home in.

"It does matter," I snapped, shifting uncomfortably on the cot. "You do not owe me anything, especially not your guilt."

Did he think I wanted sympathy? I wanted to crawl back inside myself the moment my words slipped out of my mouth. Speaking my thoughts into existence made them real, an admittance I wanted erased before I created it.

Sympathy, even my own, was useless. Caring benefited no one, not when it could be driven with tactical precision. It would do him well to remember it before I had to remind him. My head rested against the back of the stone wall.

Keahi kneeled in front of me, lowering further to meet eye level once again, where I felt the most vulnerable when it came to him. It was a rare occurrence for someone to look me straight in the eye without the feeling of fear, whether it was theirs or my own.

His concern simmered into anger through the bond. Yet I had never heard anger sound so raw, uncalculated as he said, "We owe each other nothing, but that does not mean you have to *earn* an apology from me or anyone else."

I had braved every man's face who had ever spoken to me, at times against my will. But at that, even though his face was still hidden behind a mask, I looked away and listened to the sound of his sharp and unsteady breath.

How did he not understand? Empathy toward me would be another measure to manipulate, if not me, then someone else. My voice was weak, but I hoped he would size it up to tonight's events. "Deeds are not done without repayment, even your kindness, Son of Fire."

Ember eyes dipped to the edge of my jawline as he leaned closer. I did not have to turn back to him to feel his gaze searing the side of my face. Something I noticed he did too often, even when the bruise he was searching for was now faded into my natural color.

Keahi's touch from our bonding ceremony lingered upon my jawline as if he constructed more than memories with his hands. Gloved fingertips had lightly glided over the injury his soldier had given me in the woods. The way he had tentatively mapped out the violet ache until he gently brought my chin up to him before I accepted the bond. It had made me realize something detrimental, and it crushed me as I looked at him now. Because the things about myself I wanted to hide, I found, were never hidden well at all.

My emotions were displayed against my will when no one had ever taken the time to discover them—*but he did.* Every time he looked at me.

Keahi claimed to be my ally, apologizing when I had more than enough of my own faults, even those he had no knowledge of. I could not shake it, because my enemies were the only ones who ever came close to knowing me.

"If you will not take kindness without payment, then please know this, Sabine. . ." Keahi paused after saying my name and I wished he hadn't, because it allowed me to notice a simple longing that was not his but my own. The careful way he spoke to me, but not at me.

"I know. . . what it is like. . . to be the one running," Keahi continued, pressing his eyes closed as he shook his head. "Until I was so tired that I became what I ran from. I have been told my entire life what kind of monster I am. Please allow me to try and become different from what is perceived of me." He sighed heavily. "Even if at times I fail. The guilt you speak of has *nothing* to do with you. I pay no debt but my own."

Running was not a privilege I had when I was trapped within my body by the command of my father's crystal, though I did not hold this against him. Not in the way I wished to as I watched him turn away from me and I found a part of myself in him.

It resounded like a click of a lock being opened, ringing between my ears because I understood the mechanics of what he did not fully say. Even those who run can still be trapped. I had called him a monster, but no monster I had ever met was kept inside a cage, with or without a key. So, *what would that make me?* If every time he reached out, I put him behind bars.

"Keahi. . . how did you find me?" I asked quietly. I watched him methodically stack the dish sets on top of each other, as if he had done it any other way, he would have had to restart. He clipped the brass latch of the chest, peering up at me through the small opening of his mask.

"The same way I found you the first time, and this morning in the ring. . . *I felt you.* I was in my study when I sensed my magic pull away from me, even though I had not been using it myself. I followed that tug until I found you." He hesitated before asking the precise question I did not want to answer right now. "Did you. . . did you feel the bond this time when I came to you?"

"I did not feel it," I said too quickly, crossing my arms. When Keahi had told me he could sense my lies, I hoped he had enough of his own to not see through this one.

Keahi lowered his chin, fitting his mask against his neck. "I thought. . . that maybe after we had fully removed the crystal this time, you would feel it as I do."

I did not risk lying to him twice. If he felt anything remotely close to what I did after the last piece was removed, my emotions, possibly even my thoughts, were no longer in solitary confinement through the bond. What little I had given him was still too much for one night.

"It had been there for a long time. Some effects I am sure are to be irreversible," I said, giving the room a second glance when he grew too quiet for my liking. It was a silence I searched to dissolve because even his shadow ceased its movement, fading into him at my words. "Is this your study?"

Keahi nodded absently, providing much needed distance. The end of his cloak dragged across the floor as he sat down. He placed a quill in his hand and tapped it on the desk.

The longer I felt his silence, the more I ignored the regret building in my stomach. "I think I am okay now. I can go if—"

"No." Keahi's back straightened, the wooden chair creaking against his stiff movement. "I mean—I would prefer if you stayed. If it does not bother you, you can sleep there while I work." He flicked his eyes back to me, and the end of his quill snapped at the tip. A rough sigh escaped his lips as he incinerated it before replacing it with a new one.

His wounded shyness had become somewhat of a guilty pleasure during our travel. It was almost enough to distract this feeling I could not overcome, because I could not be alone right now. Not while the dark still lived in every corner of the room where I had seen my father. I needed sleep, *real sleep,* where I was not recovering.

Keahi had either felt or noticed my discomfort. He attempted to lighten the tension. "I promise to not draw on you while you sleep. Although I would find it wildly entertaining to see how that temper of yours would react to find you had a mustache on your face the entire day without noticing."

I cracked a small smile, realizing it was the first one I had ever given him or anyone in a long time. This back and forth between us, although not always civil, made it easier. "You must be very resourceful in the art of war, General. I bet your soldiers sleep with one eye open."

Keahi looked away instantly, a flush to his cheekbones rising above the small seam of his mask. It was my favorite look from him because it only appeared so far at my expense.

"You are not sleeping?" I asked my ivory-streaked enemy who would watch over me. He tapped the end of his new quill into a fresh ink set, writing into a small leather notebook as I worked myself under the layers of fur blankets.

"It is rare that I do. Though I'm sure you are already painfully aware of it," he said with a hint of sheepish amusement.

I released a breathy chuckle, coupled with a yawn. "I was only reminded of it every hour, when you tossed in your sleep to check on me—"

"*Good night*, Sabine."

I tugged the blankets over the small smile I could not wipe from my face, just before I fell asleep. "Good night, Keahi."

Chapter Twenty-One

Sabine

I attempted to blink away the sleep in my eyes twice before I realized Iahni was bent over top of me, her vibrant red hair irritating my cheekbones.

"He was not lying." Iahni giggled. "You really do look like hell." My body shriveled as she ripped off the fur lined blankets, scrunching her face as she flicked it the opposite way with distaste. "Smell like it too," she muttered.

The cot I had fallen asleep on in the corner of Keahi's study sounded how my bones felt. It creaked and groaned until I forced myself into a sitting position. Every motion hinged, the ache burrowed deep into the pit of my magic, and I knew without a doubt I had pushed myself too far.

The pain felt minuscule in the presence of my power, and *I just wanted more*. The magic I was born with to be completely my own.

I rolled out the crick in my neck. "Are you always this forward?"

She pushed up her white fluffy sleeves and shrugged. "Formidably so, I'm afraid."

The hem of her peach-colored dress swished against my ankles on the floor. I had never personally met any citizens from the Solstice Kingdom, but her sunny disposition this early clarified my disdainful assumption.

They were *all* morning people.

A sigh parted my lips and quickly hinged shut, the conversation delayed in my head. "Did you say *he*, as in *Keahi*??" It had not crossed my mind to check my appearance in the mirror, let alone acknowledge it.

This ray of blinding sunshine wiggled her auburn brows at me, with a gleam in her eye that made me regret not making the time for it.

I argued against the odd race of my heart as I hesitantly lifted my shirt above my collarbone. My nose recoiled from the stale sweat infused within the fabric, no doubt from my run through the castle last night.

Iahni flashed me a roguish grin, her dimples appearing in the rosy undertone of her freckled cheeks. She leaned down and grabbed my left hand, holding up the wedding ring so close to my face my eyes crossed.

"Even if he did say you are such a charmer in the morning, you are *mar-ried*. By how positively fresh you look, it is safe to say he didn't mind it last night." She winked.

Married, my mind stunted on the phrase as we stared at my third finger together, going back to the first night I had camped with Keahi.

The sharp edges of the obsidian crystal had shimmered against the moonlight. Its molten strand swirled down the middle, dancing with the movement of the campfire glow.

It was beautiful, but after staring at it for so long, I threatened to rip it off just to see if I could watch it burn. I slowly slid the band to the tip of my finger, but before I could take it off. . . I placed it back on.

'You need the ring. How will they believe you are married if you do not at least have a ring?' I had reassured myself, looking over at the man who was going to pretend to be my husband. The ruse to hide the sorcerer's bond linked between us within our vengeful arrangement to take down my father.

'He's not that bad,' the small voice within me had argued again. The same one who had begged me not to take it off. A much younger version of myself, who never had the chance to dream up a future with someone else. Not when the present consumed itself with survival.

Keahi had been standing next to Aires; his towering stature made even his beast of a horse look small in comparison. The sharp rugged features of his face were mapped out by his scar; the white strand lost within his messy black hair. His burning eyes felt all-consuming; the way they flared every time he was anxious around me, coupled with the restlessness in his covered hands flexing at his sides.

He had waited until I turned on my side, but I quietly observed the secret gesture he had not wanted me to see; how he quickly tapped his forehead against the bridge of the stallion's midnight nose when he thought I was not looking. He did this every night after, their way of saying goodnight.

'Maybe not that bad.' I compromised for this small window of time I had quietly allowed. When we did nothing but listen to the sound of the forest and our awkward footsteps around each other.

Even though I knew our marriage was not real as he slept across the fire beside me, I relented against my better judgment during the quiet of the night to appease my younger self, who was far more familiar with nightmares than dreams. I kept the ring on for her and had refused to take it off since.

Iahni cleared her throat as she let go of my hand when I stared at the ring for longer than intended. I quickly tucked my fingertips underneath my thighs, out of sight, shifting away from her broadening grin.

"I think it is a little too late to be shy now, don't you think? The honeymoon phase is over, anyway. It is not like he has not or will not see worse. Though hopefully we can prevent. . . some of the worse." Iahni's disapproving eyes roamed over me.

My cheeks burned a brighter shade of red than her own as she settled on my less than unkempt hair. She thought we. . . *oh no.* "We didn't—I mean. . . we did. . ." The flush painfully deepened past the point of convincing for someone newly married.

I gathered myself, looking around the room to see what caused her to draw this conclusion. Keahi's books were neatly assembled in color coded piles against the side wall, alternating between burgundy, deep navy, and aged brown leather spines in vertical towers.

It was a sick kind of madness not to sort them alphabetically, but it showed he had a method of how he liked his space—even if it was wrong. It took up the entire expanse of the left wall, each stack higher than the next, like the stories were climbing steps.

There was his peculiar matching set of tiny, tinted glass jars filled with an assortment of tea leaves, carefully aligned on a set of shelves next to the hanging tapestry of the realm on the other side of the room. It should have been where his books were kept, but I reluctantly admitted he had too many for such a small shelf—although he could have just built more, instead of putting the books on the floor.

I swallowed as I finally roamed over to the contents of his desk in the middle of his study. How I would have had to interrupt his work in the middle of the night, to explain why I had not slept in my bed. The way he would have carelessly shoved off the pages, the ones he normally took the time in stacking, to explain why they had fallen to the floor. Throwing me up on his desk to—*that's enough convincing.*

I slowly sank back down into the cot, hoping I would disappear into the mattress. *What the hell had Keahi given me last night?*

Iahni's mellow approach was deceptively resourceful against me. She was even more formidable to wake up to than Drakkon, and I did not think that was possible.

"It must have been an interesting night by the look on your face, but there is no need to explain." She tossed a dampened rag in my direction, ushering me to clean my face, but the rag was not cool enough. "I am only teasing you. I know the Novears do not speak as openly on such topics—or so I have heard."

I wiped my face clean with one eye open as I said, "You have heard correctly." Not that the Novear Kingdom was shy about our affairs between bed sheets, but we approached it differently.

Novear sorcerers who visited Solstice before the war commonly jested about their people's unbearable romanticism, though I always found their campfire gossip contradictory, considering they all seemed to confirm the phrase *'burning with passion'* was an accurate rumor regarding their bedroom activities.

Iahni smirked. "So. . . does that mean it was good? I do not speak Novear."

My mouth flew wide open, but before I could correct myself, Iahni giggled as she snatched the rag hiding my face. Her playful gasp had my shoulders bunching at my ears. She raised a brow. "I'll take that—as a *yes.*"

I knew I could defend myself better than this. Play into her assumptions without the hint of actual embarrassment burning beneath my skin.

Truly, it was some kind of cosmic torture to be subjected to, when I had never reacted this way before at the mention of sex. Most likely it was for baiting Keahi with a piece of fruit while he was down, unknowingly fighting off the bond's rejection from the crystal pieces in my neck. *It was still worth it.*

"Let's get you dressed," Iahni piped up. "You've already slept past lunch, and Elias is highly impatient as it is. That sleeping tonic he gave you must have worked a little too well." Iahni's laughter was light, bouncing on every space it touched. "I do not think I have ever seen Keahi so worked up after he could not wake you this morning."

She pulled from a basket of fresh clothes and handed me an outfit similar to yesterday's. I thumbed the soft emerald tunic in my hands, pushing down the thought. It had left me completely unaware of my surroundings for too long.

"The Novears are forbidden to talk to any other region without my father's consent, and you look far too young to have been able to travel to our Kingdom before he closed our borders," I ventured curiously. Iahni's hands stopped before she dove back into the basket.

"I am of age," she said plainly. "Sorcerers may live longer depending on the well of power they are gifted, but you are right. I am not that old. I bedded one of your spies we had converted when I was still at the capital. He told me many stories of your land." She brushed an auburn strand of her hair behind her ear. "The good and the horrors."

She busied herself by folding the sets of clothes in the basket as I changed, but I could not pull myself away from her fidgeting gaze. I prepared myself for an answer I already knew.

"Did they send him back to my father?" I asked. Iahni nodded, and I paused at the hem of my shirt to steady my voice before I continued. "Is . . . he alive?"

Her stone blue eyes glazed over before she could pull away. "He was granted permission to safely live in Solstice, but only if we could call upon him for a favor of the council's choice. If he did not follow through, they would force him under capital punishment. When the time came, we sent him back to your armies to gather information. He never returned to my knowledge, and I have not heard from him since."

It could have been anyone, but I hoped by the way she lost herself in thought that it had not been him. Spies from Solstice did not survive long enough to report back, not with my father's vigorous screening methods. I repressed a chill at the thought.

"I'm sorry," I whispered.

Iahni hauled the basket on her hip. "I would not blame you for what happened to him just because of who you are. I had stayed with him enough nights to know that he did not rest easy, not after what your people had been through." My throat grew tight, unable to form a response from the guilt that wrapped around me. "Come, let me take you to Elias."

I stopped her when I shouldn't have because I already knew of the sorcerer she referred to. "What was his name?"

She smiled sadly. "Shiloh."

Chapter Twenty-Two

Iahni had left me outside of the infirmary door. After knocking twice and receiving no answer, the lock clicked on its own and the door opened half an inch. "Hello?" I said cautiously to a seemingly vacant room.

I looked back at the hallway, knowing that I would not know how to make it back at this point even if I tried, and stepped inside. The study was crammed with delicate glass tubes filled with a variety of liquids, glistening under the beacon of a single flame.

Elias was tucked behind a separate potions rack, his gold staff propped up against the frame of a worn desk. He leaned over a large stack of papers, purpled ink dispersed across the side of his left forearm, like he had been in this exact same position throughout the night to cause such a stain. He furiously tossed the sheets of paper to the floor as he finished writing on each page.

"It is not nice to stare."

A waterfall of vials scraped against the metal rack in rows as I startled backwards into the wall of potions. I splayed myself out on the dusty floor, able to catch two of the vials as they fell. Sweat formed on my brow. The final vial rolled over the edge, but my free hand was useless because of my injured wrist.

My shoulders tensed before glass shattered across the floor. I cringed as I looked up, trying to muster an apologetic smile with the vials I had salvaged. Elias glared at me, his pen still working the page he was on by itself.

"That was almost impressive," he said in a dull voice. "Especially considering you somehow managed to find and destroy the rarest set of vials within my study."

Heat flared across my face as I placed the vials back on the shelf. As one of the tiny vials tipped over for a second time, I became increasingly flustered. I dropped to the floor to clean up the one that had fallen, and my bare hand hovered over the shards of tiny glass.

"I would not touch that if I were you. Leave it." His voice carried over his shoulder, and though he did not spare me a single glance, he added, "Please."

The heel of my boot crunched into the glass with agonizing emphasis as I stepped back. "I'm sorry. I didn't mean to break your things."

Elias stood from his desk abruptly, upturning the pages of his desk in search of something. He appeared to be having a hard time finding whatever he was looking for; his fluffy gray brows pinched together in frustration.

"I can come back at a later time, if now is not convenient," I said. His hand stilled on the page, but not because of my remark. Elias was invested in the contents, reading it twice before he picked it up and threw it on top of the candle. The flame was too small to engorge the page, but it did.

"—Are you coming or not?" Elias's cloak barely peeked through a side door that I had deemed to be a broom closet. I rushed after the sound of his staff before I lost him altogether.

The cramped hallway we emerged from expanded into a ten-bed infirmary. The white sheets on the beds appeared to have collected a fine layer of dust over the years. It was strange, though, how each bed was formed with the indentation of a well-used mattress.

"Well, do not just stand there, sit," he urged, ushering me over to the nearest mattress; a stale puff of dust itched my lungs as I plopped down.

Elias gave me a sidelong glance as I attempted to suppress a string of coughs. The *Grand* Healer rummaged through several med-kits, squinting at the different labels that looked expired upon first glance—they probably were expired.

Elias's exasperated sigh sounded more like a curse as he patted his cloak pockets. He fitted a tiny piece of wire to his face; it framed two glass circles he squinted through. It was an odd little contraption; one I had never seen before.

"What is that?" I asked curiously.

His eyes peered over the top rim of the wire. "They help me see; when you have lived in the caves as long as I have, your vision fails you after some hundred years. . . *Ahh*, here we go." He whipped out an old wooden jar, a part of the ointment yellowed on the outer rim.

He nodded toward my bruised wrist. "Arm."

My eyes shot between the jar and my wrist that appeared a darker hue than yesterday, though the lack of light under the mountain did not do it any favors. I looked away as I held my arm out to him, withholding my grimace. He did not take his time to stop and inspect the injury as he thickly slapped the gelatinous salve on and it. . . *smelled.*

I rubbed my eyes with my other hand at the irritation. I was mid gag as he said, "Whatever you do, do not rub your eyes with the other hand, or you will only be able to see as well as I do." My hand dropped, not wanting to risk what it could do to my eyes with such an awful odor.

"Is this where you live? Outside of the capital?"

The golden rim around his stone blue eyes sparked as he continued to work the salve up my arm. "You will feel its effects by the end of the night. I will give you the jar to keep and apply a second dose before bed. Please do not forget to bring it back to me once your wrist is fully healed. The smell is rancid enough when applied. I do not wish to spell another jar."

"Is that a yes?" I asked, and his hands froze. He stepped back, preparing to rinse off the salve in a nearby pail of water. Twin black markings bruised the inside of his palms.

He caught my stare. "If you were to ask me a question, I would prefer it if you thought of something more useful to you. I am afraid I am in ill spirits after our recent travels. Those beasts in the forest were not exactly pleasant."

I swallowed the lump in my throat, feeling it drag to the bottom of my stomach. *'I know exactly what I have done. It is you that needs to accept it,'* Elias had said when he found me in the hold.

"What did you see. . . when you removed the crystal?" I asked.

He patted his hands dry and reached for his golden staff. The tension seemed to ease from his shoulders just at the contact. He relaxed into it before he spoke. "You know what I saw."

I stilled instantly. It would be treasonous not to report what he saw when he removed the crystal; if he reported what he'd seen, all my plans to enact revenge would be ruined. "What do you want from me, Elias Griselda?"

My insides shook as I waited for his response. If he knew the extent of what flowed through me, it was only a matter of time before the entire kingdom had knowledge.

The mattress sunk beside me. "I saw what you feared most, and I can clearly see it on your face now."

The power in my core panicked. My eyes shut. Crescents formed on the side of the foam. I could not bring myself to kill this man just because he knew my truth. I would never kill again if it was my choice. My grip released.

"Fear," he said, as if reading my thoughts. "It is a wicked power, cunning in the sense that it drives us to control things we do not understand. We mold it until we cage it in the form of something we can accept, that we can look at every day and make peace with. That is what your father saw when he looked inside you that day, and every day since." My head was spinning. The fumes coming from the salve did nothing to help. "Do not confuse the mold they have placed you in with who you truly are. No amount of power can corrupt what truly lies beneath."

My bottom lip quivered. "But what if I do not know what lies beneath?"

What if I do not want to know?

"Do not let them take it from you, for they have already taken too much. Even if you do not want to find out for yourself. Fight for it."

"Fight for it? Do you even know what you are insinuating? What they would do to you if they found out—Keahi, he would, he. . ."

He placed a frail hand on my shoulder. "Do not let your father's words continue to cloud your judgment when he is this far out of reach. You cannot survive our world that way. I do not believe it is the work of chance when fate carves the path. There is a reason your powers have found my nephew."

It was not just my father's judgment I had to consider, and some would seek to destroy me to obtain it. That last part, however, took me by surprise. "Keahi is your nephew?"

He patted my shoulder as he stood. "A *major* pain, but my nephew, nonetheless. My sister would have been happy to see he is married at least, even if it was by force technically, but the rest of the kingdom does not have to know that. She used to fear that he would never slow down enough in life to marry. Death became a fierce motivator."

The corner of Elias's lips lifted with a soft, beaming smile, proud of his nephew. My chest ached. I would have given anything for someone to love me that way. I did not have it in me to tell him we were not married upon sealing the sorcerer's bond.

"How did she die? Keahi's mother," I questioned slowly, fearful of his answer. Some part of me already knew.

"She killed herself," he said without hesitation. The ocean in his eyes stormed within its ring of gold. "A noose around her neck."

The way his eyebrows raised made my cheeks burn, and guilt snaked its way around my chest and into my heart a second time. I averted my eyes to smother a remorse I would not yield for Keahi, even though I understood.

Love was perishable.

Even my father, who was supposed to love me, did not, corrupted by a world that either broke you or changed you—it broke his mother.

But Keahi did not need my pity, and it was dangerous for us both. I allowed him my sympathy for a brief second before I brushed it away, knowing he had re-lived her death through me.

I turned back to Elias. "How do I know you will not tell anyone what you saw inside me?"

The smile he hid underneath his hood vanished. "Because I vowed to protect my nephew on my sister's grave. You are his sorcerer bonded, and a part of you lives within him. Turning on you, Lightbringer, would reject the very thing I swore to protect."

"Vows can be broken."

"Not all of them can be broken." His golden flecked eyes flared. "But the vows that can are worth breaking."

I shifted uncomfortably. "Are you going to tell Keahi? About what you saw?"

He braced himself on his staff with a deep chuckle. "Now, where would be the fun in that? Your secret is safe with me, Lightbringer. Now, come, I have something to show you. Do not fight me on it while I am still well."

I followed him back into his study, but it was hard to keep up with him through the layers of books and potions. I was slow behind him, trying to make sure I knocked nothing else over on the way out. The way he quickly weaved through the space led me to believe he lived here instead of the capital, and I wondered if the staff he braced himself on was for show.

"The creatures in the woods—did they cause the marks on your palms?" I asked as he searched through a twin set of shelves.

"No, they did not. Though, it would not be a stretched assumption considering how difficult they were to kill," he grumbled.

"You were able to kill them? Keahi had sent us running before they could get a hold of us, but he never exactly mentioned what they were either." I could still hear the creatures hissing at night, snaking through the forest floor.

He grabbed the spine of the last book he had been looking for and plopped it into my arms. I held in my curse as my wrist twinged from the weight.

"Thank you for that valuable piece of information. I promise to never let him live it down." He went on with a devious grin. "This one is on the foundation of Solstice magic. Brush up on these."

I turned my head to the side, reading the bindings; *The History of Volkan Fighters* and *The Art of Fire, Volume I.* I cringed as he dropped the stack of books on top at a higher elevation than necessary, my wrist throbbing.

"I heard about what happened in the training room. Kane might have broken your wrist, but you have broken the Volkans' confidence, at least." He waved a spindly finger at me. "I like that about you, but do not let one win get to your head. They will not let you off so easily a second time."

"Do I really need to read these?" I grumbled.

He paused, eyebrows lifted, as he pulled back the last book to his chest instead of adding it to the stack in my arms. "Dear Gods, please tell me you can read?"

"Yes, I can read!" I fired back.

He tilted his head. "Then stop complaining. You are worse than my apprentice. Here, this last book is the most important." It was a small, leathered notebook, held together by a single red tie.

"What is so special about this book?"

"This book will help inform you on anything you need to know about the sorcerer's bond." He gave me a pointed look. "You might need this one the most. If you do not find it useful, look in the main library for more, considering that is what libraries are for."

"I—Thank you." My arms wobbled, barely able to hold the stack, let alone argue with the old man. A broad smile broke over me, unbothered even when his snarky observance offhandedly turned to ridicule.

I preferred when he directed it at my '*husband*' the most, but I had never met someone who could dole out an insult so comforting. I could not help but let him get away with it.

"You may take your leave now and do not forget the salve. Once in the morning, and once at night." He placed the notebook beneath my chin, along with the tip of his staff, as he pushed me forward.

My hair flung into my face with force as he slammed the door behind me.

Chapter Twenty-Three

Keahi

There was a rather extensive list of regrets I had been compiling in my head since last night. Not killing the Novear King when I had the chance had been the first, and a close second was lying about my marriage with Sabine.

This morning, however, felt the worst of all after I realized I accidentally drugged my wife, who was not my wife as far as she was concerned, into a sleep induced coma. For a second, I thought I had killed her. Truthfully. My palms were still sweating in my gloves from the event.

Because she would not wake up.

Even though I could feel her through the bond and hear her heart beating. . . that woman looked just as dead as when I had found her. Although I was not directly at fault the first time, this would have been my own doing.

Elias had nearly fallen out of his chair with laughter after I came into the potion room, scrambling for a reversal, and then he scolded me from head to toe rather than offer his help. Iahni, thankfully, had been there and took pity on me. . . for the time being.

'She looks horrible!' I had frantically paced in my study after we had arrived, but Iahni would not stop laughing.

Sabine's white hair was tossed in every direction, her mouth wide open against the pillow she had smashed her face into. Half her body dangled off the side of the cot, even though I kept trying to put her back through the night.

When I picked up her hand and it dropped straight on her cheek with a small slap that echoed around the room—that's when I got scared.

'No,' Iahni said as she started kicking me out of my study. *'She looks like she's getting the best sleep of her life. Not sure a potion had anything to do with that.'*

'It was in a silver vial. Maybe it interacts with the tea. . .' I had tried to get in before she closed the door in my face. I sighed, leaning my head against the oak. *'You know I can just use shadowfire to get back in the room, right?'*

'Keahi pie, I would love to watch you keep trying to convince me, but you're about to be late for your meeting. No one, and I mean no one, likes to deal with you when you're off schedule.' She had knocked twice against the frame. *'Goodbye now.'*

My head spun as I shifted through shadowfire. I was not about to argue with Iahni when she had offered to help me because I clearly had done Sabine no favors. I materialized in front of the massive iron plates blocking the entrance to the meeting room, engraved with a portrait of the Solstice Kingdom's last volcanic eruption.

Hidden within the cliff side of Kallahni's mountain peak was the Volkan headquarters. Its scorching lava flowed down the center of the carving's crater, churning with a molten glow as it split the metal plate in half. It was the realm's most volatile form of fire, accessible only to the Volkan warriors through moltanic sorcery.

The lava was a nearly impenetrable force, curated by the ancient fire bearers who had come before us as they sealed the entrance. The Volkan's legacy, however, was greatly undermined by a much more formidable source of power as I unlocked the door to our stronghold—*my brother*, who had been waiting for me outside.

"Keahi, even I know not to give someone an expired sleep tonic," Drakkon said, the magma hissing behind us until it welded shut. *Of course, he already knew somehow.* I cursed at myself because I already knew the culprit.

Elias was only secretive when he chose to be. That was the problem—my uncle was too good at keeping secrets. He also excelled at telling secrets when the time came. The entire castle probably knew by now if it had gotten to Drakkon this quickly.

Kane was already waiting for us as usual at the head of a long metal-crafted table. A warm glow bathed the room as sunlight filtered through a vast open window panel that looked over the side of the snow-covered mountain.

"The vial looked old, but how the fuck was I supposed to know potions *expire*? It's magic," I grumbled as I sat down.

Without looking up, Kane handed me the stack of papers he had been sorting through. I gladly took it from him. Sifting through our military units' most recent reports was the only part of my routine that felt normal lately.

"Since when do potions expire?" Kane asked distractedly, trading out a set of papers to re-analyze before passing it back to me.

"Since *always*," Drakkon scoffed. "You'd think as Solstice's highest ranked military personnel, the two of you would know how to read the back of the vial."

"*Hmm.*" Kane hummed. "Last time I checked, Elias fired you as his apprentice. I'm not so sure you have room to pass judgment."

The chair legs screeched against the rock floor beside me. Drakkon glared at Kane across the table before he sat down. "He didn't fail me for something as simple as reading a vial, or do you have selective memory?"

"*We remember*," Kane and I groaned with equal amounts of exasperation. His time studying under Elias was always a thorn in the conversation.

Drakkon had demonstrated more of an affinity for healing, but after his apprenticeship with Elias ended, he struggled to find his place within Kallahni. Luckily, Drakkon's tactical maneuvers could level with any of the Volkan warriors. He withheld a high standing within our battalion, despite not being inducted into the creed.

The only way to become an honorary member without taking an oath was to defeat a warrior after invoking Volkan's ring. After Sabine defeated Kane, the Volkan warriors had bowed to her, symbolizing their acceptance of her as an honorary member.

Despite any fear that remained in my mind regarding where

her alliance with me stood, I could not help the residual pride I felt in watching her succeed. The memory glimmered through my chest even now.

There was an anxious part of me that knew if it had anything to do with me, she would not care. Not unless it involved our plans to destroy her father's reign. Sabine did not have to accept her place as an honorary Volkan warrior. . . *but what if she did?*

Maybe I could even throw in, '*The Volkan warriors accepted you as an honorary member after defeating Kane in the ring. You are the first sorcerer to be inducted who does not wield fire, and you and I are also the only sorcerers in the history of the Volkans married within the creed. . . Isn't that something?*'

I swallowed the lump in my throat.

Drakkon nudged my shoulder, and I realized I had been picking at the palm of my gloves. "Can you stop with the anxious brooding already? I promise your beloved she-demon will be fine. By the Gods, the only time I prefer your inflated, princely persona you put on at the capital is when you won't *relax*."

"Do not call her that," I warned, but caught the slight hesitation on my tongue. "Even if she can be one, Drakkon, after the way you acted, I have no problem encouraging that side of her."

"I second that," Kane piped up as he made his way across the room, comparing notes to the tapestry wall that was filled with maps of every region in the realm.

"Just for that," I continued. "The next time I go to the capital, you're coming with me and Kane to endure it. I'm not letting you hide out here at the Kallahni base."

Drakkon waved me off. "Dear old dad and I will have a wonderful reunion. Though I do not think even I could provide enough of a distraction from your secret wedding and spontaneous marriage to the daughter of our enemy kingdom. My dearest, *most considerate*, brother."

"I'm your *only* brother, even if it is just half," I sighed heavily.

"*Ah*, but I have a half-sister, at least. Although she can be a raging bitch, I miss her fiercely right now in comparison, and you. . ." Drakkon pointed at me. "Are just pissing me off."

Kane singed the edge of the page he was holding and used the ash to circle a section of the map. "Are you going to be mad at him forever because they did not invite you to the wedding?" He asked over his shoulder.

"Not just him," Drakkon said as he leaned back into the chair.

"I'm including you in all this as well, considering you were there, Kane."

My brows pinched. "He was not—" Kane appeared through shadowfire across from me, materializing just in time to slam his foot into mine.

"It was a wonderful ceremony," he said over my low curse, and I held my breath. Kane dug in the heel of his boot to further silence me before he continued. "Iahni had picked out the most beautiful dress I had ever seen. Keahi even cried when he saw her for the first time."

Even though he was still mashing into the top of my foot, a smirk broke out beneath my mask before I mumbled, "*That's not exactly how it went.*"

Drakkon, however, noticed nothing amiss. He was already storming halfway across the room. "I do not particularly enjoy the early morning meetings, especially when the company is rather rude," he said bitterly. "I'm going to the breakfast hall before I put up with you two droning on for hours."

"Drakkon, we've already told you that you do not have to come *before* we have the meetings to pre plan for our missions," Kane argued. "You are more than welcome to come in with everyone else."

"I would love to, but unfortunately my late-night rendezvous are also morning people. Once I am awake, it is hard to go back to sleep, especially when I am woken up with. . ." Drakkon's brows arched up twice. "*Incentive.*"

Kane laughed darkly as he waved his hand, separating the molten door for Drakkon to take his leave. I tilted my head toward the door and muttered, "Do you have to encourage him?"

"Not at all, but I choose to." Kane went silent before he took on a serious tone. He leaned back, propping his hands behind his head. "So. . . Sabine would not wake up this morning after you gave her the tonic?"

Over the top edge of the report I was not reading, I peered at Kane. It was the last drop of tonic I had snuck from Elias's infirmary. I had been taking it for several nights to make myself comfortable enough to lie down for a couple of hours, but it had never put me in that deep of a sleep. I could barely even find a comfortable enough position now. The pain from the wound across my chest had still not subsided.

Sabine seemed like she needed it more than I did in the moment.

I knew the terror she felt through the bond was far more painful than my own. It was the last vial, but it would have been the last vial even if I had not given it to her to sleep.

There was only one other source that brought me some measure of ease. After the last time, when the pain would not subside, I had promised Elias I would not resort to drinking again, but I could feel everything hovering over me. The stress, the pain, the lack of sleep. It was too much.

"Can we just start the meeting?" I exhaled.

Kane slowly returned to the papers sitting in front of him. "Alright. . . The capital is requesting that we report on—"

I cut him off, ripping the paper out of his hand before I turned it to ash. He cocked his head to the side as we stared at the tiny pyramid of embers it left behind on the table.

My head went into my palms as I pulled the hood of my cloak over my head. "Kane, I do not know what the fuck I'm doing anymore."

Every decision I had made so far, even if some of my intentions were good, felt helplessly wrong.

"We know," he said thoughtfully, undeterred by my outburst. "Well, Drakkon knows to some extent, but I agree. What he doesn't know does not hurt him for now. He can be just as bad as Elias with word of mouth, possibly worse when he has a temper."

"I wish I could focus on the easier things." I rubbed my temples through my mask. "If it weren't for the implications of my father and the Solstice council getting involved in warfare, I would have ripped the Novear King limb from limb by now for what he's done."

Aside from her father's involvement in igniting the sorcerer's bond through the seal on my chest, last night was one of the most excruciating experiences of my entire life. For a moment, I thought Sabine believed I was the one after her when I had found her in the hallway. The hatred I felt toward myself burned brighter than it ever had.

But then she begged me to run with her, and everything changed. I knew exactly who she had been running from. Hatred was a familiar friend, but not when it had turned my blood cold.

"Yes," Kane scoffed, "Because that's the *easy* part. Dismembering your father-in-law."

No, but it would be the most satisfying.

"I'm not the only one who wants him dead." My voice plummeted. "Sabine and I have somewhat made a deal out of all this. Once we can convince the capital and my father of our marriage, we have agreed to hunt him down."

"How. . . romantic." Kane deadpanned. "Look, the marriage was not your fault. One, you had to keep her alive, and two, you needed to initiate the sorcerer's bond." He hesitated. "I will not ask how you finished it because I would like to consider myself a gentleman, but I cannot help but be curious about how well *that* went over."

There was avoiding the truth, but the lies continued to wreck me. I did not enjoy lying to the only people I cared about, to Sabine, but I had to after her reaction. I would not let Sabine make herself a martyr by being married to me. She did not have to be a sacrifice against her own wishes for the sorcerer's bond. Not if I had anything to do with it. She was alive, and that was all that mattered to me in the end.

"That bad?" Kane asked with a hint of worry when I did not respond. "I mean Drakkon told me at least on Sabine's part it went . . . rather well, considering your experience."

"*My experience*?" My voice grew tight. "How would you even be able to judge my experience when you don't even like—" I choked mid-sentence, blood rushing to my face. A numbness sent straight to my legs, but thankfully I was already sitting down. "What do you mean, went rather well? *What* went well?"

Kane's shoulders shook with laughter as he twisted his quill between his fingers. "We weren't so sure you had it in you. Last I heard, you weren't the most vocal. . . but you were pretty good with your hands."

Fuck me.

"That's not true." I practically wheezed.

"Which part?" Kane burst out laughing.

"We're done with this conversation. We are supposed to be discussing the upcoming mission before the rest of the Volkans get here," I said.

"Excuse me, General, for asking my best friend, who is an *abhorrent* work-a-holic by the way, about one of the most important events to ever happen in his life." If guilt wielded a knife, it would have cut straight through my heart at that. "So be it though, because I have an idea, and I would like to talk to you about it," Kane finished.

"Please, for the love of all the Gods, continue," I grumbled.

I did not want to hear about my disaster of a marriage or hand. . . skills, but I did not like the way Kane leaned toward me more. Nothing good ever came out of his mouth when he propped his elbows up on the table and rested his chin on his knuckles.

"Sabine should come with us on the mission. She is clearly well-equipped after what we saw in the training room to handle her own if she gets put in danger. After she finds out a branch of the Celenia Kingdom's army has aligned with her father, she will be a formidable asset."

If the Gods were laughing at me, I could hear them now. An unfinished marriage bond was dangerous enough for both parties, but the damage was already done. I mirrored him, leaning across the table to give him a firm answer. "*Absolutely not.*"

"And why is that?" He cocked his head. I had half a mind to rip off his mask, to wipe off the cocky grin I knew he had underneath.

"Let's start with how you broke her Gods damn wrist, Kane," I growled, and he flinched at the reminder. I pressed a single finger into the middle of the table. "I haven't forgotten about that. If it would have been anyone else, they wouldn't even have the arm they touched her with to do it again."

Kane refused to retreat, though I expected nothing different from him. "When she rounded behind me, I didn't realize how fast she was as I readjusted. It wasn't intentional and you know it. You were there."

"I also watched her put you on your knees like you've never fought a day in your fucking life, but that's beside the point." I sat back, slowly lowering my shoulders.

"Jealous much?" Kane laughed.

"Entirely, but Commander, the answer. . . is *no*. Find a better option. I'm not putting her at risk. She's still on edge after what happened to her father, and she does not need to be reminded by us sticking her in the middle of this mission."

"Do you think she would feel that way, General? Because I, for one, do not," he growled back. "They have controlled Sabine for her entire life. Do not make choices on her behalf, even if it is for her own good. I would think you, out of anyone, would understand her on that."

"But they were still choices I made!" I slammed my hand against the table, surprising even myself. We both knew he was referring to my father, his king, a topic meant to be off limits.

"Not all of them." Kane fought back. "Some were decisions motivated out of fear, a direct reflection of your own father's manipulation. I will not sit and let you think otherwise. Do not take what he has primed you to do and act out of fear with Sabine."

I bristled at the sting of his words. They were a direct hit that quickly put me back in my seat. Begrudgingly, I knew he was right, but there was too much risk. Even if I told Sabine the truth, we needed more time.

"Kane, unless you find a damn good reason to bring her along, *she is not coming*. I do not care if it puts us at a disadvantage." I threw my hands up as he pushed back his chair, ignoring me. "Where do you think you're going?"

He spun around on his heels. "To find a good enough reason. Hopefully, I'll be back in time before the meeting. If not, have fun with the Volkans. They are all *very* intrigued to hear about your most recent love story after you threatened to incinerate Drakkon in front of them. Settle down on the kill switch a little if you do not want them to find out about the bond. It appears to be getting to your head."

He had no idea.

"Kane," I stopped him. "If you see Sabine, do not bring up the bond. I'm not entirely sure she remembers you were there, and I do not want to scare her. I fear she already believes we are all against her as it is. Be back before the end of the day with a solution since you are deciding to dismiss yourself."

"If she wants to tell me, General," Kane snapped his fingers as he swiftly turned away, "she will." Shadowfire consumed his figure until he faded from the room.

Chapter Twenty-Four

Sabine

As I entered the castle's library, Keahi was nowhere to be found, but another of his kind was immersed in yellowed pages. The Volkans wore their threaded face coverings, revealing only the slit of their glowing eyes. It made differentiating between them difficult, but even at a distance I would not mistake Keahi for anyone else. The warrior across from me carried no shadow but his own.

The books Elias had given me thudded gracefully onto the table, purposefully positioned in the Volkan's direct line of sight. I slipped my reddened finger-pads one by one underneath the edge of the bindings, making no attempts to muffle the sound. The library could alert its visitors with the faintest drop of a feathered quill, but the stranger still had not gained curiosity over my presence. Their hood nearly tapped against the top edge of their book.

I released an elaborate sigh, shaking the stiffness out of my arms, brought on by the multiple missed turns it took me to find my way back. It had been a very long walk through the castle, where I attempted to focus on the ache of my wrist instead of the doubts in my head.

Maintaining my ability to be withdrawn and focus on my alliance with Keahi was becoming less simple as I learned more about him. I could not blame my confusing feelings solely on what I had learned from Elias alone about his mother. It was what I felt from him through the bond that was the most confusing.

The bond was similar to my own magic. I could feel it live and breathe, but it was as if we were standing on water. Every ripple of emotion lapped against our feet as we stood opposite of each other. Stronger emotions expanded into waves, accelerating into thoughts as they crashed into me. It was a connection. A current within the magical pool, but it was not strong enough to submerge us under.

It wanted to, though. Even the core of my magic, who promised itself to me, found it alluring. I did not want to trust it, when nearly every reaction from him was the opposite of what I expected.

Mindlessly, I flipped over pages of the first book I found within reach and monitored the Volkan across from me. With his soldiers, at least, there was an obvious line. I was not just some betrothed princess who had fallen in love with their prince—I was their enemy.

That was something I could work with, at least. My attentiveness transferred to my fingers as I snagged against a gritty layer of charcoal. The smudges I had made marked the neighboring pages, but the image itself did not appear to be disturbed by my touch. I cautiously hovered over the markings, sparks traveling down my back as I traced the emblem.

It was the seal which had created the sorcerer's bond between us. The emblem I shared on the page was not only similar in detail, but in how its markings appeared to be drawn outside of their original home.

My hands gripped the frail page and begged me to rip out the memory the longer I stared at it. I turned the page instead and found what I had not been looking for but needed to. *The symbol of Rhiannon*—the leftover magic that had blessed my union to Keahi to seal the sorcerer's bond. Three golden-scaled dragons circled each other in a united flame. Together, they created the rays of the sun, powerful enough for the fire goddess to be born in the rapture of their fire. *The Dragon's Flame*, and creator of the Solstice Kingdom, shimmered against the sun-dried paint.

Rhiannon's golden scaled form was rumored to appear from time to time, turning folklore into faded legends until she disappeared from the sky altogether, just as all the Gods had done. Their portal to enter and restore their own creations split the realm forever when my father destroyed the Veil of Seven. The magic in our realm that had been so innately a part of us soon began its own timeline in my father's attempts to gain control over all the kingdoms.

The Great Fade had not begun immediately after the veil's destruction. Our children, gifted with sorcery, became weaker. Some were born without their elements at all. Magic could not flow across the veil or replenish our lands. Those already born before the Fade maintained their powers, but if their dwelling of power drained, it could never be regained. I assumed my father had not known the outcome when he corrupted our magic, risking even the loss of his own; then again, I believed he had understood it all too well and disregarded the consequences.

The King of Novear risked everything so he could have the chance to destroy the realm for himself before the Gods ever could.

My father had gotten at least one thing right. Gods were only saviors to the things they could take away. It was dangerous to believe, though, that one could overcome the very thing they despised without becoming it. I hoped to learn that lesson before he did.

The chair across from me scraped against the carpeted floor and I startled, grating my attention. Their black robe bellowed as they seated themselves across from me without invitation.

The masked Volkan slid their book over to me until it tapped the edges of my own. I tilted my head as I placed two fingers on the book and pushed it forward until I met enough resistance. The Volkan pushed it right back.

"Can I help you?" I repeated our dance and attempted to slam the book shut. As I did, his hand flattened the binding, placing his index finger on the top of the page. I sent him a daggered glare as I finished reading the line he had pointed out.

"Is that from me?" he said. I tracked his tawny eyes to my blackened wrist that was extended over the page, only a shadow of his fiery glow ringed around his pupils.

"If you remove the mask you hide behind, I am sure I could find that I have done the same to you. It is a little late for remorse from either party." I pursed my lips into a flat smile. "Kane, is it?"

Kane carefully removed his hood, the fabric piling upon his

broad shoulders. There was a black leather harness crossed over his muscular chest, the silver buckles strapped tightly to uphold whatever weapon he hid behind his cloak.

"Considering it is clear your magic does not replenish as quickly as mine, I'm not sure you would find anything," he said.

Kane leaned forward, pressing his elbows nonchalantly onto the table. I fought the oncoming urge to roll my eyes, because I knew his type too well by this gesture alone. Military men always had their hidden agendas. What was important, though, was whether he was the type of soldier who followed orders or made them.

"Were you born after the Fade?" he asked. A bold question to a sorcerer he did not know, and then I knew my answer—this soldier made his own orders.

"We all have our secrets then, because I find it none of your concern." I brushed through the ends of my white hair and tossed it back. "Unless you are looking for a little redemption?"

He pitched his voice low. "Redemption is for those who need it."

"Such arrogance for someone who cannot back up their claims, or do I need to remind you?" I smiled wickedly. Elias was right—belittling their egos was easy.

Unfortunately for them, I thrived under such conditions.

A deep chuckle rose from his chest. "You must confuse me with Drakkon—arrogance is not my vice. However, if you come back to the ring, I will be happy to meet your assumption of me."

"Did you come over here to me to make idle threats, or did you just shove this book in my face without cause?" I asked, growing bored with whatever angle he was playing at.

"Manners of a royal, I see." He studied me as he eased himself back, crossing his arms. "At this very moment, your husband, if you will, is looking for a solution to a strike made from the Celenia Kingdom. I left several hours ago when I could not take his stubbornness any longer."

I tilted my head, the news genuinely catching me off guard. "Are you sure?" I asked. When he nodded, I narrowed my eyes. "I thought Solstice had good relations with their kingdom, since they had never aligned with my father's cause?"

"To their knowledge, we still do." He paused, the heat rising off him from across the table. "They have stolen something from us. An asset that could change the tide of the war that I am not at liberty to discuss."

Keahi's commander was still rather liberal with his information, even more so because he was bold enough to work alone. I did not buy it, but I wasn't about to turn him away. "You tell me this in good faith—*why*?"

"We will need your powers for the retrieval," he said. My eyebrows knitted together, and my mouth shut when he held up a hand. "Before you answer, know I would only assume that our new *Princess* would do anything to aid her own country."

I ground my teeth. "Is that a threat, Volkan?"

Kane's eyes lit up like he was smiling through his mask. "I am Keahi's sworn second. I know him more than anyone, including you, but I also know my people. If you stepped foot into the capital right now, they would annihilate you. This is an opportunity to prove yourself before they even have the chance."

Keahi's second had a way with words, so I chose mine carefully. "What's in it for you?"

Kane took a deep breath and lowered his finger to the exact line he wanted me to read again and said, "Redemption." He slowly inched the book closer to me, and this time I did not stop him.

"You took my sight away. . ." A small shiver went through him. "This is not a power I have observed against a Novear sorcerer, and I still have yet to find a record of it. However, I found this."

He would not find any record, but he did not need to know that. My eyes widened with each sentence as I scanned the passages he had underlined with drying ink.

"You're serious." I gaped.

"You can take away sight," he argued. "I do not see the difference."

I responded with a low laugh. "Are you trying to drain my power on purpose? Something of this scale would be next to impossible against an *entire* battalion."

A condescending '*hmm*' lingered between us.

Were all of Keahi's friends like this?

"What now?" I snapped.

"I did not take you for the kind of sorcerer to submit to fear so easily," he mocked.

"I'm not—"

"—You are trained, but clearly have not learned to maintain it very well, which is surprising for someone with your threshold. We can train you to prevent the will of the Fade from bottoming you out. There are ways," he said.

Kane was too observant for his own good. I closed the book and handed it back to him. "You are challenging me as if you can wield light instead of your own element."

"That is where you are wrong," Kane said. "Fire can create its own form of light. All power is connected, no matter how differently it manifests."

"Your people might beg to differ," I argued.

"That does not make it any less true," he said just before the library doors slammed so hard even the candle flames flickered in retreat. Kane chuckled to himself as he melted into the chair, his heavy boots propped onto the table as he leaned back like he was preparing for a show.

Keahi stormed over to the table and tossed Kane's feet to the ground. He did not even turn to look at me as he pressed the tip of his gloves into the head of the table. "I expected you back several hours ago. Where have you been?"

Kane rolled his neck as he said, "If I remember correctly, you had told me to come up with a plan first." Keahi flicked his eyes over to me, then back.

"Oh yes," Kane said, undeterred. "She knows."

A low growl emanated from Keahi's throat. He looked like he was about to burst into flames at any second. "She knows what, exactly?"

As if I was not sitting right here.

"She knows Celenia has allied with her father behind our backs and has stolen from us." Kane batted his dark eyelashes. "Our Princess here is the key to our retrieval."

Keahi's entire body was so tense, the brass table bent under his touch. "What part of it is too dangerous did you not understand?" Smoke slithered between Keahi's fingers, sparking against the table as he leaned over Kane. "I said *no*, and that is final."

Kane flinched. Their years of working beside one another were evident as they communicated with silent glances. "If this goes badly, those lives are in *your* hands, General! Not. Mine. This will—"

The tension spliced in half as I reached across the table and slammed the book. "Now that I have your attention," I stated calmly, as both Volkans turned toward me, "I would like to say I accept. There's no further need to argue when it is my decision, and Kane is right."

Kane's deep laugh had my hands vibrating with restraint to cut it off at the source, but I held my hand up to him as I turned to Keahi. An opportunity to show my alliance with Solstice, not just my 'husband,' dangled in front of me, and it would better prepare us for when we presented ourselves at the capital.

"It will give Solstice the advantage. Creating the illusion we were never there to take it in the first place," I clarified, flipping through the book Kane had found and handing it to Keahi. "Through a light casting, a mirage."

"Sabine, it nearly depleted you after using your powers for the first time," Keahi said stiffly.

My power laughed internally.

Sympathy, I slowly smiled at him, *was dangerous indeed.*

"Are we sure that rancid tonic did not deplete me? The one you knocked me out with last night?" I growled. "I'm still groggy after several hours of rest, thanks to you."

Keahi pinched the bridge of his nose through his mask. His commander chuckled into a cough behind him. The General of Solstice waved his white flag as he visibly softened, reaching for the book to examine the page line by line.

Without further prompting, I looked at Kane. "How much time do I have to prepare?"

"Two weeks," Keahi interjected. "You have two weeks to prove to me you can do this." He forced the book into Kane's hands and leaned into it with one hand until it was against his chest. "Take this to the others that are still waiting on you to finish your portion of the debrief and leave us."

Kane promptly followed his command to exit the library, but not before throwing Keahi a warning gesture before he shut the door.

Keahi took a seat on top of the table, the gray tones underneath his eyes noticeable even through the mask. Wringing his hands in his lap, he steadily lowered his chest. "I cannot leave you alone, can I?"

From his remark, I ignored the twinge in my chest. "I did not realize I was causing such an inconvenience for you?"

"An inconvenience. . ." Keahi shifted his burning gaze over me slowly from head to toe. ". . . is one way to put it."

I wanted to be hurt that this was how he reacted toward me after last night, but I was more relieved he was not opting to treat me any differently. Because now I could do the same to him without the rare side effect of guilt.

"The feeling is mutual, I can assure you, but I would go as far to say this has become quite convenient for you given the circumstances." I prowled in front of him as I let my anger flare. "You are not in foreign lands, *and* you have people who are looking out for your best interests."

I inched closer to him, priding myself as his pupils dilated. I stepped between his knees, chuckling when I heard the hitch in his breath.

Two could play this game.

"The only reason anyone here would look out for me is by your extension and your extension only—*I have no one*," I said as I twirled the drawstring of his hood and smiled. "But thank you for reminding me."

Shadows engulfed his eyes, swirling in his molten stare. I let whatever thought that was running through his mind sink in as I watched the notch in his throat slide against the fabric at his neck.

"As it turns out," I whispered in his ear. "You need me more than I need you." I leaned around him, reaching for the books I left on the table.

Keahi moved quicker than I could react. He spread his fingers out wide, pressing the book I attempted to retrieve further into the table.

"*Careful*," he said in a low voice that sent streaks of fire up my skin, ignited by the faint brush of my hand against the seam of his gloves. "Your end of the deal requires a lot more than you know of. It will be no simple task to take down your father when the time comes, and we will have to do what is necessary to support Solstice to do so."

"Do you really think that the capital will believe us when even your own men see that something is amiss?" I raised a brow.

This finally caught his attention.

"You have not really been in a state where we could even attempt to persuade them or prevent their suspicion." My backside forced into the end of the table as Keahi pushed past me, pacing wordlessly in front of me. "Besides, I'm not so sure it is a problem anymore," he murmured.

"Persuasion does not conspire with words; it breeds within the finer details. Your brother saw that when you did not come to visit me while I had been sick, and your men saw when you looked like you wanted *to kill me* in front of them after I dueled with Kane," I finished. "Treat me as your enemy, and they will follow."

Keahi sighed heavily as he stared up at the ceiling. "After the meeting I had, I can promise you they did not think I wanted to *kill you*. I almost wished they had." The side of his jaw flexed under his mask as he looked past me. "The notebook on the table. Who gave it to you?"

I raised a brow at the swift change in conversation. "Elias had given it to me. Why?" There was no look of surprise as he retrieved it and handed it to me.

I tilted my chin down and removed the cover—*empty*. I flipped to the next page to find the same result and continued to search through the notebook to find not a single drop of ink displayed. "There's nothing in here. . ."

Keahi took it back from me and tied the browned knot around the binding. "The notebook is spelled with invisible ink."

"That's it?"

He gave me a curious look.

"When you write in the pages," he started off slowly. "It will produce a response and then disappear once you have read what it has revealed to you. I used to have one myself not too long ago. . . It was a popular gift among children to keep their curiosity occupied."

I hesitated, remembering that Elias had said it would help me discover information about the bond. "Why would Elias give me this?"

"He has his. . . ways of attempting to be helpful," he sighed.

I watched him as he slid the other books that I had left on the table under the crook of his arm. "If it is a children's play book, how would any of the answers be useful to me?"

Keahi spoke more softly than usual. "I would try asking it a question before you dismiss it altogether."

"I would do so," I said, somewhat confused. It was a strange comment to make about an empty book. "But it does not look like you plan on giving it back to me."

"Did you not say I need to work on my attempts at persuasion? I am going to carry the books to your rooms, as it seems the only person I need to persuade right now is you."

"It is. . . a start," I said curtly, surprised. He caught my shoulder as I headed toward the oak doors. I fought the urge to remain looking ahead as his thumb brushed against my collarbone.

"Not that way." He stopped me.

My boots dug into the carpet. "If you think I'm going to travel through that *smoke* right now, just know I would rather climb the outside of the mountain to get to my room instead."

Keahi chuckled with a hint of amusement. "You'll get used to it."

Chapter Twenty-Five

Sabine

The ocean lined tapestry inside of his study drifted as it revealed a hidden passageway beneath its waves. A soft chill dusted my skin as cool mist reached out to me from deep inside the mountain and pulled me forward. The tapestry fluttered with the last remaining light as Keahi's footsteps floated behind me.

He crept like a shadow in the night, but the aura of his magic magnified his presence to me. I could sense even the slight hesitation in his steps when my legs failed to pick themselves up, and I stood paralyzed in front of him. I had closed my eyes, creating my own darkness before the mountain could show me its own.

It was not the dark that I feared, but what I became as I wrapped myself within it. The light that was still left within me cowered as the whispers sang to me in the dark. It flooded my veins as it rattled the cage, challenging me to escape the careful mold I struggled to contain it in. *It was too much.*

I took a small step back, but a leathered hand faintly traced the back of my own. My eyes snapped open at the contact. The whispers descended into a hush as calcified pyramids of stone lit our path with a soft, lime-colored glow. Keahi and I stood side by side at the mouth of the tunnel.

"These rocks only produce a glow when light does not touch them," Keahi said softly, as if he was trying not to disturb them.

"I've never seen anything like it," I said in an equally soft tone as I melted back into my body. I turned to look up at Keahi, who was staring straight ahead, patiently waiting for me. A wisp of his shadow greeted my hesitation, swirling around my figure before it floated through the dark, unafraid. I swallowed, fighting my fears as it gave me the strength to follow as it led us deep into the passageway.

My lips parted in awe as we came upon an iron spiral staircase. It weaved around an endless stalactite, gleaming with various shades of frosted blues that glistened across tapered cones hanging from the ceiling. Light softly filtered through the last flight of steps that groaned as we made our way up their rusted frame.

There was no door covering the entrance, but a glassy sheen reflected off the glow from my night lamp. A glittering veil of magic draped around Keahi's form as he stepped past me and entered my room.

I turned back to see the portal we had passed through, realizing that the floor-length mirror I had avoided earlier while changing served a dual purpose. I tapped against my reflection, inspecting for holes in the magic, but there were none.

My eyes flew to the shadow in the mirror, but I did not have time to prepare myself as I was met with his true face. Both of his forms held its own sense of brutality, but I held my breath as I came face to face with the scarred man I had first met beneath the mask.

A small gasp parted my lips, and I regretted it instantly because I could not take it back. His appearance had not been what startled me, but rather the solace I felt within me when he came to me unarmed.

It was not something I saw in his exterior at my remark, but I felt everything as the bond between us quivered against the invisible line. A pang of regret traveled down both sides of the bond.

"You cannot go through the other side. The mirror is only one way," he said, recovering our silence. His dark brows pinched together, hovering over the flames simmering in his eyes.

"I see," I whispered. "What good is a king's passageway, if it does not serve as a way out?"

"It is not the only way out," he said, an unusual tension gripping his voice when I did not look away.

I was lost. Lost in the way I was not scared of the fire in his eyes, though it had once been the burning reminder of my kingdom's losses. Lost because his dark curls were as black as the darkness I feared, but the white strand falling upon his face looked as if it was dusted with starlight. If there was a cosmos where my people were still alive, they were whispering for me to remember what they could no longer pass down.

It was the stars who believed in the dark when the earth had feared it, but it was darkness that made the stars shine the brightest—together they found a home in each other's orbit.

He cleared his throat. "I can put it back on. . ." He thumbed his mask in his hands as he took a careful step back. ". . . if it bothers you."

I averted my eyes, realizing I had continued to stare at him despite the discomfort I felt down the bond. My hand slid, feather light, down the panel of spelled glass.

"No." I swallowed. "I prefer you without the mask." His ember eyes darted away from mine, this time in the mirror, a faint flush forming on his cheekbones.

I frowned as I turned to meet him face to face. His proximity felt strange, stronger than it had before, but different. I did not suffocate just at the thought of him being near as I had prior to the last pieces of the siphoning crystal being removed. My power wanted him near now, and secretly, so did I.

We had been alone together out in the woods, our bedrolls splayed out on opposite sides of the smoking fire. There was distance, an unspoken line drawn across the earth. It was easy to see that our paths had crossed, not as star-crossed lovers like the bonded sorcerers that had come before us, but as star-crossed enemies who had compromised on one thing; the promise of vengeance to those who opposed us, and to my father who had been at the heart of it.

I could not help but notice the way the night looked vastly different on him now, as the coals crackled in the hearth beside us.

Cages. I had been born in one, and in turn created many of my own. It was what I had known, where I had felt the safest, but a door pushed itself open inside of me. His forehead creased with a sense of worry the longer I held our silence.

The careful hand I kept on that door gradually released itself. "You have direct access to my sleeping quarters, then?" I asked.

Keahi gave me a cautious look, his scarred brow raised. "Anyone with shadowfire has direct access. We consider this the longer route. I had only made use of it to check on you during your recovery. If this upsets you, I can arrange a different room."

"No," I stammered quickly. "That will not be necessary." Keahi, however, did not look reassured as he tugged on his bottom lip. "The Volkans believe this to be your room; it would look strange if I had different sleeping quarters."

Keahi nodded thoughtfully as he placed my books on top of the nightstand. He reached toward the bottom drawer and pulled out a crystalized bottle of amber liquid. "I hope you do not mind," he said as he swirled the contents. "But I am at least going to take this back to my study."

He plucked the top of the cork out of the glass. There was a slight hesitation before he tipped it back. The notch in his throat bobbed several times before he lowered it. I could not help my gaze as it lowered to the fullness of his bottom lip. It glistened from the drink as his jaw freed itself from the tension he carried.

A desperate desire for freedom overtook me. I closed the distance and snatched the neck of the bottle from his hands in hopes it would render me unconscious. There would be no running the castle hallways tonight; I was too proud to ask for another tonic.

My belly ignited with warmth, drowning out the knowledge I had shown a weakness to him. The aftertaste of cinnamon coated my tongue as I pressed the bottle back into him, swaying slightly against his muscled chest. Dizzied, I plopped onto the bed before hitting the floor.

Keahi's shoulders shook with a honey coated laugh. "I do not mean to cast assumptions, but it does not appear that you handle the drink well."

I shrugged my shoulders as I chucked off my boots. "Never had it before."

The smirk that stretched his scar fell.

I patted the sides of my pockets, fumbling as I felt the rim of a wooden jar. My face scrunched, remembering the rotten fumes. "You might want to leave before I put this on. It was not pleasant the first time."

Keahi's determined gaze hardened as his chest moved with more force than necessary and held out his palm. "I know that container well. I am afraid the smell does not bother me anymore."

I clenched the tiny wooden jar into my chest as I eyed him from head to toe, suspicious of the olive branch he extended to me. "The smell of this stuff could wake the dead; I *highly* doubt that."

"You are telling me you would rather put that on yourself?" His pale lips lifted in a tight smirk, but his hand held out steady. "I can do it."

"No," I chuckled, and a tiny hiccup snuck its way out. My cheeks heated as Keahi pursed his lips into a fine smile. I rolled my eyes before placing it in his palm. "*Fine.* Take it." I held my chin up and turned as I threw my arm out in front of him.

When my shoulder burned from holding the uncomfortable position, I peeked at him from the corner of my eye. He was on one knee in front of the bed, staring at the single bare hand he had chosen to use.

The welts on his palm hovered over the top of my wrist . . . *shaking.* His swallow was barely audible as he shut his eyes tight and grazed the top of my skin with the balm. I did not dare look back after that. *I couldn't.* Not when I saw how far the welts traveled up underneath his sleeves.

"Thank you," I said as he turned away, frantically replacing the glove on his hands. "For. . . last night too. Comforting me the way you did. You did not have to do that. . . Are you—"

Keahi threw his hood up, fumbling with his mask in his hands. "Each morning, you will meet with Kane and Drakkon." The change in his tone was swift, strained. "If you plan to come with us, I will need you to train with them. I will be the one to work on your magic with you, no one else."

My pulse leaped in my chest. "I—Do you not have other things you need to attend to?"

A sinking feeling crashed in my chest as he looked at me with utter repulsion. The metal door handle bending beneath his grip groaned like he could not create distance fast enough, but he held on.

"I'm making time for this," he said tightly. "We cannot fail. It is too risky. I refuse to let anything happen to you—*I won't.*"

I knew that my sleep was to be restless as he left the room, his shadow fading underneath the door, no matter how strong my shot of liquor had been. Not now, when I remembered. Pulled from the darkness of night. Lost in a hell I had made for myself when fate grasped my hand. *'Don't leave me here,'* I had said into the endless sea of my eternity.

The sun had not saved me, but I heard the voice that did. I repeated it into the empty room, words I had not remembered, Keahi's whisper snaking like a shadow into the forefront of my mind.

"I won't."

Chapter Twenty-Six

Sabine

It had either been five hours, or about my fifth time around the sun, because after one shot of liquor, I was drunk out of my mind.

My head spun, and I could not stare at the ceiling any longer without feeling the urge to vomit. I had survived many things in my lifespan, but this was *actual* torture. I reached down and grabbed the base of my thigh; it was heavy as I shifted it to the edge of the bed so my foot could hit the ice-cold floor.

I groaned as I rolled over and felt absolute betrayal when I hit the air instead. My back *slapped* onto the marble floor. I knew that I should have been worried when I did not feel the impact of it, but I had greater issues at hand. I grabbed onto the nightstand, my hand knocking over the stacks of books Keahi had left for me as I slid my knees underneath my hips so I could find—*water.*

The fine silver goblet shined like it had bottled the rain directly from the clouds. My mouth watered as I cupped both hands around the stem, careful not to disturb it as I slid it to the edge. I struggled as I lifted myself just enough to place my bottom lip against the rim and tipped it back to find the sweet relief of *nothing.* The empty cup was mocking me. I cursed as I leaned back against the frame of the bed and accepted my fate.

No one had exactly mentioned I needed to stay put in my room during the night, but as I maneuvered through the hallways, it seemed someone should have.

I felt my hearing succumb to my paranoia again, but I did not run. *I could not run.* Even if I felt bold enough to give up and inevitably face plant across the floor and leave myself there for someone to peel me up in the morning, I did not want to risk alerting Keahi again.

If I had known where the kitchen was, it would have been the first place I went to—because *Gods*, what I would do for a piece of bread right now.

I had just turned the corner when the whispers were no longer a figment of my imagination, and I ducked hard in between the double doors of the training room before they could see me. Sweat trickled down my spine as two shadows appeared against the underside of the doors.

Elias's voice broke first. "If you do not tell her, I swear to you, I will. I will not let your fear get in the way. Did you really think I would not find out?"

Someone's in trouble. I suppressed a laugh into my palm—*wait, they're talking about me. . . I think.*

"I am well aware of that, uncle, since I saw you gave her my notebook," Keahi spit out in a harsh whisper.

"Do not pin this on me. I saw the letter Emric wrote back to you," Elias snapped, holding his ground.

The drink evaporated from my system at the mention of the Solstice King's name. Keahi had omitted his recent communication with the capital to me. After my reaction toward the news about him spotting my father, I'm not sure I would have told me if I were in his position, either.

Keahi did not hide his annoyance. "You went through *everything*?!"

Elias hummed with amusement. "Of course, I did. Why else would I have let Iahni help you after you gave Sabine one of *my* potions? If anything, we are even. What I find more interesting is that Iahni found the letter on your desk in plain sight where Sabine could have found it."

There was a pause, and I could feel Keahi's shoulder lean up against the other side of the door.

"I know you better than that, Keahi Aldeer," Elias said. "Why do you not want her to trust you?"

"Because she shouldn't," he said quietly.

A sharp twist grasped its hold around my gut. Regretfully, he had done nothing but make me trust him. At least I had started to, despite my better judgment.

"All I hear is your fear rolling off your tongue." Elias spoke sternly, but more lightly than before. "If the bond is not fully formed, there will be consequences. This is the last time I will warn you. Do not ignore this."

Why would we need to finish the bond? I could feel Keahi through the connection, sense his power crackling like a furnace in his core. Elias was mistaken.

Keahi's anger grated his tone. "May I remind you that for the bond to be completed, we must accept it on both sides? That is not something that will be obtained in the foreseeable future. . . Do not forget I have Zehra to worry about, and the mission, but sure, let's add one more to the list."

My shoulder sank against the door, and my stomach dropped—*Zehra.* Unexpected jealousy tangled with remorse. I hadn't thought about how Keahi had a life before he hid our bond within our 'marriage.' It was easy for me to leave everything behind when I had nothing to go back to. Keahi did, but he had given it up anyway.

"Ah, if your excuses were only currency." I held my breath as Elias said, "Do you believe that to be on Sabine's part or yours?" When Keahi did not respond, he continued, "The future changes all the time, Keahi, and this time it will be the death of you. Tell her the truth about how you feel."

No. I shook my head at the thought. *I would rather he didn't tell me.*

A single pair of footsteps echoed and faded. I panicked as the handle I held onto turned. I flattened my back against the wall as Keahi stopped in the center of the training room.

My hand reached for the door as I prepared to bolt, but I was too late. His back was still facing me when he said in a low voice, "*What*—are you doing here?"

I pushed off the door, cautiously padding my bare feet toward him. "I—I was just getting a drink of water when I heard you and

Elias approach. I was about to open the door—" My mind was fighting to ask who *she* was. *Get it together,* I told myself. *This is not you. You do not care—don't care.*

"Was there no water in your room?" Keahi ground out between his teeth.

"It was empty, though I'm failing to see the point of your irritation?" I played it off, stopping a suitable distance away from him.

Keahi pivoted on his heels with lethal stillness. He tilted his head. "*In that?*"

Heat flared down the trail he made with his eyes over my frame until they stopped at the maroon satin scrunched just above my hips. I tugged at the hem of the lace, dangerously inching toward my bare thighs.

When I had rummaged through the wardrobe earlier for something comfortable to wear to bed, I stumbled across several sets of nightgowns Iahni had supplied. No doubt they were meant for behind-closed-door activities that were not a part of the alliance I had with Keahi. I could not help myself as I tried every one of them on in my drunken state, indulging in the finest silk I had ever touched.

I was fully regretting choosing the shortest one. I pulled the strings of the matching satin robe tighter, covering the plunging lace neckline that revealed the fullness of my breasts.

"It had not occurred to me, really," I said as I found enough balance to walk over to the water canister. I could sense the alcohol returning to my system. "Though it appears to be a problem for you?"

"It is *not* a problem," he growled, looking the other way.

My core heated, because both the bond and I knew something he did not want me to know now. I finally knew what he meant because I could tell.

The Prince of Solstice. . . was lying.

I bit my lip as I hummed in disbelief, pouring myself a cup of water from the canister on top of the bench I had seen earlier.

"That is not what it sounds like to me. . . or maybe you should keep telling me about those sweet lies you keep sending through the bond. I find them very fascinating." I smirked.

Keahi materialized beside me and ripped the water from my hands. "I'm not in the mood for your banter, Sabine. Go back up to the room before someone sees you in this."

I fought against him and clumsily lunged for the water as he held it up above his head. The overwhelming scent of cinnamon lingered on his breath, invading the space between us. I dropped back down on my heels.

"Gods, you are worse than I am, aren't you? What did you do? Drink the entire bottle?" I gasped.

"I would have if you had not drunk most of it," he grumbled, stretching his shoulder out of my reach when I launched a second attack.

The weapons rack glinted with silver beside me. I smiled as I snatched the nearest dagger into my hand and pointed it at his chest.

"Give it. To me."

Keahi's eyes flared with a playful warning. "I don't think so." I turned my eyes up to see the water dissipate into a puff of steam, and his own silver dagger appeared out of thin air.

"Are you challenging me, Son of Fire? *Because it's working.*" Metal clanged upon metal as our blades clashed, our arms shaking against the force we exerted, until he shoved me backwards.

"So *eager*," he panted.

"For violence?" I said as I spun the dagger in my palm, sizing him up as I planned where I wanted to sink it into his flesh. "Yes."

"Be careful with that." Keahi nodded toward the blade. "You can barely find your footing."

The dagger in my hand slipped as I launched it straight toward his head, but he ducked out of the line of fire. The tip of the knife, once destined to meet him in the center of his forehead, embedded into the back wall.

"*Oops.*" I grinned, strolling over to the canister. His eyes trained on me as I lifted it above my head and let it flow into my mouth. It trickled down my neck, beading in between my breasts. I wiped the corners of my lips and held it out to him, and I could have sworn I heard a slight low groan from his.

"Here, drink before we decide to kill each other under the influence of whatever this dark magic is," I said, pressing the reservoir into his gloves.

Keahi's baritone chuckle hit deep inside my chest as he sat down beside me on the bench. "If that is what you want to call it," he panted. His shoulders slumped unnaturally as he pressed his back into the wall. "How much did you hear? I may not have known you for long, but I do not doubt for a second that you would not seize the chance to eavesdrop."

As I sat next to him, I tucked a strand of hair behind my ear. "I thought. . . Elias said the future could change. It was difficult to make out the exact words of your exchange." I wove some truth to disguise my lie, not wanting him to know that I had heard the entirety of their conversation. "Was he speaking of our bond? A way to undo it?"

Keahi shifted uncomfortably beside me. "From what I have found, that would be next to impossible."

If there was any truth to Elias's warning, I wanted to know for myself in the future. I twisted the obsidian ring that weighted my left finger. "If there was a way to undo it, would you?"

Keahi lowered his voice. "I do not dwell on things that I cannot change."

A pang of resentment bloomed when he did not simply say no, despite knowing that I felt the same.

"I understand," I said as I rushed to create any form of distance. "I will see you tomorrow, then."

"Sabine."

I halted at the strain in his voice, telling myself that I did not want to turn around and see if his face confirmed that he also felt whatever was roaming through our bond.

"I have killed enough men already. I do not need to kill any more for looking at my wife," he warned, almost as if it were true.

"I am *not* your wife—it would be wise to remember," I said, unsure of the game he was playing at. My warning to him was a sounding board for me to heed because he was *not* my husband.

The deep growl of his voice threatened to make me forget.

"To them you are. I would stop at nothing to make sure they pay the price accordingly," he said, and as if the fates were testing him, shouts and hollers traveled from outside of the training room door.

Chapter Twenty-Seven

I was going to have to kill them.

Every single one, if they saw my wife right now.

Sabine waved her arms frantically in front of my face, the satin robe loosening around her shoulders. Her lips moved faster than I could register intoxicated.

I guess I could replace them. . . but it would be highly difficult.

"Keahi." She growled my name like it was a threat; *it sounded. . . good*, despite how terrified I was of her.

"Keahi Aldeer, they are about to walk through that door, and as much as I don't give a single fuck if they see me or not, you are acting like a rogue animal right now. I do not want to deal with a single thing that consequently comes out of your mouth."

I wonder how pissed Kane is going to be if I have to make him train a new battalion. It might not be that bad—a handprint seared the right side of my face.

"Did I wake you up finally? *Move.* You and your shadow."

The perpetrator grasped the front of my cloak and dragged me across the room. Sabine ripped open the door to a tiny broom closet within the training room and used all of her body weight to shove me inside with her.

I touched the side of my face, still burning as she hurriedly shut the closet door. "Did you just. . . did you slap me?"

"Your eyes turned *black*," she whispered harshly as the training room outside grew louder. "I thought you were going to pass out if I didn't do something."

"I was not about to—"

"—Save it. Now use your shadowfire and transport us out of here before we get caught." The closet space diminished further. "Well?" she asked, "What are you waiting for?" Sabine pressed her eyes closed. The lace bunched at the top of her breasts as she crossed her arms—waiting.

My eyes shot to the ceiling.

"I—I can't," I stammered.

"Hilarious," she huffed. "I didn't know you could make a joke."

My heart thumped violently in my chest.

"Aww man!" Ossian, one of the younger Volkan members, called from outside the closet. "Someone drank all the water again."

"That can wait," Kane graveled on the other side behind him. "You were supposed to have this set up hours ago before I had to drag you out of bed."

"Why are you not making everyone else do this, too?" Ossian groaned. "I wouldn't be complaining right now if you would have let me go to breakfast with them."

"Because everyone else does not slack when it is their turn to set up for training," Kane shouted back. Even I flinched, because he rarely felt the need to raise his voice like that, and in doing so, I accidentally stepped on Sabine's toes. She bit down a yelp before she shoved me off.

Sabine stared a hole straight through my chest as we listened to what was taking place outside. My back met a solid wall on the other side of the broom closet, and my attempt to give her space failed miserably.

"I can't," I said between my teeth. "The last time I used shadowfire to transport while I was this drunk, I ended up teleporting myself midair off the side of the mountain."

Her muted glare split as a cackle crept up her throat, a hand thrown over her mouth.

"For fuck's sake, Sabine, be quiet unless you want them to come over here!" I threatened. *Their lives depended on it.*

She ignored me as her back hit the opposite wall, and her knees touched my shins as she slid halfway down. I fidgeted at how loud she was and knocked over a broom stick propped up next to me.

Her hushed laughter cascaded down the bond, and it warmed the space between us as she introduced me to a feeling I had never felt before. I was too distracted to notice that the wooden handle was inches away from striking against her head when I snatched it with both hands. She had not tried to lunge for it herself. Sabine placed a second hand over her mouth, snickering into her palms.

Great, that makes two of us.

Tension was plucked away from me when her rose-colored cheeks glowed in the dark. I rested the broom against my shoulder. I had felt her through the sorcerer's bond before, but not like this.

She radiated with a humored bliss that I did not want to disturb with my presence. I wanted to fall into the shadows, just so I could continue to hear her laugh, even if it was at my expense. I had not thought of her incapable of happiness. With as much fight as she had in her veins, she could take anything she wanted; happiness included. I wanted to tell her I understood its familiarity; her sadness that called me to remember my own.

I often pretended that it did not exist, that I was without feeling. Though our paths had been very different, I would never want to take away what she had been through. Fate had found the one person who matched the pain I refused to acknowledge.

In return, I exposed the worst parts of myself to her: fear, pride, reluctant jealousy. I was willing to admit it as I watched her now, because the last thing I wanted was to lie further. I would not take this part of her, and I longed to see her detain it until it became solely hers, this bright part of her soul that exuded a foreign sensation within my own. As it washed over me, I closed my eyes and prayed that one day I would feel it again. Even just for a moment.

Even if I was not the one to share it with her, because someone like me could not hold such a breakable thing as happiness.

I shattered it, every time.

"I think there's another gallon of water in the closet!" Ossian's voice resounded too close for comfort outside the door.

Our eyes clashed instantly. All humor vanished within those golden eyes. *If the fates were to spare him from me, he better be aiming for a different closet right now.*

My hand reached for the door at the same time Ossian did on the other side. The knob rattled as he attempted to open the door.

"What the hell?" Ossian cursed under his breath. "I guess I'm going to have to go get the key."

We released a simultaneous breath as his footsteps faded away. Sabine chuckled again. "What are we going to do now? He's clearly coming back."

"Just. . ." I fumbled. "Just let me think of something."

"Better hurry." She smirked.

"What? Now you're just *okay* if someone finds us in this damn closet together?"

A light sigh escaped from her lips. "I guess it is finally catching up to me, I suppose." Her smile softened. "I don't feel anything."

She didn't know how wrong she was.

Ossian's shadow peered underneath the door frame. The keys jumbled on the ring as he searched for the right one. "*Fuck*," I growled low.

Sabine stiffened.

The keys stopped jangling on the other side. I pulled down a portion of my mask so I could mouth to her. "*Did I say that out loud?*" I grimaced.

She bit the inside of her lip and nodded.

Ossian faintly pressed his ear to the door on the other side. "Is someone in there?"

Sabine looked down and peered back up with every bit of malice that relished inside of her. She steadily placed her hand on the small work bench beside us.

I shook my head, eyes wide with terror at the thought that had just crossed her mind. She licked her lips before it turned into a devilish grin and rocked the workbench against the side wall at an excruciating rhythmic pace.

"Oh. My. Gods," Ossian mumbled against the door as he pressed closer, the hinges creaking. *He was a dead man.* Sabine's chest rose. Her mouth formed in an 'oh' with a taunting shimmer in her eye. *A very, dead man.*

"Ossain!" Kane's yell echoed on the other side, and my knees wobbled underneath me. "What did I tell you about the water? Get over here—now."

"Ah-uh. Coming!"

My focus blazed its course as I released the dented knob on our side of the door. Sabine had slumped all the way to the floor.

"We're leaving," I rasped.

"I thought you were too drunk?" She breathed a delirious chuckle.

I knelt beside her. "Let's just say I think it's all burned out of my system."

Sabine lazily threw her arms around my shoulder, unthinking, catching me off guard as her eyelids drooped heavily with the need for sleep.

My arms tightened around her. It was the first time in a very long time that I allowed an embrace so simple. I did not want to let her go.

Her face nuzzled against the pain in my chest when I swept us back to her room. The way her eyelashes fluttered transfixed me, and I held her until she fell asleep in my arms. That tranquil smile remained on her lips as I gently released her onto the mattress and pulled a soft blanket over the tops of her shoulders.

"I would give anything," I whispered, fading into the night.

To see you smile like that again.

Chapter Twenty-Eight

Sabine

"It's not that I'm doting." Drakkon's smile was as wicked as they come. "But I am quite fond of the way you are looking at me right now."

I inhaled through my nose, bile rising in my throat, building until I spit on the ground in front of him. Drakkon and Kane had been training with me every morning for the past week and a half with relentless intent, and with a far greater intensity than I was used to.

I had underestimated them greatly and kept paying for it every time I stepped into the ring. It hurt my pride, but I kept coming back for more torture until I craved it. I stuck my tongue out at him. He scrunched his face and returned the proud gesture.

"Are you always this much of a complete ass, Drakkon?" I cursed, pushing off my knees to stand up straight and tighten the wraps around my fists. I held them up and readied my stance for more.

"Darling, if you wanted it easy, I would give it to you that way," he said, winking at me as he prepared his own stance. "But we all know that's not what you want."

He winked at me.

I threw my hands up and looked over at Kane. "Does he talk to you like this?"

Kane shrugged his shoulders casually as he leaned up against the weapons rack. His eyes flicked over Drakkon from head to toe. "Only when he wants something from me."

My eyes went wide as I looked between them, but Drakkon's expression gave nothing away.

"Do not bring him into this!" Drakkon laughed. "If you wouldn't have kicked Kane's ass the way you did, I would have gone easier, but I know better than to underestimate you, *Princess*."

I closed the gap between us.

"Are we actually acknowledging titles now, *Bastard*?"

Drakkon started throwing everything he had left at me. He was fast, even when exerting a mass amount of power, but I knew that if I could distract him, I was that much quicker. "I did not realize how easy it could be to wound a fire bearer's ego," I taunted. My fist cut his growl off, smashing into the side of his face. I felt the contact clang all the way to my elbow.

I really hope I still have some of that salve left.

Kane yelled off to the side, "I appreciate the two of you saying this while I'm still standing right here, but I would rather you not." Drakkon and I stared at each other, before we both burst out into a fit of laughter.

The first week of training after I accepted the mission had been brutal. Everyone thought we were going to kill each other—*I had definitely tried.*

Kane had been the only one brave enough to put a stop to our feuds, but even his patience had limits. He finally gave up and let us beat each other until the first drop of blood hit the floor. It had gone on for *hours* until Drakkon and I were both hit by a wall of exhaustion and called our temporary truce.

We were a force to be reckoned with as we snuck into the kitchens and stole extra rations to refuel for a rematch; Keahi berated us after the field chef ran us out of the pantries, loaves of bread falling to the floor as we tried to escape.

Keahi had pointed between the two of us and growled, '*Don't. Move.*'

'Is he putting us in time out?' Drakkon leaned over in the wooden chair beside mine with a smirk.

I peered over at my '*husband*,' attempting to apologize to the field chef, who was cherry red as his arms flailed in Keahi's face.

'I dare say he is, though. He probably should have tied us down before he left us unattended. How long should we let him think he put us in time out? A minute more?' I had asked.

'If it wasn't for the fact he made us return the bread we stole, I would have already walked out the door, but maybe he'll take pity on us.' Drakkon snapped his fingers. *'I have it! Start rubbing your eyes, so the next time he looks over, it looks like you're crying. He'll be so uncomfortable he won't know what to do with himself.'*

Keahi had snapped to us over his shoulder with a warning glare, clearly eavesdropping on our conversation. We both straightened. Our lips sealed until he turned back around when the field chef said, *'Are you even listening?'*

I snickered. *'As much as I would love to see how this unfolds. . .'* I pulled out a piece of bread I had been hiding behind my back. *'I say we get out of here?'*

'I knew I always liked you.' He smiled.

Drakkon was still infuriating, but we could tolerate each other after that—in brief intervals, at least. I found it was easier to converse with Kane and Drakkon more than my '*husband*' now, because we had somehow gone backwards.

Keahi took me from the training room every evening to test my magic for the mission. In front of the others, he would occasionally put his hand on the small of my back or offer his elbow to maintain appearances. It was not the best effort, but it would do for now while we were out of the capital's reach.

There was a significant change in him since our night in the training room. The distance he created, and how calloused he came off toward me when we were out of other people's sight, had affected my powers to the point I felt drained with each use.

At first, I had thought it was the residual effects from my power being controlled by the siphoning crystal for so long, but the more Keahi distanced himself, the deeper it languished.

My magic knew before I did through the bond that something was wrong with him. Before our bickering ceased, silence had taken over, long before his nervous laughter stopped. All prior to when I started missing the hesitation in his steps every time he approached me.

I missed the kindness he claimed did not come naturally to him but did. Even if he was not perfect at it, no one ever was, but when he gave it to me, it changed me. The absence I sensed in the places he had authored within my soul terrified me; I had not known it was being written.

Anytime we were alone, Keahi would constantly reach up to rub his chest like there was an ache beneath him. It made my chest burn just by looking at him. His moods were far worse during our training anytime he had his morning meetings with Elias.

After days of him being so withdrawn, I couldn't take it. I finally asked him what was wrong, and it had been a mistake. He brushed me off without a second thought and left. I only saw Keahi during our training sessions after that.

It was a marked difference in how he had acted toward me the night we were alone in the training room. I was still confused by what he had said, even if it was the drink talking. If I went based on sight alone, I would believe there had been nothing boiling underneath his mask. The bond between us said otherwise, though, and I could not help but feel turmoil on the tip of my tongue every time I turned away from him. It was a ghostly sensation, filled with unearthly anguish that kept me up at night.

Every time I tried to reach back, it dissolved, as if I had been imagining it. We owed each other nothing but what we had agreed to. I did not push him on it any further because I feared the answer. Maybe he was coming to terms with what he had lost? Whatever it may be. . . or who, considering the lie we had to hide behind in this false marriage. I understood because I was forced to come to terms with my losses many years ago. It did not mean that I had ever forgotten them.

It did not stop my heart from tensing every time I looked at him, because I had gained something that I did not expect.

I had never had real friends, and although I knew I could not really count on them as such. . . Kane and Drakkon felt like the closest thing I ever had to the word. Even if the two of them combined made me want to gouge my eyes out.

A part of me felt guilty for it. I did not want to hold on to it too tightly, for fear that friendship would always be just out of reach.

Drakkon groaned as he stirred, recovering from the hook I planted on his face. "Hardly. My ego is untouchable," he said, wiping the corner of his mouth. "But I think it is you who should answer that question."

A puzzled look crossed my face. "I don't know what you mean?"

Drakkon tsked. "Oh, little Novear, you don't have to hide it from me. I can see it all over my brother's face."

Short. Very short intervals.

I crossed my arms. "Have you now? You can't even see his face?"

He grabbed a towel, benching himself off to the side. "I have heard from a very reliable source you have not produced a light casting yet," his tone went serious for once.

I rolled my eyes. "Drakkon, Keahi is the only person who could tell you that. He is the only one helping me with my magic."

He unsurprisingly did not ease up with that. "If this goes badly—"

"It. Won't," I said with warning.

He let out an exasperated sigh. "Can you at least do something about him in the meantime? He's becoming a real pain in the ass, more than normal, and I did not think that was possible." *Maybe I wasn't the only one having to deal with his bad moods.*

"You said from the first time I met you he was an ass, so I'm not sure there has really been a change." I drank out of my canteen, but Drakkon's stare was so heavy I nearly choked out my water.

"*What*?" I snapped.

Drakkon turned to Kane. "Close your ears." His head whipped back toward me. "Have you fucked my brother or not? Because I hoped that by having someone around, he would be less of a dick. So, either my theory was wrong, or it is not happening."

My face flushed as I heard Kane spit out his own water onto the floor. My body physically attempted to melt. I had never thought about Keahi in that way, besides that *one time* when Iahni caught me off guard, and possibly the night of the training room. All entirely coincidental.

This time, though, the very thought unleashed a spiral of heated images. I did my best to shut them out—*and failed.*

Kane recovered quicker than I did from the shock, because he punched Drakkon in the shoulder harder than I ever could have. I needed to thank him for that later.

"What the hell was that for?" Drakkon grumbled, rubbing his shoulder.

"Why would you even say something like that?" Kane groaned.

"It's not like you were not thinking it too. He has been more horrible than usual lately. You cannot deny that," Drakkon said, scratching the side of his dark brown hair.

"Even if I was, I know how to mind my business!" Kane yelled back. I was not sure who wanted to be rid of this conversation more, me or the Commander, but they both turned to me at the same time—waiting. I wished I had taken a run prior to this, because there was no mistaking the heat on my face from anything but embarrassment. These two had an influence over me, and I did not like it.

"*Oh, shit.*" Drakkon's face lit with realization. "It is him. . . I'm sorry I shouldn't have said anything."

Kane mumbled under his breath. "You shouldn't have said anything. . . regardless."

"No! *No.*" I did not know how I was going to get out of this one. "Well. . ." I grimaced. "We did! *Once.* After the marriage to consummate but. . . he said he wanted to wait. Wait until we reach the capital. Some kind of tradition, an honor? I'm not really sure." A bead of sweat rolled down my forehead.

Tradition? Yes, I mean there was always some type of tradition in royal marriages. The Novear Kingdom's traditions were rather subtle with royal affairs compared to the others—*or so I had heard.*

There was no way Solstice topped what was rumored in Celenia's Kingdom. Banished for an entire lunar cycle to consummate their marriage, flourishing under the moonlight to fuel their powers to create the future heirs of their kingdoms.

Truthfully, the rumor did not seem all that obscure. Not until I learned they did this underneath a waterfall surrounded by their people, casting spells into the basin.

Every. Single. Night.

They stared blankly at me like statues.

I would never live this down.

Drakkon looked up to Kane with his mouth wide open. "Did *you* know about this?"

Kane shook his head slowly, side to side. The training room doors swung open, and Keahi waltzed into the room as if we had called for him.

"You're late! I've been waiting for over twenty minutes." I spoke out nervously, eager to be rid of the two of them. Drakkon and Kane stared at him intently, like he had grown a second head. I was looking more mortified with every passing glance.

"Is there something wrong?" Keahi looked between the three of us suspiciously.

All of us in unison responded, "No!"

Keahi paused. "I do not want to know. . . are you coming?"

"Yes! We can leave right now," I said, throwing a bold look over my shoulder. Drakkon's smile stretched with amusement as I walked away. If I could see underneath Kane's mask, I was sure he wore the exact same expression.

Chapter Twenty-Nine

Sabine

If Keahi had been talking to me prior to this, I had not heard him. Not one single word after we left.

"We are going to the library today to train," he said beside me. Keahi's gloves were behind his back, and he looked down at me from the corner of his eyes.

The Volkan normally wore the same attire every day, but today he was wearing a thinner cloak than normal. It did not fit tightly over his collar like it normally did, and his light brown skin peeked through at the edge of his mask as we walked.

I nodded in delay, too busy replaying the conversation with Drakkon and Kane painstakingly in my head. Hopefully, they would say nothing to him about earlier.

"I think you will be more comfortable there," he said.

I responded with a grunt, doing my best not to look up at him anymore as my face was telling more than I wanted to right now.

Keahi probably thought nothing of it. Kane and Drakkon were always taking shots at me now, anyway. I was fully regretting letting them get comfortable to do so right about now.

My face smashed into Keahi's chest.

The images of our bodies pressed together from earlier ran wild. My power swirled eagerly inside of me at the contact. I did not look up to him; I couldn't. I just tried to scoot around him. *Tried.*

Keahi's hand lightly pressed into my shoulder, eyes narrowing as he looked me over. "Why are you acting strange?"

"I am trying to focus and prepare for our training; we only have two days left. You are not helping with that," I said as casually as I could. "If anyone is acting strange, it's you, General."

I brushed Keahi's hand off my shoulder and kept walking, but he pinched the back of my white tunic, causing me to fall into him. My breath caught in my throat as his chest rumbled against me with amusement.

Really not helping.

"Are you trying to piss me off, Keahi?" I snapped. He tugged my shirt until I was fully backed up against the hard plane of his body. The ghost of Keahi's lips against my ear through his mask sent a coil of heat straight through me.

"If you are hiding something from me, I will find out," he whispered. "I do pay attention to you, Sabine, more than you know."

If I could wield fire, smoke would have surely been pouring out of my ears. I nudged him off, face fully flushed, as I strode toward the library. Thankfully, I had learned the basic layout of the castle recently and could get there on my own, but Keahi trailed two even steps behind me. When I made it to the entrance, I slipped through and tried to let the wooden doors close on him. His hand barely slipped through before it did.

"Did I do something?" He asked cautiously, retreating slightly from earlier as he folded his gloves behind his back.

No, but I did.

At least I assumed so, if it had anything to do with the look Drakkon and Kane gave me after I opened my mouth. Surely their kingdom's traditions were not to the level of Celenia. An entire lunar cycle of consummation was rather bizarre, even if it was just a rumor. If I was forced to have sex with Keahi Aldeer every night for an entire month, because of some ritual to satisfy the kingdom, I suppose it would not be *torturous. . . Oh Gods.*

"Considering this is the first time I am seeing you today—no, but tread carefully," I said, shaking myself internally. "If you ever grab my shirt like that again, I will perform the same magic I did with Kane and leave you there for your guards to find."

Keahi tilted his head, looking more intrigued than terrified. "Before that."

"You were late." I shrugged my shoulders.

Was I fidgeting? I never fidget.

"Before that," he repeated.

I crossed my arms, restraining them at my sides. "I simply do not know what you are referring to?"

Keahi squinted his eyes at me, turning to the library door. He began waving his hand over it, smoke curling out of his palms. The handles locked in place as his magic continued to move without his eyes on it, creating an infinite loop between the iron bars. Keahi took his face covering off, shaking out his raven-colored curls. The single white strand always fell in front of his face, just above his scar. I forcefully swallowed the lump in my throat.

The only time he took off his mask was when we were alone together, and there was no other chance of anyone else seeing. It was a tradition for all Volkan warriors to remain covered. Kane explored their histories with me in between trainings. Only family, and those that they had pledged themselves to, could see their faces. I did not mind; Keahi visibly relaxed a fraction every time he removed the mask, and so did I.

"You do not have to tell me now," he said, prowling over. "I will wait."

I barked an incriminating laugh. "There is *nothing* to tell."

"Says the woman who speaks her mind even when she does not want to." He pressed his mouth into a smug smile. "I will wait."

I scowled back. "You act like I have borne everything I have to you."

"You keep secrets, yes." He tugged at his bottom lip with his thumb, looking me over; sparks trailed along my skin as he did. "But so far, you speak your mind about almost everything that is presented."

"Do you want to know what I am thinking right now?" I bit out.

"Not particularly."

I think I preferred him when he didn't talk to me.

Keahi walked over to the center of the library and sat down on the floor, legs crossed and eyes closed. He painted himself as the perfect picture of serenity as he placed his hands on top of his thighs. I looked around the library. "I thought you wanted to train with me today?"

"What makes you think we are not?" His eyes remained closed, but he still raised an eyebrow at me.

"Because it looks like you are about to fall asleep," I said pointedly.

"You said that in order to make others see images, you needed complete focus; I have brought you here to give you just that," he sighed.

"Okay. . ." I shifted from one leg to the other. "And you act like I am supposed to know what you want me to do."

Keahi let out another deep sigh and pointed to the floor in front of him. I slowly made my way over, huffing my way down as I mirrored him. "Close your eyes," he instructed. "Focus on the image that you want to produce."

"That's it?"

"Yes."

I adjusted myself, tossing the length of my hair over my back. "This is quite the opposite from last week." I was glad for it too, since I fought with him more than I did Drakkon during training at this point.

"And I found it wasn't working."

I peeked at him through one eye, and his were still closed. "Fine."

"Fine."

I sealed my eyes shut, attempting to concentrate, but I had never been one to stay still. Silence without a task felt painfully crafted for me. When I was sacrificed in the woods, bound to the rock in ropes, it had been the worst experience of my life. I found that there was nothing worse than sitting in the wreckage of everything you refused to look at; forced to sit down and face my own thoughts that I had no intentions of returning to.

"This isn't working."

"Your eyes haven't even been closed for a full minute," he mumbled irritably.

"I think I'm distracted," I admitted with defeat. This is what our sessions amounted to, and without fail, I became frustrated by the mental block on my magic.

"It is probably *your* fault," I continued, not hiding my accusation.

"Every time you get too close to me, I get all hot, like the flames of your magic are suffocating me through the bond. It is rather annoying to be subjected to at all times of the day—"

My eyes flew open when I realized what I could have insinuated—I had meant it literally. It *was* his magic, and it *was* annoying. Being next to him was like standing beside a furnace at the peak of summer, and right now was no exception.

I found a wide grin plastered on his face waiting for me. "I would have thought you were trying to flirt with me if I had not seen you so worked up earlier."

This was. . . *new*, and for some reason, I did not mind it.

"You would *know* if I was trying to flirt with you, Aldeer," I warned, watching him dip down to the red splotches forming on my chest. "Take a hint."

"I like hints," he said, and I knew I was in for it when his smile shifted into a sly smirk, his eyes pooled with shadows. "But I will look forward to the day you try, if your flirtation is anything like your threats to me."

What has gotten into him? He hasn't been like this since we were both drunk out of our minds in a broom closet. Surely he was not drinking in the middle of the day? But we had just gone from new to unexpected.

"There's that subtle arrogance of royalty," I teased him, because it was true. "I have been wondering when it would come out to play. Besides the extensive amount of moping you tend to do."

"I do not mope," he said, but did not remain offended for long. "But what can I do to help you focus without making you feel so. . . *hot and bothered*? Would you prefer warm instead, Princess? With enough practice, I am sure to be capable of finding your desired level of heat. Do not let my stubbornness during our sessions fool you. I am quite teachable, given the right amount of motivation."

My mouth hinged open and closed, my own grin undeniable. There was a part of me that wanted to shut down this side of him immediately, but Keahi was practically beaming, as beaming as he could physically after being so worn down. Truly, it was harmless compared to his recent temperament. If I did not know him any better, one would imagine he had just received word he finally won the war. He could take my white flag, *just* this once, but not unless I could have fun too.

"Would you like to be taught right now?" I raised a brow.

Keahi's eyes widened, and his smirk fell.

"Warm is. . . acceptable," I quickly compromised before he stopped breathing entirely, trying not to laugh. I knew my *'husband'* was still in there somewhere. I looked around, hoping the answer to his actual question would pop out of thin air.

"There is too much light in here, maybe if. . ." I trailed off as the room descended into darkness, one candle at a time. My eyes centered on Keahi when he did not move, but I could feel the magic coming from him as each ring of candles above and below us dwindled until it was pitch black.

Even in the dark, I could feel him, his magic permanently etched into my skin. At first, it felt like a light pulse. A tap on the shoulder when no one was looking. A whispered caress, but my ears could not form the phrases in my head fast enough.

After I had left Keahi in the training room that night, I could finally see what I had been too afraid to look at when I had spun the dagger with my wounded wrist. The deep blue-ish coloring on my wrist that should have lasted weeks even with the spelled salve had disappeared, like my wrist had never been broken. I kept it wrapped, wanting to keep it a secret even from myself.

His magic spread like wildfire over me. I would know the feel of it anywhere. As if the fates had made it especially for me, as if it were my own, and I hated it. Hated that it skinned me alive and left me seeping with vulnerability. Hated that even without the siphoning crystal shoved into my spine, I felt weaker, trapped in a different way, because I did not know how I would feel without him.

Reaching within my power, I attempted to settle myself in the dark. Every time I tried to manipulate the world around me, it was always just out of reach. So many details overwhelmed my magic, a million particles trying to escape my will all at once in the light. I closed my eyes tighter, attempting to fight the hold.

The whispers always found me in the dark. The only thing that could drown them out was the sound of our breathing, matched in time with each other. I scanned the pages of the book Kane had found on light casting in my mind:

A mirage begins with a single stone. If you stack the stones on a faulty anchor, just like the stones, your mirage will crumble. Your image is only as strong as the anchor.

My anchor was not strong enough. I chose the strongest memory I had, but it still was not enough. "I'm not sure I can do this," I whispered.

"Yes, you can." He reassured me. "You just need to start small."

"I need some type of anchor to ground me; changing what you already see is much more difficult than creating something brand new or taking directly from a source," I said. "It will not just be one line of sight I have to manipulate on the mission."

"A physical anchor?" His volume matched mine.

"No, an anchor to create my images with—" I stopped.

A physical anchor.

Magic pulsed on my finger as if it heeded the call. The ring I had not taken off since the day he placed it there was waiting for me. I found the rough edges of the crystal with my other hand, memorizing it. If Keahi was truly my sorcerer's bonded, anything that was linked to him had to be a powerful enough source.

It was God-touched magic, blessed through the sorcerer's bond. We did not easily find such magic in our world, yet it was in the palm of my hands, right in front of me this entire time. I grasped my hand around the crystal, its magic pulsing in my palm as if it was responding to a question it had already answered.

Power flooded into the space, my light illuminating every crevice of the library until it molded itself and became what I asked it to. "Open your eyes and tell me what you see."

Keahi's thoughts seemed endless as he surveyed the room.

"This. . . is starting small?"

At first, panic flooded his voice, but I felt his eyes wandering over the room curiously. He could not see me in front of him. I used this moment to fully take him in; something I had not allowed myself to do, in fear of being seen by him. I could feel him shrinking inside himself every time I lingered on his face for too long, but I was not looking at his scar. I was looking at him, all of him.

Keahi's hood draped over his broad shoulders. He was as built as any other experienced soldier would be, muscled with honed precision. I trailed a line from his shoulder to the side of his neck, briefly wondering if the thrum of his pulse was as wild as it appeared to be right now. He looked at the room, awestruck. The same way I was now looking at him. *He was beautiful.* The scar on his face only enhanced him.

"We are in Astraea's temple, the Goddess of starlight," I said, clearing the scratchiness in the back of my throat.

A dome of colored glass surrounded us. Hues of emerald green, lilac, and turquoise glinted off the side of his cheek as if he was actually sitting inside the room.

"This is a prayer room. . . why can I not see you?" He questioned softly, staring into the space where I would be in front of him. Boring so deeply into me, I questioned if I could block him from seeing me at all.

"Because I am not allowing you to."

"*That's highly unfair*," he muttered, shifting his weight back.

Keahi stared in amazement, circling the room until his eyes landed back on me. His gloved hand twitched at his side before he slowly reached out toward me. Heat pooled between my legs at how close his hand gripped my thigh. My mouth went dry as I attempted not to lose concentration.

"I can still feel you," he said gruffly.

"The room is built the same. I am only making it appear different."

Keahi tried to make sense of his surroundings. His hand gently explored to where I felt a need for him heighten as his thumb grazed against my inner thigh. I shuttered a breath and slowly placed myself into his image.

The stained glass added color to the blank canvas of my pale skin. His breath audibly shook, and he adjusted his back as if a frigid chill had hit him.

"You are—" Heat grew in his palm against my inner thigh, quickly retreating as if he'd burned me with his touch. The glass was barely coloring his face, but red hues bloomed across his cheeks. I let go of the crystal, and the room faded into patches until the darkness swallowed it whole.

"Even with the crystal as an anchor, I can still feel it expending my magic. I cannot hold it for long," I said. "At least not right now."

"You did better than expected. How did you. . ." Keahi trailed off.

I slid the ring back onto my finger. "I used the ceremonial ring. The magic it took to forge is left inside of it, so I used it as an anchor."

"I see," he said as light began swirling around us, candles reigniting one by one. "I did not know places like that still existed in Novear."

"They don't." I swallowed bitterly. "They once did, at least until my father destroyed them all on the night of the burning."

The grief hit me as though it had never left, and by the way Keahi was looking at me, he felt the weight of it too. I had been too late to save them from my father when I found what he had done. It was a torment to hear the absence of their screams as I stared into a pit of burning chaos, their bodies wrapped in flame; the silence since then had never been so loud.

"I once believed in the Gods, Keahi." On the edge of breaking, I tested my shallow voice. "I went to that very temple and prayed for their return. As a child, I wanted them to wipe away what my father had done to the kingdom, to the future of our realm."

My hands formed a soft glow of light, growing into a fluorescent white sphere.

"I realized too late that no god with the power to create such a world, who claimed benevolence, would watch such a horror unfold. That I might believe in the Gods that gave us our powers, that my own mother can no longer pray to, but I could not believe in gods so shameless."

The tiny ball of light in my palms lifted, and we watched as it began floating toward the ceiling.

"It was told in our legends that our kingdom was created in the image of the night sky. The Goddess Astraea painted with her stars as her lover Eos held the canvas for her, creating constellations in her wake. On the longest night of the year, we would honor their story by painting the night sky in lanterns of light, floating them into the dark just as Astraea once did."

The lantern I had formed continued to travel until it became a bleak speck compared to the dark that swarmed it.

"I never had the chance to take part in the celebration. Not that I can remember. He had banned it after my mother had died by his hand, and then the Veil of Seven closed. Years later, when he fought further to gain control, embers floated instead of lanterns on the memorial of her death. My father burned every last temple to the ground. He killed anyone left who had ever loved me."

The light above us faded into the dark.

Or could have ever loved me, I reminded myself. Love was expendable. It could be sacrificed, misused, or destroyed. What it could not be is forgotten. The pain of remembering was irreplaceable, even when memories were lost. I positioned myself to stand, but Keahi reached out. I stared down at his hand wrapping around mine.

Keahi's touch was sure, compared to when he had healed my arm. He got up first, one knee at a time. He hoisted me up after him, but he did not let go of me as he turned my palm over with his and created a small flame. His ember eyes illuminated into a brighter hue than the flame itself as he morphed the tiny flame into the shape of a phoenix.

The small fire bird flapped its wings as if it were truly alive, lifting out of Keahi's hand as it began gliding circles around us. It levitated until it began soaring away in the same path as the lantern I'd created, flying until it reached its end, vanishing into fallen ash.

Chapter Thirty

Sabine

I felt one with his shadow, dragging behind in the wake of his unspoken thoughts, as he opened the door to '*our*' room for me earlier.

The change in his disposition was swift. Keahi's eyes had glazed over on our nightly venture after exhausting my magic, a window of what I had seen earlier in the library. There was no indication he gave thought to the pressing stares, blooming curiosity of others, or anything else, for that matter. Our efforts to be seen together finally gained traction. We had achieved displaying some level of our union in the abandoned castle of Kallahni, and yet he hardly noticed.

Normally, Keahi vanished through shadowfire before I could even turn around to go back to his study. Tonight was different.

He hesitated, as he stepped through the door, giving no other explanation as he made a quick bow to me and walked straight back out.

I gaped, not knowing what to make of the space he left instead. I only made it halfway to my bed before I felt the faint brush of his magic. It floated across the castle floor at a haunting pace outside my room.

Back and forth. Back and forth.

His magic escaped into the only places it could, giving his presence away. The burnt coals in the hearth smoldered more vibrantly with each inhalation in my bedroom. Heat rushed to the side of my face in waves as I waited for the source of the disturbance to return.

I felt the moment he gripped his sorcery into place through the bond, right before a faint knock pressed up against the door. I had already opened it before he could knock a second time; his hand hovered midair.

Keahi placed his arms behind his back, straightening as he strode through. He looked as if he was preparing to give a speech to a room full of soldiers, power dripping off him in every way possible. My own power sought to intertwine with his.

There was only the telltale sign of his thumbs roaming in circles behind his back. Defeat, a loss before it could become undone as he prepared to speak.

I approached him wide, sensing that for whatever reason he had turned around tonight. . . it was not good.

"Is everything alright?" I asked, folding my arms in tightly.

After his distance toward me this past week, I grew anxious. *Was it his thoughts of me? Were the things he learned about me keeping him away? Had I pushed him away?* I no longer knew if I wanted to, no matter what form I had him in. This absence through the bond was unbearable.

The notch in his throat visibly slid underneath the fabric of his mask. "May I. . . speak with you on something?"

I felt myself take a step back, not knowing how to respond. I made my way over to the couch in front of the fire, sinking into the soft velvet.

He knew.

Elias had told him the truth of what he saw beneath the crystal. Why had I not thought of it before when he first started distancing himself, or believed we would keep it secret?

"I'm listening," I called out over my shoulder. "But take your mask off. . . please."

So, I can see you—gauge more than he often allowed me to.

I did not hear him approach me. Only the weight of the couch shifted as he took a seat at the opposite end. His hands hovered over the collar of his mask in my peripheral, lingering, as if he needed to wear it for whatever he had planned to discuss with me. He pulled it off reluctantly, as if it were his own skin.

"After we invade Celenia's camps, my father ordered us to arrive in the capital. He has placed us on a timeline; he grows impatient."

The ease I felt was almost crippling. The conversation was laced with concern, but not over what I had been expecting.

"We need to discuss how to move forward from here. There will be a lot more eyes on us at court. I know we did not—*I did not* start us out strong enough here, but that will change once we step foot on capital soil. Leaving room for questions about how we came to be will leave more for us to cover up in the end," he confessed. His jaw tensed as he forced himself to face me. "Will you be ready for that?"

"I will have to be. We both will," I said firmly. I would not give up on what had kept me alive, to avenge what had been destroyed, even if it made me just as bad as my father. I knew Keahi felt it just as much as I did, because I was not the only one who had losses in this war.

Distance edged his voice. "I hold myself differently in the capital compared to the Volkans. I behave as who I am supposed to be seen as. Where you fit into that mold. . . I do not know yet. Whatever my father's response may be, we cannot back down."

Our eyes clashed like the weight of a comet, unable to look away from the tension swirling in my magic. *Our magic.* I knew he could feel it too, possibly more than I could perceive within its invisible touch alone.

Keahi looked between us as if the sorcerer's bond spoke to him in only a language he could understand. I was still putting the pieces together, learning what it sought to bring into the light. I drew my legs further onto the couch as his voice dropped into a near hush. "Behind closed doors, Sabine. . . it will always be completely up to us. To you. I want you to know that."

I caught my breath in my throat. Thoughts raked through me, spinning in multiple directions; I did not know where he was headed.

His tone grew stronger, forcing me back in. "You may be bonded to me, but this. . . I know this is not what you may have wanted. I am sorry that you are burdened with it. I will do everything in my power to make this worth it for you. You have my word."

"Are you saying this to me because that is how you feel? Burdened? You may be bound to me, Keahi, but I do not want you to feel you are chained to me." Especially after what I had learned of him. My own burdens were heavy enough. "We are not married. . . even if we are pretending to be."

A torturous burn found me while waiting for his admission, and a hollow longing ached my soul, but it was not my own—it was his.

"I do not know how I feel, but I know it could never be that. . ." his voice grew distant. "I cannot always be your friend, nor do I really know how to be one for you. . . but I want to be. Someday at least, for you, no matter the state of our relationship. I do not want you to feel forced to be with me, any more than you probably already do. You, out of anyone, deserve better than that."

I felt the low and unexpected hum of disappointment. The bonding ceremony invoked a vow that only called for submission, falling as your powers drained, or heeding to the call of the magic binding us by fate. I did not hear or recognize at first, but it grew so loud I could not ignore it even if I resisted.

My soul connected with his. There were pieces of him I felt like were still missing. Each time I looked at him, my magic begged to discover what those pieces were, but I was my own renegade, still hidden in our half-truths and blatant lies. All we would have was each other in the end, under the secrecy of our imitative marriage.

Despite how his kingdom would feel about my ties to Novear, *to my father*, I trusted the part of Keahi that would burn with me in vengeance. I sensed his own quietly within him, but it was the only thing I fully knew how to trust about him.

The empty feeling it caused tunneled deeper, turning me into the hollow weapon I had once told myself I would not be. *It hurt too much, I felt too much.*

Keahi's genuine notion was filled with good intentions, but all I could summarize from it was the ache in knowing that even if I had him, I would always be alone. That we would be alone together in this, bonded in our path toward vengeance at whatever the cost.

"This is not one sided, Keahi." The words left my mouth quicker than I could think of stopping them. "Is there someone?"

It felt odd as it tumbled out, but I could not help but draw myself back to his conversation with Elias that I had overheard outside the training room doors when he spoke another's name.

I did not have feelings for Keahi, but I needed to know now in times of weakness. I needed to draw that line, if we ever needed it, in between the loneliness of our lies.

"You can tell me the truth."

He expected my question as much as I had when I said it, shifting his weight multiple times before leaning into the question.

"No," he said firmly, but did not elaborate.

Keahi sat so quietly, I thought he was going to dissipate into his own shadow. His bottom lip dropped before he slowly dragged his teeth across the inside of his lip. "Is there someone else. . . that you left?"

"No." I closed my eyes tightly. "Maybe once before, but not anymore."

That was the painful truth. I had taken others before, but I have never truly loved someone. I wanted to. So desperately that I would have crawled on my hands and knees just to reach for the opportunity. I had feared I would go through my entire existence, not knowing what it was like to be loved and feel it in return.

The molten line in my ring flared as I ran a light finger over the obsidian ridges. I would not be the one to stand in the way of that for anyone else. I looked over to him to find that the wick of his gaze had burned down to ebony in my silence.

"If there ever is anyone, you can tell me. . . I promise." I continued, "There will be many eyes on us at court. I want you to have what you want, just as much as I do in my own life. Being truthful with each other in this part of our lives; I feel it is important for our situation."

The fire beside us dimmed, and the room crisped with a sudden chill as he dipped his chin low with a slow nod. "If that is what you wish, then that is what you will have. I will not get in your way if you wish to be with another, despite our alliance."

I forcibly gave him a soft smile. "I need to ask you for one more thing."

He eyed me cautiously, but I did not retreat.

"I have said this before, but I have to be the one to kill my father when the time comes. It has to be me, and no one else," I said.

He took the change in conversation with stride.

A language we both could understand.

It was Keahi's turn to smile, but his was genuine. I hoped to never encounter whatever evil that made him produce such a sadistic grin. "I will count it as one of your 'wedding' presents."

"One of?" I raised a brow.

"Yes. For now."

"I don't even get a hint?" I chuckled.

His dark eyelashes fluttered from the weight of them as his back hit the upholstery. He looked past the point of exhaustion. Even the coloring of his face was backlit with the gray tones of someone who had not slept in days—weeks, maybe.

"I have never been one to give hints," he said with a lazy smile, pushing through the sleep threatening to take him.

I pulled on the edges of my braid, loosening the strands one by one. "That's too bad, but since you have told me of one of your 'wedding' presents, I would like to tell you one of mine."

The white strands of my hair fell loose. Keahi was staring at my hands as I worked through the fine knots leftover from the braid.

"And what would that be?" He slouched further, closing his eyes briefly.

"You are going to sleep in your bed again."

Keahi's eyes snapped open instantly up toward the ceiling. "I cannot—"

"Yes. You can. Do not refuse this."

He slowly inched himself up onto his elbows with a grimace. "Sabine, it's fine. Really."

"It's not. You look like death could take you any day now. You can barely keep your eyes open." He let out a repulsed sound, but I continued. "And before you say anything, everyone else has noticed too. We will have to stay in the same room eventually in the capital. You can't just not sleep, or sleep on that thing you call a bed in your study."

"Who is 'everyone'?"

I twisted in my seat. "Your brother. . . Kane. . ."

Keahi was not amused. "What did Drakkon say this time?"

I flattened my hair nervously against my side, a lump growing in my throat. "Nothing out of the ordinary, it would seem."

"*Right.*"

I started melting into the couch. "I might have. . . defended you. Maybe a little too well."

I could not stop the flush forming across my cheeks, but I had to tell him, eventually. Kane I could count on, but Drakkon did not know how to hold back. Neither did he ever show an ounce of subtlety. Keahi would find out sooner than later, since his brother did not know how to keep anything to himself.

"He might have said you seemed rather. . . grouchy for a newlywed. He might have also asked what I was doing to. . . help. . . with that." I thickly swallowed the tension building in my throat. Keahi looked like he had stopped breathing.

"That I possibly have helped. Once. In the past, on our wedding night, of course. I had to make it believable." I tried not to grimace. "I said that you wanted to wait until we reached Solstice. It felt more. . . traditional? I don't know. You know how your brother is."

I was practically rushing to finish my sentences now. The gray in his face was turning a deadly shade of pale, nowhere near the natural color of his skin tone.

"Please say something." I sank lower into the couch.

He blinked slowly. Twice. "You are just now telling me this?"

"Yes?"

His palm dragged down his face, pinching the bridge of his nose. "Drakkon, unless threatened with his life, spills more secrets than the barmaid did. The entire camp probably knows now." I slumped lower into the couch. "You could have left that last part out. Thanks to you, I will not be able to sit at a campfire for the next *several months*."

"How is this my fault? If you were not having one of your mood swings, we would not have been in this situation! You could have at least tried to act a *little* happier." I stood up, needing the distance. "I'm not that hard to look at."

At least I hoped. Keahi made no means to make a response as his mouth parted slightly and then closed again.

"There is nothing we can do about it now. Now get in bed and go to sleep. Also, maybe you can stop giving me that *exact* same look you are right now when other people are around." I painted on a smug smile. "At least now you can say that we share a bed at your little bitch fire, or whatever they are called."

His eyes danced between the end of my pointed finger and the bed, letting out a rough sigh as he muttered the words *bitch fire.* "Mouthy, for someone who does not even know what she agreed to. . . on more than one occasion." He kicked off his boots to plop down on the right side of the bed.

"What is that supposed to mean?"

The bed was enormous enough to fit four people comfortably, yet he still placed himself all the way along the edge. His hands were flat against his stomach as he laid on top of the covers and closed his eyes.

I stomped behind a cream paneled changing frame, throwing on an oversized sleeping gown. I threw my training clothes over the edge as I came out on the other side. "You are on *my* side, by the way."

Keahi did not respond. His breathing had already turned deep, peaceful even, despite how uncomfortable he looked.

I took a quilted blanket from one of the sitting chairs in the corner and floated it over the top of him. There was something that I had noted on him before as I leaned down to pull the cover over his chest; the overwhelming scent of cinnamon lingered on his breath. I inspected him out of the corner of my eye as I opened the drawer to the nightstand, noting the liquor bottle that had been refilled to the brim with whiskey the night prior was completely empty.

I pulled out the notebook Elias had given me and created a bed for myself on the couch. I held the ink in my hand, blots dripping on the page, not wanting to put the pen to paper. I had avoided it, working up the courage to find answers I may not want to know, as I wrote down a single question.

What would it take to destroy a sorcerer's bond?

For what felt like hours, I waited, flipping back and forth through the pages, thinking that a response would appear, but it stared blankly back.

Chapter Thirty-One

Sabine

My phantom shadow disappeared before the sun could rise. He had slipped into the night before I could wake, along with almost any evidence that he had ever been here at all. The warm blanket he had wrapped me within on the couch, and an emptiness that plucked away at my subconscious, said otherwise.

It was not his absence though, that caused me to beg for numbed mercy as jagged pain coursed through the remnants of what I had not wanted to accept. Each word was heavier than the last as I scanned the faded response to my question in the notebook. My fingernails scraped against the coarse surface of the page before I shredded it from its binding. I threw the notebook halfway across the floor as I slammed the door and left for the Volkan's training room.

My fingers glided across the cool glinted metal, the weapons clinking as I scanned for the balanced edge of a dual bladed staff. It had been the weapon I was most drawn to when I trained under my father's army, and although this one did not have a drop of magic to ignite my power, my blood sang with recognition as I grasped the center of the pole.

I charged across the floor, whirling the weapon through the air as I barreled toward my target. The tip of the blade struck against the ground as I used it to vault over the assault trainer and sunk its twin blade into the crown of my opponent. The staff was nearly twice my size, but I used my weight as a lever to shred its center wide open. I strangled the core of the staff's beam, dislodging it before I wreaked havoc upon its ripped chest.

'Again!' My father screamed in my ears.

I thrashed violently against its sternum, piercing it repeatedly to find a sense of release before it found me.

'Again!' His voice cracked like a whip.

My chest ached as my blade tore through the other side. I looked down upon the false image of myself.

I hated her.

Shredded upon the realm, torn from the inside out as I was supposed to be—the jealousy was paralyzing.

I was a liar.

I was poison.

I did not deserve to feel.

I did not deserve to want him.

My father's smile, incandescent with fallacies, lowered to my ear. The inhalation of his breath pricked my skin as I prepared for his command.

The back of my neck scorched with heat. *'You know what you have to do, Sabine.'*

My arms shook as I held the point of the blade above her chest—let mercy fall like drops of rain upon us.

"Again!" I screamed.

A dull vibration stopped the force of my attack. It was Kane who I found at the end. I jerked away from his grasp, but he was fixed in place. I gritted through my teeth, "Let. Go."

"I can't do that," he said evenly.

A sob broke free. "Today is not the day to find your redemption, Kane. *Let. go.*"

He gripped it tighter.

"*Please.*"

His eyes flared; warmth turned into searing heat as I winced away with burning palms. I twisted on my heels. "What is your problem?!"

"Do not do this," he said as he sent the staff clattering across the floor.

A hostile laugh worked its way through my ragged breaths. "Do what exactly?"

"Do not let them see you like this."

I sucked in my coursing rage. "What would it matter, Kane? I am nothing but a pawn in a game we all are playing."

He stepped forward. "Not all of us."

I matched him. "Then what are you choosing to hide?"

Kane's eyes dimmed from their Volkan flare, transforming into a vale of evergreen that could pierce the most crowded of souls. He lifted his chin, searching my face. "Come with me; you need to get out of here for a little while."

I felt the urge to retreat, but the light of my power swirled inside me. It urged me to go with him no matter where he planned to take me, because it trusted him.

"There's no way out of this damn city," I said finally as my shoulders fell.

He leaned into the back of his heels, placing both hands behind his back. "And how would you know that?"

"Because I've looked," I bit back.

I had looked for almost the entire first week after I had first agreed to the mission. There was no chance of an exit I could access without being met with a solid wall.

"It is almost disappointing you did not find one." Kane exhaled a small laugh as he fixed his eyes on me. "Let's hope you can keep up, then." He turned on his heels and broke out into a sprint without another word.

"Wait! Where are you going?" I called out, but he had already turned down the hallway. I cut off the enraged rumble in my chest as I drove my feet into the ground and rushed after him.

The air had gone thin by the time our strides synchronized, climbing in elevation as we ran through the castle in the mountain. We had maneuvered our way through a maze of dead ends until there was nowhere left to turn, but Kane did not slow down.

"Do not hesitate," he said between breaths as we neared a slab of solid rock.

Kane's hands crackled with a ball of flame as he blasted it into the center of the wall. It dispersed into a wide circle, unlocking a portal in the earth for us to escape the castle walls as we ran through a ring of fire.

The winter air assaulted my lungs.

A path unfurled at our footsteps as we hit the gravel, weaving over the abandoned castle of Kallahni. It carved against the mountain peaks, stretching farther than I could see as snow covered meadows and evergreen forests emerged in a muted haze through the fog we sprinted through.

Our unanimous goal was forward as we conquered the icy wind pushing against us. I wanted the pain to intensify until I could bury the thoughts in my head. I needed my legs to burn until I left my father's voice far behind, and by our third peak, I felt nothing but sweet exhaustion slamming into me.

Kane's pace retreated until he staggered to a stop, his hands over his knees as he attempted to catch his breath. I relented, only a few slowing paces further before I did the same.

He lifted the bottom of his shirt and used the hem to pat the sweat that had gathered underneath his mask. I averted my eyes as I saw the muscled lines of his warm brown skin, because it led me to wonder whether Keahi looked similar underneath his Volkan attire.

The wind cooled the side of my face, my cheeks burning beneath from the exertion. My white hair whipped through the crystalline flurries floating through the air from the last snow. I breathed deeply as the crisp air woke my lungs.

I wiped away the beads of sweat and condensation from my

forehead, eager for conversation. "How far did we run?"

He pressed himself up. "At least six miles. . . You are in a lot better shape than I would have ever given you credit for. No offense."

I held my tongue. "Your underestimation would be considered an insult to most, Kane."

"I will never underestimate you."

The rocks crunched beneath his feet as he made his way over to me and held out his hand. I stood on my own, brushing the sweat from my palms against my legs. The edge of the clearing we had stopped at was cold and distant. Sun rays fought to battle through the clouds while there was a stillness below, and shrill guilt overtook me.

All I saw was peace before the destruction my hands would bleed with. The blood of my predestined wrath flowed onto the land until it turned cold and painted the realm with its darkness.

Kane stepped quietly behind me. "Wherever you are going in your head, know that we have six miles back to run it into the ground. I know that this has not been easy for you. It will not be easy."

"Do not speak as if you know me," I said. Or as if he cared to, no matter what motive it held.

"I do not claim to know you, Sabine, but I know him." I could not stop myself as I glanced at Kane. "You may feel your pain, but do not let it destroy you," he said with a solemn look in his eye.

There was not much left of me, and the parts that were still alive wanted to hide. I spoke with the dying wind. "Did it destroy him?"

"Every day," Kane said without hesitation. Spoken as if it still did.

I faced the gray ridgeline, a canvas for the ever-changing sky behind him—freedom. A constant metamorphosis of color, untouchable, but even the sky was at the mercy of its limitations, redesigned but defined by elements outside its control.

"What if I do not want to feel at all?" I asked weakly. It was a coward's choice of a way out, but it was what I had always told myself I wanted. To feel was to change like the sky, knowing the past clouded control. Not all skies were beautiful.

He turned toward our trek back. "You will. At least one day, I hope."

"Kane." I hesitated to ask before we started our descent down the mountain.

"Yes, Lightbringer?" He said over his shoulder.

"What do you believe in? To give you hope?" Because I wanted to know. Some believed in the Gods, others found hope in fate, but I had found no reprieve in either, even if others did.

Kane was quiet for a long time. He waited until I stepped beside him to speak. "I believe we all can live to one day create our own existence. That is where my hope comes from."

"And have you created your existence?" I asked as we took our first steps.

"No," Kane said as we became lost within the rhythm of our footfalls. "But I'm trying. We all are."

We became lost in our path. I remained captive to my pain, and I used it to push myself forward. It was almost as if Kane felt it too, keeping up beside me every step of the way. When my physical body could no longer maintain my mind's punishment, the faded response swept its way back onto the page of the notebook I was trying to forget.

"What you seek to destroy requires a harmony only death can produce. A soul cannot survive the threads of unwoven fate without unraveling the consequences of time itself. As is the balance of life and magic, the chosen must endure what cannot be undone, for it is the fate that they bear for all."

Chapter Thirty-Two

Sabine

"There's my darling sister." Drakkon appeared, plating pieces of dried meat and bread onto his breakfast tray across from where I was sitting.

The kitchen was nowhere near the training room as I had originally thought, living within the same tunnel section as the library. Keahi had been even more reserved as of late, but I lingered outside his study when I could not sleep. The early morning trail of bread toasting in the furnace drifted through the bookshelves on the wall. I found myself here instead, not wanting to bother him if he found rest better than I did.

Extending from the kitchen was a little dining nook tucked off to the side. It was the only place inside the castle that grew life. A Tellurian sorcerer originally spelled the layout. His home had been in the castle before the Veil of Seven closed, and war had not stretched across the realm.

Green vines dotted with floral leaves hung from the ceiling, brightening the small cave without sunlight. The colors changed daily, but today was a soft yellow. Sprouts of lavender and vegetable bushels were planted within tiny coves carved into the walls.

Their field chef, Samuel, had somewhat forgiven me for my earlier altercations with Drakkon after I had complimented him on the lavender butter that he had made too much of, using the overgrown herb in his kitchen.

He continually set out an earthy, sweet concoction for me every morning, even though we were the only two people in the castle who enjoyed it. The Volkans had long grown tired of it, and Drakkon acted as if he could barely tolerate the smell of it.

After I kept using the lavender butter despite Drakkon's complaints, a fresh cup of coffee appeared on the table beside the butter dish as a reward. The beverage waited for me every morning in the spot I had claimed against the back wall, poured into a steaming red painted mug.

When I asked Samuel how he knew my favorite color was red, he smiled and said he didn't—my '*husband*' did, but I had never told Keahi my favorite color.

"Drakkon, we've met here almost every morning now, and for the love of all the Gods, do not call me your sister," I said. I took a second to inhale the bitter aroma of fresh grounds before Drakkon ruined my morning ritual with his antics.

"And every morning, you are just as divine." He batted his eyelashes, fingers laced to prop up his angled chin. His eyes widened when he took me in. "*Why are you wet?*"

My sweat drenched clothes squeaked as I shifted against the back of the chair. "Kane took me for a run this morning. You would have known if you had showed up."

Drakkon squinted at me. "He took you over Slayer's Ridge? What did you do to deserve that?"

I slowly picked up the knife in my hand. "Nothing out of the ordinary. Perhaps he just grew tired of me."

Drakkon leaned back. "Cruel—even for him. . . was it raining?"

"Drakkon." I placed my silverware back down.

"Yes?" He said far too innocently.

"Do you ever, just, not say what you are thinking?" I asked.

He waved around his breakfast on the tip of his fork. "That is the wrong question to ask, considering I may have many more thoughts that I do not say out loud. Though I tend to feel it is a reflex I gained after spending so much time with my brother; I believe Keahi spoke maybe two words his entire childhood."

"I'm not really sure he had room to talk," I mumbled. His gold-rimmed eyes flared, letting me know he heard my remark.

Drakkon shrugged. "He was a good listener, at least. . . but speaking of my dear brother, did he not tell you we had the day off?"

My fork screeched against the ceramic plate. "We leave tomorrow. . . I need more time."

"Novear, I was giving you a hard time the other day. We cannot afford to extend further—you are a force to be reckoned with. Seeking appraisals never seemed to be your way of reassurance and giving them is not really mine." It was as uncomfortable coming from him as it was for me to hear him say it.

"Is Keahi taking the day off?" I sat back.

He barked a laugh. "I would think you'd know him better by now. He had already called a meeting earlier this morning in preparation. I am not sure if we will even see him today."

I nodded as I pushed the dried berries to the perimeter of my plate. Not that I wanted to see him after reading what the notebook had written back, fading from its invisible ink. The strain I had been feeling on my magic had disappeared last night, knowing he was there. And though Keahi had fallen asleep so quickly, I was almost sure he felt the same.

The silence coming from across the table was jarring. It forced me to look back up, knowing that whatever it meant, it was not good.

Drakkon pinned me with a wicked grin plastered across his face. "We are going out tonight."

I had to cover my mouth to prevent my food from expelling. "And where could we possibly go, surrounded by rugged terrain for miles? It is not exactly a short walk to the next town."

"That is where you are wrong. There are miles of underground tunnels here; you just apparently have no sense of direction. I would know because I followed you between your breaks for a period," he said between bites. "And then I realized why would they send a spy who cannot even find the city. I am surprised Keahi has not taken you to Kallahni himself yet out of pity."

My following sigh was strained. He was lucky Kane had worked off what I had felt this morning. "There is an actual city here?"

"The outside is practically a decoy." He gave me a condescending wave. "The castle itself was abandoned almost a century ago when the capital moved further north from the border. It has been used as a military base ever since, and as for the city beneath it—it turned into a black market during the dark age. They have continued to reside there."

I stopped mid-bite. "What sorcerers willingly live underground year-round?"

"The worst kind." He grinned wider. "Solstice has never intervened in their affairs; it was a collective decision by our councils to let them go about their activities where it could be hidden under close military observation. Though we have found it has become a symbiotic relation, if you will."

"That is where you plan to take me?" I gaped.

He rolled his eyes. "The entire guard is going out for dinner tonight. After you humbled them into the ground these past two weeks, you owe it to them to show up tonight and be a part of it. It is one of our traditions."

I threatened him with the end of my fork. "As long as there is no drinking involved."

His wicked grin remained.

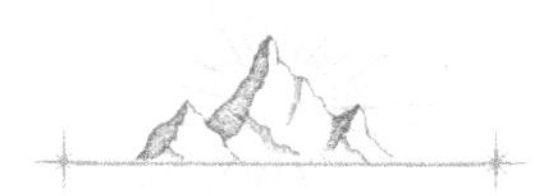

"I swear if you get me sick and I have to ride horseback tomorrow, I will find a way to burn you alive," I called out to Drakkon as Iahni handed me a dress from across the changing panel.

"Just bat your eyes a couple times at my brother," he said lazily back, "and I'm sure he'll do it for you if you ask."

I already felt nauseous, not only because I had vowed never to consume a drop of liquor again, but because I had convinced myself that I needed to do this.

My father had kept me under his thumb my entire life, traveling within his military ranks. They were not the best conversationalists, and admittedly, I would not win over the Solstice court with brute force when the time came.

I palmed the fabric between my fingers, holding it up to the skylight. It was a bright ruby gown with elongated sleeves, paired with a deep v-neckline that left little to the imagination. The back was less revealing, at least. I still could not bring myself to look at the emblem my father carved, and I did not know if I ever could.

I inched the bodice on until it hit the apex of my hips. The fabric clung to my frame as it slinked to the floor. My right thigh peeked through as I stepped out. "I think I ripped the dress?"

Drakkon issued a long, appreciative, but aggravating, whistle.

"It is meant to be there, Sabine," Iahni chuckled.

"My entire leg is supposed to be out?"

"The *entire* leg." Drakkon placed his hand underneath his chin, assessing me from head to toe as he circled me. "Yes. This will do." He spun on his heels with a curious look in his eyes toward Iahni. "Don't you think?"

"*What*—will do," I said.

Drakkon loosened the collar underneath his black cloak in the mirror, the interior embroidered with gold cross stitch patterns that no doubt matched his eyes on purpose. "Calm down, Novear. You already stick out like a sore thumb. It would not kill you to look the part." He turned back toward Iahni. "Besides, the slit was a nice touch."

"I thought so too." Iahni's grin turned more devious by the second.

"I'm seeing that I cannot trust the two of you, especially together." I breathed out.

"Why would you ever trust me at all?" He smirked. "But I will not leave you unarmed in case you decide you cannot tolerate me further."

Drakkon lifted a long wooden box he had stowed away when I had not been looking from underneath my pillow and placed it in my hands.

"I talked Elias into getting one made for you. It is the twin to Keahi's." Iahni spoke first, following the long pause of my confusion after I opened it.

"It was my idea," Drakkon interjected. "Elias does not particularly like many of my ideas, so I had to go through her." He grunted as Iahni elbowed him in his fourth rib.

I clutched the box tighter in my hands. "I . . . do not know what to say."

"You do not have to say anything. . . yet." Iahni smiled softly. "Let me help you, at least."

She retrieved the gift from my stunned hands and kneeled beside me. I stepped through the black leather harness as she slid it above my knee to fasten it.

Iahni held out the remaining object to me once she was done. "You get to do the honors," she said.

I faintly brushed my fingertips against the cool edge of the golden dagger before my palm greeted the twin serpent at the hilt of the blade. It was nearly identical to Keahi's, but along the edge of the hollow grind was a small foreign transcription. If Keahi had the same phrase etched into his silver dagger, I had not noticed.

"Thank you," I said weakly.

The blade produced chills along the skin on my thigh as I glided it into the harness. I had never received a gift before, and I did not know what to make of it.

Drakkon motioned toward the door. "Well, I am afraid I cannot travel through shadowfire like my brother, but at least we won't smell like ash."

"I heard that," Keahi called out as he opened the door. I straightened as he entered, suddenly feeling self-conscious at the thought of him seeing me like this. It was a prolonged torture when he did not look over toward me, transfixed by the stack of papers in his hands.

The room was still as he poured himself an amber drink, setting down his papers to lean against the furnace, and he was still pouring when he finally acknowledged my presence. The invisible line between us sharply pulled against my chest and drowned any residual confidence I had mustered. His gaze darted to the floor in front of me, roaming up my bare skin to settle on the twin golden dagger strapped to my outer thigh.

The silence broke when the liquid he had been pouring waterfalled over the rim of his glass and onto the floor. Keahi jumped up with a curse as it splashed onto the table where his papers had been.

Drakkon and Iahni snickered off to the side, but something rooted me in place. Pure horror struck through our bond on both sides. Keahi's eyes burned a line of detestation up my form, and I would have taken any other reaction when he reached my face.

I pulled at the edges of my sleeves, suppressing the urge to wipe the vibrant red that painted my lips. It had looked strange to me, but they both had insisted it was the final touch. Their eyes shined as they told me I looked beautiful, and it was such a rare word to me I wanted to hold on to it.

The upbringing I had did not allow me to grow used to the royal customs set by those before me. I had slept in the dirt of fields covered in blood and bile; as my father sought his next target, I wore only what I could carry. I had no mother or confidant who eased me into womanhood. This was the first time in my life that I had ever looked like this. When I not only saw, but felt, the way he looked at me. . . I crumbled on the inside.

"Smooth, brother." Drakkon leaned up against the doorframe as his eyes bounced suspiciously between us. I swiped away the hurt from my face, not wanting him to note anything further amiss. He pointed toward Keahi's glass as he made his way over and swiped it from the table. "Were you planning to drink this? Or were you just throwing it all away on the floor?"

Keahi barely registered him as he gaped at me. "Where are you going?"

Drakkon spoke up on my behalf, still inspecting the overfill of the drink he had stolen, and I had never been more grateful for his inability to be quiet than right now. "I am taking her to the cavern tonight. Or were you too busy not paying attention when we had that conversation?"

"The cavern? I thought you were—" Keahi said as he whipped toward Drakkon, but he was already a step ahead in whatever scheme that was played out before him.

"I did not exactly say *where*, now did I?" Drakkon waved his fresh drink around. "Besides, she has been training with us every day. She's coming with us."

Keahi turned toward me, but promptly pivoted away, his jaw flexing underneath the mask.

Drakkon sipped from the rim curiously. "If there are any objections, Keahi, we would all love to hear them. Preferably out loud this time."

Keahi's eyes followed Drakkon as he placed the glass in my hand, but his gaze did not reach my face. I swallowed the lump in my throat, immediately regretting agreeing to go out tonight. "I do not have to go if you need me to stay. It's just. . . I've never really been—" He turned away from me mid-sentence and stormed over to the soaked stack of papers he had abandoned on the table.

"What you do on your own time is your business," Keahi spoke like he was out of breath. "As I said before, I will not get in your way when it comes to your personal affairs, but do not be a hungover mess tomorrow, like you were last week. We cannot afford to have you slowing us down."

My face burned as Drakkon and Iahni flinched beside me. Their exit from the room was swift after they heard the glass in my hand form a crack near my thumb. I drowned the drink in my hand as I prowled over toward Keahi.

The magic from the sorcerer's bond roped between us grew slack. For once, it finally stepped out of my way, removing the ache from the combative pull at my chest to see what had grown when I let my guard down.

Caring benefited no one, I repeated to myself, *but you did it anyway*.

Keahi was still attempting to salvage the papers he had ruined when I placed the empty glass in the center of the table. His frantic hands paused as I bent over his shoulder to retrieve the bottle on the other side.

"Clearly," I whispered, finally feeling like my old self again, "you cared enough the other night. Do not think I ignored the way you looked at me."

I poured the drink to the rim, sliding the crystal glass directly in front of him.

"Can you feel it?" I lured him in. His dark eyelashes fluttered at the low and soft lull in my voice. "How *fucking* angry I am."

I trailed my fingertips lazily along the ridge of his shoulder, and heat sparked against my feathered touch. The sharp inhalation of his chest as I lowered my lips to his ear filled the greed of my temper.

"You are going to need to drink this, because I don't know what made you think I would ever allow you to talk to me like that," I darkly chuckled.

"I—I'm. . ." Keahi couldn't finish his sentence; he was breathing too hard.

"Have a good night, my shadow," I said as I removed myself from the room with the rest of the bottle at my side. "Start watching your back."

Chapter Thirty-Three

Keahi

I shredded the liquor-stained papers in half and flung them through the air, my hands restless to touch the comfort of cool glass after Sabine took the only bottle left with her.

Kane's door smacked the back wall as I stormed through without knocking and went straight to the back of his room, cursing as the oak stands of his dresser screeched against the stone floor as I shoved them aside.

"What are you doing?!" Kane yelled, tossing the book he was reading to the end of his bed. I searched for the hidden compartment I had carved several months back into his bedroom wall. Elias had monitored my drinking habits again, and it wasn't safe to keep everything stored in my room for him to find. The pain from the drainings after I visited the capital had lingered longer each time I went. I could not bring myself to let Elias continue to use his magic to heal me and exhaust himself.

Elias never wanted to give up on me. Even as the larger wounds stopped healing altogether over time. He did not give up when I had left the capital the last time in excruciating pain, traveling to the border of Novear. Not after he discovered I was still inflicted by the same wound I carried when I found Sabine, frozen in the same state from when he last worked on it.

'Tell her,' Elias warned me. But what good would it do? Sabine did not feel the sorcerer's bond the way I did. She did not know we were technically married. I was supposed to just tell her I lied, and then worse, admit I refused to regret it? Because I would have regretted it more if I had told the truth.

There were two paths I could have taken after I realized she lied about knowing the full extent of the sorcerer's bond when she accepted it. Neither were good options, but I chose the one where she didn't have to keep sacrificing herself to get what she wanted.

I had already sacrificed myself greatly for others. Though I had torn myself open with a willing blade to prove I was not a monster, I always became one. Not all sacrifices bled in return, and I would not watch her become one.

The tension in my shoulders relaxed when I stared at the tinted glass. It glinted back at me as I reached for it in between the cut out of the rock wall. There was a tremor in my hands as I used the underside of my cloak to remove the gray film at the top before I popped the lid off, hungry to drown myself until it made my eyes burn and my head spin. The drink numbed my pain the quickest, but it collected everything else in the process.

"Keahi, what the hell are you doing? This is *my* room. . . when did you even put that there?" Kane's dark brows pitched forward as he shifted upright on his bed. "I thought you quit months ago?"

My right heel tapped into the ground as I squeezed the neck of the bottle and lowered it to my side. *I had quit*, but quitting was never easy.

"Iahni and Drakkon caught me drinking some time ago, but I had some leverage to pull." I wiped the corners of my mouth with my sleeve to catch my breath. "Elias—he. . . has been suspicious lately, but he does not know I'm drinking."

Kane interlaced his fingers through his black hair, his mask still on his bedside table. "I thought the bond would have fixed you having to self-medicate. . . or at least I had hoped it would." His mouth opened and closed. "*Wait*—what leverage?"

"Do you remember when Elias couldn't find the mushrooms he uses for his tea? From the black market," I added.

"Yeah?" Kane shrugged. "So what? It tastes like dirt anyway." He threw the quilts off his bed, quickly attempting to get dressed even though I hadn't asked him to go anywhere.

"Well." I took another swig, the warmth finally catching up to my core. "Drakkon and Iahni *ate* them. Elias only uses a small dose in his tea, and they had the whole jar. They were so sick for days. I had to take care of them, so he wouldn't figure out who stole them. It was unbearable, listening to them yowl their heads off, believing they saw a dragon. Drakkon's been covering for me ever since."

"Has he now?" Kane released a long-suffering sigh as he finished rolling on the shirt he picked up from the floor. "They never learn, and neither do you, Keahi. You are not supposed to be drinking. It messes with you. . . you're not the same person when you are."

I paced from wall to wall, the space more cramped than I remembered as I took several sips in between. Kane cluttered his room with art supplies that were thrown into every corner, with mix matched paint tins and brushes stacked into discolored jars. It was hard for me to look at, which is exactly why I now remembered putting the last bottle in his room.

Kane was good at everything, but the only thing he was not good at was art. But none of us were brave enough to tell him after he explained it was '*therapeutic*' for him. He had even tried to get me to do it once, to help me when he first noticed how anxious I got before leaving on missions; he thought it might calm the pressure I felt on my shoulders to make sure everyone made it back to the base.

It ended rather quickly because Kane had gotten a little wild-eyed when we showed our finished project to Drakkon and Iahni. He had been painting for several years at that point, and they went on about how much they liked mine. I had never picked up a brush a day in my life, but they went unnaturally silent when he showed his.

If I wasn't completely mistaken, the same painting was hanging above his desk right now. The muted browns that were originally supposed to be green blurred together. I squinted at it, but I still couldn't make out what it was; drunk or sober. Kane coughed, diverting my attention back to him.

"Drinking helps. . . with the pain in my chest," I said finally. "You know that."

It normally helped when I looked at Sabine too, but it hadn't today. The mistakes I had made, the lies I told to protect her, and the past I was at the mercy of, would not let me have her, even if it was a possibility. *I was selfish.*

Slowly, I placed the empty glass on Kane's desk, unable to let go of the rim of the bottle like it was the only thing that could keep me standing.

I didn't even know how to try without hurting someone else. A strangled sensation climbed up my throat. I pulled at the edge of my mask, unable to breathe as a low choking sound left me.

Kane hesitated before he lightly placed his hand on my shoulder. Panic edged his voice. "What's wrong?"

Me, I thought before I took another drink and pressed my eyes closed, "and she was wearing red."

Kane turned his head. "I don't understand. . ."

"Sabine can't know." My breath trembled when I found the bottle was already empty in my hand. "She can't know that I want her so badly; I needed her to hate me right then. I thought I could do it. . . but I just can't. That fucking dress—"

"—But why would you want Sabine to hate you, Keahi? I know this is not something you are familiar with, but you have feelings for her, and I do not believe it's just from the sorcerer's bond."

The way he said the last part without question sent dread curling up my spine in a wave of heat. "She looked at me like I was something more—I felt like something more." I shook my head. "But then I finally felt the way she wanted me to look at her through the bond, when I have already looked at her like that a million times before."

"Isn't that a good thing?" Kane asked, confused. His hand was still on my shoulder, but he kept his distance.

"*No*, it's not," I rasped. The glass tipped over onto the desk as I pushed him out of the way. "I don't know how to be someone worth wanting. I wouldn't know the first thing about how to make her happy—I'm *not* happy."

My footsteps halted midway through the room when I realized what I had admitted out loud. They had known for a long time that I wasn't happy, but they hadn't always known, and then they felt guilty when I did not want them to.

Happiness was a moment, not a feeling for me. Because when I looked at my friends, I saw what made their faces light up. I knew what made them laugh. I felt myself smile when they were around; and then there was me. The times where I could not feel happy but enjoyed the moment despite it. Still, they saw me at my worst, and I saw how the happiest pieces of my life, my friends, were infected by my sadness.

Happiness didn't always feel worth it after that. My chest grew excruciatingly tight as Kane took a deep breath and slowly approached me.

"Keahi, that's not how this works," he said as soon as he stopped at my back. "You don't just get to push people away to spare your own feelings."

The sorcerer's bond had not spared me; it wrapped around my soul against my will. It was agony to know it consumed every part of me. I snapped back toward him, a prisoner inside my rib cage. "It is not my own feelings I'm trying to spare—*it's hers.*"

The only things I could give her with confidence, what I knew she deserved, was what I had already promised. Whatever I could say, or do right now, would hurt her less in the end. I shouldn't have tried to be anything else in her eyes.

Kane's eyes widened, taking a step back. "Oh Gods. What did you do??"

I turned away from him to clear my throat, working my clenched jaw.

"Keahi," Kane snapped. "What did you do?!"

I rolled my shoulders, biting the inside of my cheek. "I might have implied. . . that she can do whatever she wants. . . or whomever she wants, and I could not care less."

He blinked at me twice. "Keahi—"

I folded my arms tightly. "I might have also—"

"Fucking fates, I don't want to hear any more of it!" Kane held both palms out to me. I swayed on my heels. The room was blending into shades of gray, attempting to take me from the realm. My vision spotted as I anchored my shoulder to the nearest wall, but I missed. Kane caught my arm to steady me.

"I don't care what you think is good for you right now. I'm not letting you sabotage yourself. Tell me where they went. *Now*," he demanded.

A low rumble started in my chest and worked its way into a deranged laugh. "She went to the *cavern*, and she was already planning on going before I got there, so what does it matter?"

"*The cavern*?!" Kane cursed. I felt my legs grow limp, begging to melt into the floor and disappear for an eternity. "You're telling me you couldn't just be honest for two seconds and ask her not to go? Maybe tell her why you wouldn't want her to go and just see what she said in response? What if she was waiting for you to finally speak up?" he groaned.

It wasn't that simple, but when he put it that way—Kane jammed his finger into my chest. Right where he knew it hurt.

"I am so fed up with you right now, Keahi. I don't care that I am about to manipulate your stubborn ass under the influence," he said.

I lifted my chin. "Do your worst, Soldier."

He released a rough sigh. "Fine. Do you not remember the last mission we were on when Ossian told us how he slept with three women in the same night after he went to the cavern?"

I shrugged. "People can have casual. . . relations." *Not that I would know the first thing about it.* "That's not your place to judge."

"Normally I would agree." He narrowed his eyes at me. "But you are forgetting something."

My eyes rolled back. "And what is that, exactly?"

"Ossian told everyone, in great detail, about how they were worthless whores to him, and they *laughed*, almost every single one of them. He had no respect for them, despite his own involvement. Where do you think they all are right now?!" He threw his arms up. "Let's not forget that she's also *your wife*, the future queen of the Kingdom of Solstice!"

My jaw clenched so tightly I felt like it was going to crack open, because as far as she was concerned, she was the farthest thing from my wife in her mind—especially now.

"It was already agreed upon. If she wanted to be with someone, *she could*, and Sabine was the one who brought it up. If that is what she needs, I can deal with the political consequences later," I said roughly. "She has been through too much for me to stray her away from that."

"What if *you* are the one she wanted, and now she is with someone else right now at the cavern?" Kane argued.

"I could never be what she wants me to be, and it's best I let her realize that now," I said, folding in my arms.

"Really?" Kane piped up. "That's how you feel."

"*Yep.*"

He tipped his head to the side. "Then why is my chair on fire?"

I glanced out of the corner of my eyes and back to him. His desk chair was indeed firewood. With a snap of his fingers, it turned to smoke, clouding the room.

"I am waiting, Keahi."

I nodded. "You're right."

Kane clasped his hands together. "Finally. Come on, let's go—why are you going through my stuff?"

I slung his clothes out of the dresser—he desperately needed to reorganize at some point—until I found a dark brown cloak at the very bottom.

"What do you think?" I asked as I worked off my old cloak. "This looks different enough, right?"

"Um. . . it's brown?" he said.

"Good enough." I dimmed my eyes until they no longer glowed red from my magic, revealing their true color. "What about now? Do I look different?"

Kane looked up and down at me. "Your old cloak was fine. You just need to go down there and apol—"

"I'm not apologizing," I said flatly. "What's done is done."

"And how," Kane growled through his teeth, "is that going to fix anything if we go all the way down there?"

"I'm going to go in a disguise, and we will stay out of her way," I said. "You are right, others may not have good intentions for her; we will just have to kill them off one by one."

Kane placed his hand over his mouth, and then he started laughing—*really* laughing.

I ignored him. "After the act. Not before. If that's what she chooses. As for them. . . Well, they slept with my wife. I was going to murder them, regardless. Might as well do it quickly."

Their deaths would not be quick.

Kane was inching to the floor, one hand on his knee, the other wiping the corner of his eye. Once he caught his breath, he straightened to see me standing still. His expression gradually flattened the longer he stared. "You are serious right now?"

"Deadly."

"This isn't war, you idiot!" Kane's temple pulsed.

I finished tying off the end of my new cloak. "It might as well be."

Kane pivoted away, throwing back the covers of his bed. "I can't watch this. If that's what you intend to do, I'm going to bed."

"It might be important to know that Drakkon is the one who took her to the cavern," I said, slowly rocking back on my heels.

Kane's hands stilled on the sheets and kept his voice steady as he spoke to me over his shoulder. "Why would I care if Drakkon was at the cavern?"

I took a step closer, placing my hands behind my back. "I didn't ask if *you* cared."

Kane whipped around to face me, searching for me to say more when I wouldn't.

"I will never ask that. . . not unless you want me to. I care far too much about the both of you," I told him, and it was the truth.

He narrowed his eyes, an expression blooming over his face that I realized I had never seen from him before but had always known was there when the corner of his lip lifted. It stretched across his face until he replaced it with the mask we were sworn to wear.

Kane threw his hood over his head with an exasperated sigh. "*You* are a bad influence, Keahi Aldeer, and please keep your mouth shut for the remainder of the night. You are uncharacteristically chatty when you're drunk. It is unnerving."

I mirrored him, lifting my hood. "I am not quite sure what would give you that impression."

Kane's chuckle softened before mine did. His eyes hardened and my chest stung before he spoke, staring at the slit in my mask. "Your scar Keahi. . . it is a dead giveaway."

"We can stop by Elias's study," I said without missing a beat. "I think I remember seeing something that could work precisely next to the missing mushroom jar I was attempting to help him find."

Kane held the door open. "Was this before or after you knew Drakkon and Iahni ate them?"

"After. *Definitely*, after."

Chapter Thirty-Four

Sabine

I knew I had more than enough liquid courage when Drakkon and I used the cave's acoustics to our advantage. Our song, even with a drunken ear, was less than advantageous. We passed our stolen bottle without care as we descended into the underground city of Kallahni.

Keahi had pinned a rage-filled glance to my back as we left him alone earlier. It was not out of the ordinary for men who spent their nights out in the field to hold their drink, fighting the cold and dull ache of violence coating the blood on their hands, but Keahi held his differently. He acted like he needed it. Although I am sure he had more than enough to spare, I hoped to believe he suffered with the frugal ration of a glass I left him with.

Drakkon squinted through the bottle, shaking it. "Empty." His shoulders slumped. He flipped the bottle over his shoulder and spun around. "What happened to our music?" He pouted. I had stopped mid song, as the city emerged from the dark.

Bright rings of ember burned in circles around the dome, encapsulating the city as it guided my gaze to follow the ribbed vaults of iron intersecting into its natural mold. Pointed arches with ornate detailing climbed the frame of the cave walls and burrowed into the very core of the mountain, where a cider-colored glow cast upon river lined streets, supplied by a waterfall flowing into the city.

"This. . . is not a good idea," I said. My nerves had finally caught back up to me.

Drakkon took my hand in stride, our footsteps wavering against the stone. "This is, *most definitely*, the best idea I have ever had. You'll see." His speech slurred as he guided us through the streets below in a zig-zag formation. "The look on Keahi's face before we left was enough to make the night. It can only go up from here—well, down." He looked up, shielding his eyes with a wince as the light from the fires blinded him.

"You couldn't even see his face, Drakkon," I argued.

Or what I had felt.

"Nooo," he drawled. "This was different—*trust me.* I don't have to see him to know him."

"He could barely even look in my direction." I slowed, feeling the need to turn back.

A lazy look overtook his gold-rimmed eyes, his cheeks fully flushed. "When he looked at you, though, it said everything."

Keahi's look had said everything I was afraid of, and it had felt even worse finding I had wanted something different. I pulled at the end of my red sleeves, reaching down to twist the obsidian ring on my finger when Drakkon wasn't looking. The molten stripe along the crystal dimmed as I took it off before I could change my mind and placed it in the small gold clutch Iahni had given me to match the dagger.

We passed over the mouth of the sparkling reservoir, banking behind the small hidden entrance at the side of the waterfall. I did not know what I had been expecting of a cavern in the hub of Solstice's most defiled sorcerers, selling their trades on the black market, but it was not this.

Drakkon guided me out onto the floor laden with multiple hand-woven rugs and soft white furs. It was not the most sanitary choice for a crowded bar, where customers would undoubtedly spill their drinks, but it made the room feel warm and relaxed.

A deep maroon velvet lined the walls, creating an intimate feel as the waterfall rushed over an exposed side wall. The soft moving light from the ember city glowing beyond the waterfall illuminated the dim cave. Hazelnut couches surrounded the fire pits placed off to the side of the bar. Not one seat was empty as several couples sat around enjoying themselves.

My head recoiled—*enjoying themselves a lot.* An undeniable flush crept into my cheeks as I twisted away. Drakkon caught me in his arms and shifted us to the left as one couple slammed into the wall behind us. Their tongues clashed as their greedy hands roamed without limitation.

"Drakkon," I half whispered as I grabbed onto his sleeve. He reached for my hand, locking me in before heading straight for the bar without a remark. *Was it normal for the people of Solstice to have sex at their dinner locations?*

I trained my eyes on the glass topped wooden plank that served as a bar top, cupping the brew Drakkon had slipped into my palms, but I could not resist turning to the next couple in the room's corner who were moaning into each other's mouths.

The hands of her lover tousled the woman's auburn hair, spreading his fingers into her crown as she straddled him. She tugged at the back of his head, holding him captive by her essence. A sultry smile curled her dark red lips as she played with the necklace she wore, lifting it to her mouth as she bit the cork off the tiny glass charm.

I had thought her shoulders were bare because of the dress she was wearing, but as she lifted herself up over top of him, her breasts were on full display. Her hand slid to the angle of his jawline, lifting the bottom of the Volkan's mask by her thumb as she sprinkled a white powder onto his tongue. My eyes widened when she leaned down to lick her share before it dissolved, grinding her hips as she did.

My hand was already on the dagger at my thigh as I turned to find him watching my realization unfold with his wicked grin. "You've got to be fucking with me," I whispered harshly, pulling him back up by the collar of his shirt. "This is not a bar!"

He patted me on the shoulder. "Where else would a group of soldiers be the night before they leave?"

My anger turned into a flightless panic. Amends of this betrayal from Drakkon could wait. This was a compromising position I could not afford to be in, and the fact Keahi had not stopped me from going made my blood boil beneath my skin. This carried the potential to derail our plans of a convincing marriage if rumors of me being unfaithful spread to the capital. I was already on the line for being from an enemy kingdom, and the consequences of this night would be fatal if someone saw me.

"Not so fearless now, are you, Novear?" he teased, followed by another rumble of deep laughter. "I know your customs are a little different from ours. Many of our women who take part in battle still come to the brothels. Take a deep breath, will you?"

"And I'm sure that those women are not married to the crowned Prince of Solstice!" I hissed through my teeth with one hand up to my face.

"Calm down," he said, halfway offended. "They are all too drugged to recognize you; I am sure over half the kingdom does not even know what you look like yet. The fun hasn't even started."

It would be *fun* to stab the crowned Prince's brother in public, but that wasn't an option. "I cannot be here, Drakkon!"

"Awe, is the Princess scared of the royal ramifications? It's nothing I promise. Try being the bastard some time." He chuckled darkly. "Plus, you haven't met my sister yet. I have heard she frequents more often than I do when she's here. Just be glad you are not her type whenever you do."

My mouth hinged open. He hooked one finger underneath my chin and closed it.

A tap landed on Drakkon's shoulder as a woman in a sheer teal robe engaged his attention. Her sleek, chestnut brown hair covered the peaks of her breasts and stopped just above her hips.

"Where have you been, Drakkon?" She said in a low voice. "You know we cannot start the game without you."

"Is everything set up for me?" He leaned back, breathing her in.

Drakkon played with the ties of her robe as she prowled around his shoulder, her painted fingertips playing with the collar of his shirt. "Just how you like it. . . master," she purred.

I was going to be sick.

"Just have fun, Novear," he said as he ran his hands down her hips and abandoned me at the bar. Their mouths were a moment from connecting as they dipped into a private room near the stairwell.

I have to get out of here.

I jumped down from the bar, ready to make my escape, when Kane walked in.

The leg of my seat groaned as I sprung back on top of it. I

flailed my hair to cover my face and lifted the glass to my mouth as I leaned down. This was already mortifying enough, and Kane was the last person I expected to see here.

That was until I straightened from the prickling sensation gliding down the scars of my back. Kane and the guard that had entered with him headed toward the farthest corner directly across from my position.

Keahi did not know that I could feel him, that the bond was no longer one way, because I had lied to him. Our gazes clashed with magnetized force as he sunk down into the couch facing the bar and bolted his attention away. He had done his part; the complexion surrounding his left eye was slightly darker to cover the scar through his mask. His eyes had turned into pools of shadows, swarming around his iris to change the fire that raged underneath him.

My chest ached as my gaze dropped to his hands—he had forgotten to find a solution to the gloves. Keahi was the only one who wore them.

A sick sensation drank straight from the source of my vile volition at the thought of why he would come here disguised. Why he had lashed out when he found out I was coming to a brothel house. Keahi had known I was going to be here, and he was upset because he had not wanted me to see him with someone else.

My face burned with unwanted betrayal.

I had no right to require his honesty after I asked it of him. There were many things he did not know about me. If there was one thing that I needed from him, though, it was his honesty in this. Because I was not prepared to face this part of my new life with him that I had been trying to ignore. The one where I had to watch him be with others in secret because of our false marriage. I realized I had drawn the line in the sand too late as I looked at him now.

I slid to the edge of my seat, a dull ache in my chest, with no ounce of rational thought to stop me as I headed straight toward them. Keahi may have not aimed to make me suffer, but I was going to start with his friend, who helped him first.

"Kane," I said his name in a sultry voice. "I did not expect to see you here. Is Keahi not making you be his errand boy tonight?"

The "guard" with Kane choked on his drink, and I could feel his heart race through the bond.

"I get the night off every once in a while," Kane responded casually. *I'm sure he did*, but not tonight, not anymore if I had anything to do with it.

"I see . . ." I sauntered down onto the couch beside Kane until our thighs touched. The slit in my dress dangerously rose to the top of my hip bone as I crossed my exposed leg. The golden dagger on full display was a warning to the man I was bonded to sitting across from us. "Do you frequent here often on your nights off?"

The blush Kane was wearing crept all the way up and over his mask as I softly ran the tips of my fingers over his shoulder. "Not always." He coughed as he attempted to shift further into the arm of the leather couch.

There was a small amount of guilt that pricked the back of my mind as I saw the fear in Kane's eyes when he looked to his accomplice for help, but my hunger for revenge was stronger than any guilt I would have later.

I tipped my head over in *his* direction. "And who might this be?"

Kane cleared his throat, fidgeting in his seat. "This is my brother. . . Erik. He's visiting."

For his second, he was not even close to a decent liar. Kane may not have underestimated me, but I had overestimated him.

"Interesting. You never told me you had a brother," I said flatly. "I must have miscounted when you told me there were only thirteen of you, too. . . *hmm*." I shrugged my shoulders. Keahi was doing his best to ignore me, but the tension rolling off him was like a match waiting for the first strike. I watched him follow my dancing fingers over Kane's chest. I licked my lips. "It is nice to meet you. . . *Erik*."

I shifted my attention back to Kane. "I'm sure even you know what I am about to confess to you now." A sensual laugh escaped me. My vision blurred as I leaned forward. "But I know you two can keep my secret. If it is even a secret by now."

Kane tried to speak up, but I pressed my fingers firmly into the side of his neck to suppress his windpipe. "*Shhh*. I'm sure he would think you were doing him a favor. You don't have to be shy. I know why you're here."

"Doing *who* a favor?" The depth of Keahi's voice was on the fatal line of resistance, his concern radiating when he was supposed to be pretending that he and I were strangers.

"My husband," I sighed. I tracked his gaze as I picked up the gold clutch I had laid beside my thigh, opening it up to pick out the ceremonial ring I had taken off. I slowly dipped my chin, closing one eye as I held it out for him to see, and looked through the silver band at him on the other side.

"What about him?" My bonded said so quietly, so still, I could barely hear him over the cadence of the surrounding brothel.

I lowered the ring and frowned. "He stopped wanting me the moment we said our vows. In more ways than one, if you can imagine."

"No, I can't." Keahi's breath turned shallow. His broad shoulders slumped forward in his brown cloak onto his knees.

"Can you believe it? He doesn't even care that I'm here." My voice turned bitter. "I believe his exact words were, 'what you do on your own time is not my business.' I took that enough as a hint."

Kane was actually sinking into the upholstery in an attempt to pry away from me as I leaned back into him, my grin full of malice. *Erik* took a deep breath through his nose, the fine tremor of his control slipping.

"Is that why you are here?" Keahi's words were brittle, uncertain as his gloves flexed on his lap, and I stilled.

That's when I saw it. The matching ring to my own, still on his finger, when he should have thought to take it off if he planned to be here.

He always wore it, just as I did, even though the fabric of his gloves bunched around the ring. It might have looked odd on anyone else, but not him. Keahi had always worn it proudly, in the same way he did now.

My plan of attack fully derailed as I heard his voice, stripped bare by the core of his magic, reaching out for me to hear him through the bond.

'Please, say no.'

'Please.'

My palm burned. The crystal was waiting in my hand to be acknowledged as it broke down the walls he had built for me. Our minds unlocked with requited heartache, dripped in the mitigation of this heavy stillness on both sides. I felt everything all at once, and I wanted it all. *Just for tonight.* I leaned away from Kane as I slowly slid the obsidian ring back on my third finger and looked back up toward Keahi.

"It depends," I said in a low voice, "on what you are offering?"

I knew my match had finally struck a flame when all the color drained from what I could see of my bonded behind his mask. A temporary vice for what was to come.

Kane urgently jolted from his seat. "*Erik*, I think it's time we—" I pressed a firm hand onto Kane's shoulder and forced him back into his seat.

I leaned down into his ear. "No need to panic, Kane. It'll be our secret for tonight." My smile was malicious for a different reason now. "I'll take care of him."

Kane whispered a desperate plea as I stood from the couch and fisted my hands into 'Erik's' cloak. I dragged Keahi up the stairs I had spotted on my way in and shut the door behind me before I could change my mind.

Chapter Thirty-Five

Sabine

A heady scent of spiced berry filled the private brothel room with a pulsatile sensation of lustful magic on my skin. The draw of incense blazed in tantalizing circles across my core, coiling through the air in wisps of smoke. It veiled us in silence within the cramped entrance way we confined ourselves in.

Resentment sliced through me, bitterness coursing within my veins as I imagined Keahi here in the arms of anyone but me. My intent was to shred him from the inside out with my words and expose that I knew it was him all along. To finally reveal I had lied to him when he asked me if I could feel him through the bond; including the way he felt right now.

Keahi had been armed with his own omission before we stepped foot into this room. What we were to each other, the lines we had created in the truce of this feigned marriage—*ceased fire*, combated by a side of him I was unfamiliar with. Weaponized with the dark smolder of his gaze that trailed my body with decadent heat. The man who stood before me knew what he wanted, and it was a fatal discovery on my part for us to learn he was not alone. My body lost all ambition to keep up my mind's defenses.

I had been with women and men alike, but it had been only a means of release. I felt only what it gave me in the moment, a mutual distraction, but this would be nothing of the sort. There was no numbness to keep me disoriented as his soft leather armor grazed against the silken fabric of my red dress. The tension crackled through the air as he flexed the stiff material of his gloves, his hands dutifully restrained at his sides when our gazes did little to hide our desires.

An altar meant for the kind of sin that felt like worship was lit with scarlet candles that surrounded the bed in the back of the room. The glow outlined our silhouettes as our breaths turned heavy in the warm glow surrounding us, and then my mouth went dry. There was no mercy to be found for our thoughts when the moans of another couple's arousal passed through the paper-thin walls of the brothel.

We spiraled into a storm of chaos, his magic simmering against my skin until all I felt was him, everywhere. Together we were intoxicated by the bonfire full of mystic and misery between us through the bond. Panic synced with our desire, as I knew he felt it too, but he was the first to break through.

"Wait," he said, his voice rough but fragile. "I need to tell you something."

My eyes fluttered as I felt his arousal firmly pressed against my hip through the thin material of my dress, memorizing the feel of him. The scent of the spiced incense fused with the familiar taste of cinnamon I wanted to explore on his tongue. I bottled it up for a time when I knew I could not touch him, but instead think of him.

In the confines of his fantasies, he craved not only my body, but my soul. He had been keeping these thoughts to himself, but I selfishly wanted them. Needed them. A sweet torment I intended to repay him for through the bond when I made use of them. Keahi's entire body vibrated with an insatiable need as he tilted his head back. A low, tortured moan escaped him as I pressed him into the wall.

"What is it you need to tell me that I do not already know, *my shadow*?" I teased in a low voice. Keahi stiffened as I drew my fingers over the seam of his mask. I hooked a single finger underneath, lifting the dark fabric slowly and deliberately without removing it entirely. I admired the sharp edge of his jawline before tracing the outline of his lips with mine, imagining the feeling of them far lower.

The succeeding growl of warning that came from him confirmed he knew the direction of my thoughts just as much as I did his. I pressed my body closer, rocking my hips against him, gliding my fingers over the seam of his waistband. His eyes rolled back, his head following the motion as he rested against the wall.

"If I told you I did not want to know, Keahi, would you believe me?" I whispered across the chill I created on his skin. "I do not want to know what you have to say, and I am begging you not to. I just want to feel you."

Keahi's eyes lowered to mine in their true form, hunger derived into a molten heat I could feel pooling between my thighs. I stilled against him, ceasing the urge to move as I waited for his response. The lack of friction peeled back the final layer of his and my sanity.

"Do you promise me?" he said in a gruff quiet. His gloved hands trembled as he tucked the fallen strands in front of my face, fingertips brushing across my cheeks and behind my ears. The steadfast beat of his heart against me roared in time with my own.

I shook my head, my lips parted with a murmur of truth. "I do not make promises, but you can be my exception. . . for now." Ember eyes searched mine for mutual damnation as he slammed his mouth into mine.

My tongue danced along his lower lip with a permission he lost himself in, as Keahi claimed my mouth fully. In one fluid motion, he splayed his hand up the nape of my neck with a fierce desperation, raking through the strands of my hair and tugging me closer. He roamed the contours of my body with a recklessness that bordered the line of helplessness, because Keahi touched me as if he would never get another chance.

I wrapped my legs around him as the veil of his control incinerated. He thrusted me against him, holding me up by my thighs as he slammed us into the wall as if time would take me away from him. He moaned into my mouth as my dress rose above my hips, leaving nothing to stop us in between, because I was bare beneath this dress.

"*Gods*," was the final prayer that left his lips as he realized it, too.

Our lips never parted as he carried me across the room and lowered me onto the mattress, my hands gripping the bed rail behind us. His thumbs teased the peaks of my breasts, drawing a circle over them before his hands lowered to the tops of my hips with a possession that said '*mine*.' I moaned into his mouth as he cursed on my lips, "*You are so fucking beautiful*."

At his words, I froze, lined up over top of him.

It hit me with instant regret as I interpreted the devotion in his voice. The way he looked up at me, like he trusted me. He told me I was beautiful. Looked at me as if this was unrequited. The problem being, it was not.

The vulnerability severed the moment, and I recoiled from his gaze. There was selfishness, and then there was shamelessness. A new fear bloomed within me, worse than the thought of him not being mine, because I could not promise him safety within my heart, even though I wanted to. We were both a lie, and I was the one he wanted to believe in.

His eyes clouded in lustful confusion as I pulled at the edge of his mask further, leaning down to savor the way my lips molded to his. A baneful distraction as I uncovered his face to me.

Damn the Gods that did not care.

It did nothing but make me want him more.

"We can never do this again." I shook my head. I did not want the guilt of tearing him apart more than once, because it was already enough to wound us both.

Keahi's lower lip quivered against the sharp exhale of his breath. "Did I do something wrong?"

Anguish tore open my chest as my face hardened, digging my nails into his mask to conceal the war in my heart. The pain radiating through the sorcerer's bond led him to search me for physical injury, frantically scanning me from head to toe.

"Did I hurt you?" he rasped.

The lump in my throat thickened because nothing could be more harmful than the truth. "I'm not hurt. You just are not what I expected, Keahi. This can never happen again."

He made no attempt to hold me back as I headed toward the door. Keahi's hands wrung together in his lap as he said, "Sabine, I know I might not be what you want, but I could try if you wanted me to. I swear if you just give me a chance—"

"No. I do not want you to try again." I threw the mask at his feet as I watched the pain of my words strike him down. A coward. I was a *coward.* "Once was enough."

The door was not all the way shut as I heard him speak across the room.

"I'm sorry."

Chapter Thirty-Six

Sabine

Kane had been blocking the entrance leading up to the stairs when I fell directly into his arms. His forest eyes flared underneath the veil of magic that coursed through the Volkans as soon as he saw my face.

"*Please*. I know your loyalty lies with him, but I am *begging you* to take me anywhere but here," I pleaded with him. The magic-filled lust was rapidly depleting in my system from the bond.

Kane made a quick scan of the room, and any gaze that met his was quickly averted. He doubled back with heavy eyes, looking for someone within the crowded brothel he could not find. His focus snapped back to me as a single tear landed on his hand that held me.

That was all it took.

He whisked me away through the smokey air until we landed within my rooms. Kane gripped me by the shoulders until I was eye level with him, shaking me to grab my attention as I became inconsolable.

"Sabine, *what happened?*"

I went to answer, but it was too late.

Words turned into a fountain of regret as I vomited at his feet, the hangover already crushing my skull with its fists. Kane grabbed a bucket and kneeled behind me, drawing the fallen strands of my white hair away from my face as I lurched until there was no poison left in me. I peered up at him through damp lashes, my mouth hinged open, feeling woozy and lightheaded. "Don't ever—let me do this again."

My stomach returned to its vicious cycle. Sweat dripped from every pore as it rejected the abuse that I put it through.

There was a faint crack of the door, and despite the bodily urge to continue, I willed myself frozen in place until my body shook with its punishment.

No words had been said, but Kane must have given a look full of warning from behind me as I felt him shake his head. I knew who had been on the other side, but I was not ready to face the sobering effects that would linger from my actions.

Thoughts I had whispered to myself and believed to be untrue flooded through me. I was desperate for a feeling I had never been given freely. No one had ever chosen to love me on their own, and those that did were no longer here. Love was a want out of reach, but it was still a want, and Keahi felt like something I needed.

How weak you truly are, Sabine, to finally admit it.

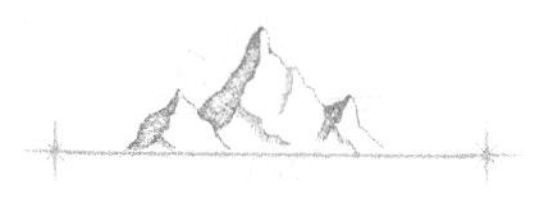

The few hours of sleep my body allowed after Kane woke me up, was not enough. Yesterday had turned into a nightmare that would not stop. I slung my pack across my shoulder. It was unnerving to watch Kane check on me out of the corner of his eye, hovering beside me as we walked toward our exit point.

"Can you stop looking at me like that, *please*? You are not making me feel any better about last night," I said. He looked away briefly and returned with a worried side glance, like he couldn't help himself. "*Kane*. I will not tell anyone what happened."

He paused, his boots churning into the dirt as sounds of commands and beating hooves echoed near the edge of the tunnel. "That's not what I'm worried about," he sighed.

"Then what is it? Because I can't take the looks you are giving me for the entire trip," I said, weaker than I wanted to. *It was killing me already.*

He lifted his chin. "I'm worried about *you*." Kane said it like he meant it. As if I was just as much of a friend to him as Keahi, and I couldn't take this from him right now.

"I'm. . . fine," I said, pulling at the edges of my sleeves as a stiff wind swept through the tunnel.

Kane did not look reassured as he watched me start toward our exit, but he stopped me. "How did you know it was him?"

I looked at him out of the corner of my eyes. "Did you actually believe I would not recognize my own husband?" *Or feel him through the bond.*

I could not see Kane's expression, but I became increasingly aware of the footsteps coming up behind us when he stiffened.

Drakkon's voice called out, "How was everyone's night? I couldn't find you when I went to leave." He hoisted his pack up onto his shoulder.

Kane ignored his greeting, a questioning expression under the shadow of his mask. "I will find you later, Sabine."

Every ounce of feeling drained from him as he turned to Drakkon. "*You*—You have done enough the past twenty-four hours, and I need to prepare the rest of the crew. If you're coming with us, stay out of trouble, because I'm done apologizing for you. *Give your brother a break*—he can't take on anymore, do not make him."

There was a fierceness about Drakkon. It did not matter whether it was in battle, love, or laughter, he made it known. When his stare settled between Kane's shoulder blades as he walked away, that fierceness deflated. Drakkon's wicked smile, I appreciated, vanished.

"How long will we be traveling today?" I asked to break up the unusual tension.

"Past nightfall," Drakkon said gruffly. He shook his head. "We have run into a predicament with the Celenia camp that we have been monitoring. I'm afraid we cannot afford to stop for long."

"What have you found?"

His mouth thinned, pausing his train of thought for the first time since I had met him. "I'm not supposed to tell you," Drakkon said finally.

My interest sparked. Keahi had given me the layout of our plans during the two weeks we had been training, but they strictly kept any of the inner details between him and Kane. I was only privy to my part of the plan, to create a mirage within the enemy camp so the Volkans could search undetected. There would be no room for error. Their lives and my plans depended on it. If Celenia fully aligned with my father, we were doomed. All of us.

"Does that mean you aren't going to?"

Drakkon's eyes hardened. "I know what I had said to you when I first met you, but this mission is personal."

"I promise not to say anything," I said, knowing I could not be trusted.

The crew was getting ready for our departure, out of earshot, as he said, "Your father's General was seen entering their camps last night."

I kept my voice even. "Are you sure?"

"Yes." He swallowed. "He was carrying the staff of malachite, in a full set of black armor. Your General is hard to miss among Novear's gold and white crests."

"I know the General. . . unfortunately well," I said, deflecting the memories as they swarmed into my mind.

Drakkon's eyes softened but did not implore me to explain. "He was the one who gave Keahi his scar. I have seen no one like him on the battlefield. If they catch us—Celenia will outnumber our crew and with him in their arsenal, they would slaughter us."

I pinned my eyes to the ground. "I will not let you down. I promise."

He hesitated, reaching a hand up to grip the side of his neck. "Keahi rarely ever speaks of that night. He has not had a simple life. I am sure you have seen the rest of them. He was not the same after, but I am glad he has someone like you, Sabine. You do not fear him, and that brings more healing to him than you realize."

His warm smile made my stomach drop. "Come, I had some guards prepare a horse for you."

The horses bucked with anticipation as the Volkans hitched their bridles. I ran my gaze through the Volkans, scanning for Keahi, my nerves wringing with mortified anticipation.

Drakkon led me to a midnight mare, speckled with white constellations on the bridge of her nose, as she nudged her way into the palm of his hand. "This is Meira; she is one of my favorites."

"Hello, Meira," I said. Her eyes met mine with a sense of knowing as I fastened my pack to the back of her saddle. Her temperament calmed me as I signaled her to line up with the rest of the horses to face the massive stone wall, and then smoke curled out of the darkness into the shape of a man—*Keahi.*

This was the man that had come for me in the woods. The legendary warrior that turned campfire stories into nightmares across the realm. He was someone to be feared, belted in black leather, lined with plated weaponry, and a series of silver dipped knives strapped to his outer thighs. He carried himself like a god prepared for rapture. If only they could see their Serpent in the Shadows in the light, unmasked. They would be down on their knees in terror, instead of waiting for him to force it upon them.

A piercing grind screeched through the air as light poured into the cave. The rock wall split in two at his silent command, his fist raised in the air.

An icy chill gusted through the opening, his cape billowing behind him as a solitary onyx-colored stallion approached him through the row of horses.

He grabbed hold of the reins, mounting the horse to turn toward us as he looked down the row of Volkans, and stopped at Drakkon. It wrecked me with shame when he could not be bothered to find me—I deserved it.

We mounted our horses as they trampled eagerly in place, and he directed his own reins toward the door. The howling wind was a reminder that the elements were to be unrelenting.

The stallion's front legs lifted off the ground with sheer power and bolted into the thick of winter's peak, and we began our descent out of the mountains into the Valley of Arcane.

Chapter Thirty-Seven

Drakkon should not have trusted me.

It was his weakness; the way he held his emotions on his sleeve, said what he felt, and I envied him for it. It was a freedom I had been so desperate to maintain for myself, but what I did not realize was how even my own thoughts could learn to disguise themselves.

My truths, the ones I miserably held onto, were corroded by the lies I built them on. My father had taken everything from me, even the core of who I was supposed to be. I wanted to mourn her, just like I had mourned my mother. I wanted to believe there was good in her, but what good was there to return to if I did not remember who I had been? Deprivation of the soul was its own form of poison, the only source I had to drink from, and it starved me anyway. So, I became what they had caged me for, but they never expected me to get out.

If the General of Novear was within Celenia's camps, as Drakkon had naively disclosed, I would not lose my chance to kill him. The light casting we had been preparing for weeks, to safely maneuver the Volkan warriors in and out of the camps, would be dropped the moment I found him. The mission tarnished, and my short-lived alliance with my bonded destroyed as I exposed them. Keahi would never be safe with me because revenge would always be my first choice.

Snow crunched beneath my boots as I pulled Meira toward the fires. Her warmth pressed into my side, severing the restlessness of my thoughts for what was to come, and the premature guilt I vowed to ignore. I would not rest easy tonight knowing what I had to do. Celenia would see it as an act of war from Solstice, but we had already been in the making of war for far too long to acknowledge the inevitable.

They made their choice when entertaining the idea of aligning with Novear. I would not surrender, even if it meant I was going to destroy the things I loved along the way.

It was well past midnight. The Volkan's magic warmed the camp as they set up their tents. I reached for my own, searching for the skeleton of my shelter. My shoulder dipped further into the pack as I shuffled through the pit of my supplies, and when I did not find it in my blind search, I dumped the contents onto the ground.

My gaze slowly traveled upwards to Meira as panic swarmed inside my chest. She huffed through her snout, batting the eye that I could see.

"You think this is funny, then?" I whispered to her, nearly out of breath as a small puff froze in the air in front of me.

I spread my hands out onto the ground, checking once more. Meira's head bobbed up and down next to me, but a shiny red apple quickly drew away her attention. Keahi's horse Aires made his way over, cradling it between his teeth to share. Meira's soft nose nudged the side of my face before she trotted over to him.

Even my own horse abandoned me.

"One, two. . ." I scanned the layout of the campground, compiling the grievous error in my head. "Thirteen, fourteen. . . fourteen."

Keahi ducked out of the tent he had set in the center of our camp to disappear into the edge of the woods. The notch in my throat scraped against my airway. His tent did not differ from the other single tents it was surrounded by.

I had not considered what an oddity it would have been for me to stay in my own tent without my husband. Which was precisely why Iahni had not thought to pack a separate one for me. Winter had taken its full hold of the realm, and I either had to sleep in that tent or risk a frosty death. Any other night, I would have.

Damn Drakkon for being the one to give me the will to live through tonight.

It took longer than necessary for me to make my way over, awkwardly making small talk with some of the Volkans in between to delay the inevitable, but I did. I slowly opened the tent folds, cursing myself when there was only one bedroll laid out in the middle. At least I had not been the only one to not think this far ahead.

I chucked off my boots, inching over in the dark as I hugged the bare corner of the tent, and waited. I attuned my ears to pick up any hint of his approach when he did not immediately return. *Where was he?* I shivered against the cold ground after another hour passed by. I was too stubborn to take his bedroll for myself, fearing he would think it was an invitation. After last night, proximity would be a tragic test to my will; it would be too difficult to fight this regret when we were both already wounded.

I did not hear my shadow when he finally approached, but I felt the moment his footsteps halted in front of the tent. *He knew I was in here*, and from what I could feel, he too was considering death before he slipped inside.

Keahi went straight for the opposite wall, leaving the bedroll untouched in the middle to remain as our unspoken divider. He had to crouch a lot lower than me because of his size, uncomfortably scrunched up in the corner with his knees to his chest. Neither one of us dared to look at each other as we stared at the opening of the tent flapping in the wind, wondering who was going to jump through first.

A sound came and died in his throat. My pulse rose out of my chest as I waited for him to try again. His next swallow was audible, broken when he could not speak. Normally, it was something I prided myself on when I left him speechless, but not tonight. Keahi flinched as I shifted my numbed foot out from under me, preparing to retreat if needed.

"Iahni did not pack me a tent." I swallowed as I tested the cramped space. "You know, since we are. . . married."

He pulled at the neck of his mask like it was suffocating him, attempting to clear his throat. He settled for a single nod.

"I did not know what to do," I confessed. The deep silence

coming from him was unbearably tense. What I had felt from him through the bond in the brothel, the clarity of his emotions, was completely sealed off now. Safe and out of my reach.

"We do not have to talk about it," I said gently. Keahi's features dropped, his shallow breath simmering the full extent of my regret. "It was my fault."

"What happened could never be your fault, Sabine," Keahi said, panicked, his head snapping toward me.

"Don't say that," I said almost breathlessly, pushing through the ache in my chest. "Do not look at me for what I've been through and believe that I could never own my mistakes."

What I could still do.

Keahi bristled beside me. He stared at me for a long time before he finally asked, "Do you still feel like it was a mistake?"

I knew my actions for what they were, what they had revealed to me. Whether it was the bond between us, or the subtle ways he exposed the pieces of himself to me, I had wanted him in all the ways I could not have him. It was a mistake.

A chill ran through the tent as all the warmth left the space when I nodded my answer to him. I resented the way my emotions were on a string. The noose grew tighter by the second, because the way he looked at me right now said he saw straight through me.

"Sabine. . ." he said my name in a low, knowing voice. The same way he always did when I was afraid, soft and far too patient.

"Maybe you could sleep with Kane?" I offered quickly. "He knows what happened last night. Or Drakkon even. He would believe you if you said we got into a fight. But then again, he might also question you to death faster than you could freeze outside."

Keahi's stare burned the side of my face. I hesitated before I slowly turned to look at him; his head was shaking side to side.

"What?" I snapped.

He took a stabilizing breath.

"Their tents are out of the question. We will have to make do." *This was not an option,* his tone said, but not what I could accept when so much was at stake tomorrow.

I rocked back, shocked that he instantly refused. "It couldn't be *that* bad. I mean, I know you would much rather—"

"*No*, I promise you I wouldn't," he said firmly.

I straightened. "So, you're saying after what happened last night—"

"Sabine. I can't stay with them," Keahi said with no subtlety in his exhaustion toward my persistence. "We are just going to deal with it for tonight."

"Why not?" I pressed, because for every second I was within his reach, I was that much closer to caving against my better judgment. Keahi instantly looked the other way, fueling my annoyance. I tilted my head, "Well. If you do not want to provide me with a reasonable explanation for a very *reasonable* solution, assuming you would not like me to blow our fragile attempt at a cover and sleep with someone else, I guess we *can* talk about last night." I clasped my hands together in my lap. "Where would you like to start?"

He leaned his head all the way back and sighed a puff of cold air. "It's not that—"

"Then *what* is it?" I asked impatiently.

"Promise me you will not say anything to them," he pleaded. I raised a brow at the way his shoulders slumped forward, his apprehension coating the bond. Keahi lowered his voice. "I can't sleep in either of their tents, because even though I can guarantee one of them is empty, they do not know that I know."

My eyes widened.

Keahi tilted his chin down. "Don't—"

"*Drakkon and Kane*??" I gasped.

"Could you say it any louder, really?" Keahi bit through his teeth.

"But they're so. . . different from each other," I thought out loud. Keahi relaxed slightly, but not much as I quieted my shock.

He shrugged. "They've known each other for a long time. It just happened one day; I think."

"They didn't tell you?" I asked.

"No." He sighed. "Drakkon crawled, and I mean that literally, out of his tent on a night I took third watch. He was always attempting to scare me, so I thought nothing of it and turned the other way. When I came back from my perimeter check, Kane had forgotten to turn off his lamp inside the tent. . . Drakkon's was the only one left wide open."

My mouth hinged, the earlier events piecing themselves together. Keahi chuckled at my surprise. "Is it so hard to believe?"

"I guess not," I said as I pulled my knees in. "I would have assumed there would be no hiding it with Drakkon."

Keahi's laugh was so warm and gentle, it almost sounded foreign from him.

"Do not give them too much credit." His smile faded the more he continued. "I started to loath anytime I knew we were going out on missions together. It was not the first, or I'm sure to be the last time I caught them. They have both made me miserable trying to cover for them over the years, but Drakkon is my brother and Kane is my best friend. If they wanted others to know, they would have shared it."

Keahi's eyes dimmed with hesitation. "It can be easier to hide the things we care for, because we believe that if it is hidden, we do not have to admit the pain of it being taken away. Others never truly had it to begin with, and I fear learning which is more painful. They will tell me when they are ready."

The dull knife in my chest twisted because I knew exactly what he meant. It was easier to lose what you did not have, but what I felt for Keahi was not easy. It was painful.

Keahi pushed the bedroll over toward me. "Take it. I will go take watch for the rest of the night; I can use my magic to stay warm."

I pushed it back. "You can't do that. If you expend your magic before a fight, you could risk your life."

His hands were at the ties of the tent when he said, "That's why we are not looking for a fight."

"*No*," I said tightly, and his hands froze.

Keahi's gaze lingered on the side of my face before he sat back down, a little closer to me this time. He pulled off his mask and shook out the length of his hair, his white streak brighter under the moonlight drifting through the seams.

When he looked at me with eyes full of remorse, I could not stand it any longer. I stopped him before he could say something we both would come to regret.

Shuffling under the cover from his bedroll, I gave him enough space to lie next to me in the night if he changed his mind. I heard Keahi do the same on the ground next to me, listening to his breath even until he turned on his shoulder.

"I forget you cannot feel it the way I do—the sorcerer's bond." He spoke so low I could hardly register the longing in his voice. I did not tell him otherwise; it was better off that way.

"Can I ask you something?" He asked carefully after a stretch of silence from the other side of the tent. I considered telling him no, not wanting to risk giving him the truth, but I turned on my shoulder to face him. The curls in his hair softened his features as it toppled over his forehead.

There was no accusation as he said, "You blame the Gods for what has happened to you and your people, but what if they were forced to watch it unfold, all this time, to protect what they could still save. . . would you blame them then?"

I nestled into my shoulder, unsure of where the question was leading.

"Yes, I would. For all the good they have created, they have always allowed suffering to those who did not deserve it and watched as those who walked away. I will never forgive that, and I hope they pray to whatever Gods they serve for forgiveness." I trailed off. "I would not be so merciless."

A half-smile stretched his scar. "I'm sure that even the Gods fear you, Sabine."

"They should." I smiled back. "If they do not."

Keahi's dark laughter was untamed. "I know who might fear you the most." His chuckle turned raspy, uneven, followed by a shaky breath as he averted his eyes. "Your husband."

I hesitated. "You are not—"

"Especially him. When he saw you wearing that dress." His throat bobbed, turning his lips into a thin line. "Even if he knew you were not his, and he was desperately trying to remind himself of it when he saw you, he could not help but to make a complete and total ass of himself. . . could you forgive him, with time?"

I played with the band of my ring underneath the wool. Maybe at night, when our hearts were not listening to the fortress of our minds, he needed to pretend just as much as I did.

"Jealousy is not a trait I admire, nor will I forgive it easily, especially if it is taken out wrongly upon me." I pretended with him.

"Rightfully deserved." The side of his jaw tensed, holding his tongue as he trailed his gaze to my lips. "I'm sure he would do anything to make it up to you, except that which he cannot promise."

"That does not sound like anything." I countered breathlessly, my eyes traitorously dipping to his mouth when I caught him staring at mine.

"I am not merciless, either," he said in time with the wind. "I will not be merciless to those who aim to know your soul, not when it has been attached to mine. I am selfish, and I promise to hold myself to that torture when I do you wrong, because I cannot learn to be something I am not. I cannot stop myself from being jealous.

Not when others have the privilege of knowing you so freely, without the pressures of what we have been placed under. I felt threatened of that the moment I saw you."

Keahi sat up, placing his mask back on. "You will have to forgive me again, more often than you would like, but please know it is your happiness in the end that I want. Even if it is with someone else."

I did not want anyone else, but I could not have him either. My nails dug into my palms as I turned over. "Why are you telling me this?"

Keahi drew closer to me, and I held my breath as he tucked a fallen strand of my white hair behind my ear. Before I could turn back to him, I felt him fading away as he whispered, "Because even if you cannot feel it, I have, and it has taught me to hope when I should not."

Chapter Thirty-Eight

Sabine

The trees whipped violently, and snow battered against us with brute force. Gushing winds slithered across the forest floor, wrapping around barren tree trunks as we approached the edge of the wood. The realm bared its teeth in warning, producing its own sorcery we would not heed.

Keahi was up ahead, leading the front line, but I could sense myself in the shadow of his thoughts. It whispered gently over my skin, a phantom caress I had believed was fabricated by my sense of worry. The bond was layered with the weight of what he had said to me last night, charging the air between us.

My allegiance was to no one. My loyalty was unknown, even to myself, because I was in the crossfires of the heart—bladed between my long-held belief in the protection of indifference, and the sharp sting of want as his ember gaze locked with mine. I glanced away, questioning everything I was prepared to do. The pressure between my shoulder blades knotted together with my guilt.

"The full moon is upon us," Kane said. He had ridden up beside me without me noticing, quietly watching my distant exchange with Keahi.

Celenia's powers waxed and waned with the moon. We were already at risk by nearing their territory unannounced; this was the peak of their power.

"Celenia will not expect it," I said, and neither would Solstice.

I planned to betray them.

Kane brushed the chestnut mane of his horse, scrutinizing my silence. It was a powerful weapon against one's enemy, and right now, I was not his friend.

"We will remain hidden. Your light casting will veil us," he said to reassure me. I had no plans to go unnoticed, not after Drakkon had revealed the General of Novear was with them. This could be my only chance, and no amount of displaced loyalty I felt for them could stop me.

"Are you sure we have thought this through?" I asked for the both of us, his trust in me, despite my better judgment. Opening myself up for his response to strike me without a shield.

"I will fight with you even in times of darkness, Lightbringer," Kane vowed with a fealty I could not return. "We are the flame, and you are the light to bring us home."

There was an affirmed gleam in his eye to match the soft smile I imagined beneath the Volkan mask. Kane exuded the pride of a soldier who swore himself to honor, and I would risk his slaughter, exposing our position for my vendetta. The pang of guilt festered into an open wound.

"Kane," I said in a hush, for I feared the answer he was to give me when I was already on the verge of unwanted strife. I took a breath. "You know. . ." *About the bond.*

Our conversation lingered in the frosted air as Kane's eyes left mine, his gaze now pinned upon my bonded's back, his friend. Keahi's black cloak waved against the snow-flecked wind.

My shadow held his head high, a portrait of strength to those who closely followed behind him, prepared for the fight to come. They could not feel him though, not as I did. What we saw and what we knew to be true were never the same. A head held high was not negated by the turmoil it took to remain lifted.

"Yes. I know about the. . ." Kane's whisper trailed off. His gaze was still pointed in Keahi's direction, watching him as if he could hear us from several riders ahead.

There was a comfort in Kane's omission I did not expect, almost as if he had been waiting for me to ask him. I lowered my voice to match his. "How long have you known?"

Kane dipped his chin to the scars we both knew were underneath my cloak, permanently etched on the skin of my back, prickling with shame. "I was there when we found you." He struggled with the notch in his throat. "I carried your body to Elias."

My father had left me lifeless, a discarded reminder to taunt them with. The soldier who I urged to kill me before they found me had left me unrecognizable. They had known who I was after Elias removed a portion of the siphoning crystal, the daughter of their enemy kingdom. My secret, the truth of what lived beneath my skin, kept only between me and Elias.

They could have kept me alive to save their Prince's life after I accepted the bond, but there was no key to throw away. No cage they intended to put me in.

"Then you must have truly meant it in the library," I said uneasily, a shaken smile playing upon my chapped lips. "To have seen straight through our poor attempts at convincing the others. We were doomed from the start." Because when it came to this man I was bonded to, tactics were lost to feeling. I could not allow myself to feel when caring was the catalyst to pain; my own personal weakness.

Kane tilted his head, slowly searching my face. Evergreen eyes, honest and pure, peered through the fire of his creed. "You are the only one who needs to be convinced, Sabine."

Yet it was no longer the truth. I had not allowed myself to be convinced until last night. My indecision rattled the confines of my haven. My past, the creator of my future, one where I would be forced to betray him in the end because I refused to ask for permission. This fate was mine. What I had chosen to live for—revenge.

'I only care about one thing,' I had warned him.

Neither of us had listened.

I ventured back to our beginning. When I believed he was once the king my father sought to steal power from. Our fates had irrevocably changed the night they found me massacred upon the rock. There had been three cloaked soldiers in the woods after my father failed to sacrifice me for power, and I had lived.

"Who was the third sorcerer?" I asked quietly. I looked toward

Drakkon, who was always at his brother's side, his dark brown hair peeking underneath his hood. He had been completely surprised when I arrived. Surely it had not been him.

Kane suddenly reared the reins of his horse, an abrupt altar of his stance.

"What's wrong?" I asked as I followed his gaze, roughly making out the clearing up ahead. The others in front continued toward the riverbank, their sights set on the land bridge connecting Solstice and Celenia's territories.

A chill lifted from the river, fogging my breath with the night creeping toward us. Kane had not said a word, but his hand slowly lowered to the hilt of his sword. The General went still at the same time without warning. Keahi held a gloved hand up in a fist and froze at the front.

Meira became restless beneath me as the rest of our battalion held their breaths. I stroked her silver mane, failing to calm her as her hooves grated the ground. I yanked the reins in my burning hands, tightening my grip as she knocked her head back and forth. She was inconsolable; it was a warning.

The source of Meira's distress resounded with a fatal click, the stretch of a bow once it reached its threshold. The tip of a stone arrow was hidden within the tree line, aimed and ready toward—

"*Keahi!*" I screamed his name before I could think.

The General immediately turned at my distress, searching for a threat angled at his heart and not mine, but it was too late. The arrow flew true, cutting through the air, straight toward his chest.

A glow reflected in his pupils from the heat of his magic, incinerating the arrow just before it struck home. Keahi's stare did not escape mine as the ash of the arrow dusted his armor. My breath caught in my throat at how close it had been, and what I had just seen.

For it was the first time the famed Prince of the Solstice Kingdom had truly wielded his element in my presence. I wanted to tell him right then.

I could feel him, too. The way his soul was on fire, and I was not afraid to burn.

Fear collided between the bond as another arrow flashed in my peripheral, humming at the side of my face, a near miss. The first of many, as a storm of a thousand arrows soared through the twilight.

"Get her out of here!" Keahi yelled as Meira kicked on her hind legs, missing another arrow at her hoof.

The Son of Fire shared what felt like a goodbye in his eyes as he turned toward the sky, hands uplifted with the wind before he doused it in an explosion of orange, twisted flame and chaos. Arrow after arrow, ashes rained over his men, blackening the fresh snow.

Kane ripped me from Meira's back. His hold was firm at the collar of my cloak as he dragged me from view until I found my footing. The Volkan warriors we left behind lit the bank with fire and the river turned red from the afterglow.

"We can't leave them!" I yelled at Kane, fighting against the death grip he placed on my forearm. Together we sprinted through the forest, brush scratching my face as we ducked through a series of pine branches.

"Just a little farther. I need to gain enough momentum," he panted, "to project my shadowfire at a far enough distance." There was no emotion in the Commander's voice as we fled. The Volkan's sorcery diminished as we disappeared into the dense wood. My chest burned as we lost sight of them.

"No!" I yanked him back through sheer force of will. Kane's body tumbled over top of me, my ribs grating against the rocks covered in snow as I intercepted his momentum. My nails dug into the front of his chest, snow and dirt slinging from my cloak as I stood upright. "We have to go back. Did you not see how many arrows fell from the sky? That was an entire army!"

Kane latched himself onto my wrist, pulling me back toward him. "*It was an order*—the mission is off."

"Since when have you ever followed orders in the face of what is right?" I ground my teeth into a snarl, and he narrowed his eyes at me.

I didn't care about the *mission.* I never cared. Not after Drakkon had told me the General of Novear was found in Celenia's camps. I was on a mission to kill when there was no order to do so. I had been willing to risk their lives for this chance. As the fires roared behind me, my heart gave way and the ice in my veins melted.

"Do not make me fight you," Kane said with lethal stillness, pleading, analyzing my every movement as though I were a cornered animal.

"You fight *with me*—remember?" I lowered myself down beside Kane. Frozen moss splayed between my fingers behind a rotted tree.

The forest was catching fire, a volatile path so bright I could barely make out the figures colliding with each other in the clearing we had run from. We watched the smoke rise like a fog drifting over us. Warm water droplets formed a film of condensation on my bare cheek as it passed.

"Celenia's sorcerers are here," I panicked, brushing away the water droplets on my brow bone. "Not just their army."

The moon was the tide of oceans, the cycle of water and life. Steam clouds formed over top of us. Water greeted fire, sizzling from the opposing force of the Celenia Kingdom. Dread pooled through me as the full moon high above gleamed through the intertwined branches. The opalescent rays fueled Celenia's powers.

Why had they been prepared to this scale? Someone could have intercepted information about our movements. At worst, someone within the Solstice army had betrayed them before I could. "They knew we were coming, Kane," I said breathlessly.

Kane sank further behind the log, his stare blank.

"I can't leave him," I gasped out loud. A choice I made, long before I had made it or intended to betray him.

"Sabine—"

"*I said*—" pausing as I tilted my head slowly toward him, enunciating my speech so he would not miss my threat if he tested me further. "I *can't* leave him."

Kane grabbed my shoulder, desperate to get me to understand motives I would not hear. "We knew this was a risk, but I promised him if we failed, I would make sure you were safe. *This* is a death sentence. Not all of them are going to make it, but Keahi will handle his own. *Trust me.* There are things he has not told you yet, Sabine. We have to—"

I kicked the air out of his lungs. My boot connected to his sternum, burying him in the snow. The ice beneath me threatened my stance, but I recovered.

"Then let us give him the chance to tell me for himself, because I trust *no one.*"

"*Wait!*" Kane screamed behind me, but the wind howling in my ears turned his plea faint.

We had fallen directly into a trap, and if Celenia had been waiting to ambush us before we invaded their camp. . . if Drakkon's information was correct, if they had seen the General of Novear at their camps before our arrival—*he was here.*

'It would be a slaughter,' Drakkon's voice crept into my racing

pulse. My hands balled into fists, digging into the flesh of my palms as I pushed my legs to run faster toward the fight.

Mist combined with the night, clouding the bank. Only the fire bearers were visible as they eviscerated heat from their hands in streaks of vicious sorcery. Celenia reused the mist, drawing the source of their element from the water lingering in the air. I unsheathed my golden dagger from its harness at my thigh, glinting in the moonlight. I headed straight toward a Volkan fighter drowning in a sphere of their opponent's power, a massive body of river water gyrating around their head.

I vibrated with adrenaline and power as I zeroed in and took away the fighter's sight. The sphere of water lost its shape, and he crumpled to the ground. The splash from the release boiled the side of my face, infused with the Volkan's magic who had been fighting for his life. I enveloped the Celenia sorcerer, yanking the root of his blonde hair to gain access to his windpipe. River water and blood coated my fingers. I slit his throat clean through with swift precision, bleeding him dry until I felt his magic succumb to the death I gifted.

War was haunting, death was hollow, but vengeance was retribution. My eyes darkened with the first taste of bloodshed, overcome by the uncaged power humming in my veins as his body thumped to the ground at my feet.

Elias probably should have exposed my truth.

The Volkan violently coughed beside me, the water still suffocating him from when he was drowning. I dragged his body to the edge of the clearing behind a tree, rolling him on his side before he leached over, vomiting the occlusion out of his lungs.

The enemy army outnumbered us; they had triple the amount of soldiers. Celenia had been prepared, but they were not the only ones. The power crackling with fury inside my chest as I ventured onto the battlefield was not just my own. Keahi's power was lighting me from the inside out.

Embers rained down all around him, like molten flames erupting from an immeasurable source of power. The energy he bent to his will was so strong it pulsed in waves through my fingertips, the center streak of my ceremonial ring glowing in the night.

Keahi was surrounded. Six figures emerged through the glare of smoke and vapor. Water flayed from their hands as they attempted to submerge Keahi, but it evaporated around him. The General's crimson eyes illuminated through the veil of steam, his hands moving viciously, keeping a circle of fire around him for protection. I took a hesitant step back at his magic on full display.

I thought back to the times he could have used it but didn't when he ran in the woods instead of fighting. The pit of Keahi's power seemed endless. I had never seen another sorcerer wield that much power on their own, even before the Veil of Seven was destroyed. Why then did I feel so much *pain*, like a hot iron rod was being dragged across my chest?

Keahi. . . was hurt. . .

Two of Celenia's troops emerged behind him from the riverbank as their versatile lungs breathed in the air. They sliced through his ring of fire with swift precision, breaking his stance. His hands and feet dug into the mud, attempting to withstand the weight of the current until his knees hit the ground.

Keahi's flames extinguished.

How long had he been hurting? I took a step forward from my vantage point. Rage ignited as Celenia's sorcerers closed in on him. *Why had he hidden it from me?* The amount of pain I felt from him as he used his magic. . . *how had he—*

Three blazing paths of fury ricocheted from behind me. Kane rippled through the battlefield like he was made of wrath, his flames engulfing three of Keahi's attackers as fire found its fuel. Their agonizing screams pierced my ears until their faces charred.

A sharp sting bit at the side of my face. My palm quickly jolted up to the touch of an abrasion forming. Keahi's body flush to the ground, Celenia sorcerers dangerously close to encapsulating his body with river water, preparing to drown him on dry land.

Get up. Get up. I pleaded as I hesitated to go to him, frantically searching the grounds for the engineer of this attack and back to my sorcerer bonded.

He. Was. Here.

It was the only thing that made sense.

He knew I was with them.

The strain Keahi was exuding lacerated. His power flickered within me. My ring dimmed on my finger. The loss of his control was the loss of mine; it triggered my decision as I willingly stepped further into the trap designed for me.

A tether broke loose inside, something so primal the power within me took over in response. I aimed for the beating heart of the battle, prepared to burn through the sorcery natural to my kingdom.

For there was another power dangerously wading within me, free from my father's crystal cage, and it wanted out.

My skin surfaced a glow, the same shade as the stars casting down upon us from lifetimes away. The starlight still left within me compelled my senses, and my eyes turned a glowing white. Kane's scream erupted beside me, *"Nooooo!"*

My concentration severed.

I thought he had been trying to stop me as my power flourished to breakthrough, but I followed to where he was now running to, trailing behind Drakkon's point of attack.

Time felt as if it slowed around me.

Our stares collided from across the bank, on the other side of Celenia's territory.

The one I had been waiting for. Dressed in the exact armor he had made me wear. Except now, it was especially fitted for him. The staff of malachite, absent in his other hand.

A sheer cry released from across the bank. His fists entangled around long black hair, dragging a woman's body across the sleeted mud with him. I gasped as I saw a flash of the woman's face—the resemblance was irrefutable.

The mission the brothers did not want me to fail them on, to retrieve their sister, who I had not known was captured. Buried into the ground, her mangled body stomped over *like she was nothing* as Drakkon raced toward her.

Keahi riled against the waters cascading over him, dangerously wading in up to his neckline when he too noticed her from his position, pinned to the ground. He was physically burning to prevent them from covering his face, forcing water into his lungs.

Drakkon trampled through the river waist deep, choosing to go after her regardless of Kane's screams that begged him not to. Kane was still too far away, battling his way forward to intervene. But Drakkon did not need him. He scooped her up in his arms without a fight and ran. Because the one they believed to be the *General of Novear* did not care as they took his bait, because he was prowling straight toward me.

The white of his hair fell past his shoulders as he threw the black helmet into the dirt. His teeth gleamed with a snarl I felt rumbling within my chest from across the bank.

Fury solidified in my core because my father, the King of Novear, and *Destroyer of the Veil,* was here, pretending to be what he had created. The very thing that scared me the most, what I became because of him.

His daughter, *General of Novear*, was no longer his to wield. I was a symbol of the power he was still pretending to have under his control, but we both knew he no longer had in his possession. Power my father had feared, the balance of the scales, and his sin for destroying the Veil of Seven.

The destruction of the Veil of Seven lived within me. And he needed his sin wiped clean by another's hand, one powerful enough to destroy it.

For he had already learned a valuable lesson after closing the Veil of Seven; the hand that struck was the hand that bled. If the King of Novear had destroyed me himself, it would return to haunt him. Just as it had once before when the curse of the veil claimed my mother, and he murdered her for it. My father could not destroy me when it passed on, in fear his sin would return.

It was why he never allowed me to die, even when I begged him to let me take my own life over the years I served under him. One of many commands he gave to the crystal was for me to be unable to take my own life. That was until he released me from it on the day I was pledged as a sacrifice, and I had not realized until now why he had lied to me about the sorcerer's bond ritual.

The King of Novear had wanted me to believe he was using another siphoning spell. To convince me he was to become more powerful the longer I remained alive during the siphoning, what he knew I ultimately feared. A dual victory, when concretely it was a ploy to destroy his curse for good.

My father had beaten me within an inch of my life on the day of the bonding ritual to make sure I was not worth saving or could be saved with the siphoning crystal still in my neck. The King of Solstice left with no other choice but to murder my father's sin for him, but it was the Prince who had found me instead.

The King of Novear's final command had only been a failsafe. A calculated risk. On the deadly chance he failed, and I survived. . . I would become bonded to one of the most powerful sorcerers in the realm.

My father had tightened the ropes around my wrist before the ritual and whispered a chill across my neck into the crystal that bent me to his will. If I was to survive the siphoning. . . I was to take my own life. *And I had tried*, because he and I both knew it was what I had always wanted.

'I would rather die,' I had told the prince. Even after the crystal had been removed, another failsafe of my fathers, because he knew I could not live knowing the things I had done—forced or not.

After he discovered the magic of the veil had transferred within me to haunt him, he punished me with the murders of my people. He bandaged me with the siphoning crystal as he forced it into my spine to "fix me," turned me into string and bones, until I became a means of his control. Death would always be my path, but I chose the revenge fate had offered me first.

My father's commands drifted from across the riverbank as he drew closer over the land bridge, and I became surrounded by an entire clan of Celenia's troops. His boots prowled at the edge of the water, watching me from a distance like the coward he was, always getting someone else to do his bidding.

It benefited me, because not only did I not have to enact war on behalf of Solstice. . . I no longer had to betray them to get what I wanted.

Death.

My power glittered into an intangible rage as the cage inside me swung wide open. *Hungry—for vengeance.*

A battle cry ripped from my lungs as I clamped my hands above my head, palms to the sky, as a beam of light radiated from them. I spared my father a malicious grin as light split the sky. I was running on sheer determination that my own power could not fend off.

The sky opened as I channeled the starlight above, bringing my hands down to the center of my chest. I set my feet wide and sweat trickled down the sides of my face. The stars swirled, dragging their light across the night sky as I redirected their path. Feeding my power until it bowed to me and no one else. Cursing life itself.

Light surged erratically around me; the outline of the warriors was faint as Kane commanded the others. I used the distraction as an opportunity, fighting their way through, as I summoned all of my power for this one chance.

Keahi swiftly knocked the sorcerers pinning him down, gaining a second wind the moment he made the connection I was here. His power detonated, lighting his attackers into piles of scalding flesh.

"Sabine!" Keahi screamed my name, sprinting toward me. But no matter what he wanted to say. . . I knew I could not hear him for much longer.

Starlight crackled through my hands. The sound of the electric current blocked out the dying on the battlefield. My vision narrowed on him as if he was the only person left in the realm, the bond barely holding on to the thread of fate between us.

My magic answered in recognition, just as it always had for him—I overpowered it, growing the sphere of light in my palms.

The fear in Keahi's eyes grew as he slowed his sprint to a stammered halt as he watched me, a tug of realization between us. It was a shame; this was going to be the first and last time I was going to be honest with him. Keahi's hand went to his ring, at what he now knew, because I had sent two clear words through the bond.

The electricity between my fingers webbed and sparked inside the sphere. I attempted to press its way into my palms, feeding it more and more to the brim. It hissed with an intensity that threatened to split me in half. I could barely hear Keahi when he bellowed his command, "Pull back!"

A deafening scream erupted from my chest. *More*! I screamed into the pit of my power, using all the strength I could gather, as I slammed the splitting light into the ground.

The realm shattered in revolt.

I peered up as I held the light to the ground. Electricity searched for its targets in viper like motions. My limbs detached from their sockets as it tore through my center, as I forced the starlight to bend to my will as the ground illuminated underneath Celenia's army.

As the light electrocuted them, I could feel *everything*. The way my magic found its final destination, like they were metal in a storm. The world rapidly dimmed as I held their bodies in the frenzy of my power. My palms remained on the damp earth as I looked up to make eye contact with my father. A malevolent smile widening on my face as I stood with lightning and starlight crackling all around me.

I knew it was coming. The power that prowled underneath my skin threatened to overtake me. Because this was the second time in my entire life that I had seen genuine fear distort my father's face. The magic I had been cursed with because of him, the sickness unnatural to any sorcerer who wielded power from my home, the Kingdom of Light and Starfall.

The white light in my hands transformed into a dark glow. As the sky closed into darkness, the realm plunged into gloom and corruption. The electricity rattled through me, signaling my nerves. I could not hold on for much longer. My control finally slipped as my magic gave way into its hidden form, the duality of my powers rallying against each other.

Only death will stop us, I called to it as the fall of an entire army dropped unanimously, finally deciding to release them from my magic. *I would no longer fear the darkness. I would become it.*

Black lightning, darkness, surged deep from within me, untamed with fury as it crackled toward my coward of a father who was abandoning his allies.

Dark magic, the balance fate had designed for the closure of the veil in the form of sin, crackled at his heels, avenging its freedom from his control—

A solidified *snap* broke through me.

Pain hammered into my skull, splitting me in half, folding in on itself at a seismic proportion. It ate away the light of my power still left inside of me, betraying the freedom I gave it. It wanted to devour me and use my body as a vessel.

The King of Novear disappeared into the woods beyond, out of sight. My outstretched hands dropped to my waist. The power rebounded, radiating toward its beholder; crackling, seizing with a force that was going to end me and the rest of the realm with it.

Power—the frailest of illusions.

The fall from power, a stark reality, as it barreled toward me, returning to its home.

The core of my magic cracked inside of me, and it allowed the briefest moment for me to watch as the darkness closed in, claiming what it had wanted all along. It did not just want me to become it; the darkness wanted to become *me.*

All the anguish that had fueled my power looked vastly different as I watched it transform into something I had not expected long before it made contact. It was not anger that had fueled the darkness I had hid myself within, but soul shattering grief as I accepted my fate.

It dissipated when I turned to see Keahi screaming, tearing the earth with his hands as he fell to his knees, because he felt it too—*the end*—the consequence of choice.

A shredded hand extended, reaching toward me in a futile attempt to take me from it. There was nothing more he could do but watch it unfold, and for the very first time in my life. . . I wished I was not about to die.

True regret sanctified in the pit of my stomach as he threw off his mask, tears flowing down that beautifully scarred face I would never see again. Ember eyes that could make the world burn with despair held onto me like a beacon of life in this shroud of darkness I had unleashed upon the realm. My tears salted the corner of my lips as I repeated the earlier words I had sent down the bond.

I'm sorry.

Chapter Thirty-Nine

Keahi

Darkness conquered.

Sabine's magic capsized the night, sparked with the same deadly reverence she unleashed upon the realm. Black lightning encapsulated her body within a dome of electric gloom. It drove deep into her bones with a vicious crack of thunder, unrelenting.

The last of Sabine's magic radiated over her skin in ebony waves as she went still, and the echo of her voice rippled through the bond as she fell onto the riverbank below.

I'm sorry.
I'm sorry.
I'm sorry.

My heart shredded in two as I crashed down beside her, gripped at the seam of my bleeding chest wound, and was torn apart as the beat of her pulse faded—a constant I had not known until she was dying within me. Tears streamed down the side of my jawline. I pulled Sabine's limp body onto my lap and bunched her pale face into my gloves, searching, begging for any sign of movement. The stars above reflected in her vacant stare.

"You don't get to say that to me. Not when it is my fault." I wept into her shoulder, uncaring if there was anyone left to watch me break. My throat, raw from my screams, forced to watch Sabine's power turn on her. The magic on her skin simmered against my bare cheekbone as I pressed my ear closer to her heart, counting, listening to her life on a timeline. "I'm the one who is sorry. *Do you hear me?* I'm sorry, not you, okay?"

My life flashed before my eyes; not the one I had lived, but the one I wanted to live with her. A life where I was not bound to fear but conquered it daily on the tightline. Each step was scarier than the first; hell beneath my feet. But it did not matter when Sabine was on the other side. I wanted her despite it. Golden eyes like the first ray of sun, the sweet smell of her skin in the wind of her long white hair, and a smile that dared the realm to cross her. Sabine had a heart that death itself feared, and I was begging it to fear her for one more day.

Kane jumped down next to me from above. Dank sand from the riverbank and fallen snow slung across my back as he landed. His worried gaze bounced between Sabine and my unmasked face as he hesitantly rounded in front of us. "Keahi." He exhaled shakily. "Is she. . ."

"She's alive," I shuttered against her, whisking away Sabine's hair clinging to her forehead with my thumb. The residual spark of her magic hummed against my fingers, the darkness far beneath her skin now, taking root inside its home. "She's alive," I repeated because I needed to hear it again for myself.

"Not for long," Kane kneeled beside me, his hand on my shoulder. The other pressed tightly against a gash he sustained on his thigh, the ripped material of his cloak around the wound saturated in blood. "We need to go to the capital before it is too late. Elias cannot save her this time, she needs help—"

"*No.*" I pulled Sabine's body closer to me. My father would take one look at her and order her execution. After tonight, Sabine was more than just his enemy. The pain was excruciating, both mine and Sabine's, and I would be too weak to stop him right now.

"Keahi. . . you had already sent your father a letter telling him you were *married* to her for the Gods' sake." Kane shifted uneasily beside me, boots sinking into the bank. "The King of Solstice himself knew he was going to be forced to give up the throne eventually. This ruse of power he *stole* from you to maintain his image was not meant to last—*you know that*. We will stand beside you."

"Emric did not *steal* from me," I threatened, pain seeping into the hollow spaces of my unrest. "I *willingly* gave it to him; do not paint me with valor because I will fail you." Power was poison, and it had already ruined me.

"It is true you are no peacemaker of the realm, Keahi Aldeer. For one man's peace is another man's hell, and there is no valor in that. In your father's peace, your scars refused to heal for you. The reign of kings was not meant for eternities."

There was no such thing as time in the face of eternity.

There would be no peace in my mistakes.

"I can't," I rasped.

The truth was there, a weight on thin ice, but *I was too late*. I was always too late, and it was always *my fault*. My mother had said so herself before she took her life, and I have only ever proved to myself she was right.

"Elias is a powerful Healer, but he has not been the same since he removed the siphoning crystal from Sabine. I do not think he could heal her in his current state, even if he tried." Kane paused, holding a single breath. "Please, do not do this."

My fault.

"I am begging. . ." His voice was a tether, ready to fray. "Sabine is going to die if we do not do something."

My fault.

"We can fix it, Keahi. We can fix it," he repeated. "Do not let your father get into your head. Emric holds no power over you—he never has! *Please*, we have delayed long enough!"

"*Stop*," I growled. Sabine's chest shallowed further against my palm. "You don't think I can feel it? It's *killing* her. This is my fault. I refuse to take her to the capital." My chest heaved, and the truth set itself free. "We did not *finish* the bond."

The sorcerer's bond required three bindings, and Sabine and I had only completed one. Kane's breath quickened as he stared at me with confusion, at my betrayal. I had not once lied to him prior to this, and he and I both knew it. "What do you mean you have not finished the bond. . . you were supposed to the night of the ceremony to secure the tie? Sabine had said—"

"She lied; we both did." I lifted her up further into my arms. My body wanted to collapse into the earth as I attempted to stand, searing every breath in my lungs from the weight of my chest wound. "We did not complete the process, I wanted to tell her, but she was—"

Kane stuttered out a string of curses, kicking the ground with his bleeding leg, shoveling the ice and mud. "But nothing! She might die because of this and *you*—" he pointed at my chest, "had barely survived in your current form after your father drained you from the last visit to the capital. Elias said the bond would heal you before I left that day, and I had found it odd when you told me the other night it hadn't, but I thought it would just take time. . ."

My body had refused to heal long before then, and Elias had tried to mend me the best he could every time I offered the magic in my veins to my father. But I had healed, even if each time took longer than the last. The laceration on my chest was frozen in the exact same state as it had been the night I met Sabine.

I knew the moment we made it to Kallahni it would remain. When it still did not heal after I removed the last piece of the siphoning crystal out of her neck, and I could not numb the pain, I was certain. I did not heal because we had not finished the sorcerer's bond, but I was willing to live with it.

"All this time, you chose to lie. . ." Kane's eyes widened. "Knowing an unfinished sorcerer's bond would put you *both* at risk. No wonder Elias has been angry with you. . . That you didn't want her to come on the mission, you knew, and you didn't tell me. I never would have asked her to come with us if I had known. . .why would you do this?!"

"She was *scared*." My voice cracked. "Even if she did not want to admit it. She pretended to know what she had agreed to upon accepting the bond, and it was too late when I realized it. I would not force her into anything while I had the upper hand—you saw what her father did to her. I am not a monster!"

Yet every voice in my head reminded me I was.

Every memory of those I failed believed it to be true. I was empty, and if emptiness was a monster, it had clawed its way into my soul. All I wanted to do was be better, but even my better was not enough. I made the wrong choices. I said the wrong things. I failed.

And I hurt people because of it.

I hurt Sabine.

"I know you, Keahi Aldeer," he whispered, lowering to retrieve the object I had left buried in the snow. "I know you stared in the mirror and saw your father staring right back. Sabine made the choice to accept the bond, but after she made it, she deserved to know the extent."

Kane stood and placed the cold, dark fabric of our creed over my face. He took a step back, his black cloak drifting against the chill as we faced each other. He and I both knew I would never forgive myself. Not for the pain I have caused others, or for the life of the woman I planned to take from death's arms.

I had never needed forgiveness to try one more time. This time, I wasn't just going to try. I was going to *win*—for it is the vow to her I have made.

"I will take her to Elias. In the meantime, go to the capital," I instructed Kane. "Give warning to my father's troops. Tell them, if my father does not grant us safe passage, then I will break down his doors." I looked down at Sabine, still tucked tightly into my arms. "I will not let her die."

The Commander of Solstice nodded as he grasped Sabine's dangling hand and placed it on her chest. Kane leaned down toward her ear. "I will see you again, Lightbringer. Do not leave us just yet," he whispered as he faded into shadowfire. "I won't be able to forgive him if you do."

The embers leftover from the fight floated through the abandoned battlefield. Fog lifted from the raging river behind me. Soldiers on both sides of the land bridge bled into the snow. Not a single sorcerer from Celenia on this side of the bank had survived the blunt force of my bonded's attack. Sabine had risked her power in order to save my soldiers. . . to save me while she watched her father slip away. I would not fail her.

My shadow trailed behind me as I broke out into a sprint through the night, Sabine in my arms. It wrapped itself around us in the tailspin of my shadowfire, hanging on for dear life as I forced my footsteps to run faster until they faded from the realm.

'You are not a weapon!' Elias's words broke through me, ignoring him as I ripped us through the first round of ash and flame. Tearing through the space that divided the realm with no ounce of mercy, my sights set on the safety of Kallahni.

The air morphed and tunneled around me as I rivaled against the odds, dragging my magic behind me because I refused to fail her. I did not know where the realm ended as we became one against the force of time in a sea of stars and fire.

'Stop punishing yourself!' Elias's voice grew stronger as I continued to run with Sabine in my arms. I did not hesitate as I unleashed my magic without consequence—repeatedly until there would be nothing left of me but this fragile chance of fate.

Pain eviscerated me, igniting across my chest from the abuse of my sorcery when I was already injured beyond repair. Wounds had never stopped me before, but this time I knew deep down it would not heal.

'You are not invincible, Keahi Aldeer!' Elias flared in my memory with a final warning as my knees slammed into the rocks. I stared up at the mountain of Kallahni, my body trembling as I faltered from the travel. Sabine's back smacked into the ground before I could splay one hand against the earth. The weight of my pain was too heavy to remain standing, to breathe, forcing my ribcage to expand.

You are going to make it, I told Sabine through the bond. She could not hear me trembling above her. I lowered my lips to her forehead through my mask to give me strength. *I promise.*

My shadow thrashed in the moonlight, attempting to grasp onto me, prevent me from making the final jump. The aftermath of fire cowered around me as I bent my magic to my will. We were so close, but as we materialized through a ring of fire. . . we hit the forest floor only a few feet away.

Chapter Forty

Sabine

We didn't make it.

The glowing snow-packed mountains of Kallahni were unwilling to bend for us in retrieval. A white haze dusted upon the ridgeline, shimmering through the treetops with an icy, unmoving reflection. We were too far out of reach for the mountain to take mercy on us as we landed at the edge of the forest, just outside the entrance to the Volkan stronghold.

The sin of the veil had paralyzed my body from the inside out, conquering my veins, humming with an electric current inside of me. The darkness had wanted me to watch as Keahi begged my heart to keep beating. It wanted me to know I was not alone, as it took hold of my soul. It trusted that my bonded would not abandon me regardless of what power I possessed, who I was—now it was going to make me watch him die.

We shared an unspoken apology between us when he too knew it was over. The firelight in Keahi's eyes dimmed, looking me over with a pained remorse. All power required sacrifice, and I had foolishly believed there was nothing left of me for it to take—I was wrong.

An eternity went by as I remained frozen at the mercy of my power that was eating me alive. Keahi collapsed onto the ground beneath me, his chest lifeless against mine upon impact. There was nothing I could do but feel the warmth bleed out of him as his magic left his body through the bond, eviscerated from the realm. The death of his magic detonated within the connection between us. My bonded ripped out of my soul like he never existed upon this earth, violating me as I screamed until I felt the inside of my skull stripped raw.

Keahi was gone.

Then I screamed—*louder*, knowing he could not, his chest motionless underneath me. Lost were the words he had said to me through the bond. When Keahi had told me he was the one who was sorry, while I was stunned in his arms; I had heard everything.

Louder, as I told him how I hated him, even if we were both at fault in this. Hated him for keeping me alive just to watch one more person die. Hated him because I never deserved to live for what I had done under my father's rule, even if I had no choice. Hated him because it should have been me. It should have been me, not him. I was nothing. He had died for nothing.

You should have just killed me when you had the chance! I screamed into the empty void where the bond had been. *You can't leave me!*

When that did not wake him, I begged.

You promised.

I heard you the first time. When you said you wouldn't leave me. You were the shadow that grabbed my hand when the sun could not save me.

I heard you.

My numbed fingers pushed away his mask, tracing the outline of his scar as I regained enough mobility to reach for him in the snow.

Don't go.

Don't leave me.

Broken; I felt broken as I quivered against the jagged line, remembering how I had been the one to carve the mark into his skin. Keahi had almost killed me then, but on the last strike I had gained the upper hand and struck him beneath his hood with the staff of malachite.

We had not spoken—I had not known him then. I had believed him to be the King of Solstice on the night they ambushed our camp, for the General of Solstice was rumored to be the Serpent in the Shadows. The one who was unseen. A presence that felt like an omen on the battlefield. Not the man who had gone bone chillingly still, the hood of his cloak hiding him along with the peak of night as I brought him to his knees.

I will forgive you if you forgive me.

It had torn my soul in two when I had first seen his scar, when I realized he was the one I had dueled that night, not his father. A clashing memory of who I would always be, forced under my father's corruption as the General of Novear. I had nearly left him for dead then, and now all I could think of was how I would never get him back.

Please.

Now all I could think about was how I would never learn about his other scars. The ones he hid underneath his cloaks. The aged welts that traveled up his sleeves and were lined on the surface by someone who took their time in carving each individual one. I hated him for that too, because now I would never know how to repay their creator.

I lowered myself down to the corner of his mouth, placing my cracked lips at the edge of where I had left him scarred, kissing his jawline. It was the only place I could reach because I could not physically pull myself up further through the stark, grinding pain.

'I'm sorry,' I shakily mouthed into his ashen skin. I counted the seconds between the imaginary breaths I forced him to have, commanding his lungs to fill with air and let go.

Breathe in. Breathe out.

I was still counting as the sun rose above us and his body bled cold.

Breathe in. Breathe out.

Chapter Forty-One

Sabine

My head was submerged underwater—*I could not breathe.* Shockwaves ransacked every fiber of my being as I woke beneath the frigid waters.

The roots of my hair wrapped in a tightly wound fist against the nape of my neck. The water suffocated me, slamming into my nose, flooding into my lungs. Pinpricks sliced open the back of my scalp, uprooted for a sliver of air as I broke the surface.

"Open your eyes, daughter of mine. . . before I grow impatient." The urge to open my eyes constricted, my lashes crystallized shut by the plunge. But that deathly octave, my father's voice, forced them open. "Ah, we aren't quite awake yet. . . are we? Let's try this again."

The solid slab of ice beneath me sliced into the flesh of my knees, forced to obey the alarming pressure on top of me. My upper body re-submerged in a mesh of roaring, glacial heat, as my lungs broke the water's surface. River water gushed out of my mouth, and I gasped as my father's fierce grip forced my head back.

"You have kept me waiting long enough, Sabine," my father snarled behind me. I thrashed away from him, but the rope fibers binding my wrists cut deeper the more I writhed to break free.

The vapor of my father's breath grazed my ear, and I stilled. The fog traveled across the frozen river, swept away by the oncoming winter storm. Dense thunder clouds blanketed the sky. It was too dark to see beyond the night's summit; too cold to feel the sting of my wounds. There was just the absence of him. A hole in my chest where his magic had once been, warmed by the flames of his sorcery through the bond.

Keahi was gone.

"Don't be shy." Lightning split the sky. A shadow of my father's figure flashed against the ice as he leaned closer. "Tell me just how much you have missed me. He removed the siphoning crystal, but the scars from my knife remain; what a relief it is." He laughed in time with the thunder. "For you to know, I will *always* be with you."

A single sharp nail started at the base of my spine, a deliberate and slow upward trail. I shivered as his metallic rings scraped against my damp tunic.

"Ah, if I remember correctly, I believe it was right—" My scream echoed across the frozen river before he could finish. *"Here."*

The ornate silver talon my father always wore on his thumb punctured into the soft flesh of my neck like a viper, twisting in the space where the siphoning crystal had been; right where he claimed my magic and buried his past. He dug the tiny blade into my skin until I was sure he was hitting the bone underneath, carving his name.

"That's much better, isn't it?" He hissed through his teeth, piercing the metal deeper. "You don't have to tell me. I know you missed me—but do not worry, my little star, for as long as you walk upon this realm. . . I will always find you."

The King of Novear snatched his thumb from my wound, and fiery blood flowed beneath my collar. Every bone in my body stiffened from the swift release. His strike made of venom. Crisp winter air burned my nose as I attempted to slow my breath, to regain an ounce of control. My body shuddered uncontrollably, waiting for the next blow, listening for the waiver of his next breath.

How had he found me?

My father had sprinted in the opposite direction of the Solstice mountains which Keahi carried me to, before he collapsed on the forest floor. When I lost myself in the pain of his death, I passed out on his unmoving chest. There was no way the King of Novear could have found me so quickly. Keahi had used his shadowfire to project us several days' ride ahead and drained his magic of the realm. I swallowed back a cry and took a deep breath.

This was not real.

A weary laugh parted my lips. "Do you think I don't know the game you are playing at father? You are the one who taught it to me."

Only a powerful sorcerer of Novear could manipulate the light within your dreams, change them. The means by which you could torture someone in this state were endless. As my father's General, I had done it many times to retrieve information. The souls I had tormented did not know they were dreaming, and nightmares were real until you woke up.

"Who did you murder this time, to siphon enough power to find me in my dreams this far away?" I smiled. "Do not act as if I didn't see you run from me. *You. Miserable. Fucking. Coward.*"

The King of Novear's mocking laughter echoed in the prison he had constructed within my mind. "You are just like your mother, aren't you?"

My cheek seared as his fist slammed into my frozen jaw. Blood trickled out of the corner of my lips. Each drop of crimson was a ripple against the frost, crystallizing in the thin layer of snow, transforming into a bed of ruby crystals within the dreamscape. I would not break for those who had sacrificed to set me free.

Elias's voice echoed in my mind. *'Fight for it.'*

"Powerless," I whispered. "You are powerless. Not even a siphoning crystal could stop the darkness from taking over now. How did it feel, father? To finally see the power of the veil unleashed upon the realm, the sin for your destruction?"

"Those who oppose the Gods, do not fear sin." My father's growl thrummed against my back. "I taught you better than that."

"Then why did you *murder* my mother, after the curse of the veil found her first?" I seethed. "Why did you place the siphoning crystal in my neck to control me? Why did you keep me alive for all those years if you did not fear its escape? If you do not fear the power of darkness, what do you fear?"

The King of Novear's calloused hand reached around my neck, tightening until I was gasping against his hold. Death was not a mercy he had ever given me, not even in my dreams, as his hands shook with restraint. He did, however, do something I did not expect. My father finally gave me the answer to what he feared.

"Bring. Him. To. Me."

Tears streamed down my face at the memory of the sorcerer's bond being ripped apart. My chest cracked open. "The Prince is dead."

There was no more calculation, no ounce of control for my father to grasp hold of in the face of what he truly feared. *"Bring him to me.* Before I find another way for you to bring him to me myself. You both should have died the day he found you!"

Fear was a valiant tool in the face of feeble men, and the weapon of my choice. For it was my father who taught me to wield it and took advantage of me until I craved it. The King of Novear had just shown his hand.

It was time to wake up.

"You have a lot of fear for a man who is dead, but I'll play your game. . . Do you know what I will do to you, father, if I wake up, and my bonded is still dead? *I will hunt you to the ends of the realm.* I will not stop until I have you on your hands and knees praying to the Gods you have betrayed. I will be your *King.*"

The slate of ice beneath us cracked, splintering into a thousand directions across this nightmare.

A wicked laugh crawled out of my chest. "And if the Prince is alive? I will bring him to you, just as you have asked. I will watch him shred you, limb from limb, and I will feed it to you until you choke from the suffocation of your own sins."

My father's laughter mimicked mine. "I do not fear your threats, because you do not even know *what* he is, child. *Bring him to me."*

I clawed at the edge of the ridge, fighting against his weight, inching me closer to the hole cut in the crystalized ice, the river raging beneath.

"I know what his soul looks like." A single tear traveled along my jawline and fell into the water below. "I saw its very core, the monster hiding underneath his skin, peering through the gateway of hell in his eyes. . . but do you know why I was not afraid?" My shoulders were punched forward, bracing my head to resist the christening of icy waters. "Because I am the monster you made me!"

A violent strike obliterated the crown of my head, my vision shooting an array of colors through my skull. I ripped open my eyes just in time to see his reflection staring back at me through the river.

It was not my father who I saw in the glimmer on top of the water.

It was Keahi.

My limbs thrashed as my body gave way to the surface, resisting the rush flooding into my lungs as I gurgled out the remaining air I had left.

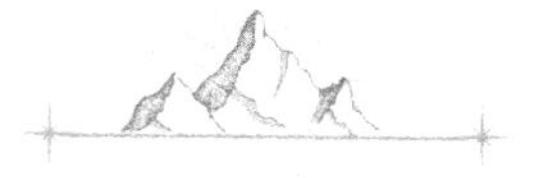

"Elias! She won't stop seizing!" A female voice I did not recognize cried.

"Hold her head, do not push her limbs down. I need to pour another tonic into her," Elias commanded. Hot liquid poured into my mouth; the acid mangled my tongue until I fought to choke it out. A warm palm pressed against my chin, forcing my mouth to stay closed.

"She wasn't like this when we found her—why is she getting worse?!"

Drakkon?

"She's still feeding her magic to Keahi. We must sedate her before she kills herself in doing so. She is overexerting her magic." Elias released his hand.

"Why won't she wake up?" The female voice was full of panic.

Elias sighed out a long, loose breath. "She will. I can already feel it."

A door slammed open. Iahni spoke with a tremor in her voice. "Elias, hurry-please. Something's wrong with Keahi. . . he's losing it. He won't stop screaming her name—the chains." I could hear her swallow from across the room. "They're not holding."

"Zehra." Elias's voice surged with urgency. "Can you stay with Sabine? Are you well enough?"

"Elias, I did not forget years' worth of knowledge in a month's time," the woman who Elias had spoken to responded. "I can manage—*go*. My brother needs you."

Elias wasted no time, his staff tapping swiftly across the marbled floor. "Drakkon, come with me; Kane has not arrived yet. I am going to need your help."

Drakkon's footsteps followed Elias, but there was a lingering pause before the door slowly closed in on its hinges. "Zehra," he called back. "Do not let her die. I need her alive just as badly as I do

Keahi right now. . . I need to tell her I am sorry."

"Sabine is safe with me."

Chapter Forty-Two

Sabine

The iron barred skylight steeped the walls in midnight. The moon hung low among the stars, unable to glisten through the ceiling window of my room in Kallahni. A gradient of the day slipped into a seamless slumber, undeterred, as I listened to quiet footsteps drift in and out of the room to check on my healing. This endless cycle of wakefulness, bleak and unforgiving.

It compounded with my agony until each beat of my heart became unbearable. In every breath, there was grief. In each movement, I felt his absence. But it was when I closed my eyes that I found him. These dreams were archived from another kind of pain, cutting deep into my soul, carving into my battered heart.

Dreams that were not nightmares, but a sanctuary to a soul that was not my own.

Each time I dreamed, honey-filtered rays combed through magenta skies, flecked with a thousand stars. Night and day were eternal as the phases of the moon lined the atmosphere, colliding with a stream of indigo and lilac planes of spiraled luster.

A soft breeze brushed through my hair, with the perfume of fresh rain and fields of spring. The crust of the earth beneath my feet suspended itself without anchor in the air, and many more clouds roamed beside me. I was gliding through a life filled with many strings, each strand of glowing light connected to every living thing.

And it felt like *home.*

As I slowly forced my body to turn, to wake, emerald eyes found mine in the mirror from across the marbled floor. The owner's stare was full of tension. Her dark brows furrowed deeper as I kept my gaze pinned. The small expression sent a dull ache in my chest, because it was the same look Keahi gave me when he was worried.

A look I took for granted.

Missed.

Keahi's sister. The woman Elias had asked to stay with me, who I had known to exist, but had not known was captured by my father. . . she had not left my side or this room. When I saw her on the battlefield with my father's hands strangled around her long black hair, it was the same shade as Keahi's. Drakkon's determination to cross the river only confirmed my suspicions, despite the stark resemblance.

'He's alive,' she had murmured each time she checked on my injuries in the following days. I was too weak to move. Darkness both flourished in and corroded my veins, staking its claim over me after I had set it free, and now I was forced to lie with it. But every syllable beneath her words was a promise of Keahi's survival, an anthem. *'Do not give up now.'*

Alive, I repeated to myself, He's alive.

When his chest stopped moving, his magic died in my heart—*I felt him leave.* Keahi was gone from the realm, and no matter how many times I begged him to stay, he would not come back. But it was the same recurring dream I had that finally made me believe he was truly alive.

There was no home without him, and I had not known one existed until I felt his return every time I dreamed. The Prince of Solstice's eyes were made of fire, but his soul was my oasis.

If my bonded had not died. . . where did he go?

The hearth flickered, and a flare of amber heated the side of my face. A swirl of embers floated away from the fireplace, dancing through the night lit room. The magic drifted in sparks, gliding across my frame, and over the bridge of my nose until she whisked it away.

"Welcome back, Lightbringer," she whispered. "Or so I have heard, but it would seem to be the opposite. . . would it not?" She lowered her palm, and the embers curled into smoke between her fingertips. "My name is Zehra Aldeer, Princess of the Solstice Kingdom, but I have already foreseen you know of that."

I was frozen. Not by what she said, but how she said it—*empty*. Zehra's mouth thinned as she crossed her legs, her knees tapping against the ornate metal frame of the floor-length mirror. The mirror I avoided when I first woke up in this room after my travel with Keahi. I had feared my reflection then and refused to see myself or the scars on my back from the ritual.

Zehra turned and stared into the mirror straight on, like she had been doing so this entire time just to make peace with what she saw on the other side. But as her hands trembled at her sides, her chest faltered with her breath. It did not look like fear, not the kind I knew. Her features echoed with hatred.

"You have not talked for days despite us telling you my brother is alive. . . but I am going to. I need someone to listen, and I'm afraid—" She paused, releasing some tension from her shoulders as she took a deep breath. "I'm certain you already know what it was like."

The thought lingered in the firelight: what *he* was like. A deep burgundy bandeau wrapped around her chest, crisscrossed right beneath her bony shoulder blades in the back. The tips of her fingers lightly pressed against the tops of her thighs, her left hand steadily circling an obsidian dagger belted against her black tights.

"I feel like I already know you." Zehra swallowed.

Unbeknownst to her, I felt the same. The scream she made when my father had thrown her into the dirt was enough to remember her by, so different from the fragile rasp of her voice now. I shut the memory away.

"He talked about you, your father. I wish he hadn't. Because when I look at you, *I see him*. Worst of all, I see what he has done to us."

Zehra shook her head as she reached up, roving her hands over her dark raven hair. The tremor in her hand steadied, her grip tightened on the hilt.

A chill traveled up my spine, and my stomach sank as she slowly lifted the knife. My body screamed as I shifted upright, but she swiftly held up her hand to stop me from injuring myself further.

"It isn't fair, is it?" She whispered with a tainted smile. "To be at the hands of others." Confusion fought to the surface as her hand went to the dagger and pulled a section of her hair taught. "Fairness is only as valuable as the mirror they place in front of you."

Zehra raised her dagger to the side of her chin and sliced the strands of her hair at an angle. The gasp on my lips disintegrated. I quietly listened to the sheer of the blade, and I heard what she needed to say until the final lock of hair fell to the floor.

She pushed a portion of her fringe behind her ear as she turned to stand and face me. Her frame was long and lean as she stood, but her ribs protruded like someone who had been starved. "I could not look at it anymore. . ." Her voice grew quiet. ". . . knowing he touched it."

My voice was weak, out of practice, from the time I had not used it. I looked back up to her emerald eyes in the mirror. My lip cracked as I forced the words past my heavy tongue. "You look so much. . . like them." *Her brothers.*

There was so much more I needed to say, but my weakened body refused. I stared at Zehra's hair on the floor, the strands now dull and lifeless. At every turn, I had wanted to cut myself free of the fate my father had tied to my body; a phantom string I could not grasp hold of or forget when I had felt him through the siphoning crystal tugging the other end. But even if I had the chance to cut it myself, it would have never been enough. It still was not enough.

She cleared her throat after my long, unfinished pause. "I hope you do not blame them for not telling you about my capture. The Volkans were as shocked as you were."

My chin slowly tilted up to her face as she carefully made her way to the side of my bed, her jagged ends swishing just above her collarbones. "Why did they not want anyone in the capital to know?" I managed to ask.

A sleek arched eyebrow rose. "Drakkon said to be careful when you woke with questions, but he refused to tell me why," she responded almost amusedly, but her tone was hollow. The corner of her lip twitched, and sadness muddied her emerald eyes.

The Darkness faintly whispered to me as she drew closer, but it was not strong enough yet for me to hear. After what I had demanded of it in battle, it would take its time cultivating my offering—we would become one.

I strained between words, using her as a crutch when she extended her hand. "It feels. . . like I am bruised from the inside out," I huffed.

Zehra lifted me the rest of the way to a sitting position. I released a pained groan as I moved to dangle my limbs over the side of the bed. Her hands propped up against my shoulders and gently squeezed them.

"My brother is not easily killed. . . and neither are you," she said uneasily. "I can only hope you're not just as stubborn."

"More so," I panted. "Depending on the day."

A hint of an honest smile finally broke through. Zehra's eyes were knowing and wise, despite the young appearance in her cheekbones. The pit of my stomach sank deeper. It was never a good thing to see someone both young and wise. I was not much older than her, but I too had been stripped of my youth far too soon.

"Do you. . ." Zehra hesitated. "Would you like to see him?"

More than anything, but it had to wait.

"There's something I need to see first," I said, on the verge of reluctance, slowly nodding toward the mirror.

Zehra stiffened beside me. "Sabine, before you look in the mirror, know Elias said it would go away. It is just going to take some time."

Elias had always known my truth. This part of me was hidden beneath my skin, and I refused to fear any longer. I pressed my eyes tightly and shook myself. Zehra guided me closer to the mirror after I gave her a silent nod. I caught a glimpse of my bare thighs as I fought to take my steps across the room.

"Is it all over?" My breath shook.

"Yes."

The woman I looked up to face was unrecognizable, but I had never felt more connected to the reflection I saw. This is what I had felt alive beneath me, when I had been nothing but a hollow shell.

Black veins spread from the center of my torso and branched out like tree roots into my limbs. The curse from the Veil of Seven had planted its seed in the garden of my soul when it contacted my chest. The Darkness would not wither; it would grow, and there was nothing my father could do to stop it now.

"I don't remember." I swallowed. "If Elias said anything about my hair."

On the right side, my hair reflected that of my father's lineage.

Porcelain white strands made of starlight tapered at the top of my hip bones.

Zehra tensed at the back of my arm. "He was not sure about the hair. . ."

My magic split itself in half when the vessel of my power broke inside of me, forced to share a home with its opposite. The left side of my hair, now pitch black, darkened into a shade as lightless as the sorcery itself. The sides of my cheeks were met with hot, steaming tears.

It was time.

"Can you turn me around, please?"

Zehra gave me an unsure nod in the mirror as she rotated my frame, my back facing the mirror for me to see out of the corner of my eyes.

The red angry welts had turned black from the magic. I dropped the white sheet I held onto lower, exposing the symbol my father had carved into my skin with an enchanted blade; an attempt to destroy us both by igniting a sorcerer's bond.

My heart clenched, remembering the matching mark my shadow had developed on his chest. A black dragon, wrapped in front of the sun's flames, engulfing the sun into an eclipse.

The urgency to see him heightened, but exhaustion buckled my knees instantly. Zehra reached beneath both of my arms and helped me walk over to the bed. I was not the only one who kept secrets in our alliance. His conversation with Kane pushed its way to the forefront of my mind: *'We did not finish the bond.'*

"Elias has not been able to leave his side," Zehra said as she helped me lie back down. I had made no mention of Keahi out loud, but the worried look on my face was enough. Zehra added, "He will make a full recovery thanks to you."

"Because of me?" I mumbled, my vision fading. I wanted to remain awake enough to see him, but I was losing sight of the room. The whispers from the Darkness grew louder, but not loud enough. My head collapsed onto the pillow.

Tired. I was so *tired.*

Zehra's weight settled next to me on the bed. "It was possible he could have recovered on his own, but you healed him faster than he would have healed himself. Elias believes you transferred some of your power to him."

The whispers silenced.

"He can heal himself. . . what kind of sorcerer has that ability? But he has—"

"The scars?" She knew the direction of my thoughts before I went quiet. "Only elements crafted by the Gods can truly mark him."

I touched the side of my face, goosebumps trailing along all the places I had witnessed the touch of a blade on his skin. Then to my mouth, remembering the kiss I had planted on the single scar I had given him. I had marked him with the staff of malachite the night we had first met, the weapon my father had given me when I became his General.

Desperate and confused, even still. "Strange," I echoed my thoughts, "I have never heard of such magic existing."

She tilted her head. "Some might say the same about you. I have never seen someone be able to wield magic as black as night. Though no one in this castle will be brave enough to try and question you through your marriage to my brother, not even me."

My eyes drifted close, even as I fought to keep them open. If I was to recover, to see him, I needed to keep fighting this constant cycle.

"Tell me something, anything," I pleaded. "I need to stay awake. I keep falling asleep."

Zehra tucked the soft fur blanket underneath her chin, and after a long silence she took mercy on me. "I will tell you a story then, Lightbringer. One I rarely tell, because it is not just my story to tell. You must promise to keep it until the other half is given to you."

My eyelashes attempted to flutter shut, but I nodded my head. "I promise."

"My mother was a powerful seer," she whispered, as if someone was in the room to hear us. "After the Veil of Seven was destroyed, the messages from the fates were broken. Her visions became erratic and painful. In the end, she lost her ability to piece the future together. My mother took her own life, and Keahi was the one who found her."

I held my breath. Elias had told me of her death, but not why. There was both guilt in hearing of her passing from everyone but Keahi and shame because he had never told me himself. Worse, I never gave him the chance to.

"My first vision appeared the day after she died; the gift could only be passed on through a female sorcerer's lineage. The visions did not affect me the same way. I have never been able to see the future, only bits and pieces of what could be. It is like staring into a shattered mirror, each piece reflecting its own path through fate, but I could never see the entire image emerge. There was always one piece missing."

A shadow darkened over her hollowed features. "Sometimes I would be right as I fit the messages into their frame, and other times I was wrong. The night your father captured me was the night we found you. I had left Keahi and Kane on my own accord. . ."

"I'm sorry." My voice hushed into the pillow.

"It destroyed me; in the same way it had destroyed my mother, I suppose. I finally knew what it meant to know what could have been, and see it ripped away by a thread of fate. I could have changed it." She loosened a breath. "I had never been more wrong a day in my life."

"We can change it," I said firmly. "My father can be stopped. I know it."

Zehra's eyes turned to glass as moonlight cast into the room. She reached over, tucking a fallen black strand behind my ear. "Not all fates change—some are finely woven."

"It was you," I hesitated. "You were the one who saw us coming. How my father knew."

The hitch in her breath beat the stillness in my own. "He forced me to do many things I am not proud of." Zehra's touch lingered on my cheek as she rolled onto her back. "And for now, that is as far as the story goes."

Chapter Forty-Three

Sabine

A soft magic intertwined with my soul, calling me forward. My feet were soundless on the ground before my eyes could open, roaming the night-lit hallways of Kallahni in a barefoot slumber. The somber notes sang the abandoned castle into a deep and quiet melody as I explored the depths of the mountain.

Each key strummed with my steps, building into a crescendo, descending into a madness that enchanted me. Cool, gritty soil pressed between my toes with my next step as I gazed down a dark and narrow tunnel.

Monstrous caves lined the tall, strange corridor. Rusted metallic chains glittered against the sphere of light illuminated within the palm of my hands. Each one was bolted into the walls with massive archaic fastenings, ringed with silver spikes meant to inhumanely anchor its slaves. Though there was nothing human to be said about the ghostly beings who had been imprisoned beneath this mountain.

A faint orange glow crept out of the final cave cell; this one was neither open nor empty. I twisted the hem of my nightgown and hesitantly approached the magic it beckoned me to find.

The music stopped.

My hands flexed against the cool metal bars, transfixed. Chains scraped over the dirt floor, jarring me fully awake. White powder encircled Keahi within the cavernous cell; markings that were not of my language were written on the inside of its rim to spell him in place.

He was shackled to the floor, the cuffs around his four limbs armored with wrought iron nails embedded into his flesh. I inhaled a sharp breath as Keahi rose from his knees, covered from the waist down in shreds of ebony fabric.

The metal chains grew taut as he slowly ventured to the rim of the binding circle. A shadow cast over his face as he ascended from the darkened corner. Each piece of his disheveled hair found a different direction to masque his expression.

Keahi silently swayed against the metallic bindings, his body tensing, trying to find the balance to stand. He looked *drained*, even more so than when I saw him in death. Unrefined guilt emerged within me. This pain was a measure of years. Keahi was caged in the same way I saw myself; an unending torment. I would rather spend another lifetime under my father's command, then see him like this.

My lips quivered as I whispered, "Who did this to you?"

Each inhale appeared to cost him with the exhausted way the sides of his rib cage flexed in and out. Sweat glistened along the lines of his muscles, rippling down the sharp angle of his hips. Each movement dragged heavier than the last, but his scars were the heaviest of them all.

A tear streamed down the corner of my face. My breath caught as each bladed wound took shape on his skin, fragmented across his entire body.

The worst scar extended from the apex of his right shoulder to the top of his left hip bone in a jagged curse. It looked ageless compared to the others, curated into a horrific welt that had not fully healed. Not all of his scars were bare to me, though.

Some were hidden within the black serpent, scaling from his left wrist that twisted in intricate bindings, merging until it coiled around the matching emblem on his chest. The same symbol forever carved into my back, except his looked as if it had always been a portion of the design; like it had always been there.

"Are you done yet?" The deep threat in his voice seared my hands. I hissed as I withdrew them from the bars, unbearably hot from his sorcery warding me away.

This was the same man who died for me, forced to witness his unending devotion by the darkness's will. He sacrificed himself for me, even after he saw the truth of my magic. Keahi tilted his chin toward the empty cave wall, unable to look at me.

Did he regret saving me? My heart collapsed. *Had the darkness been. . . wrong?*

"Your magic," I said breathlessly, unable to process this detached side of him.

I expected him to welcome me. Maybe I was too late; it was what I deserved. But I refused to believe my life would always be reactionary.

"Your magic," I repeated firmly. "It called to me, and I followed."

It slipped into my dreams and invaded every space that had been uncertain. I heard the magic that led me here. *'I would have known it anywhere, as if it were my own,'* he had once said to me.

"You should not have come here." His voice was cold, as if I meant nothing to him. As if his soul was not bound to mine. *"Leave,"* he growled through his teeth when I refused to obey.

A faint shadow pulled my attention, its hand stretched out in the amber firelight, begging me not to listen. Keahi was not the one who called to me after all, but if my shadow wanted to continue to lie. . . I was going to make him suffer for it.

Because I suffered when I lost him, when I found I was not the only one who lied with an unholy tongue. I bit back the sob in my throat, including the lie where I said I did not want him.

My face twisted into anger—truth, because I was sick of pretending. I slipped past Keahi's portrayal and curled my fists tighter around the rim, challenging his worn and uninviting exterior. I seethed low through the space between the railings.

"Tell me, Keahi, why would a prince be kept underground in a cell like an animal?"

Keahi's red, glowing eyes snapped up to mine in an instant. A flicker of hurt vanished from him as fast as it appeared. Lost between the lava, swirling in subsequent torment at the outer edge of his sunken eyes.

Internally, I crumbled at the faint loss of his composure with hope. I was not used to this weakness. I had not allowed it, but neither had he.

Keahi's teeth flashed, rattling the chains in unison. "I could ask the same of you, Princess, although. . ." He let out a staggering, pained breath. "You were not raised within the shadows, were you?"

I raised my chin in defiance. "No, I was not."

He leaned forward, careful not to cross the white line in the sand. Keahi's white curl fell over his left eye. The bite harbored in every word. "You need to leave—now."

Had he learned nothing of me on the battlefield? The corner of my lips lifted. I was not someone who followed orders.

I tapped the back of his shoulder.

Keahi whirled on me in an instant, debris of black sand flying the opposite direction. Anger, replaced by the truest sense of fear, as he found me within arm's reach. His eyes darted back and forth between the metal cell bars staked in place, and the woman who was unafraid to trap herself with him.

When he fully turned back to me, all the color had drained out of his face. "What have you done?"

I took a step forward and smirked.

"Nothing. . . yet."

Keahi jerked his arms out to the side, the heavy chains clashing on the ground. His gloves were nowhere to be found as he tore into the lengths of his hair. He pleaded as he looked down at his scarred hands, analyzing the strength of the chains as he pulled on their hilt. "You can't be here," he rasped, edged with panic.

"I heard you the first time." I tilted my head with a slow, predatory gaze. The sound of the chains lost all their momentum. The quiet abrupt. "You. Lied. To. Me."

Warm, glowing eyes roved over the changes already taking place in my magic, at the proof. Black veins coiled up my bare legs, spiraled up the curve of my hips, and faintly disappeared beneath my nightgown. The white fabric was translucent in the torch glow. I swallowed as his gaze trailed further. The lengths of my black and white hair tapered over my breasts.

"And you didn't?"

The whisper of my laugh sent a visible chill across his skin. He attempted to steady his breath and failed. Keahi's deflection did little to distract me from what I needed to say, because the light within had not fully vanished yet. "I have worn many faces, except for my own, and it terrifies you just as much as it does me."

Keahi's jaw flexed, but there was no mask for him to hide behind now.

My tears muddied the earth. "I am the sin of my father when he closed the Veil of Seven, the balance the realm required. This darkness I carry could swallow the entire world if I let it."

His face did not change as he said, "And if you had the chance, would you watch the realm burn?"

I went into a familiar, unfeeling place. "I wanted to die before I had the chance to say yes."

Keahi grew unnaturally still. "Did your father realize it, when he had closed the Veil of Seven, what remained?"

"He is starting to remember." My mouth thinned. This was about us. "You were dead, Keahi—*I felt it.*"

The notch in his throat slid to the base of his neck as he quietly said, "What exactly. . . did you feel?"

"Everything, and then nothing." My voice cracked. "It was like your soul had been expelled from the realm entirely—you were gone, and I could not bring you back. I *wanted you* to come back."

The firelight crackled in the background, his shadow nowhere to be seen. His ember eyes were heavy, lost to faraway places. "You should not have come here," he repeated.

My chest stung, but I did not need his words. I did not need him to tell me he wanted me back. I had already seen proof through his actions and actively ignored them. We were not finished.

"I had asked your book a second question about the sorcerer's bond. After the night you left me to wake on my own, when I invited you to stay with me. But you already knew what I asked your book, don't you, Son of Fire?"

Keahi stifled his next inhale.

"If I could not undo the bond, as the first answer claimed, I wanted to know how I could finish it," I said as I prowled toward him.

"It seems you lied about overhearing me with Elias outside the training room, too." He released a tired laugh, but I could sense his worry tremble through the bond. "Though I was a fool to believe you had not otherwise."

"No, I was the fool. I refused to believe we had not finished the bond even after I heard you with Elias, or when the book answered me the second time." I shook my head. "I can feel you, Keahi, even when you are gone. There is a hole in my chest where you are supposed to be. It was not until I heard what you said on the battlefield when you thought I was dying in your arms. I heard. . . *everything*."

Our gazes connected.

"And if I interpreted the second answer correctly. . ." I held out my wrist, pulling at the sleeve of my fragile nightgown, lightly gliding my fingertips over the blood in my veins. "An offering is due for the second binding of the sorcerer's bond."

The hold Keahi had placed on himself shattered, undone at the sight. He frantically shook his head and stepped back, chains grinding against the iron hilt.

"No Sabine—Stay. Back." He demanded.

I stilled my trailing fingertips, raising a single brow. "I'm sorry. Was it something I misunderstood? Or are you only honest when you think I cannot hear you or you are writing answers in that book Elias gave me?"

Keahi turned, muttering curses to himself in a language I could not understand. "Whatever answers you are looking for, I—I cannot give to you. Not right now."

"Is that so?" I tilted my head to the side. "And if I undo those chains. . . will you talk then?"

Keahi's shoulders dropped as he reached the end of the barrier. The white line in the sand sifted. Its enchantment triggered the grains to levitate around us, preventing him from stepping away further.

"There are three bindings to the sorcerer's bond: of the blood, body, and soul. It was written by your hand. Was there a reason you couldn't tell me yourself?" I lowered my voice. "Or do you enjoy playing games? I'm not opposed."

"Sabine," he groaned. Ember eyes pleaded for dissolution, searching for my actions to be disinclined.

They were unwavering. My previous reluctance was rewritten with absolution. This is what I wanted to return to. This was my choice when I thought I had nothing left. "I already have your soul, my shadow," I said softly. "What more is there to be afraid of?"

Gold sliced through the copper in my veins and blood fell like drops of rain, creating an oasis in barren sand. The muscles across his chest flexed, straining into a tremble. His knees plummeted into the sand, the metal burning against his wrists as it glowed a bright white. He struggled to create the distance he was not fated to find between us.

My hand darkened in the dim light, covered in my blood, dripping into a pool of offering as I circled him. "I am the one who gave you your scar, the one on your face."

"I know," he relented without hesitation. Keahi tore his hands deeper into the ground, but the black sand slid through his fingers. "I remember the scar on my face the most."

"When?" I pressed. My golden dagger sickened red. His focus shattered as he watched a drop slide off the knife. "When did you know I was my father's General?"

"The day you were in the ring. . . Lightbringers are not supposed to succumb to the dark side, and I had only witnessed it from one other—the night I received my scar." Keahi closed his eyes tightly. "I had only suspected you then; it is why I questioned if you were working with your father. It confirmed my suspicions when I witnessed your powers on the battlefield."

I held out my bleeding hand to him.

"Then take it. Take the second binding for the sorcerer's bond," I rasped. "It is only fair. I cannot heal the scar I gave you, but we will finally be even."

Keahi's dark brows furrowed with confusion, bare hands flexing at his sides.

"That is *not* the scar I am worried about." The cave walls shook against his ragged breath. "It is the one I will be left with if you leave me. If you believe this to be transactional. . . because I assure you, it is not."

I sunk myself into the sand, one foot at a time, as I crossed over to him, backing him toward the edge of the circle. I dipped my unstained hand into my bleeding wrist and painted my bottom lip red.

Fear was replaced with hunger as his pupils dilated. His mouth went slack when I gripped his jawline with my bloodied hand.

Keahi looked at me; full of agony and pure unrequited desire. It was a look that should have had me running back to my chambers as it did before when I saw it for the first time, but my own knees crashed before him in the sand.

I pushed my other hand into his hair and gripped the back of his neck to pull him forward. Keahi let out a small gasp right before I sealed my lips onto his mouth. He tensed, unmoving, as I held him.

My fingers curled into his dark hair, my touch gentling, willing him to understand. We were both afraid, but we were not alone. "When you cannot speak it," I whispered into his mouth. "Show me the truth."

His eyes squeezed tight, melting against me. The kiss was slow, a brief meeting of our lips. Each touch lingering, hesitant, and needing more. It dismantled into urgency, our lips parting and the tip of his tongue brushing the seam of my mouth. A low rumble sounded in his chest as he fisted the back of my hair and sucked on my bottom lip, tasting the offering I gave him in blood.

I moaned as the chains rattled, dredging through the soil as his powerful arms encircled me. He pulled me closer, my curves yielding to his hardened muscles. Keahi's kiss roughened at the sound, desperate as he pressed, forcing me open. His tongue swept past my teeth, exploring my mouth.

The fire in his blood slid through his touch, igniting every part of me until the heat of his kiss pooled between my thighs. Keahi tugged me into his lap with a low, penetrating growl. His hardened length ground against my aching center to where I needed him the most, but then he wrenched himself away from me.

His molten pupils widened as he looked over my swollen lips. Pain clouded his eyes from the truth he revealed to me. My bonded let out a breathless whisper, "This. . . this is not real."

A throbbing ache pierced my chest. I pressed off the top of his shoulders and took a grievous step back. The form I had placed in front of him dissipated into the hollow spaces of his cell. Keahi had been asleep when I found him, lying within the circle until I entered his dreams. I could hear the hitch in his throat as he looked over his shoulder. My hands were still pressed into the metal bars, having never left.

"I asked your book a third question about the sorcerer's bond, Son of Fire." I gently released my hold. "It has not answered me yet."

As he turned, I could still see the hot flush of his cheeks. Sadness twisted in my chest as he lowered his head away from me and sunk into the binds. His voice was barely audible, broken. "Did you find the answer you were looking for?"

"Not yet," I said as I lifted my unharmed wrist. "Thank you, though, for thoroughly explaining the second one. . ." I backed away from his cell, preparing for the long journey back to my rooms, the pain rapidly setting in as the magic I followed faded.

I spoke directly to him through our bond:

But if you do not tell me how to finish the sorcerer's bond. . . I will.

A shattered wall of terror fell on the other side, but I could not afford to falter. I had to be certain, and what I had learned through this interaction was still not enough.

I would not lose him a second time.

Chapter Forty-Four

Sabine

Truth is what others create. Written within their assumptions, they refuse to change.

'Dismember the urge to correct them, General,' my father would repeat in our lessons. *'Let them disclose their purest motivations within the stories they have created for you. Only then can you expose the weapon forged by their idle hands, plucking the realization from their tongue before they can formulate the cost of their own error.'*

'That you have only told one lie, and they. . . have told legions.'

The faces in this room did not realize the cost of their error, but I did. It loomed over my shoulders in a blanketed awareness. I was not the only liar in this room. Their gazes wandered across the round table in passive silence, waiting for Keahi's delayed arrival.

A full week had passed since his disappearance.

The air in the castle turned bitter as I passed through each corridor with dulled senses, knowing I would not find the monster who breathed life into his kingdom of shadows. I had peered into each of the cells with frantic intent, searching for him in vain, unable to accept the painful truth.

My shadow was not there.

A weak apology hovered between my lips and the weight of it desperately clung to me without remorse. I felt guilty for baiting him to answer me, but I could not find him shackled anywhere, to force him to hear the words I wanted to say. I searched every inch of the prison's labyrinth, each cell as empty as the one before. When I reached the end of the prison's tunnel, I realized I had overlooked something in passing.

The metallic chains whose shackles were once clasped had been left wide open; *every last one of them.*

There was no beast, no hint of man or sorcerer alike, hidden within the cells I had passed the night I approached him. I searched through each possibility in my mind of why the shackles were now open when they were already empty. Each conclusion ensued more chaos than the last.

'Did he realize it when he had closed the veil what remained?' It was not a question he had posed when he already knew the answer, and it traveled deeper than the curse in my veins.

The sin of the Veil of Seven was now visible to the table of sorcerers who sat before me, sharing their secrets with me when their eyes did not widen at the violent black markings on full display. The vine-like bruising was just now fading to my skin's natural shade.

My truth did not terrorize them, not how it should have. So, what secrets had they been hiding behind? What truths did I create? And how much was it going to cost me in the end when I swore there was no price too high for vengeance? Would it be worth it in the end to be surrounded by those who wanted to see my father's reign end as much as I did, or would the depths of their secrets prove more fearsome than the world I had escaped from?

If I had even escaped at all.

The round table anticipated Keahi's entrance into the room before he appeared. We were seated at the edge of its silver-finished borders, casting a glow that resembled the surface of the moon. It glimmered in defiance of the void it carried in its center, home to the shallows of ink-colored waters that were richly dyed with a single drop of night. It evoked such an emptiness that not even a reflection was visible if one directly looked upon the waters.

The deep magic within stirred its viscous form, swirling with the undercurrent of a cosmic whirlpool that not even oceans could replicate. The water eddied to a funeral pace when Keahi seated himself directly across from me.

Zehra's emerald eyes softened toward me, a gentle squeeze of the hand in affirmation. I did not have the strength to return it. Our greeting was fragile, but when Keahi had disappeared, she checked on me every night and promised his return.

My limbs had been nimble, restless upon the first call of our meeting. Keahi had not sent for me upon his arrival, to Gods knows where he had found himself away under such conditions. Elias had refused to offer the slightest bit of information, only that Kane had never returned. Dread gripped the vessels inside of my chest as my shadow emerged—his second nowhere in sight.

Unfeeling eyes flickered toward me, draped in his Volkan robes. Elias braced a hand on Keahi's shoulder, using him for support as he leaned forward to dip a single aged finger into the oily reservoir. The response to his touch was not immediate, but his eyes tightened as he grabbed hold of whatever he found within the stained waters. Elias's breath deepened, changed with each solid inhale as the water churned from the force of his magic inside the moon's circle.

The hair on the back of my neck spiked as his sorcery warped the darkness until it glowed with the radiance of the surrounding sun, blasting its sparkling rays through the seams as the pool of water levitated from the table.

Its shape became clear as it continued to drift above us, molding itself to fit every crevice of the room. It drew itself like a curtain once it expanded from ceiling to floor, shading us from the outsiders now banished from entry. The marbled floor illuminated beneath us in a white omniscient light, as darkness enclosed itself around us. As one, it sealed us within a formidable eclipse, bottled by the Gods themselves.

The wrinkles on Elias's forehead showed the onset of strain. Keahi reached up to grasp the hand he had placed on his shoulder, giving him a subtle nod as he pulled away. Concern heated the tops of my ears as I looked Elias over, the painful grimace on his face from the act aging him beyond his years.

Elias's eyes had always held a shaded stone blue hue, now they were entirely gray. I shot a worried glance toward Drakkon. The frown at the corner of his mouth twitched, but he offered nothing as he stared at the seat Kane should have been in beside his General.

Keahi placed his elbows on the moonstone rim, resting his chin on his gloves as he clasped them together. "I am sure most of you are wondering why I have gone to such lengths today, or where I have been." Ember eyes found mine. The fire within him had revitalized since our last encounter. "All you need to know is there is nothing I would not sacrifice to destroy those who oppose me in the coming war."

That familiar power radiated from across the table, even when there was no tell from his exterior. Warmth greeted me as if he carried a portion of the sun somewhere deep inside of him, easing the vacant tundra aching in my chest in his absence. I knew he felt my response flicker down the bond when his eyes softened a fraction before they turned to flames.

"We have been betrayed." His wrathful shadow curled around him, scanning the length of the table. "More than once."

Grumbles and muffled whispers erupted around the circle. Keahi's voice hollowed out to its very core. "Kane is not here to barter for you in such circumstances, so if there are any objections—now would be the time. *To. Speak. Up.*"

The Volkans quieted. The tension in the room was volatile at the mention of the Commander's absence, their brother in arms. If there was a traitor in this room, they would find their prayers useless. Keahi's shadow prowled, weaving in and out through the soldiers at the round table, hungry for blood. It swirled around me. The front strands of my hair swayed as if I was cliff-side, caught in the summer wind.

"I'm okay," I whispered under my breath. The oncoming storm of their General occupied the soldiers. *"I promise,"* I whispered again when his shadow did not leave me. It slowly unwrapped itself from me to finish its vetting.

This silence was unbearable from the men who claimed they did not fear. If no one could draw the courage to speak, I would.

"What is this?" I asked. The entire room turned its attention to me. Their abrasive stares nearly caused me to flinch.

My shadow remained entirely still. "My apologies, Princess. I forget you are not familiar with our histories." He ignored the succeeding chuckles, training every ounce of his attention toward me.

"Rhiannon is the Goddess of Solstice and the source of the Dragon's Flame, but she is not truly a dragon herself, unlike the so-called legends have otherwise claimed. She has the gift of clarity, purification through fire gifted in her veins; anointed with unfathomable power from her gravitational pull, born inside of our sun. Her light within our realms exposed the truth for all to see. Her rays burned so brightly, she not only gained the power to see one realm. . . but all her realms, even the future itself."

Zehra spoke up, continuing the story as if she had heard it a thousand times. "This is how the Seers were born. As she walked our realm, she passed on her gift of sight to the female sorcerers of her line for the Solstice Kingdom to carry on for generations."

"One night each century, her powers vanished. The night all of her realms descended into total darkness—*the eclipse*." A hush reverently circled the table as Keahi continued. "It was in the pit of darkness where she found what had always been missing. Some truths were only meant to be found where they are unseen. To remember her discovery, our round table was born, a piece removed from the last total eclipse before the Veil of Seven had been closed, brought down to our realm by the Goddess of Solstice herself."

Acid burned the back of my throat as Keahi said, "Only truths can be told inside the circle of the eclipse. As some truths are meant to be kept in the dark, they cannot be heard from those who are outside of its capsule; nor can they enter. Only those who have spoken truthfully will leave freely."

"And if you lie," I countered. My hands shook underneath the table. *What game was he playing when he and I were the guiltiest of them all?*

"If you lie? Let us hope no one in this room finds out." His eyes darkened. "Now, is there anyone who would like to make this easy for us before we begin?"

Keahi's Volkan robe dragged against the floor as he began prowling beside his phantom executioner, taking his time before he found a clear vantage point. His shadow curled greedily over his shoulders. The Volkan he stopped behind straightened his spine; his muffled breaths shuttering under his mask. Keahi leaned down to whisper, his red glowing eyes scanning each one of his soldiers, one by one.

"Is that a no?" Keahi hissed.

The soldier's gulp was audible to the room as it hit the pit of his stomach. I saved this man during our battle. He had nearly drowned on dry land, choking on Celenia's hydromanipulation during the full moon.

"Did you have something to say, Ossian?" He prompted coldly into his ear. Ossian's pleading eyes bounced back and forth between Zehra and I. "Do not look to them for help. *Look at me.* They will not help you."

The dark waters created a storm in Ossian's eyes until his pupils capsized the Volkan magic, heating his eyes. Even if we wanted to help him, the truth was already spilling from his lips.

"They-were-going-to-torture-me!" He panted. "They said if I told them, they would let me go—" Keahi ripped off his Volkan mask.

The room pitched to a furnace as the Volkans shouted for his blood. Ossian was barely a man among the sorcerers in his creed. The soft angle of his cheekbones had been hidden, a face he would not have the chance to grow into. The flesh tone of his lips pursed together. His chest violently hurled up and down. The Volkan writhed into his seat as Keahi pinned him with one hand, unable to fill his lungs with air.

Keahi fisted the roots of his long blonde hair and twisted his neck back at a snapping angle. The Heir of Solstice was consumed with rage, a death grip locked on Ossian's chin, forcing him to look at Zehra as he snarled, "And in your weakness, someone else suffered the same fate!"

Smoke, as dark as coals, poured from Ossian's mouth, trickled from his nose. Blood-stained tears streamed down his red, bulging eyes.

"Ah. Ah," Keahi mocked the man he burned from the inside out, pressing his thumb with both hands into the socket of his jaw. My bonded's speech flowed with sorcery, a disembodied chant. *"Do. Not. Fight. Me."*

Gurgling sounds rolled in Ossian's throat. Keahi cracked his jaw open and tarred bile seeped out of the corner of his lips. A malevolent, baritone laughter gutted the room as Keahi said, "That doesn't sound like an apology to me—"

"Enough!" My scream reverberated against the dense curtain of magic encapsulating us. Every eye in the room averted. Keahi's shadow halted briefly. My chair scraped against the marble floor with a loud thud.

Ossian slumped over as Keahi released him. Black bile ejected from his mouth, pooling onto the moonstone. I was no stranger to torture; I had been on both sides under my father's rule. The things I had done—been *forced* to do. . . but the sound of Ossian's body seizing against the table drove my mind into a maddening click.

"Hand me. The knife," I demanded, knowing I had my own strapped on my outer thigh. Keahi's eyes flared with an unusual curiosity, but he did not argue with me as a silver scaled dagger materialized before me, smoke billowing off the table.

Briefly, I lingered on the transcription written across the twin blade to my own, the one Elias had forged. The dagger was cool in my sweating palms as I picked it up and walked toward Ossian. The Volkan's eyes no longer held fear. They were solely vacant as Keahi pressed his hand over the crown of his skull into the table.

"Move," I gritted through my teeth. Keahi's palm twitched briefly before the Prince obeyed without retaliation. An action that would not go unnoticed by any soul who made it out of this room.

I gently leaned over Ossian's body, palpating the edges of his rib with the tip of the knife, until I found the exact spot I was looking for. There was no hesitation, only a slight give, before I drove the blade home. I watched the light leave his eyes before ripping out the blade, discarding its bloodied remains on the table with a clatter.

Zehra looked up at me through hooded eyes. An unreadable grin formed on her face as I slowly walked away and anchored myself back down to my seat. I placed my elbows on the table, leaning down into clasped hands, positioned straight across my bonded. Keahi's gaze adhered to me the entire time.

Elias placed his palm on the moonstone, and the black enclosure seeped from its domed ceiling. Dripping its magic over Ossian's blood and body like honey until he levitated over the center of the table. I barely had enough time to look away as the bright light glowing beneath our feet beamed up through the center and eviscerated his body to dust.

Keahi leaned into the table, and a low growl emanated from him—one that would have cleared the room if we were not trapped inside. "It appears *my wife* does not appreciate my methods. Unless you would like to risk being interrogated tonight. . . I suggest all of you leave."

The entire room held a collective breath.

"Now."

Chapter Forty-Five

Sabine

The shield rippled as they rose one after the other, chairs striking the marbled floors, and curses alike fled the room until there were only two sorcerers left. Keahi picked up the bloodied knife, spinning it on its sharpened peak.

"If it is not the little liar herself, or should I address you as your title now, *General*?" he asked quietly.

The tension between the bond was a taut thread, ready to snap. I gave him a narrowed look, resentment for his disappearance coiling around my heart. Even if I did not deserve to feel this way after the night in the cell, at least I could admit that. "Call me what you wish—your words hold no merit to me, Son of Fire," I spat back.

Keahi took off his mask and shook out his raven curls. His lips parted with a sadistic grin. "Does that mean I get to choose what you do to me, then? Because I would prefer it if you made me say your name."

The whiplash from the exchange of his blatant reserve and forwardness caused my mouth to fall open. *"Who are you?"* I shook my head. "You left me for an entire week without a trace after we both nearly died, dropped a body on the table, and you are choosing *now* as the optimal time for seduction. . . Are you drinking again?"

Ember eyes sparked with defiance.

"I assure you my head is *perfectly* clear," his deep voice on a fine edge. "The sorcery detaining us in this room has, unfortunately, made sure of it."

He propped his heavy black laced boots up on the spelled table and pointed his silver dagger at me with a wolfish grin. Keahi placed his other hand over his heart.

"Forgive me, my enchantress." He lowered his voice further. "For I may not be able to subdue thoughts no gentlemen should ever be allowed to have. You have given me too much to think about while away."

My mouth went dry as the heat of him transcended his thoughts, palpable from across the table. The feel of him beneath me in chains flashed through the forefront of my mind, but it was not my thought, it was his through the bond. I crossed my legs, attempting to subdue the wicked sensation building between my thighs. Keahi leaned forward, tracking the subtle movement.

"Do you aim to torture me now as well?" The leather of his gloves flexed as he pressed them into the table, and he took a deep breath. "As you had when I was chained and on my knees the other night? I did not take you for such lowly antics to extract information, but. . . I cannot say that I am truly disappointed."

My face flushed further. *Did I regret it?* If he continued to keep looking at me like *that*. . . no. I attempted to divert the conversation. "Ossian did not deserve the death you gave him."

"Technically," Keahi sighed heavily, disappointed with my choice of deflection. "You were the one to kill him if we are keeping tabs."

"That's not the point," I argued. "This side of you is a stranger to me. I want to know your reasons."

"That is the point, Sabine. Every single sorcerer in that room needed to see it," he hissed, slamming his hands on the moonstone. "They needed to see what would happen if they crossed the line. If you want to know me, understand this—I am loyal to a fault, but when those I care for suffer, I am not the same man who found you. . . do not mistake me for him."

His admittance embodied every malefic rumor made about him among the war camps. A brutal General and scathing Prince of Fire. The serpent could not tame the vengeful shadow of himself. A warrior who would not offer repentance.

The darkness within me found it all too alluring.

"You do not know the secrets Ossian shared, whose lives it has now put at risk—*yours included,*" Keahi snarled as he continued to pace the room. "He deserved worse than what you gave him."

"A lecture on torture?" I mused, rolling my eyes at his drawn-out display. "How fitting. Are we still pretending I have not manned entire armies as well? Made choices which would make anyone with a soul's skin crawl? Or would you like to continue being condescending? It was just an observation. I want to know this side of you."

Even if it means you are the walking definition of infuriating.

Keahi's pacing stopped; his scar lined brow flicked up. "I heard that."

Good, considering I was still angry with him, he was meant to. So, I continued.

A deeply infuriating, sadistic, son of a bitch.

A broad smile crept on my bonded's face. His brother's methods in the training room to rile me were put to a burning shame as he threw a fiery wink across the table.

I am sure to be all of those things except one, my little liar.
I will let you figure out which one.

Keahi turned into a whisper of smoke before I could blink, materializing in front of me before I could turn around. His hands gripped at the side of the round table with lethal swiftness, backing me onto the edge.

"Stay out." I paused, cursing myself as I succumbed to his very nearness, breathing in his amber scent. "Of my fucking head."

"Then maybe don't play with the fire when it's hungry?" He tucked a strand of my black hair behind my ear. "Do not feign me, knowing you also lack innocence. You lied to me on multiple occasions, claiming you could not feel the bond as I did. We can make this even. You stay out of my head, and I will *gladly* stay out of yours."

The dark curtain thundered above us—a warning for the blatant lie on his tongue. Keahi dropped to the teasing pout on my lower lip, his own mere inches apart.

"I take it you are angry at me for the other night?" I inclined.

A gloved finger lifted my chin. *"Furious."* Keahi leaned into me, and his soft lips brushed mine. "Fury, however," he said roughly. "Is dull compared to the memory of you dying in my arms—*I could have lost you.*"

My eyes snapped open as he pulled away before my lips fully met his. Keahi's words provoked me, stretching his scar with a smirk.

"You would have kept silent if I did not extract the information from you," I shot back. "Our sorcerer's bond was unformed. You kept us vulnerable. In limbo." I pointed at his chest. "You told me to leave knowing full well I could have been the one to lose you!"

"Answers." Keahi rolled his shoulders and tilted his head from side to side. "Well, I am standing here right now, am I not? Let's start with this. Ask me why I'm not easily killed."

Keahi's unsheltered arrogance forced adrenaline to seep out of my pores. "Do not challenge me, General. It was I who walked away the night we first met. I could have killed you if I wanted to."

"How the truth flows from that pretty little mouth under the right conditions. Tell me. . . would you enjoy killing me?" He propped himself up against the edge of the table, arms and legs crossed; *amused.*

"*Yes,*" I challenged. Lightning rippled across the dark curtain, enclosing us in, crackling with static until it fizzled out.

Keahi hummed thoughtfully. "You might not want to try that again. The eclipse is not so lenient the second time."

It wasn't lenient at all, defiantly enacting against me, tugging at my subconscious. The onset pulled me under. I pulled at the root of my black and white hair at the growing pressure. The truth rioted to be set free under the spell of the eclipse, and I barely had enough time to catch the first layer of shock written on Keahi's face.

"I could not kill you, even if I wanted to, because I need you," I confessed. "This side of you does not scare me. I have felt glimpses of it before, deep within the bond. I chose you regardless, against everything I claimed to live for."

"Sabine." His eyes widened as he took a step closer toward me, the playful smile wiped from his face.

"But I do not know if I can make that choice again. I need your help to destroy my father more." I gasped hard, out of breath. "He has siphoned too many sorcerers. He is too powerful, cunning beyond measure, and beneath my anger I fear I cannot stop him."

My knees crashed into the cold marble; the same memories always returned. This time, I offered the truth of my volition. "I tried to run away when he found the curse had returned after he killed my mother. He tried to take it from her the first time."

"Sabine, stop." Keahi shot crackling fire through the center of the dome. Darkness retreated, slithering into its nest inside the table, but I had already drunk enough of the tonic's truth.

"He burned my people *alive*. . . I thought that—I thought I would have been just like my mother. That I would not survive my father's sin when it followed him for destroying the veil," I cried silently. "I lied to you when I said I fought him the first time. I had laid down on the ground willingly—*I let him do it*, shove the crystal into my back after I watched him murder my people when I retaliated against him.

I laid myself down in front of him with *certainty* the magic would incinerate me from the inside out. Just as my mother had. It is what I told myself when I headed to the gallows, and when I walked myself through the halls of a kingdom already on the brink of downfall, overcome with the guilt of my failure to protect them."

Keahi attempted to retrieve me from the floor, but I would not go with him. I gripped the tops of Keahi's shoulders as he kneeled before me instead. I looked into his eyes.

"But I did not lie to you when I told you I did not sit down and take it every time after that, not unless it forced me to. My father used the siphoning crystal, not to take power from after his failed attempt on my mother, but to seal the magic within me. A frozen capsule in time, but it would not hold forever. . . pieces of it had already broken off, migrated inside of me. It is the reason you found more within me, and why my father attempted to destroy me before his sin found another way to reincarnate."

Keahi's other knee hit the floor; the sound thudded through me.

"I was dying within the crystal's hold. I always have been. Just as I am dying now. The darkness will take me if I do not let it claim me fully."

My bonded remained silent. Shadows danced around the room in revelation of his wicked thoughts. He studied the darkness that took root from within. Anger, resentment, betrayal—we felt it all together in waves. I reached for his hand and removed the soft leather of his gloves.

Keahi's face did not change when I gripped his bare hand. There was only the sharp inhale of his muffled breath. Small, delicate bumps chilled my skin at the contact, brushing against his leathered and uneven scars. It was the first time he had ever felt cold to me when I pressed closer and closed my eyes. I needed him, even if it was the worst decision I ever made.

Fate had birthed me to be inherently evil by design. I let him see the side of me that was corrupted by darkness. I let him feel through the bond the blood that had been taken by my hands, and how I bore not only the weight of my sins, but the inherited treachery of my father's reign.

He looked at me like he had the night in the library, like he saw me through stained glass; peering through the broken pieces stitched together. The parts that did not fit but somehow remained intact, glued together by burdened indignation. He saw what it left of me, the only thing that I could offer.

When I thought he would pull away, the pads of his fingers pressed further into my skin for invitation. I took a solidified breath before I let him feel the desire of what I had always denied myself the most.

I have never feared death, but I have always feared living. Living meant I had *hope*, and hope has always been a far heavier burden than death. There would be nothing for me to regret if I never allowed my desire to exist.

"You may think that I am selfish for not telling you when I thought we had secured the sorcerer's bond. Even though it would not have mattered when the process had already begun—you deserved to know in the alliance I vowed to uphold."

This time, I could live a little longer, just to hope for something, *anything*—even if that meant putting my father into the ground.

"Do not abandon me now." The guilt overrode my shoulders; my face dropped. "I will stay on my knees and beg you for it if I must. I cannot let him slip away again."

Keahi's palm bloomed with revitalized heat. "Look at me when I tell you this."

My eyes snapped up to his, and my fear reached a new depth when I saw nothing but the fury he beheld. If murder could embody a soul, Keahi would have swallowed it whole with the way his eyes burned brighter than the sun's wrath.

"You will not beg anyone, *for anything*, ever again. You will take what you want, and you will not feel sorry for it." His voice shook. "I will uphold my original promise as I have already made, but I need you to promise me." He gently released his hand from my chest, standing to tower over me as I sat on my heels and stared up at him.

"When you find out what I truly want, and what I will do to get it, you will not run from me. Just as I have chosen not to run from you. I have allowed myself to want many things, but never the way I have wanted this."

Through the looking glass, I stared back at him. I feared the darkness that I knew lived in him just as it did me, and somehow that made me trust him more. He extended his hand to me.

This time would be different, and he knew it, too. This time it was *our* choice, one that could spiral and destroy the realm if we let it.

I took his hand, using the weight of him to pull myself up; my decision was locked in place. "The sorcerer's bond. . . a part of you will die because of me. I will weaken you when the darkness takes me. It is only a matter of time."

Keahi's eyes lit with unwavering mischief. "Stay alive long enough to find out, Novear. You may find that you will have to wait in line before you get to kill me."

"And if I don't?"

He lowered himself down to me, mere inches away from my face as he flashed the line of his scar with the curl of his lip. "Then you better make it interesting. I would hate to have anything less than a valiant death by you, General."

"Your book did not answer my third question. What is the third and final binding of the sorcerer's bond?" I asked him again.

"The other side must have been tied up with all the laboring questions you have been asking recently," he said distractedly, lowering his eyes to my lips, as if he knew I desired the taste of him.

Unfortunately for my shadow, he was going to have to write me back, because I had a thousand more. When he raised his eyebrow at me, I let out a small, breathless laugh. "Where were you? I feared you would not come back for me."

"Tied up, perhaps." He worked his jaw, unable to hold back his smile. "But I will always find my way back to you."

"Are you going to answer me now, then?"

Keahi's mouth hinged softly and pressed together. A worried expression took over his face, but he did not falter from me.

"You may not like the answer," he said firmly.

It was too late for that. We both needed to accept it. "How do we finish the bond? We will not be strong enough if we are to go up against my father."

He stood straight, his eyes drifted over me from head to toe. "Do not insult me, Novear."

"I never wish to see you like that again. I can feel it, the pain on you now." Before I could take them back, I released my thoughts. Something in him snapped inside our connection.

His eyes glowed a soft orange. "Don't make it your fault. I had kept that information from you after I realized you lied about knowing the conditions of the sorcerer's bond. My wound is healing for now. I can manage for the time being. The magic you transferred through the bond has given me enough strength."

My brows pinched together. "Do not hide from me, my shadow. I cannot aid you in completing the bond if I do not know."

Keahi's jaw tensed. A faint hue of red crossed his cheeks. My worry grew when I felt his emotions drumming on the other side of the bond. My head canted to the side.

"Why are you afraid to tell me?" I asked, his refusal to answer me insistent.

The Prince of Solstice shook his head in protest, attempting to release his answer as he grew unnaturally still, determination set in his stance as he worked to loosen his jaw.

Keahi was cut off mid-thought.

A steady ripple went through the night-touched waters one after another, as if someone had dropped a stone in its center. The answer hung on his lips just as the entire castle trembled.

Chapter Forty-Six

Sabine

The familiar sensation of smoke consumed my senses and burned down my throat. Iahni was in my bedroom as we materialized into the space, her face a mask of shock as she held on to the bed-post. The laundry she had been folding had fallen to the floor.

The look they shared between them sent warning signals through my power for the threat they clearly knew invaded the castle walls. A second rumble went through the mountain, but this time it was not from impact. A low growl erupted, followed by a bone-chilling screech and crackle of wildfire.

"Stay here. Do not open the door." His footsteps faded as he whispered into smoke. I tried to reach him, but he slipped through my fingers. "Do not open the door," he repeated. "Even for me."

"Keahi!" I screamed, but he was already gone.

I whirled toward Iahni, who was stagnant, her lower lip trembling. Her eyes pierced straight through me. *"They are here."*

"Who is here?"

A stillness had invaded the room.

"Do you hear that?" she whispered to herself. Her eyes glazed over.

I gripped her shoulders. "Iahni, look at me. Tell me who is here?" I began shaking her out of the spell she had put herself under in fear, but she did not budge. She placed both of her hands on mine, her voice distant, trance-like.

"The army. Keahi's blood."

A sinister heat snaked up my spine.

"I can *hear* them." Iahni dropped the towel in her hand, brushing me to the side. One foot led in front of the other as she tiptoed across the room.

"Iahni. . . do not move. Let me find Keahi. Stay here."

"*Shhh*. You are here and they know it. They want you dead. You will free him," she sang in a disembodied whisper. "The others are coming."

Her arm floated in front of her, one finger pointing to the mirror within the room as she glided toward her reflection like a ghost. *"It's too late."*

The moment her fingertip pressed into the glass; terror raked through me.

"Iahni, no!"

I did not have time to react, as a scaled hand reached through the other side of the mirror. Sharp nails embedded into her skull, gripped with death. I screamed as her cheek bone crushed into the mirror. I did not know if it was her face or the mirror that had cracked first. Her vacant eyes found mine as the scaled hands pushed her face back.

"Stop!"

Her skull demolished in a clean blow as the creature went in for the second strike. Red streaks smeared down the mirror until her body dropped to the floor in a pool of her own blood. I sprinted toward her, flailing onto the floor. I could only hear my heart roaring through my head as I came atop of her, dragging her body away from the mirror.

No, please no. Please no.

I grabbed her crushed face in between my palms.

The crunch of broken glass was a faint echo as I began rocking her back and forth as the rest of her body dangled from me. *You're safe-you're-safe-you're safe*—I wanted to whisper back to her as miserable as the lie it was. My back revolted in pain as I threw her underneath my arm, blood sopping down my shoulder.

"Pathetic."

My hand was on the doorknob when a twined rope sunk its thread around my windpipe. A choking sound escaped me as it embedded into my skin, laced with the burning singe of magic. The owner of the collar pulled the rope from the other end, *tighter*, bringing me down to my knees.

I yearned to fight the pull at my neck, to gasp for air, but I would not let go of her. *I would not let go of her body.* I struggled to breathe; a high-pitched sound throttled from my throat as I fought for air. My body was spent. My magic was raw from its last use, and it revolted against the rope pressed against my airway.

Heavy footsteps rounded out of the corner of my vision. It was not a scaled monster who knelt beside me, but his tawny slit eyes were still mutating from the change, a window into what kind of monster he could be.

A crown made of fire burned in a halo around his head. The King of Solstice grinned into a callous and fanged smile. His hand had grabbed the rope he held onto and twisted the other end around his palm three times before he cinched the collar in place. "You can be dragged, or we can do this the easy way. Your choice."

I clutched Iahni's body into my chest, taking the time to brush a lock of her auburn hair away from her glass encrusted face. The magic burned against my neck when I did not immediately obey his command.

I could feel his weight shift in irritation when I held my gaze to her, unbothered by his presence. The rope tightened, and my dark lashes fluttered momentarily at the sensation. This is what honest pain felt like, and it blurred the line of reality into the numbing rage my mind instinctually fled to. My eyes turned black as I looked up at him, the light of my power nowhere to be found.

"Careful," I said with violence edging my throat. "I do not let any man speak to me like that. I make no exception for kings."

The flaming crown around his dark, long curls flared in challenge. He shared the same eyes that Zehra had, except he exhibited a darker green which bore a fountain of envy.

I braced myself as I traced the corners of his face and fell to the unscathed hands that held the other end of the rope. A memory flashed through my mind as my skin contacted the magic, but it was not my own; it was Keahi's.

A low, deranged humming sound drew from my throat. "I see. . . you have been stealing. . . and I am a threat to your supply." A hungry grin formed on the lower half of my face as my grip tightened on the rope. "You should know I crave the death of kings more than the Gods themselves. I will let you choose which of your makers you would like to meet, King of Solstice, because it would be in your best interest to be certain it is not me."

He strangled the leash, forcing me to stumble upright onto my feet. My fingers pressed into Iahni's body as she dangled between us in my arms.

"Is that what you told yourself, Princess, when your people nearly died out? When your father waged a war while you were sitting up in that porcelain castle of his, as the realm rotted with the death of our power source? I do not heed feeble threats. You would have already killed your father if that were the case."

The healed split in my lip cracked as my smile broadened. "You may not want to show your hand too soon, Emric. It makes me eager to play with a king who never realized he was his own damsel, sitting up in his guarded castle as he sent his son to fight a war on his own."

I would know. I was the one who gave him a battle scar, but it was his father who made him a martyr instead.

The King slammed his fist into my temple, but only because I allowed it. My vision flurried in black and white until I caught my bearings. The rope tugged when I reached the end of the line as I stammered back to set Iahni down on the floor. My forehead brushed against hers as I did, hoping she would forgive me in the next lifetime as I let go of her. When I finally looked back up at him, his breath was ragged.

The King of Solstice snarled into a confident grin. "And how eager are you now?"

Even though he was several feet above me, I stood taller. The rush of my power pulsed underneath the collar, fighting the temptation.

"I'm starving."

The magic that spelled the rope slowly unraveled as it morphed under my curse. The twine encircling my neck turned black, spiraling until it transformed the other end of the rope into the same shade. Satisfaction coiled inside the pit of my curse when the King looked down at his blackened hand. He held it out in front of me, frozen in his own lapse of judgment.

"Only fools will think they will not fail when they rise to such heroics. Who did you think you were saving?" I reached up to the twine that now served me. "Better yet, why do I have the feeling you were so simple-minded to believe that it was yourself? Because I promise you, it was not my people."

I snatched his force of gravity as I jerked the end of my rope. His shoulder dipped in succession when his entwined hand pulled toward me. My boot pressed into the back of his shoulder blade as I sent him in the other direction, looping the black rope around his neck.

A humiliating sound whimpered out of his throat. I drove my knee into his spine before his body could hit the floor and wrenched his neck up with all the force I had left in me. The leftover pain from the battle worked its way into an agonizing tremor as I let his body fumble underneath me.

'The others are coming.' Iahni's warning rang through my ears. I knew I did not have long, or enough power left in me for the forces barreling toward me. But I would not let that stop me from stripping his pride in the meantime.

"Do you want to know what I thought as I watched my people die from my so-called 'tower,' knowing that one of the most powerful kingdoms had stood by while they watched my father do it? When you so poorly underestimated him as a threat then, and now look where that has gotten us." The rope loosened momentarily to let him catch his breath before I strangled him again.

"I see no difference compared to what he has done when I look at you." I breathed out this last part down his spine. "So let me ask you this. Do you plan to underestimate me as well?" I watched the hairs raise on the nape of his neck as I smashed his forehead into the marble.

The door was forced wide open, and I stood in time to spread my arms out wide, ripping the collar off my neck with a slight bow. It fell on top of the King's back as I said, "We have been waiting."

Chapter Forty-Seven

Sabine

I locked eyes with the King of Solstice as his Kingsmen peeled his chagrined body mass off the floor. He thrashed and spat at the bloodied foam building between his splintered fangs.

"Off of me! Get off of me! Grab her now!" He roared, jamming his elbows against his own soldiers as he staggered into a crumpled position, watching him piece together his balance from the blow to his head. A matching angry welt flowed down his temple, shards of glass jabbing from his wound where I had attempted to drag Iahni's body away from him.

I anchored myself into a tranquil stillness as I watched the scene unfold. It redirected the attention in the room toward me at his command. I stretched my arms out wider, hinging into a graceful bow as I observed the energy in the room peak with lividity. I met his intangible snarl with a crimson smile as his Kingsmen shoved a leathered sack over the top of my head.

It was pitch-black when I felt the brush of cold metallic chains against my torso. The heightened contact caused my abdomen to clench as a fervor of magic went through me. A rush of awareness lit the rest of my skin on fire as a piece of memory transferred through the spell's binding.

My composure broke under the mask, hiding the uncontrolled panic I did not give them the privilege of seeing. I could not stop the frightened gasp that escaped past my lips, or the dark laughter charging through the surrounding room in response.

I knew the curse of the veil could not overtake the chains this time, not when I had seen a glimpse of what they could hold through the enchantment.

My breath was rough in my throat as I attempted to contain what came next. I pinched my eyes closed despite not being able to see the inner workings of the cuff scrape against my lower limbs, along the soft inner portions of my wrists.

They forced a strangled groan from me when the first metal thorn hammered into my skin. The following spikes of pain drew out the strain that was holding my body together, within an inch of my life, as I collapsed. Their hands cupped underneath my arms with a bruising grip. When I could not stand, a brass knuckled fist slammed into my stomach; a high-pitched cry throttled from me. Hot blood dripped out of the four puncture sites the hit created.

My knees buckled as they dragged me across the floor, leaving a trail of blood behind as I sucked in shallow breaths of suspended pain. They wanted him to find me. That much was clear, but they did not know the regret they would feel when he found me like this.

The Kingsmen let out a string of grunts as they struggled to push against the lock they had placed on a massive set of creaking doors. A palpable hush descended over the occupants in the room before a single scream of agony blistered my ears.

It was a reverberant echo. A piercing sound. One I would have to spend many nights trying to forget if I survived. An ache carved itself into the crater of my chest as they drug me up and over a set of stairs onto a hollow platform. I flinched before I even heard Iahni's body thump next to me on the ground.

"My daughter!" His devastation sent a stabbing sensation through me, worse than the one I had physically received. "Not Iahni. My daughter!" Elias wailed until his voice was a shrill and fragile murmur of pain. "*Please, no!* I'm begging you. Not my little girl. *Nooo!*"

My stomach retched inside of my hood, convulsing as it burned through my nose. The King let out a disgusted, disapproving scoff beside me. It did not matter how much I wanted to hold myself together. It broke me in the exuding presence of the pain, grating the repetition of her name so thoroughly into my mind I was convinced it would haunt me into the next lifetime as I saw her stone blue eyes in him for the first time.

Emric's impersonal voice barreled over his cries. "Remove him. I cannot stand to hear him anymore." A struggle broke out, but all I could hear was his own chains rattling as they dragged him out of the throne room. *"Bring me my son!"*

"You will regret this!" Elias cried from a distance, "You will not come back from this, Emric! I will not protect you from him this time!"

Fire crackled like a furnace, building outside of the doors as if in response. Screams of terror were no longer a muffled sound in the distance as a familiar force came within reach.

Even from a distance, I could feel the pain Keahi was battling through as he fully expended his magic with a piercing rage. I had to swallow the acid building in my throat when *I felt it*—his gaping wound. My magic had not healed him at all. *How was he still standing?* Elias's struggle quieted as the Kingsmen hesitated to unlock the door, knowing what was waiting on the other side.

A hardened laugh came out of him. "You should have thought about that before you allied with my son, Elias Griselda. *I said, remove him!"* The double doors slammed open from the outside, sending a lashing crack through the room.

"The prodigal son returns; it is a pity I had to come to you though, isn't it?" the King said as he ripped my hood off like I was a captured prize. "As you can see, I have become well acquainted with your *wife*. My apologies for missing the wedding. I now see why you allied yourself with our enemies, Keahi Aldeer. She's so. . . *spirited.* I can only imagine what she is like elsewhere."

My shoulders slumped forward as I grasped the fresh air into my lungs. I looked up through tear coated lashes as my vision fogged, taking a moment to acknowledge a glimpse of the diamond-like crystals embroidering the floor. I could barely see the pebbled red and clear quartz crystals through the thick layer of dust coating it, similar to the ones I had seen when we had united the sorcerer's bond in ceremony.

The King shifted on the silver throne next to me, a hood thrown over his head in a useless attempt to hide the markings I had given him.

The bond pulled taut as Keahi stared at me, completely drenched in blood, as if he had bathed in it. His eyes burned like coals, dropping to the line of flesh purpling around my neck. A rumble went through the castle as his gaze dropped lower to the silver spiked cuffs around my extremities.

"What have you done?"

"You brought this upon yourself." The King clasped his hands together and leaned forward. "You all did."

Zehra and Drakkon were flanked behind their father. The Kingsmen crushed their metal staffs against their windpipes. Their own clothes dripped with blood from the fight, but not how Keahi's did.

"It was so much more than you refusing to give me your blood, was it not?" He dropped his chin toward me. "So much more."

"It was never yours to take."

He slammed his fists against the arms of his facile throne. *"I am your king!* It will always be mine to take. Tell that to your second in command, as I ripped your schemes from his throat. Did you think you could finally overpower me with the sorcerer's bond? *You couldn't even finish it."*

A strangled whimper broke from behind me. Drakkon's tear-filled eyes flashed with hurt as he looked between me and Keahi as he sobbed against the metal beam strangling him.

Emric flicked his gaze over to Zehra. "*You*, I am so very disappointed in, but I will overlook it just this once." Zehra grimaced underneath the bar, her words set in a chokehold. "When we return home, I will crown your sister as the next heir of Solstice, strip you of your title, Keahi Aldeer, and I will chain you in that prison for an eternity if I have to."

As the King twirled a piece of my white hair between his fingers, I shivered. "I might even let you keep her down there with you—on good behavior, of course. . . after I'm done with her."

Keahi tensed, holding himself in place as the slicing sound of a sword drew from its holster. "You remember this. . . don't you? It has been far too long." He placed the metal exactly where the rope marking welled against my skin.

"Put the Sword of Rhiannon down, Emric," Keahi growled in a low threat.

His breath was hot against my skin as he neared. "I will drain her right here and make you watch. Did you really think I wouldn't notice once you brought her to the capital? That you could hide her? You can see the magic from the Veil of Seven on her skin, the one that her father is responsible for."

Keahi took a step forward but stopped at the sight of Emric pressing the side of the blade deeper into my throat. A light trickle of blood fell from the very tip where it connected. Keahi's pupils dilated as he watched it hit the floor.

"I will not let you have her power." Emric shook his head. "When I reopen the veil to the Gods, I cannot wait to see what they will do to you, Keahi Aldeer. It will be a reward enough for me to know I will not need your blood anymore. . . perhaps Rhiannon herself will give me the ability to turn freely."

Emric turned his lips up, his fangs vanished from his twisted smile. "A *gift* for returning the beast to his cage after he betrayed them."

A line of torches blazed with flames as Keahi's power funneled within him into an intangible depth. Wrath lit the entire room. His voice was turbulent against the rage building inside of him. "Have you ever considered the Gods might have been the ones to betray me *first?*"

The fires blew out all at once.

Chapter Forty-Eight

Sabine

Warmth flooded through me as Keahi opened the pathways between our connection. My vision flooded with a haze. It coated the between like he had blown out a match; the entire world had gone gray. I could still feel the sword at my neck, but I could only see Keahi as we crossed into the edge of time before each other.

The torches he had diminished flooded the between with black clouds of smoke. It poured onto the floor as it curled, wrapping itself until it wound into the body of a serpent underneath him. It slowly snaked itself up the wall behind Keahi when its ember eyes snapped to me while Keahi's remained closed. I could not fight the tremble in my voice, even as I spoke through the bond.

What are you?

The serpent tilted its head as Keahi remained still at my question, his voice resonating around me.

I cannot hold us like this for long. The scar you see could not heal—frozen in its state unlike before. I have been weak since we accepted the sorcerer's bond. You had asked me what we needed in order to finish it. . . and I had wanted to give you more time before we entered the second binding. I cannot give you that, not this time. You had offered it to me once before, as a test, but it must be your choice, Sabine. I will follow the path you decide to take.

Distrust placed a wall between us. I reread the pages in my mind; the response he had written in the journal I had been given.

Even as I tried to make sense of it all, I could not shake the feel of his wound, even with my eyes closed. I homed in on the dark line painted across his chest from injury, knowing I had the key to relieve the torment he bore. It was glowing with the dark magic that had ripped him open, even under the layers of his clothes.

I swallowed hard.

Tell me what you are, and I will give it to you.

The serpent in his shadow danced back and forth as it hovered behind Keahi on the grayed wall. A growl ripped through the bond, reverberating, as the serpent behind him bred wings out of its shadow; the peak of it was sharp, talon-like as it tripled in size.

You—you're not a sorcerer. . . my eyes trailed over the wings. . *. you are not even human.*

A grim smile appeared on Keahi.

Not originally, no.

As he walked toward me, the ground shook with each step as the beast followed. His shadow grew until the serpent tore itself from the wall, its wings stretching as it pulled itself out into the open.

They have disgraced my kind, using my blood to shift into monsters. I am not an abomination, but I cannot claim the same for what they have done with my power.

The shadow's tail coiled, whipping back and forth.

Are you one of the Gods, in human form?

The serpent growled behind him.

I cannot lie to you, Sabine. He paused before he kneeled before me. *I am not a God exactly, but I might be worse.*

I thought Rhiannon. . .

Keahi's jaw tightened, sweat beaded on the side of his forehead from holding us in this space of time. On the verge of collapse—the rest would have to wait, as I confirmed my decision. I swallowed just before I pressed my neck further into the blade on the other side.

Are all dragons this cryptic?

A low sound tore from his throat as he lowered his head to my neck, his lips hovering over the blood welling at the base of my collarbone.

I may speak in cryptics, but your answer must be clear to me. Keahi opened his true eyes to me now. The shadow dragon blinked in time with him. *I will not take from you, not unless you ask me to. You are my sorcerer bonded, and I will always choose to honor you in my promise for lifetimes.*

I shuttered a violent breath at the last word.

You will take my blood, Son of Fire, an offering of my bond to you in the second binding of our fate.

Keahi kept his eyes trained on me as he lowered his lips, hovering over the side of my neck with a deep restraint, dipping his lips into my blood softly with a full body shudder.

"Which one of them caused this wound?" Keahi's words muffled through time as he spoke out loud. His fingers traced the four puncture sites of my abdomen as he drank from me.

"Which. One."

The magic he bore crossed over in waves as I felt our connection through the bond strengthen. It was so powerful I felt it tearing at my soul, restitching itself with his. Keahi swept his thumb across his bottom lip and slowly placed it in his mouth. The dragon's wings arched up as a pained moan slipped between my teeth.

"Which one is it, my little liar? Or I will make sure that no one else in this room survives the night."

The power building in him at the blood offering was spiraling out of control. I sucked in a sharp breath as he lifted away, dizzied by the power rippling from him. My skin burned where his lips had touched me.

On second thought. . .

He leaned back, running his tongue across his bottom lip, staring at my neck.

I might just kill them all.

I felt the exhaustion hit me all at once. My thoughts unanchored as he turned to walk back to the spot he still stood in on the other side of the realm.

The dragon wrapped itself in its wings and began spiraling—morphing until it changed into a shadow that matched the outline of Keahi's form, turning simultaneously until two pairs of glowing eyes faced me.

The serpent's shadow melted into his form, stitching the sliced wound across his chest from the inside out, until it sealed itself inside of its home. Keahi rolled his shoulders with a shiver. The tension coursing from him unraveled through the bond in an instant.

Undiluted power flowed between the bond as his ancient power coiled inside the newfound depths of his magic. I could not see the future, but we would be the realm's reckoning. We would not only make those who have wronged us pay, but even the Gods themselves. His thumb and forefinger came together, preparing to merge us into the present time.

Wait.

I could feel the release of his power coming to a boil beneath him, but he stopped himself for me.

Yes, my little liar?

Leave one.

Keahi's scarred brow arched. *Your conscience is quite endearing, Novear. . . I will see what I can do.*

One, just choose one to keep alive.

With a snap of his fingers, the haze lifted. The room appeared just as it had been, but the point of the knife was pressing deeper into my neck.

Emric shouted, "I will never forgive your mother for accepting the deal from Rhiannon to let that thing inhabit you. You are just as much of a curse to me as what runs through her veins from closing the veil, and it will make no difference to me when I strip the magic from her!"

Keahi took his time as he picked at the tips of his gloves to pull them off, tossing them one by one on the stone dais in front of us. "Do not worry yourself, Emric. I'm sure you will have time to work it out between yourselves very soon."

He extended his right palm until he turned it upright, motioning two of his fingers in a slow curl. The pressure of the knife against me eased as the King's hand shook, struggling against the force as he re-arranged his grip on the sword with two hands just to keep his hold. Keahi rotated his fingers with the knife until the King had reversed the blade on himself. His next words came out in a disembodied hiss. "I would let them go now if I were you."

Keahi had spoken to no one in particular, but the nearest Kingsman ripped the chains off me and Elias. Zehra and Drakkon toppled over as soon as the staffs were released from their throats. Keahi's magic still froze the rest of the room in place.

As soon as Elias's chains crashed to the floor, he rushed toward the dais, dragging his bad leg behind him without the support of his golden staff. His hands trembled as they drifted over Iahni's body, a cry itching the back of his throat. The weight of her did not seem to deter him, as he used all his strength to lift her. Drakkon had turned to offer to carry her the rest of the way, but Elias shook his head, pushing him away until he stopped before the closure.

"Keahi, I never believed this was the way, but I do now." Elias's voice deepened with grief. "I was wrong."

He brushed the deep red hair out of his daughter's face, lightly tapping his fingers on the glass freckles at the bridge of her nose.

"Be the monster they called you, become the weapon he made you, and then you learn how to control it." Elias spoke with a proclamation, "Let this be where the beginning and the end find each other. Take the power that has always been yours to wield and make them pay for it."

Even the flames were still as the Prince and his Healer bowed to each other without another word.

"Elias!" Keahi allowed Emric to scream as he watched Elias walk through the doors without looking back. "Elias!"

Zehra's arms crashed around me in front of her father. A heavy stare impelled between them as she lifted me up, turning without delay to remove me from the horror that was about to unfold in this room. It was the King's undoing as he watched her. "Traitors! All of you! Trait—" The blade drove through the top of his stomach. He gurgled blood in his throat, drowning within his screams.

"This is for every time I believed I deserved it, when I let you take from me." Keahi's outstretched hand twisted, slowly lining up the blade, and sliced his father straight down his center. Emric attempted to hold his entrails as they dumped out onto the floor, sending him to his knees.

The Serpent in the Shadows prowled toward the King and picked up the Sword of Rhiannon. "And this—" He paused, readjusting the hilt in his hand. "—is for touching my wife."

I turned just in time as Emric's blood stained the dais, but a portion of it splattered against the side of my face with every swing. Each strike of the blade purposefully placed an inch above the last until the sound dulled against his broken flesh on the side of his neck.

The crown above Emric's head, no longer attached to his body on the floor, dimmed until it became a ring of ash in the crown's place.

A swirl of black fire and smoke bloomed into a halo above Keahi's head as he stood and tossed the Volkan's mask to the ground beside him.

The new King of Solstice was crowned.

An inferno of power answered to him as he consumed all the fire producing light within the throne room. My darkness shook internally. The entire ceiling erupted in flame and fury as he breathed out a volcano of fire.

Drakkon was preparing to close the doors. Zehra and I barely escaped from the heat he produced at our heels. The dragon made his way up to his throne, stepping over the disemboweled body of his predecessor. A shadow of his wings stretched out across the mountain's fire lit ceiling as he claimed his place. He captured my gaze between the slit of the closing doors.

Do you remember your own promise?

Zehra let my feet settle on the floor before releasing me. Screams of terror began all at once as he released his initial hold on the Kingsmen.

I will not run from you or what you want.
I am not afraid, my shadow.
The darkness within you . . .
calls to the darkness within me.

Keahi's scar-lined grin rose to one side before the doors slammed shut. Fists began pounding frantically against the door. Screams erupted into a symphony as fire burned into an orange glowing rage beneath the door frame, and I did not run as I blocked out the sounds of the dying.

A dragon's battle cry shook the mountain.

Acknowledgements

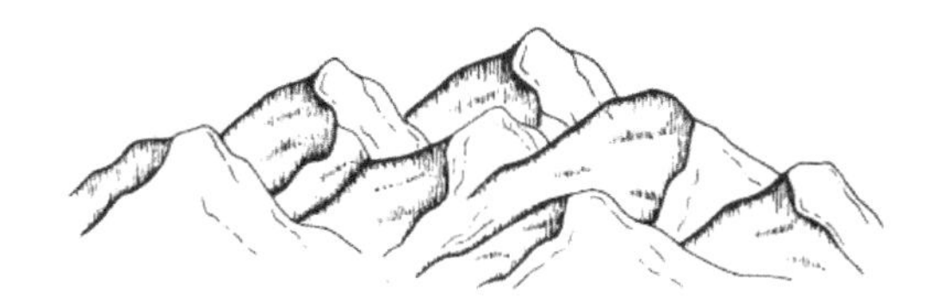

To my readers—it is because of you that my reluctant words become stories. I hope you find yourself lost in the characters, but not the world (maybe not them either, depending on their mood. . . questionable) because that shit would suck. I mean did they have to die like that? Brutal. Personally, I wouldn't live past page one.

To my husband—you anchor me on solid ground. Thank you for being the first person to ever read my stories. Your advice and reassurance is astounding, I quote: "If George R. Martin can write about tits and ass babe, so can you, so can fucking you."

To my cats—Peter and Lilly. Thank you for pretending to edit my book as you cuddle me and stare at the screen. I know you two can't read, but good try.

To my family—I love you with all my heart, let's hope you didn't even get to this page. If you did, we can both pretend you didn't. P.S. The first books in my series, now and future, are the only ones remotely safe if we want to make eye contact ever again. Proceed at your own risk.

To my critique partner—Kalista Neith, Author of Invoking the Blood, the K-money, Dragon Mommy, My Wife, and Raging Insomniac. REST BITCH. But also, thank you for being my loyal counterpart. For the dedication it takes to tear apart each other's stories, while also simultaneously building them up. This is how we move our mountains, and of course write porn. All my love to you my beautiful and talented friend. Forever your chaos demon.

To my personal bookish community—Did we stay strapped in? Are all titties safe and accounted for? (The ones who get it get it, and to the ones who don't you are invited). Thank you for being so uplifting. For providing a space where we can enjoy books together, and not feel judged. Reading is the foundation of what fuels me, and you are the ones telling me "you're doing great sweety" while we binge read fantasy romance at 2 am with work the next day. Fueling the soul and staying ~fresh~ is not synonymous, but ITS WORTH IT.

To my Alpha, Beta readers, and Editors—Thank you for reading my book in its rawest form. Feedback is so important in crafting the end result, and I value you all beyond measure. I could not do this without you.

Editors:

Faemance—Keahi's biggest fan.

Honorable mention Kelsey—You are an editor in my heart and thank you for making my English teachers proud.

Alpha reader:

Taylor (taylortotsreads) you are the best cheerleader, and an amazing story strategist. To many more books to come, and sports romances to read.

Elizabeth—I'm sorry for traumatizing you, hopefully I made up for it by dropping a huge secret for book two, stay strong lone soldier

Beta readers:

Developmental: Raeanne—1/2 of team gay moms. . . (Katie?), Arley—my soul mate when it comes to book tastes, and Amanda—my dm away when we are ready to scream about all things books.

Line: Author Madison Wright—I'm obsessed with you, and that's why I promise I'll try and watch outlander, Courtenay—my Capricorn, you could ask me to jump off a cliff and I would ask what time, and Brooke—to the books we have read and to the alcohol we should not have consumed, to your barbie dream house and my goth mansion.

Proof: Brooke—Thanksgiving turkey ain't got nothing on us my golden retriever, and Steph—your dedication to Dramione inspires me, it does not go unseen.

May Darkness be with you all.

J.D. Ronan

www.jdronanauthor.com

CPSIA information can be obtained
at www.ICGtesting.com
Printed in the USA
BVHW031007090223
658119BV00020B/202/J